# UNDER THE WILD SKY

*For Megan, Jack and Adam*

# UNDER THE WILD SKY

A SAGA OF
LOVE AND WAR IN
REVOLUTIONARY
IRELAND

MARY RYAN

ERRIS BOOKS

First published in English, 2016 by
Erris Books
Blackrock, Co. Dublin, Ireland



| | |
|---|---|
| Paperback | ISBN: 978 1 911013 280 |
| eBook – mobi format | ISBN: 978 1 911013 297 |
| eBook – ePub format | ISBN: 978 1 911013 303 |
| CreateSpace paperback | ISBN: 978 1 911013 310 |



Produced by Kazoo Independent Publishing Services
222 Beech Park, Lucan, Co. Dublin
www.kazoopublishing.com

Kazoo Independent Publishing Services is not the publisher of this work. All rights and responsibilities pertaining to this work remain with Erris Books.



Cover design by Andrew Brown

Printed in the EU

'He shall not hear the bittern cry
In the wild sky, where he is lain,
Nor voices of the sweeter birds,
Above the wailing of the rain.'

FRANCIS LEDWIDGE
from *Lament for Thomas MacDonagh*

# *Part 1*

# *Chapter 1*

*County Monaghan, Ireland, 2 September 1901.*

Ellen put her bicycle in the turf shed, took her books from the basket, dodged the gushing drainpipe and ran for the house. The kitchen was empty, but the hot range was blasting enticing smells – soup, baking bread, boiling mutton and apple pie. She hung her cap and waterproof on the peg by the back door and sat to unlace her boots. From the hall came mellow Westminster chimes, reminding her that her father would be with her in a couple of hours. He was coming for dinner, a special one for her birthday.

She heard footsteps on the tiles and Aunt Harriet came into the kitchen, her black dress whispering on the floor and an open letter in her hand. Ellen recognised the writing and her heart gave a small, painful start.

'Ellen dear,' her aunt said, 'your father will be bringing someone to meet you.'

'Oh Aunt …'

'He's bringing a lady. Her stepson is coming too. He was at school with young Mr Wallace and is to stay at Clonshule.'

Ellen's thoughts strayed to Clonshule, the great house hidden behind an avenue of beeches, home to the Wallaces who had been local landlords for hundreds of years. If their young visitor had been to school with the heir he would probably be Protestant or English.

The back door rattled and Maggie entered, her coat over her head. She was bearing a basket half-filled with new eggs to which bits of straw and chicken dirt were clinging. While she washed them at the sink, her mistress conferred with her about the meal – instructions for the caper sauce, warnings about lumps in the custard – and left the room with a warning to Ellen to change her wet skirt. Ellen rummaged in the bread bin, cut a slice of brown bread, went to the range and moved the smaller of the two cast iron kettles to the hot plate.

'Where's Harry, Maggie?'

'Not far off!' said a youth who had come quietly into the kitchen and who now clapped his sister on the back. 'Cheer up, Sis. Fifteen isn't so old. You'd still give a run to the Sugar Plum Fairy! Fran and I got you a present, but you'll have to wait until she's finished making your card, which should happen sometime before nightfall!'

'Has Aunt told you the news?'

'It's the widdy woman, Sis! The one he mentioned in his last letter?'

'Her stepson's coming too!'

Harry sighed, lifted the lid of a saucepan and peered in. 'Is that mushroom soup, Maggie?'

'A grand crop this morning. Franny got to them one second before the maggots.'

Harry made a face. 'O Maggie, Maggie, how thou doth prod the appetite!'

Ellen laughed. The maid slapped Harry with a dishcloth and bustled into the pantry. Harry sat into the carver at the head of the kitchen table and watched as his sister put milk and sugar in her tea and buttered her slice of brown bread.

'What do you think, El? You don't suppose it means … we'll be a family again?'

'It's seven years, Harry. How well do you even remember poor Mother?'

Harry dropped his eyes. After finishing her tea, Ellen put her hand on his shoulder, picked up her books and left the kitchen. She crossed the hall and peeped into the dining room where the table was set with the best damask cloth and silver cutlery. A fire had been lit and tendrils of turf smoke were escaping to the discoloured mantle shelf where a sepia portrait of her parents on their wedding day stood among her aunt's photographs. She looked at it for a while before climbing the creaking stairs to her room.

Harriet Murphy, foster mother to her brother's children, heard her niece go upstairs. She was sitting in what she liked to call her 'study' – a small room where she kept her desk and where she did her household accounts. She had left her birthday present in the child's room and hoped the fit was still perfect. A good girl, she thought; in a few years she'll be thinking of marriage. Young Jimmy MacMahon already had an eye for her and she could do a lot worse.

She glanced at the yellowing photograph of Mathew, her husband, and felt the longing for him that had never left her, that even after ten years seemed to leach from her bones. Since their daughter, Clare, had married, the care of their younger child, Frances, and that of Harry and Ellen, her brother's children, filled her days. Frances she thought difficult to rear, far too headstrong for a girl. Harry was a dreamer. And Ellen … well, Ellen was a lady, reserved and fragile yet determined for a scholarship to Carysfort College. She was now a pupil-teacher, but her chances of a scholarship were slim and failure would go hard with her. They would eventually get her a job behind a counter in one of the bigger shops in town, a genteel enough occupation while she waited for a husband. But it was only right to let her try for the scholarship. She could not deny her that.

Ellen shut her bedroom door. She loved this room, overlooking as it did the short driveway, the front gate and the fields sloping to the Multeen. Once it had been her cousin Clare's, but a year ago Clare had married Frank Ahern, a journalist with the *Irish Independent.* She was now living in Dublin and expecting her first baby.

The room contained a chest of drawers with a cheval glass, a white iron bedstead with brass finials, a toilet table with basin and ewer (black ships on a blue sea), a table where she kept her school books and a worn rug before the slate fireplace. She inspected herself in the mirror, searching for new maturity, but saw only the same freckles and the same brown hair curling, as it always did, from the rain.

The mirror also reflected two parcels on her chair. Wrapped in brown paper with her name in bold letters and tied with twine, they had the immediacy of love. Unused to gifts, she picked them up with emotion. One bore her father's handwriting and had the shape and feel of a book. The other parcel was soft. She excitedly untied the string and removed the paper. It was her aunt's birthday present – made from a McCall's Misses pattern, Ellen had chosen herself – a dress in powder blue merino, with sleeves that puffed gently below the elbow, a high lawn collar and a flounced, mid-calf hem. She took it from the tissue paper, removed her blouse, stepped out of her wet skirt and pulled the new frock over her head. After tying the cinch at her waist, she ran to the mirror and caught her breath. She was somehow a different person, a young lady.

From outside came the sounds of wheels and the screech of the gate.

'Father!' she whispered, and rushed to the window. But it was only Farrelly's horse-drawn van. The boy got down to lift out the box of groceries and was helped by Jimmy MacMahon, the young neighbour who lived in Culgreine down the road and came every day to muck out the stable and do other odd jobs. Jimmy wore his dead father's greasy cap and was, as usual, in wellingtons. He took the box from the boy, put it on his shoulder and began to whistle the popular tune, 'Barney O'Hay'. He glanced up, tipped his cap to Ellen and his careless tenor filled the air.

Impudent Barney
None of your blarney,
Impudent Barney O'Hay …

Ellen laughed and moved back from the window to unwrap her other present. It was a Morocco-bound journal with a small brass lock, which she recognised as having once belonged to her mother. Pinned to it was her father's letter and a small brass key.

*Dearest Ellen,*

*I hope you have a happy birthday. Your mother would have wanted you to have her journal – which is far too handsome to be wasted! I hope to see you on your birthday, but am sending this through the post in case anything should happen to detain me.*

*I will have company on this occasion. Mrs Forrister, the lady I mentioned in my last letter, will be coming with me. We intend to marry in the spring and it's time she met you and Harry. She has made me very happy in consenting to share my life. I'm sure you will both welcome her.*

*I need hardly mention that your mother's memory will always remain sacred.*

Oh Father! Ellen threw the letter on the bed, ran her hands over the volume that had been her mother's diary, sobbed as she took the key and turned the lock. The brass flap fell back. She found the last entry – the spidery writing of the dying: *I think it will be soon. Dear kind God comfort John. Dear Jesus look after my poor children.*

She remembered the day she and Harry had returned from school to find their mother installed in the garden shed, a shed cleaned and stripped of tools and prepared for an invalid, an invalid seized by a paroxysm of coughing who had waved them away – 'Don't come near. Don't touch me!' – and Mrs Quinn had rushed with a towel to catch the bright blood. Wiped clean, their mother had lain back wearily and looked at her terrified children.

'You see,' she whispered, 'I'm sick … but I will be better soon … Darlings, go back to the house.'

Next day at school the girl with whom Ellen shared a desk, announced reproachfully, 'My mam says your mother has TB. I don't want to sit beside you.'

Ellen put the journal on her table, picked up a pencil, turned over a stiff new page and wrote one line: *Dear Mother, I am your daughter Ellen and today is my fifteenth birthday.*

She closed the book and laid her head against it. Her mother's funeral was with her, the hearse with its glass windows, the horses tossing black-plumed heads, the coachman in a black silk hat. Afterwards Aunt Harriet had taken her and Harry home to Kilcrannagh. It was like yesterday – the train journey in the dark, the smell of mothballs from her aunt's black coat, their reflection in the window, the wheels beating out, 'Your mother is dead … is dead … is dead … dead … dead …'

For weeks afterwards Ellen could barely speak. Her cousin Franny, who had taken immediately to Harry, had tried to comfort her, while Clare, then fourteen – the most beautiful creature Ellen had ever seen – had made no secret of her resentment.

'My home is invaded by cousins I don't know and don't want to know!' she had said. But, when Ellen had burst into tears, her lovely cousin had added, as though assessing the foibles of a distant third party, 'I'm afraid I can't help being spoilt and selfish!'

With time, Ellen began to find her mother's passing fitting into the past, as though her death had been part of a strategy known to God. She and Harry became settled in the local national school and accustomed to their father's infrequent visits. Based two hundred miles away in Tralee, he sent letters with his monthly cheque to Aunt Harriet for their keep. His absence gave him a mythic status. Once he had come to see them wearing the dark green uniform of the Royal Irish Constabulary, his Webley at his waist, and they had nearly burst with pride. But their aunt had not been impressed.

'I really would prefer, John, if you didn't come here in uniform!' and she had muttered something about people crossing her threshold who were armed to the teeth.

Ellen knew that winds of change were blowing through the country her father was policing. She knew there was a resurgence of interest in all things Gaelic – language, history, legend – which was all the nearer to home because of Jimmy. Jimmy lent Harry books and talked to him about Irish history until Harry was filled with passionate resentment. On their father's last visit he had demanded, 'Why do people call you a "Peeler", Father?'

'Because a prime minister called Sir Robert Peel founded the police force.'

'The boys in school hate them!'

'Rabble sentiments, my boy.'

'No, Father. *Rebel* sentiments!'

Ellen had pulled him away. She knew, because Maggie had told her, that their father had once been attacked, fired on by men who had appeared from nowhere and disappeared as suddenly. They had never been apprehended and the wound had taken months to heal – one of the reasons why they had not seen him over a long period.

*

'El … Can we come in?'

Ellen thrust the journal under her school books.

'Is this a princess I see before me?' Harry inquired, entering the room and pretending to shade his eyes. Franny, coming in behind him, looked at him scornfully.

'I told you the dress was lovely!' She kissed her cousin and handed her a small box tied with a ribbon. 'Happy Birthday, darling Ellen!'

Frances Murphy had the same colouring as her sister, Clare – chestnut hair, green eyes and translucent skin – but she did not possess Clare's extraordinary beauty. Right now she looked dishevelled. Her thick plait had come undone, and her hair spilled over a pinafore blotched with paint.

'It's from Harry and me! We saved up! So you'd better like it!'

Ellen untied the ribbon, found a hand-painted card – rioting pansies and daisies – and a small flat box containing six lawn handkerchiefs, their corners embroidered with tiny flowers.

'Oh they're so lovely! You shouldn't have been spending your money on me! I'll keep them until I'm a grown up lady ...'

'You're nearly there already!' Harry exclaimed. 'With a waist that tight you'll end up puking.'

'No I won't. I'll wear the dress for Father. Will you do me up, Fran?'

Harry left the room and Franny did up the hooks and eyes at the back of the new dress. Then she brushed her cousin's damp hair, searched in her top drawer for a ribbon, which she secured with a bow, and surveyed her handiwork in the mirror.

'Why are your eyes so red, El?' she asked gently. 'What will the visitors think?'

'Oh Fran, I don't care what they think. I wish Father were coming on his own!'

Franny sighed. 'What can't be cured must be endured! If this woman makes your father happy, isn't that what counts? The stepson's only coming because he's been invited to Clonshule, so he'll probably be very grand, but curious about the leprechauns!'

'Leprechauns? You mean us?' Ellen demanded with a laugh.

From the driveway came the clatter of hooves and carriage wheels.

'Oh God, they're here.'

The girls sprang to the window. Ellen saw her father alight from the carriage and watched as he gave his hand to a lady in a loose coat and fashionable hat. A young man stepped out behind her. He was as straight as a ramrod and was carrying a box.

'That's the stepson!' Franny announced and skipped to the door.

'Change that filthy pinny,' Ellen called after her, and went back to watching the young man who was now mounting the steps to the hall door and who suddenly looked up into her face. She backed away from the window, bathed her eyes, gave her hair a few more strokes and went nervously downstairs.

# Chapter 2

Ellen was greeted on the drawing-room threshold by the scents of whiskey and turf. She saw the young man by the window and the handsome, tightly laced woman in the fireside chair. Her father was standing by the mantelpiece with a glass in his hand. He was trim in a dark suit and waistcoat, across which stretched his familiar silver fob watch on its chain, but his whiskers were now grey and new lines had etched themselves around his eyes. Bursting into tears, Ellen ran to him and threw her arms around his neck, powerless against a surge of emotion that had its own will.

'Dear child … don't upset yourself like this …'

'It's been so long, Father … and mother's journal made me remember …'

John Healy took out his handkerchief and wiped his daughter's eyes. 'There, there. No more tears …'

The door opened. It was Harry and a newly tidied Franny who had removed her dirty pinafore and put a yellow ribbon in her hair.

'Lilian, my dear,' John Healy said, smiling at the lady in the fireside chair, 'this is my daughter Ellen, my son Harry and my niece Frances. Children, may I present Mrs Lilian Forrister, my fiancée, and,' he added, gesturing to the young elegant by the window, 'Guy Forrister, her stepson.'

'I'm delighted to meet you,' Mrs Forrister said languidly. 'I've heard a great deal about you. As has Guy.'

The young man came forward to shake hands. He had brown eyes and a square chin above a winged collar.

'How do you do, Miss Healy,' he said, raising her hand to his lips. 'My compliments on your birthday!'

A rush of crimson went to Ellen's hairline. Franny giggled. Mrs Forrister straightened in her chair and rearranged her skirts.

'The young ladies are not used to continental ways, Guy!' She glanced around the company. 'Guy spends his summers in France where he has learnt gallantry towards the fair sex!'

Harry extended his hand and asked, 'Are you French?'

'He's English, of course!' said Mrs Forrister, 'But he has a French château, a bequest from an elderly cousin. And he speaks French fluently!'

'It's not a château!' Guy said.

'I don't know any French!' Franny announced. 'They turfed me out of school and now Mother teaches me, but she doesn't really know any French either.'

Harriet Murphy directed a warning look at her daughter and suggested that the young people might like to show the garden to Guy, now that the rain had stopped.

'Much better if I could take him fishing,' Harry muttered. 'Jimmy says there's great trout rising!'

Guy smiled at him. 'You're a keen fisherman?'

'Second best in the county!'

Franny led the young people to the garden while Harry talked of reels and rods and how to tie flies. Ellen was silent, but acutely aware of the stranger. She was aware of his bearing, his confidence, his politeness and the sense that he belonged to a rich, foreign world.

They were almost at the stables when Maggie's voice erupted from the kitchen door, 'Young Harry ... I'm needin' turf ... Will you come in out of that and be some use to a body!' She appeared on the step with the creel against her hip.

Harry groaned and excused himself. Franny ran after him, leaving Guy and Ellen alone.

Guy looked at the young girl in the blue dress, at the blush only now ebbing under her collar. Searching for something to say, he gestured to a profusion of pink hydrangeas by the garden wall.

'I'm sure you have had a great part in the creation of this lovely garden, Miss Healy.'

She shook her head. 'It's my aunt's garden. I've no time. I have to study.'

'Indeed?'

'I need a scholarship.'

The colour rose again in her face.

'What scholarship are you aiming for?'

'The King's Scholarship. So I can become a national school teacher. I'm a pupil-teacher at the moment. I have my Senior Grade exams still to do … and then the scholarship exams.'

'So you're headed for university?'

'No. A teacher training college for women. There's no proper university in Ireland for Catholics. I would have to go to France or Belgium, but Father couldn't afford that!'

'But I thought Ireland was mostly Catholic?'

'It is,' she said with a small shrug. 'But they don't really count.' She glanced at him. 'I suppose you're a university man?'

'I'm headed for Sandhurst actually. Next year. Royal Military College.'

They passed into the stable yard and a workman, forking out manure, stopped to lean on his pitchfork.

'Grand soft day,' he said, regarding Guy curiously.

Ellen smiled at him and turned to her guest.

'This is Mr James MacMahon,' she said. 'Jimmy, this is Mr Guy Forrister.'

Guy was uncomfortable with the way the fellow raised his

head and narrowed his eyes, as though he were a prince vetting an intruder and not an underling in a greasy cap. But he exchanged nods and followed his guide to the orchard, bemused by the formality of the introduction, the informality of the workman and the strange taste left by their brief encounter.

'Who is that chap, Miss Healy?'

'Jimmy lives down the road. He does jobs for us in return for the grazing of some land. He's a great reader. He goes fishing with Harry and they lend each other books.'

Guy looked around the orchard, but he was not thinking of the Bramley seedlings or the Victoria plums. He had seen the way the Jimmy fellow had looked at the slender girl who moved ahead of him with her curling hair down her back. He was surprised by a rush of protectiveness. When next Ellen turned to him, he reached out and took her hand.

'Such a little hand! Tell me, Ellen, what do you think of Mrs Forrister?'

Ellen caught her breath. Guy's hand, warm and decisive, seemed to speak to her. But she removed her own, sliding it gently from his grip.

'I thought her pleasant. But she is already your stepmother, so you know her better than I do.'

'She became my stepmother two years ago, and graduated to being my father's widow twelve months later. She has had a busy, and reasonably lucrative, two years.'

'Why did you come here with her?'

'It was an opportunity to meet you all! I had arranged to stay with a friend locally – someone I was at school with.'

'Is your friend the young Mr Wallace at Clonshule?'

'You know him?'

'No. But everyone for fifty miles around knows Clonshule.'

'Such an odd place name! Does it mean something?'

'It's Irish – *Cluain Siúil*. It means The Haunted Meadow.'

They went back to the house. The fire was now burning brightly in the dining room and Maggie had just placed the soup tureen on the table. John Healy took his place at one end of the table and his sister at the other, with Mrs Forrister at her right. Ellen sat next to Guy. Her father said grace and then her aunt ladled out the soup. Guy said it was delicious and Franny demanded that he say it in French.

'I have to be sure you're not codding us. There's lots of people go around pretending they know French!'

'*La soupe est vraimant délicieuse, Mademoiselle!*'

There was a ripple of laughter. Mrs Forrister looked around the room.

'What lovely miniatures! They would be your Protestant grandparents I suppose? Were they people of substance?'

When the question did not elicit an immediate response she pressed on, 'John told me once that he was born in a castle, but maybe he was ribbing me?'

'It's true,' Harry said in a quiet voice. 'The castle was built on his ancestral lands. But his family were dispossessed.'

'And John tells me you have a relative in America,' Mrs Forrister continued. 'A very rich man. A gold miner, is he not?'

Harriet Murphy looked down the table at her brother.

'We have no contact, my dearest,' he replied gently. 'He left Ireland a long time ago.'

'But he is still family, is he not? And the Irish Americans never forget family.'

'Maggie,' Mrs Murphy said to the hovering maid, 'I told you to bring in the wine!'

Maggie scuttled off to the kitchen, muttering, 'Lord save us: *Wine*!'

John Healy carved the mutton.

'A nice piece for you, my dear,' he said to his fiancée, handing her plate down the table. Ellen passed the caper sauce. A flustered Maggie returned with an opened bottle and said she'd had grand work getting the cork out of it.

'It was very kind of you to bring us a case of wine, Guy,' Mrs Murphy said. 'We are not used to such luxury. I'm afraid we have no wine glasses ...'

'I'm sure these tumblers will do perfectly,' Mrs Forrister said. 'You know, Guy is a wine connoisseur. His experience of France has been remarkably educating.'

Guy wished this torture would end. 'I'm no expert,' he said. 'But I chose this wine for a reason. If you look at the label, you will find that reason.'

His hostess searched in her pocket for her spectacles.

'Cuvée O'Byrne?' she said laughing. 'Have you brought us an Irish wine, Guy? One with a label that says Bordeaux Superieur?'

'The wine is certainly French. But the vineyard was founded by an Irish emigrant in the seventeenth century, one of a number of Irish people whose descendants have châteaux in the Bordeaux region. Many of them have French titles of nobility.'

'They'd be descendants of the Wild Geese.' Harry said. 'It's a nickname for the Irish soldiers who joined the Irish Brigade in the French army after the Williamite Wars. The unfortunate people left at home had nothing after that little Dutch fart, King Willie, was finished with them.'

'Harry!' his father exclaimed.

'If you are referring to William of Orange, you will have to educate me,' Guy said, startled by the boy's passion and dismayed that the wine should have prompted such tension. 'I'm not sure he was particularly popular on the throne of England, but I know nothing of his Irish exploits.'

Fixing stern eyes on his son, John Healy said the wine was excellent and stood up to pour it, offering some to Ellen to celebrate her birthday.

'The French drink it every day, I suppose,' she said, sipping the ruby liquid carefully. 'I've never tasted it before.'

Guy smiled at her.

'My dear girl, over there it practically flows in the streams! May

I propose a toast to wish you many happy returns?'

She shook her head, laughing.

'You can drink to *my* health instead if you like!' Franny said.

He raised his glass. 'Your good health, Mademoiselle … And what do *you* do, Miss Murphy? How do you occupy your time if you are not at school?'

'I read and sew, and I paint. And mother teaches me the boring stuff. But I have plans for when I grow up.'

Guy raised his eyebrows. 'Indeed?'

'I will fight for women's rights!'

'Unlike your quiet cousin beside me?'

Franny laughed. 'It would be a mistake to underestimate Ellen!'

Guy leaned towards Ellen and confided in a voice that only she could hear, 'Not everyone is cut of the same cloth as you, Miss Healy.'

She looked embarrassed.

'You flatter both of us with your shrewdness, Mr. Forrister!'

Guy felt he had made an ass of himself. I hope she didn't think I was being insolent, he thought. The firelight in her hair, the colour in her face, the delicate curve of her cheek, neck and bosom, stirred him. On her open lower lip was a drop of wine; its incongruous rakishness prompted a rush of desire. He glanced around the table. Mrs Murphy was talking about the war in South Africa.

'They've put the Boers in the most dreadful camps. Women and children!'

'It's true,' Guy said. 'My brother Nigel is serving out there.'

Mrs Forrister moved restively.

'Why talk of such dreadful things, Guy?' she said with a light laugh, 'When you can tell us all about your wonderful house in France?'

# *Chapter 3*

Guy loved his French inheritance, his amazing piece of luck, and hated having to conjure it because his stepmother wanted to impress her new family. He saw Ellen's grey eyes on him. Most beauties had powerfully calculating mothers and it was damned odd to meet a diamond who automatically assumed she had to make her own future.

'My house in France is called Fontebelle,' he said. 'It's about a hundred kilometres southeast of Bordeaux, was built in 1850 by my French cousin for his bride, who unfortunately died in childbirth.'

'And he nursed his poor broken heart to the end of his life?' Franny said eagerly.

'Franny's been reading too many novels,' Harriet Murphy said with a short laugh. 'Is it a very pretty place, Guy?'

'Why not come and judge for yourself?'

'It *is* a pretty place!' Mrs Forrister said with a gesture. 'It has an avenue lined with lavender, and *acres* of private parkland!'

'But,' said John Healy, 'how will you manage to spend any time there, what with the distance and your cadetship at Sandhurst? Would you not sell it?'

'As you know, sir, I cannot sell it until I am of age. I would prefer to keep it. And there is always the summer,' Guy added with an inviting smile, 'when anyone inclined to travel to France is welcome to join me!'

He did not glance at Ellen although he longed to do so. Would she come? It was an exciting thought. Why not? Properly chaperoned and all the rest of it.

'Oh can we go, Mother?' Franny cried, putting down her fork. 'It would be such an adventure!'

'A long and expensive journey. Crossing to England and over to Calais! And then the journey through France.' Mrs Murphy shook her head. 'I do not think any of us will ever see your Fontebelle, Guy, but thank you for the invitation.'

It was only common sense, Ellen told herself. I will never see this magic place. It seemed a great and unnecessary loss and her own existence small and insignificant. She would have to slog for a life she could bear to live, while the youth beside her was already the proprietor of a romantic house with a lavender-lined avenue, a private park and days of endless sunshine in a country where wine flowed in the streams.

'You're very quiet,' Guy said in her ear. 'Penny for them?'

'They're worth more than that!' She met his eyes shyly. 'But only to me!'

Guy held her gaze and she looked away.

Why was she drawn to him? she wondered. Why this inexplicable homecoming? He was present to her in a way no one had ever been. It made her feel visible and powerful, as though she had been touched by magic and summoned to live. She looked down the table and saw that Mrs Forrister's eyes were on her.

The discussion about the Boers resumed and Harry raised his voice, 'It's the same gobshitery as in Ireland, Father. They should leave the Boers their land.'

'I will not have my son use such language! Especially at the dinner table! Nothing can be done about the past. But we can make the present a safe and proper place to live.'

Ellen tried to catch her brother's eye to shut him up, but could see he had the bit between his teeth. Ever since Jimmy had lent him that book, *The Story of Ireland*, he had been like someone with a mission.

'So, we should let them continue to walk all over us ...'

'That's quite enough Harry! We are at table!'

'For God's sake!' Harry jumped from his chair and threw down his napkin. 'Why are you so blind, Father? You must know what really happened in this country! The horror of it – the horror! Century on century! Or don't you care?'

He looked at his aunt with a kind of bewildered apology and left the room. Franny made as though she would run after him, but a look from her mother kept her on her chair.

'What has done this to him?' John Healy demanded. 'Every time I am here, it is worse. Is it the Brothers in that school of his?'

'But everywhere you go it's the same,' Mrs Forrister murmured. 'John and I went to the theatre in Dublin recently and the production was full of political innuendo. It was a play by Mr Yeats – *Caitlín Ní Houlihan*.'

Guy looked incredulous. 'What was wrong with it?'

'It was an irresponsible piece of theatre,' John Healy said. 'The whole thing was propaganda inciting young Irishmen to rebellion, but as only the natives understood the message it is unlikely that Dublin Castle will arrest the author for sedition.'

'Would you put him in jail, sir? Mr Yeats?'

Franny giggled and a ripple of laughter went around the table. Ellen laughed too. Her father looked pointedly at his sister.

'It's just that I fear my son is being contaminated by radicalism. I saw Sullivan's history book in the drawing room ... now there's a book designed to foment unrest among the young.'

'It belongs to Jimmy, our young neighbour,' Harriet replied. 'But if they won't teach our history at school, John, how can you blame young people finding it themselves. Now if you will excuse me, I'll fetch our young man.'

Mrs Murphy rose and left the room, returning a few minutes

later with a sheepish Harry who apologised and resumed his seat in silence.

'You fairly put the cat among the pigeons, old chap!' Guy said to him in a whisper. 'And I thought you were a fisherman – patient and wise!'

Harry brightened, 'Guy, there's heaps of trout in the Multeen. I'll show you tomorrow … if you're around.'

Maggie came in with a tray holding the apple pies, a jug of cream and another of custard and the dining room filled with the scent of cloves and cinnamon. The dinner ended with coffee and then the company retired to the drawing room where Ellen, by popular request, sang 'Love's Old Sweet Song', accompanied by Guy on the piano. But the atmosphere remained uneasy and the evening out of tune with itself.

When Mrs Forrister absented herself before departure, John Healy took his son aside and said, 'This is a social occasion, not a political meeting. My job is to enforce the law, not question it!'

'I didn't mean to upset you, Father.' Harry glanced at Guy. 'Or you Guy. I hope you didn't take offence?'

'Not in the least, old chap! I had no part in that history.'

'You would be much happier, Harry, if you would accept the improvements in this country,' John Healy said. 'We will have Home Rule soon. Don't you think so, Guy?'

'Well, sir, the prime minister ruled it out in May.'

'I saw that. But Salisbury wasn't then addressing Parliament. No, it will come, and soon I think!'

Harry sighed and turned his face away. 'Don't bet on it,' he murmured under his breath.

En route to the kitchen, Ellen met Lilian Forrister in the hall. She was already in her coat and pulling on her gloves.

'Well, my dear girl, I am glad to meet you at last! I was particularly charmed by your singing. As indeed, was Guy …' She glanced through the open drawing room door to where the men were talking by the window. 'He was to go straight on to Clonshule

House. The heir is an old school friend – Harrow you know. But now he's decided to stay overnight in town in order to go fishing tomorrow with your brother.'

Mrs Forrister compressed her lips and lowered her voice.

'I doubt his interest is entirely in fish. But it would be useless to set your cap at him, my dear girl. There are young ladies in London, young ladies with tidy little fortunes.'

'You'd have got on grand with your father, only for that awful Mrs F,' Franny announced when the visitors had left. 'She was a real pain in the fanny.'

'No language like that in this house, if you please Frances. You have disappointed me enough this evening with your brashness.'

'Oh Mother ... I can't pretend to be a good little mouse. In my veins runs blood, not water!'

'Go to bed, Frances. You have the dentist tomorrow, the one person who may be able to curb your tongue. And as for you, Harry, you should write to your father and apologise.'

Harry made a face.

'Guy will be calling after school tomorrow. He's staying over in the Westenra. We've arranged to go fishing.'

'Write the letter now! And make tomorrow's expedition brief. Young Mr Forrister may be on holiday, but you are not!'

Ellen lay in bed and relived the day. Her father's news had reinforced in her the sense of being alone, and her short conversation with Mrs Forrister had made her feel nauseous. Set her cap at him? What did that mean? She thought of the clasp of Guy's hand in the orchard, the way he had looked at her, the way he had listened, the ease with which he had deflected the tension at the dinner table. Realising she had forgotten her prayers, she got out of bed and knelt down.

She prayed for her dead mother, for her father's happiness, for Harry, her aunt and her cousins. And then she prayed for her future.

'Dear God, grant that I may get the scholarship to Carysfort. '

The fitful moonlight filtered through the curtains. The room and its contents were ghostlike. She rose and went to the window. The countryside was quiet, the shining river wending its way near the MacMahon farmhouse where a solitary lamp was still burning. She pictured Jimmy by his hearth, book in hand. He borrowed books from Harry, from Father O'Dowd, from the Master and from the new public library. He would be the best person to go fishing with Guy. He knew the river better than anyone.

In his small, thatched farmhouse at Culgreine, Jimmy built up the fire. He sat at the kitchen table under the picture of the Sacred Heart and reached for his current reading matter – *The Book of Erin*, by Morrison Davidson – an Irish history written by an Englishman, which the curate had lent him. He knew that his ancestors had been the hereditary lords of Monaghan and that the clan lands had been seized by the English after the devastation wrought by Cromwell. He stiffened while reading a contemporary eyewitness account:

> Lord Hugh Mac Mahon, the chief of his illustrious race, a brave and noble military leader, was, after two years imprisonment in London, half-hanged, and ere life was extinct, quartered; his head was then placed on an iron spike on London bridge to feed the ravenous fowls of the air; his four quarters were placed over four of the gates of London.

Jimmy kicked a smoking sod back into the fire and closed the book. Our ancestral lands used to pay Cromwell's foot soldiers, our civilisation destroyed; our people starved, defamed, murdered;

our religion and our language outlawed …

He could no longer put off what he must do. He looked for the New Testament, which was kept on a shelf by the churn, went on his knees, laid his hand ceremoniously on the Bible and took an oath to Almighty God.

# Chapter 4

Cycling to school the next morning, Ellen thought of her father's engagement to Mrs Forrister, and the latter's astonishing caution. Had Mrs Forrister set *her* cap at her father? She thought of him with wistful love. How often would she and Harry see him once he was married? The old bicycle creaked along a puddled road where the barefoot schoolchildren walked in cheerful groups. She heard the song of the Multeen and thought of Jimmy and how his meadow would be affected if it burst its banks.

It was a school day much as any other. The rain had settled in by lunchtime when Mr Corrigan, the Master, joined Ellen and the assistant teacher Mrs Gallagher, by the classroom fire. Above the wooden mantelpiece, dark with years of smoke, was a faded portrait of the late Queen. The children were outside, eating their cuts of homemade bread and jam in the school shed, or chasing each other in the drizzle with shrieks of laughter. The Master commented ruefully on the weather. Ellen told herself there would be no fishing today. Guy Forrister would go on his way and she would never see him again. She did not hurry when school ended. She marked some specimen English compositions for Mrs Gallagher before finding her bicycle when the rain eased and then headed home.

Ellen always loved the sight of Kilcrannagh's chimneys emerging from its trees. She saw them from the little rise in the road outside the school and wondered hungrily if Maggie would have delivered on her morning promise to cook griddle scones. When she reached the turf shed, she put her bike in its accustomed place, noting that Harry was not back yet.

Almost before she saw him, she knew Guy was there. He was seated by the range talking to Maggie who was rolling dough for the griddle. Of course, Ellen thought, Aunt Harriet has taken Franny to the dentist, and Maggie had been fool enough to entertain their visitor in the kitchen.

Guy stood up. 'Hello Ellen. You see how hard it is to get rid of me!'

I'll strangle Maggie, Ellen thought, aware of the untidy kitchen, with the table floured, the griddle hot on the range, and the line of drying clothes.

'Here,' Guy said, 'let me help you off with your wet things.'

Ellen put down her books, let him help her with her coat and felt his fingers touch her shoulders.

When Harry came home he found his sister and Guy Forrister in the kitchen, drinking tea and eating hot buttered scones while Maggie plied the iron. He sighed. He was not in a sociable mood and had hoped Guy would postpone the promised expedition. His right hand was swollen where he had been caned for inattention by Brother O'Flaherty.

'This isn't an opium den, Healy! To think a daydreamer like you has plans to be a teacher … Ha!' Each time the cane came down, the same 'Ha!' accompanied it, until there were three weals across his palm. Now it was hot and swollen and he longed to bathe it in cold water.

'I thought you would change your mind about fishing,' he said to Guy. 'What with the rain …'

'If you show me the best spots today I can try my luck tomorrow without bothering you,' Guy said. 'It can't rain forever.'

'This is Ireland,' Harry replied with a grin. 'It can!'

'Guy's been telling me about his school in England,' said Ellen. 'It sounds like the army!'

'Aren't they all like the army?' Harry drew his breath through his teeth and put his sore hand into his pocket. 'Is poor old Fran still at the dentist?'

Maggie nodded, thumping the cooling iron down on a folded sheet. 'Aye. They'll be back any minute and it'll be straight to bed for the *creaturín*!'

Harry went to hang up his coat and Ellen rose from her chair.

'I'll leave you with the famous fisherman!' she told Guy. 'I have to study or I'll fall behind.'

'If I come tomorrow will I see you?' he asked, his voice very low.

Ellen shrugged, glanced at Harry and left the room. Lingering in the hall, she heard her brother describing a pool where the trout were hiding, '… little buggers think they're safe because of the overhang,' Guy's deeper voice replying, Maggie clattering as she made fresh tea and her sudden warning, 'Don't be goin' near Duff's Pool. Jimmy says it's twelve feet deep if it's an inch!'

Ellen reached her room and closed the door. She was still warm from Guy's confidences during that blissful half-hour before Harry had come home. She had a window on his life now – could feel for him in the sudden death of his barrister father two years ago, was able to visualise his London home and his elder brother, Nigel, who was getting married as soon as the South African war was over. Nigel would take over their uncle's estate, a place called Lindthorp in Yorkshire. Guy himself was looking forward to his career in the army.

'It's in the family,' he had said proudly when she asked him why he was so keen on a military life.

'So you won't be living in your lovely place in France?'

'Fontebelle is for when I'm old and retired.' Squaring his

shoulders he'd added, 'It is an honour, you know Ellen, to hold the King's Commission.'

'And your friend in Clonshule House? Has he military ambitions also?'

'Bertie? No. He's more the sort of chap who'd do the Grand Tour, then spend the rest of his life playing squire.'

'I saw him once,' Ellen had said.

It had been a wintry Sunday. People on their way to Mass scuttled out of the way of the flying Clonshule coach. All except one old man, who had struck the bowling vehicle with his stick and, as the wheels rattled by him with inches to spare, had cried out fiercely in Gaelic and spat. The only thing she recalled of the young man who stared through the small back window of the coach was the curl of his lip.

She positioned her table by the window, opened her books and tried to apply herself. When the rain eased she heard the back door open and the footsteps coming around the side of the house. She could see the two aspiring fishermen clumping through the front gate in wellingtons and raincoats, Harry carrying a fishing rod and Guy a net. They were talking like old friends. She concentrated on her work and did not feel the time pass until she heard her aunt's trap turning in at the gate and saw Jimmy jump to the ground to let down the step.

Aunt Harriet shook out her umbrella and helped her daughter. Franny was holding a scarf against her face and seemed close to fainting. Jimmy put a brotherly arm around her and guided her towards the house.

Thank God for Jimmy, Ellen thought. She did not know how he always found time to look after the Murphys when he had ninety stony acres of his own to manage. But he seemed to have boundless energy. 'He's the kind of man who'd find the source of the Nile,' Harry had once said about him, 'if someone else hadn't got there first.'

Ellen ran downstairs. Fran's impacted molar had been giving

her intermittent pain for weeks. It had been Harry who had persuaded her to have it extracted. But now she was slumped in a kitchen chair, looking white and ill, her scarf covered with black blood clots. Aunt Harriet, still in her hat and coat, was stirring something in a cup and its pungency filled the kitchen.

'Poor Fran! What did he do to you?'

'Oh El, he took my poor tooth out! My mouth was bleeding all the way home.'

'This will ease the pain,' her mother said in a practical voice, spooning laudanum into her daughter's mouth.

Fran made a face, 'Yeh … ack …!'

'Bed for you now, my girl! The best thing is sleep!'

Ellen filled a stone jar from the kettle, wrapped it in a towel from the line above the range and told her cousin she'd help her upstairs.

'Good girl. I'll be up in a moment.' Aunt Harriet paused and looked around with a frown. 'But where's your brother? Not back from school yet?'

'He's gone fishing with Guy Forrister.'

'That young man must think Harry has nothing better to do than entertain him,' her aunt replied with a snort. 'And on a day like this too.'

'He's all for showing him Duff's Pool,' Maggie muttered. 'I couldn't stop him!'

Ellen saw Franny safely into bed, pulled the curtains and left a cup beside her so she could spit into it.

'Don't go,' Franny whispered when she was comfortably settled. 'Tell me about Guy!'

'What do you want me to tell you?'

'El, you're the reason he came back today. I'm sure he doesn't care if he never saw a fish.'

Ellen was spared replying by the arrival of her aunt who propped her daughter up with a second pillow, stroked her hand and said, 'Sleep now, Frances dear.'

When Franny's eyes closed she whispered, 'The laudanum is doing its work. She'll be all right now, providing the bleeding doesn't start again. One of us should stay with her.'

'I'll stay. I can study here.'

Ellen fetched her poetry book and sat near Franny's window, lifting the edge of the curtain to avail of the light. Part of Tennyson's 'Morte d'Arthur' had to be learnt by heart. The verse was full of music and soon she was immersed in its story of the majestic dying king, the sword, Excalibur, thrown back into the lake and the mysterious hand that rose to catch it.

Half an hour later Franny stirred, suddenly turned on her pillows and whispered, 'El, is Harry back?'

'Not yet.'

Ellen glanced out at the overcast sky. The light was failing. Why weren't they home? Seeing that Franny had gone back to sleep, she went to her own room and stood at the window where she had a better view of the road. In the distance, emerging from the shadow of the arching trees, she saw two young men. She lifted the sash and leaned out, wondering why they were moving with a drunken gait. And then she was racing from the room, down the stairs and into the yard, calling to Jimmy who was leading the pony in for the night.

Jimmy looked in the direction of her pointing arm, dropped the pony's reins and vaulted the fence that bordered the meadow. Ellen saw him take her brother from a staggering Guy. Her aunt, who had come to the front door to see what the fuss was about, stood on the front steps, clasping both hands to her heart as her nephew was carried into the house.

Ellen tried to run but her legs would not obey. Guy approached, water squelching in his boots, his clothes sticking to his shivering body.

'Slipped on a boulder in the river, Ellen … Hit his head …'

When Ellen made no response, he put out an icy hand and drew her towards the front door. Jimmy came around the side of the house on Harry's bicycle.

'I'm getting the doctor!' he yelled, standing on the pedals as he shot out the gate and down the road.

'I pulled him out as quickly as I could and pumped him, Ellen,' said Guy. 'I think I got the water out of him.'

Ellen heard his uncertainty. She was in the terrifying space she had known before, where reality was only illusion and where people you loved could slip away. She wanted Guy to tell her Harry was fine, but Guy, no longer the urbane and privileged young Englishman, was just a shocked youth with chattering teeth. Maggie came with towels. Ellen left Guy to her and went to the drawing room where her brother was on the sofa by the fire. Aunt Harriet had already removed his wet clothes and wrapped him in blankets. Ellen knelt to take his hand. Except for the blood clotted along his hairline, he looked as though he were asleep.

'My poor child, don't look like that!' Aunt Harriet said, putting motherly arms around her niece. 'Harry's cold and concussed. The main thing now is to keep him warm and to pray there is no internal bleeding.'

Ellen's tears soaked between her lips. She chafed her brother's hands, whispering, 'Harry, Harry, wake up …'

Doctor Dempsey's voice could be heard in the hall. Ellen showed him to his patient and went to the kitchen where Maggie had put tea and ham sandwiches on the table. The atmosphere was taut. Guy, his hair in drying spikes, was wrapped in an old Foxford Wool dressing gown that had once belonged to Uncle Mathew. Jimmy, red-faced and breathless, was standing by the range.

'So what happened?' he demanded.

'The bank gave way. He hit his head. The river was high …'

'Thank God, Guy, you managed to pull him out!' Ellen said.

Jimmy gave a snort of contempt and said, 'But who was the eejit who persuaded him to go out fishing in the first place?'

Guy tried to think of a fitting response. He was unfamiliar with the fellow's vernacular and did not want a contest of words with him. He heard the front door close as the doctor left and then Mrs Murphy was in the kitchen doorway asking Jimmy to help Harry to his room.

Ellen jumped up and followed them. Harry seemed lucid, joking as he was helped up the stairs that he had finally found the cure for boredom.

'Tell poor old Guy I'm sorry I made a mess of things. And tell him thanks,' he whispered to Ellen, 'for saving my bacon!'

'Your brother needs to sleep now,' Aunt Harriet said when he was safely in bed. 'I'll stay with him for a while. Thank you, Jimmy, for your help.'

Jimmy, muttering that his cows would think he had died, went downstairs and Ellen saw him to the front door.

'You shouldn't have spoken like that to Guy,' she said in a low voice. 'It wasn't his fault. And without him, God knows what might have happened!'

'Ellen, if that English fellow hadn't pestered Harry, he'd never have gone out on a day that wasn't fit for a dog! What's he doing here anyway? When he's not damning your brother he's looking at you like a sick calf!'

'Don't be ridiculous.'

'If it's admiration you want,' Jimmy went on, putting a tentative hand on her wrist, 'you can find it much nearer home!'

Ellen shook off his hand. She shut the door and heard Jimmy clump cross the gravel. She returned to the kitchen where a dishevelled Guy was fingering his drying clothes on the clothes line hoisted on a pulley above the range.

'Don't mind Jimmy, Guy! He's had a fright and he's not himself.'

'Quite frankly, Ellen, I'm not interested in whether the fellow's himself or not!'

'Harry said to thank you,' she murmured. 'You took a terrible risk.'

Guy's eyes softened. 'My dear girl, I could hardly have done otherwise.' He took her hands and drew her to the fire. 'Poor

Ellen. Your fingers are frozen! You should be tucked up in a warm bed. And I,' he added, eyeing his wrinkled garments, 'should be on my way'.

'Your clothes are still sopping! Maggie's making up the box room for you.'

They stood together in immobile silence, inches apart, staring at each other.

'I'll say goodnight so,' he whispered when they heard Maggie's step on the stairs.

Maggie gave him a candle and Guy found his way to the box room where a trunk and three suitcases were piled on top of each other and where a narrow bed had been made. The room was cold and smelled of camphor. The door did not close properly against the jamb. Guy put the candlestick down on the old leather luggage, threw himself onto the bed and in the flickering candlelight studied the cracks in the ceiling. He was still smarting at the barb handed out by the workman, particularly as it had been delivered in front of Ellen.

But it had been a rotten day to go out, and he had done so with an ulterior motive. He'd wanted to stay near Ellen. He'd wanted to know her brother better because it would bring him nearer to her. He'd wanted to be part of her odd little world. Trying to work out why it appealed to him, he had decided it involved the absence of cant; it was a circumscribed world, but it was real. And she was real, a little warrior with her back to the wall, depending on an enormous personal effort for her future. It was that gallantry, allied to her fragility and beauty, that riveted him. But how could he have foreseen that Harry would come a cropper in that damn river, or how close a thing it could have been for both of them, the current so powerful and the water so cold?

He heard the stairs creak and, looking through the crack in the door, he saw Ellen, candle in hand, move along the landing. She paused at a door and her aunt emerged. They had a whispered conference and then the girl continued on her way and slipped into the room beside his own. He heard her small sounds as she prepared for bed. He closed his eyes and imagined her in a white nightdress, a cold little angel. He groaned softly. He would warm her, love her …

# Chapter 5

Ellen was far too tense to sleep. The house, she felt, had become a hospital. In one room lay Harry, emerged from the shadow of death. In another Franny slept, drugged with laudanum. And in the box room beside her was an exhausted Guy who had risked his life to save her brother. Filled with gratitude for what he had done, she wondered at the tenderness he had shown her, the feelings he had awoken in her and the strange excitement of his nearness.

Eventually she slept. But her sleep was troubled and she woke before dawn, emerging from a dream where her mother had taken her journal, written Harry's name on a blank page and ringed it in black. In the dim light she could see the diary resting where she had left it, but the lingering horror made her afraid her brother had died while she slept and that her mother had come to tell her.

She got out of bed, tiptoed to Harry's door and turned the brass knob. Her aunt had left a night light burning on the chest by the window and she could see that Harry was lying on his back, one arm thrown over his pillows. She listened and heard the strength of his breathing, the grip he had on life. From outside came the first cheeps of birdsong and the first shy light.

Relieved, she went back to her room to wash and dress quickly. While going downstairs she was mindful of the creaking steps and the sleeping household and wondered if Guy was up yet. In the kitchen she found a sleepy Maggie brushing the hob with an old goose wing and Guy at the table eating porridge. He stood up when she came in and wished her good morning, but he cut a sorry sight in shrunk and matted clothes.

'Oh Guy! Your clothes are ruined!'

He shrugged. 'No matter. I'll change at the hotel. How is Harry?'

'Alive. Thanks to you.' She lowered her voice and added, 'I've just had a horrible dream.'

'What was that?'

'It was very queer. My mother was crying and ringing Harry's name in black ...' Maggie started and crossed herself. 'So I went in to check on him,' Ellen went on, 'and he's fine.'

Maggie pulled back the curtains and let up the smoke-discoloured blinds.

'It'll be a grand day,' she muttered. 'Thanks be to God!'

Guy said he should be on his way and Ellen told him he could take Harry's bicycle and leave it at the Westenra where Jimmy would collect it.

When Maggie went to the pantry he whispered, 'Could I accompany you to school, Ellen? I would very much like to talk to you.'

The air was fresh. The cottages had their half-doors open and the thatches were dark and damp after the soaking. Down the road in the morning sunlight came the schoolchildren, tramping along the wet road in bare feet, their books in satchels made of sacking, a single sod of turf under each child's arm.

'That's Jimmy's place,' said Ellen, indicating the modest thatched house set back from the road and accessed by a stony boreen. Guy saw the MacMahon fellow, bucket in hand, come around the side of his house and dip the pail into one of the barrels of rainwater at the gable end. He had a military bearing, he acknowledged, the sort of fellow who, if properly trained, would make an excellent soldier – provided, of course, he learned to keep a civil tongue in his head. Ellen waved at him, and Jimmy raised a hand. He glanced at Guy, nodded briefly and turned away.

When they had negotiated the bend in the road and were out of sight of the house, Guy dismounted.

'Can we walk?' he called.

Ellen braked and dismounted. A few children passed them, smiling shyly and saying, 'Good morning, Miss Healy.'

'I don't know how their poor feet can take it,' Guy said indignantly. 'On a stony road … And why are they carrying peat?'

Ellen looked at him reproachfully. 'It's not out of caprice, Guy! They are very poor. The government keeps down the price of farm produce so people in England can have cheap food, but the rents paid for the farms here are very high. The turf is for the schoolroom fires. It's the parents' contribution. This isn't England you know.'

'There are poor people in England too, but not on this scale!'

Ellen lifted her chin. He was afraid he had offended her. Her profile was proud and beautiful. He loved the way her hair was caught at the back of her head with a ribbon, loved how it flowed down her back. She could grace a court, he thought, and yet here she was on a wet, stony road at the back end of nowhere.

'Ellen,' he continued, lowering his voice, 'I've wanted to have time alone with you. It was the real reason I came back yesterday. I am utterly gone on you. You make other girls seem like cardboard dolls.'

'But you don't know me!' Ellen exclaimed after a moment. 'And I really don't know you either.'

'I need to see you again, Ellen. Is it possible?'

She looked at him and looked away, dropping her eyes to the potholes.

'Guy, you are leaving here today. So it's not possible.'

'But Clonshule is only four miles away. You like me … Ellen … don't you?'

She nodded. He made to take her hand but she pulled back. As they neared the school, Guy said in an urgent whisper, 'What time do they release you?'

'It's not prison!' she said with a laugh. 'I get out about half three, but …'

'I'll see you then,' he said, mounting Harry's bike and pedalling away.

Mr Corrigan, the Master, was waiting for her in the school hall to tell her that Mrs Gallagher would not be in today, so she would have to manage the junior classes on her own. Ellen called the youngsters into the big, single schoolroom that served the Infants, and First, Second and Third Classes. The fire had already been lit by one of the senior boys and the room had the familiar smell of turf smoke and chalk dust, but today Ellen was barely cognisant of her surroundings.

She gave Third Class an arithmetic test, Second Class a spelling test and conducted reading with the rest. Father O'Dowd came at eleven to give a catechism class for the half-hour permitted by the Board of Education, and Ellen dutifully hung before the class the mandatory card with the printed legend: 'RELIGIOUS INSTRUCTION IN PROGRESS'.

Afterwards the priest drew her aside.

'I'm sorry to hear Harry was in a spot of trouble yesterday.'

'Oh yes, Father. But he was saved by his companion … a visitor.'

'A young Englishman I understand? Who escorted you to school this morning,' the priest went on whimsically. 'A youth of many parts evidently.'

'He's a very nice person, Father.'

'I hope he wasn't filling your head with any nonsense?'

Ellen saw the dust motes dancing in a sudden shaft of sunlight.

'No Father.'

'That's good anyway,' Father O'Dowd said. 'I'm sure a sensible girl like you, Ellen, doesn't need me to tell you how important it is to keep young men in their place.'

Ellen turned indignant eyes on him and said, 'He did nothing out of place, Father.'

'Good. So I will see you in confession on Saturday?'

Ellen nodded politely. But the priest had intruded into her innermost sanctum and her heart filled with a new rebellion. This was not a matter for confession and she was not going to gratify curiosity.

At the day's end the Master dropped in to the junior classroom and watched while Ellen conducted the needlework class. She went from one child to another, demonstrating running stitch, hemming stitch and showing the older girls how to turn the heel of a sock. Expertise at needlework was a prerequisite for obtaining a place in Carysfort College.

Mr Corrigan let the children off five minutes early, then stood by the hearth as Ellen put her sewing materials away. She was wondering what he had to say to her, this middle-aged man in a grey worsted suit and waistcoat who personified authority. She prayed he was not about to find fault with her teaching.

But the Master merely asked, 'How is Harry, Ellen? Father O'Dowd tells me he had an accident.'

'He fell in the river. But he's all right!'

'That boy was always too spirited for his own good! I remember him when he was a little fellow here. Too ready by half with the quick answer. And physically foolhardy too.'

Ellen sighed, thinking of Harry's recent outburst at the dinner table, and his showing off to Guy, which she was sure had caused his accident.

'Does he still want to be a teacher?' When Ellen nodded the

Master added, 'He's lucky he doesn't have to get a scholarship. Unlike his hardworking sister.'

'It's all right,' Ellen said stiffly. 'My father can't afford to pay college fees for us both.'

'Well, hopefully everything will be grand. You're an excellent pupil-teacher.'

Ellen heard the forced cheerfulness. And the doubt. She was used to it. She often saw it in Aunt Harriet's eyes; she even saw it in Harry's. Sometimes when her aunt was very kind to her she felt it was to cushion her against eventual, almost certain, disappointment.

I will, she told herself. I will. I *will*! But, all the same, the old panic jittered. What if she failed? Where could she go? What could she do? Get a job behind a counter if she were lucky. If she was not lucky she might get some kind of position in service in some rich household, some variety of skivvy work. She certainly could not burden either her father or her aunt. Or she could marry some old farmer.

Dan Corrigan saw the girl pale and wondered what would happen to her if she did not fulfil her dream. The climate did not favour Catholic education. The Erasmus Smith scholarship scheme had recently been withdrawn from them and Protestants, north and south, were still objecting to the idea of Catholics having a university. Longstanding government policy in Ireland had sought to create an ignorant population out of one of the most literary minded people in Europe. Even the primary school system had been intended as a force of anglicisation. But over the centuries, the people had flouted the Penal Laws, to the extent of founding a succession of Irish Colleges on the Continent.

'I know you have set your heart on winning a scholarship,' he went on gently, 'but you must realise there is fierce competition for the few there are.'

Ellen thought of the evening ahead, the pile of books, the long hours of lamplit study. She thought of her Senior Grade exam next year. She thought of the big test, the King's Scholarship examination, in another two years.

On the chimney breast was the dead queen's portrait. Only last year the sovereign had visited Ireland. In Dublin, Miss Maud Gonne – the English beauty who had become a fierce Irish patriot – had addressed a great crowd and urged them to protest at this visit by what she called 'The Famine Queen'. The constabulary had baton-charged and several people had been injured. Ellen was well aware that, had the venue been elsewhere, one of the injured could have been her father.

The Master went back to his classroom. Ellen tidied things into the brown-painted cupboard where the schoolroom stocks were kept, took off her pinafore and hung it on its peg. She donned her coat and went to find her bicycle, looking around nervously, as she passed through the school gate, to see if Guy had kept his promise. But there was no sign of him and her sense of disappointment was tempered by relief. After all, the Master would have seen him and in no time at all her aunt would have heard of it, not to mention Father O'Dowd, who would raise it in confession whether she liked it or not. And anyway, the turmoil he caused her was something she did not know how to deal with, and her spirits were too low for company. Despite all her determination, her conversation with the Master had left her feeling that her ambition was absurd and her future dark and hopeless.

But Guy was waiting. As Ellen passed the point on the boreen where the verge was wide and hawthorn created a kind of dell, he was there, leaning on Harry's bicycle. With a quick glance over her shoulder, Ellen dismounted and wheeled her bicycle out of sight of the road.

'Someone will see us and I'll get into trouble!'

Guy's face was full of delight. He took her bike and propped it against a tree.

'One day we'll thumb our noses at the lot of them!' he said, taking her hands. 'You don't really mind, do you Ellen – that I lay in wait for you?'

'No. But you should go now.'

'Not until I give you this.'

He pressed a small box into her hands and closed her fingers around it.

'What is it?'

'I bought it in the town today. Open it when you get home. Use it to remember me.'

Ellen looked at the little box and found herself suddenly in Guy's arms. She gave him her lips and felt the hunger from the very depths of her that cried out.

'Is there anywhere I can write to you that my letters will not be read by your formidable aunt?' Guy whispered when he released her.

'She does not read my letters,' she replied breathlessly. 'But, of course, the only ones I ever get are from Father. Oh Guy … I'd better go!'

He reached out and touched her hair.

'Bless you Ellen. Don't forget me. Don't give up on me. Promise me that? Promise.'

She bent her head. Her whisper was so low he could barely hear it.

'I promise.'

Franny was up and about when Ellen got home. Although a bit pale, she was as ebullient as if she had never had a tooth extracted, been dosed with laudanum and slept comatose through yesterday's drama. She was in an armchair in the drawing room, wrapped in a rug and reading a library book. Harry, she said, was still in bed, but only because her mother had insisted that he remain there.

'He has a grand lump on his skull,' Maggie said. 'But otherwise he's as fit as a gosling. Jimmy's upstairs with him at the moment.'

When Ellen had removed her boots she hurried upstairs, turning over Guy's little gift in her pocket. But first she needed to see her brother. Harry's door was open. His forehead was bandaged and he was propped up with pillows. Jimmy was sitting by his bedside and rose when she entered..

'How are you feeling?' she asked, deliberately ignoring Jimmy because she was still angry with him. 'You look the picture of the wounded hero!'

'It's true that I'm wounded,' Harry responded with a grin, 'if untrue that I'm a hero! I'm getting as much attention as a nabob so I don't think I'll bother recovering!'

Ellen, feeling suddenly bad about snubbing Jimmy, turned to him and smiled. Jimmy looked uncomfortable.

'Where's Guy?' Harry demanded suddenly, turning to the door as though he expected him. 'I did not thank him properly.'

'He's gone to Clonshule. I thanked him for you.'

Franny appeared at the door in a sociable mood and Ellen excused herself, saying she had heaps of work to do. In her room, she took Guy's gift from her pocket and slowly unwrapped it. Inside was a jeweller's box and a small gilt-edged card. She stared at the writing: *For the only girl in the world! All my love forever, Guy.*

She opened the box. Secured in black velvet was a piece of jewellery unlike any she had ever seen.

'How strange it is!' she whispered, picking it up and holding it to the light.

It was a gold ring in the shape of a coiled snake. A shaft of sunlight from the window picked out the miniscule diamonds along its coils. The red stones of its eyes were like tiny drops of blood.

She slipped the ring on her left hand, admired it, held it up so she could see it in the mirror. Her heart quickened. A whole world, one she had hardly dared to imagine, was taunting her with the prospect of being loved.

She did not hear her aunt's bedroom door open, nor her own,

until her aunt was already in the room.

'What is that, Ellen?' Aunt Harriet asked in a low voice. 'Has someone given you a ring?'

She crossed to the bed, picked up the box and the card and held out her hand for Guy's gift.

'Oh Ellen. You know you cannot keep this. You must return it to him.' She gave a low compassionate laugh, 'You have only known the boy for three days!'

'But he means what he says, Aunt. He has asked me to wait for him!'

'Of course he means what he says,' her aunt replied, studying the ring in the palm of her hand. 'This is very pretty, the gift of a young man who has fallen in love. But young men make a career of falling in love. You must not read too much into it,' she added, sitting down on the bed beside her niece and putting an arm around her. 'You come from such different worlds. The truth is that he will forget you and you must forget him!'

'You think it's some silly infatuation.' Ellen said angrily. 'But he has kissed me and I have kissed him back. And I won't forget him,' she added in a low voice. 'I will never forget him!'

# Chapter 6

*October 1901*

Kilcrannagh returned to normal. Harry forgot his brush with destiny and Ellen heard nothing further from Guy. Her aunt had confiscated his ring and had advised her to put the whole episode out of her head. But this, coupled with his silence, only made him more mysterious.

In mid October a wire arrived from Frank, Clare's husband, to say Clare had gone prematurely into labour. Aunt Harriet packed her bags for Dublin and left the following morning, a misty autumnal Saturday. Harry drove her to the station in the trap and returned to a house buzzing with female conjecture from which he was excluded.

'It must be queer having a baby,' Franny opined suddenly in late afternoon, putting down *Sense and Sensibility* and looking out of the drawing-room window at the falling leaves. 'Poor Clare. Mother is so coy. She wouldn't even talk about it this morning. But it must be awful – blood and bits and *total* agony …'

'Fran!' Ellen exclaimed from her chair by the piano where she was mending stockings, indicating Harry with an inclination of her head.

'Mercy!' Harry pleaded in a woebegone voice from the sofa where he was reading his father's letter for the third time.

'Men never confront reality,' Franny announced scornfully. 'They invent versions that meet their requirements. Then they worship the versions.'

She looked to Ellen for endorsement, but the latter did not respond. She was thinking of Clare, wondering when her ordeal would be over. Women often died in childbirth and she was praying silently that all would be well.

'Speaking of worship,' Harry said suddenly in a coaxing voice, 'I could really venerate some toast. You're so good at it, Fran!'

'From the significant to the mundane!' Franny exclaimed, but she got up, went to the kitchen and returned with a loaf of shop bread, a bread knife and some butter.

'Maggie's bringing in tea,' she announced, kneeling on the hearth rug, where she took the brass toasting fork from its hook at the corner of the hearth, skewered it with a thick slice of bread and held it to the fire.

'Fran,' Ellen said irritably after a moment, looking up from her darning in response to the stench of burning bread, 'you're scorching it!'

Franny exclaimed under her breath, removed the burnt slice to a plate beside her, attached another and held it to the fire.

'You're very cross these days, El,' she muttered, adding in a low voice, 'You don't need to be, you know.'

Ellen was galled by Franny's ceaseless chatter. She was under a cloud. Her aunt had confiscated Guy's ring, but had subsequently mislaid it and accused Ellen of having secretly repossessed it. Her denials had been waste of breath.

'I know I left it in the top drawer of my dressing table, Ellen. It's not there now.'

'I think it's too bad that you should lose it, Aunt, and then blame me.'

But when the weeks had passed without any word from Guy, Ellen had begun to painfully suspect that her aunt had been right about him all along. He had probably thought things through, she told herself, and realised he had been the victim of a ridiculous impulse.

She heard voices in the kitchen, Maggie's and what sounded like Jimmy's, followed by a crisp, male footstep in the hall. Jimmy came into the room carrying the tea tray.

'I was hoping the "quality" might invite me to partake of tay with them,' he said mockingly, putting the tray on the table and executing a bow. 'Ladies … Young master …'

'Sit down, Jimmy,' Franny said, 'and stop behaving like an eejit.'

Ellen put away her darning and rose to pour the tea. She noticed how lean and handsome their visitor looked, how well-dressed for a change. She had been uneasy with him since his outburst on the evening when Harry had fallen into the river.

'My goodness,' Franny added, looking their visitor up and down, 'you're all dressed up!'

'Fresh from the sacrament of penance, I suspect?' Harry said. 'Freshen the body. Shrive the soul!'

Jimmy grinned. 'Can't a man go to confession in peace? I'm calling on my friends,' he continued, directing a coaxing smile at Ellen, 'and that's what I'm dressed for!'

'Well, I'm glad to see you anyway!' Franny said. 'Ellen's like a wet weekend and Harry's digesting another tetchy letter from his tetchy dad.'

'Bad news?'

Harry sighed. 'Father promises us another visit and no doubt I will have the riot act read to me yet again.'

'You're being unfair!' Ellen exclaimed as she poured the tea. 'What is he supposed to do? He pledged himself to the maintenance of law and order in this country.'

'There's more to law and order than supporting a regime predicated on expropriation,' Harry replied darkly. 'And there's more to fatherhood than sending a few pounds to someone to rear your children for you.'

'He had no choice!'

Franny fixed another slice to the toasting fork. 'Why don't you just read us the letter?' she said.

'It's the usual parental exhortation,' Harry replied, but he began to read, mimicking his parent's dignified tones.

> *I am relieved you have fully recovered from your accident, Harry, and I have written to thank Guy for his part in saving you. I hope to see you at the end of the month. Right now we're being kept on alert with a spate of cattle driving …*

'What's 'cattle driving'? Franny demanded, handing Jimmy a piece of toast at the end of the fork.

'It's a subversive activity,' Jimmy replied mildly, 'designed to punish landlords who have cleared their land of people. Desperate men come at night, drive off the cattle that have replaced the tenants and plough the pastures so that they can no longer be used for grazing.'

'Poor Father,' Ellen said. 'It makes the work of the police so dangerous.'

'He knows that,' said Harry, picking up the letter again. 'He says as much here at the end of his letter.' He resumed reading aloud. Ellen could almost hear her father's tired voice.

> *Be careful of what you allow to influence you, Harry. Sedition has only one outcome. This country is like the sea, waiting only for a wind big enough to forge a cataclysm!*

'Sedition!' Franny exclaimed with a laugh. 'That's a grand word!' She crunched a bite of toast, licking the butter that dribbled over her fingers.

'Cataclysm is an even better one,' Harry said. 'Fran, stop gobbling the toast and fire another piece over here!'

Franny said she wasn't his slave and that he could make his own. But Harry lost interest. He turned to Jimmy, lowered his voice and said cryptically, 'Did you bring it?'

Jimmy nodded, took from his pocket a book in a brown paper cover and passed it to his friend.

'I got it from old Sweeney,' he muttered. 'The ex-sergeant major!'

'What's the book?' Franny demanded, sitting back on her hunkers to drink her tea, her cheeks red from the fire.

'Mathematical calculations of an advanced nature! Of no interest to young ladies.'

Harry added that he had to stretch his legs. He rose from the sofa and Jimmy rose from his chair. 'Anyone else for walk?' he asked, looking at Ellen who shook her head.

'Ellen and I have urgent ladies' talk,' Franny said. She stared at the youths who suddenly seemed inclined to linger and added, 'of no interest to young men!'

When the two friends had left the room Ellen looked at her cousin apologetically. 'I'm sorry I've been like a wet weekend, Fran. But what's the urgent ladies talk?'

'More than you dream of. I happen to have in my pocket something that will set your little heart pattering!' She sat at Ellen's feet, put her hand into her pocket and extracted something in her closed fist.

'What is it?'

Franny opened her hand. Nestling in her palm was Guy's little ring.

'I pinched it from Mother's dressing table. I overheard your conversation with her the day Guy left. It was very mean of her to force you to give up his keepsake.'

Ellen picked up the ring. For a moment she wondered if honour demanded she return it to her aunt. But her aunt would only send it back to Guy and he would think she had broken her word.

'Ellen,' Franny burst out anxiously, 'you're not thinking of telling Mother I pinched it? You couldn't be so craven. I know we're supposed to be good, obedient little girls, but, since obedience is about pleasing other people, it is really quite immoral as a lifetime option.'

Ellen laughed, tucked the ring away in her work basket and put away her darning.

'Don't go,' Franny said, in evident relief. 'I'm not finished yet, dear cousin!' She pulled a letter from her pocket and announced triumphantly, 'This is a missive addressed to a Miss Ellen Healy. As it is not her father's writing, I fear it must be from an admirer. I very improperly intercepted it some time ago, but thought it was better to wait until Mother was out of the house before passing it on.'

Maggie's step could be heard in the hall. Ellen snatched the envelope and shoved it into her pocket.

'Thank you, darling Franny. But you have taken an awful risk!'

Maggie came in and the two girls helped restore cups and saucers to the tray.

'What did you think of the dashing Jimmy in his Sunday best?' Franny asked the maid slyly, 'With his snow-white shirt and his boots polished …'

'Sure he'd take the sight out of your eyes!'

'Was he eyeing you, Maggie? '

'Divil an eye, Miss,' the maid replied, glancing at Ellen. 'He keeps it for someone else not a million miles away.'

'Oh Maggie, you must have something better to do than filling your head with nonsense.'

'There's a lot to be said for nonsense!' the maid replied tartly. 'At least it's harmless.'

She gathered up the tray and left the room. Franny rolled across the carpet until she had reached the sofa and then searched among the cushions for the book Jimmy had brought, found it and opened it curiously.

'*On War*,' she intoned after a moment in a puzzled voice, 'by a Mr von Clausewitz. I thought they said it was maths. But this,' she added, leafing through it, 'is all military stuff!'

Ellen muttered that boys would be boys. She picked up her work basket and hurried upstairs. She shut her bedroom door, put Guy's ring on her finger and opened his letter.

*Sunday 8th September, 1901*
*Clonshule House*

*My dearest Ellen,*

*Even here in the splendid home of my friend Bertie all I can think of is you. Whilst out cubbing yesterday I took a toss at a ditch (I am blaming the horse!) and today I have to rest the knee, which gives me the chance to write to you.*

*My room overlooks the park here, which has heaps of interesting trees – oaks, monkey puzzles and south American pines, imported many years ago. The room itself is full of antique furniture, some Georgian, some French, but the bed is fit for a Borgia – a mahogany four-poster with crimson hangings.*

*I will be returning to England tomorrow. I will write again from Sandhurst and you can write to me there. I long for a few lines! Everything I said to you holds true for now and for ever. Trust me in this, my lovely Ellen. I will come back as soon as I can.*

*I'm enclosing a small snap which I found in my pocket book – so that you don't forget me.*

*All my fondest love forever,*

*Guy.*

It was like a reprieve when hope was gone. Ellen looked at the little photograph, kissed it and wrote Guy's name on the back. Then she put the ring to her lips in fervent happiness, before looking around for a good hiding place.

# *Chapter 7*

Harriet Murphy returned from Dublin ten days later, bemused and delighted at having become grandmother to a baby boy.

'They're calling him Mathew after his grandfather,' she told them tearfully. She embraced Franny and Harry, and added, 'He is a very handsome little fellow, and although a few weeks premature, should do well. Clare is also fine, although exhausted, and Frank is walking on air.'

But she did not embrace her niece and later, when they were alone together, she said to her coldly, 'Well Ellen, the ring has not been returned to my dressing table! Have you anything to tell me before I write to your father about your conduct?'

Ellen was appalled. One glance at her aunt's face told her she was serious. She could not risk her father's ire so she bent her head and shamefacedly confessed she had the ring.

'And to think I would have staked my life on your integrity! Look at it from my perspective,' her aunt went on when Ellen was sullenly silent, 'I have charge of a young girl who is carrying on a clandestine relationship with a young man. I am very worried because I know that these things can have extremely serious consequences.'

'But I'm not "carrying on" anything, Aunt Harriet.'

'Ellen, I have intercepted several letters to you from Guy Forrister, the content of which makes it perfectly clear that there is more between you than simple friendship!'

Ellen fought back the tears. So Guy had written again … and again. He did love her still! He did! 'Please give me the letters, Aunt,' she said, her voice rising. 'They're mine!'

'Don't take that tone with me, child. It is quite improper for a young man to be filling a decent young girl's head with notions. Now, if you would return that memento to me I will say nothing of the matter to your father.'

'Guy is the only person who ever understood me,' Ellen cried, dabbing angrily at her tears . 'Oh, please let me have his letters!'

'I will make a bargain with you, Ellen,' her aunt said with a sigh after a moment. 'Hand up the ring, and promise never to deceive me again! If you do this, and keep your word, I will keep the ring for you against the day when both you and Guy are older. I will also allow you to write him one letter, advising that I am *au fait* with the situation and that any further letters will be opened by me.'

Ellen knew when she was beaten. 'All right,' she said dully.

'And you promise you will turn over to me any further letter from him?'

Ellen promised and that evening wrote to the young man she loved.

*Dear Guy,*

*Aunt Harriet is minding the ring you gave me until we are older. Your letters have been opened by her and will continue to be read by her. She has asked me to let you know this and to ask you not to attempt to contact me again without her knowledge.*
*I hope your studies are going well.*

*With every good wish,*
*Yours very sincerely,*
*Ellen Healy.*

Aunt Harriet scrutinised the letter, put it into an envelope and addressed it. 'I forbid you to discuss this with Franny,' she said. 'She is excitable enough as it is.'

The year deepened into winter. Despite his earlier plans, John Healy did not come to see his children until after the new year. He came alone. Mrs Forrister was busy preparing for their wedding, but she sent small presents. Harry asked after Guy, and Ellen's ears pricked up at news of his doing well at Sandhurst. But her father did not know where he had spent the holiday period.

'Perhaps he went to France. He hunts wild boar there you know, in the forests near his house.' He added with a chuckle, 'Makes a change, doesn't it, from the poor old fox.'

Harry whistled. 'Wild boar! Like a medieval potentate! So that's why he didn't come to Ireland for Christmas!'

Ellen imagined Guy in his manor house, sitting by a log fire, a prince in a fairy tale. He had not replied to her brief note, but with her aunt in the role of watchdog it would have been pointless. She was beginning to feel how glamorous his world was, how simple her own and how ridiculous and pointless it was that she should love him.

'Old man Wallace has just died, Father,' Harry added after a moment. 'Day before yesterday. So Clonshule now presumably belongs to his son. Wouldn't you think Guy would come for his friend's father's funeral?'

'Not if he has to come from France,' his father said, raising his grey eyebrows. 'But, tell me, what's the new squire like?'

'He's young,' Harry said, privately cavilling at the word 'squire' as an imported label, 'and that's all we know about him.'

*

It snowed the first day back at school in January, a desultory sprinkling that covered the fields for most of the day. The children were delighted and, at morning break, gathered what they could for snowballs, seemingly impervious to the icy cold on their bare feet. Ellen stayed indoors by the fire, chatting to Mrs Gallagher who regaled her with stories about her own Christmas.

The Master came in during this conversation. He was carrying a photographic portrait of the new king. He stood on a chair and exchanged the portrait of Victoria for a portrait of her son.

'Edward VII,' he intoned in a voice full of irony, 'By the grace of God, King of Great Britain and Ireland.'

When the children came in, glowing from their break, they remarked on the changeover.

'Sure th' ould queen's dead for more than a year!' Dickie McCabe, one of the third years, informed his classmates scornfully. 'An' she's been sitting up there looking down at us, when it should have been the new fella all the time!'

It was Dickie's job to replenish the inkwells and when he went to the cupboard for the ink bottle he whispered to Ellen, 'I have something for you, Miss. A gentleman asked me to give you.'

He reached into the pocket of his patched trousers and produced a small envelope. It was sealed, but bore no writing. Ellen took it swiftly.

'Where was the gentleman?'

'On a horse. He came to the gate at the break.'

Mrs Gallagher was writing on the blackboard. Ellen muttered an excuse and went outside, looked down the road where the snow was turning into slush. There were hoof marks, ruts made by cartwheels and footprints of many young feet. But no one was in sight except a man driving a donkey and cart. Shivering from the razor wind, she hurried back indoors. From the hall she heard the geography lesson in progress in the Master's room – What was the highest mountain in Ireland? What was the longest river in the

British Isles? She tore open the envelope.

*My darling girl,*

*Despite the contents of your note, it was wonderful to hear from you! I have written you more letters than I can count, and am glad at least to know the reason for your silence. I will wait for you for as long as it takes – on condition only that you do not forget me!*

*Guy.*

When she got home, Ellen handed the letter to her aunt without a word and went upstairs to her room. Her heart felt as though it would burst. She looked at the algebra waiting for her, but instead wrote the name of the boy she loved across her blotter – Guy, Guy, Guy, Guy, Guy – until it fell off the edge, and then she wrote it across the surface of the table, uncaring that the pen scratched, until the nib broke.

Her aunt found her a few minutes later, her head resting on the table, her eyes red.

'Thank you for honouring your word, Ellen.'

Ellen tried to hide the scratched varnish with a copybook, but her aunt saw the repeated name across the blotter. She bent over her niece.

'Ellen, my poor dear. I do understand, whatever you might think.'

'I can't forget him, Aunt!'

'We never forget to order! Instead, try to understand … why he made such an impression on you, why he was himself so smitten, because he is, of course … very young.'

'So that's why he loves me, Aunt?' Ellen exclaimed angrily. 'Because he is young and has no sense?'

Aunt Harriet looked at the girl's woebegone face and her face softened, 'Ellen, let us examine the facts. Firstly, you are both far too young to undertake lasting attachments. Do you accept that is the case?'

Ellen sighed. This was an adult perspective, and she did not share it.

'Secondly, he is rich. You are not. It is not insurmountable, but it creates an imbalance.'

Ellen shrugged. 'If he doesn't care, why should I?'

'Because life is long and people change. Thirdly, the boy is a Protestant and you are a Catholic and you know the Church's requirements regarding the children of mixed marriages.'

'He mightn't care.'

'True! But he might. Fourthly, he is English and you are Irish. No matter what you may think, there is a gulf between you that would be very difficult to bridge.'

'England isn't on the moon!' Ellen said, now angry at the forces apparently aligned against them.

'No. But the centuries of bloodshed have marked us, more's the pity and the sorrow of it. It will take longer to heal our history than you have years to live.'

Ellen felt the impertinence of history. She burst out, 'In that case Aunt, why didn't you just make me send the ring back to him, tell him I could never see him again?'

Aunt Harriet sighed. 'I see the pitfalls, Ellen. But I do not pretend to be God.'

When her aunt was gone, Ellen gnawed at her thumbnail. Her mind kept repeating the words, 'I will wait for you for as long as it takes.' A wild impulse rose in her. She could run away, go to England, find Guy. She had a little money saved, and Franny would lend her what she had. If Guy sent her to his house in France she could stay there until they could be married. She saw herself cutting back lavender in a broad-brimmed straw hat.

But this mood did not last. The voice of common sense suggested that her aunt knew things about life that she did not; that she was too young; that if Guy were really serious he would wait, as he had promised.

A few days later, Guy Forrister crossed the parade ground of Sandhurst's Royal College. He was tired after his Christmas break in Ireland. The festivities at Clonshule had been marred by the sudden death of Ernest Wallace, Bertie's father, and by the frustration of not being able to see Ellen, although she was only four miles away and he had haunted Monaghan town in a vain hope of surprising her. He would have liked to have been able to call on the family, to have met Ellen again in a family setting. He felt offended when he dwelt on Mrs Murphy's excessive caution. Who did she think he was, he thought, some kind of Bluebeard?

He wondered if his beloved had even received the note he had dropped by the school. He had given the barefoot boy a sixpence and warned him to give his missive to no one except Miss Healy, but he knew that guaranteed nothing. Perhaps the letter had gone astray? Perhaps she had got into more trouble over it, although he had been careful not to put her name on it.

His breath misted in the cold air. His boots made crisp sounds and he heard the shouts from the rugby field. He looked at the long lines of the Royal College – its pillared portico, white stucco Georgian architecture, its purposeful immensity – and felt proud before a statement of such power. He knew the Empire depended on the machine that was honed here and he loved the atmosphere of duty, discipline and collective, unconquerable might.

The work was arduous: study, drill, night marches, immersed in military company, absorbing the rules of combat, being saluted by experienced non-commissioned officers twice his age, and learning, with all his intellect and all his instincts, how to become a leader of men.

But there was more to it than that. Sandhurst, its hierarchy, had become his world. The part of him orphaned by the death of his father, and even earlier by the latter's marriage to a woman he disliked, had found in this tightly knit community, a home. He had his place here; he had a natural understanding of command, how to cut a good figure, how to inculcate confidence and how to play whist without losing his shirt. He was 'army barmy', as he told himself ruefully.

Sandhurst had also sharpened his aptitude for horsemanship and he was in the process of honing his ability as a fencer. He was determined to get on the college team and take on Oxbridge. But he did not neglect the academic work: passing out would be in order of merit, and his promotion prospects afterwards would depend on it, as would his choice of posting.

But in the midst of all this Guy had kept within him, as a kind of shrine, the image of the angelic girl he had met in Ireland.

'Who is she, for God's sake?' Bertie Wallace had demanded, when he had returned to Clonshule after delivering his letter to Ellen's school, and had rather foolishly divulged to Bertie the reason for his excursion. 'You haven't had your head turned by some little minx? We're all pretty frisky by the time we get out of school, but don't let it addle your brains.'

Guy had clammed up. He'd been on the point of opening his heart to Wallace, but his old friend's next remark had winded him.

'If you really have the hots for the girl, why don't you just roger her?' Then Bertie had added with a laugh, 'Don't look like that! I'm just pointing out the options.'

Guy was increasingly uncomfortable in Wallace's company. It had been one thing to have befriended him in Harrow where Bertie was often mocked for being Irish, something he always denied.

'No Irish blood in me,' he would insist in the exaggerated accent he adopted while he got rid of his Irish consonants. 'One hundred per cent English on both sides.'

But it was another experience altogether to be with him on his own turf, and to see the cupidity with which he had come into his inheritance. He felt he did not know the Bertram Wallace of Clonshule, who hardly mourned his father and who lorded it over his household although he was still only nineteen, and would not be the legal master of Clonshule for two more years.

Guy felt himself subtly altered by this experience. It had drawn a line between his old self, and the self he knew he must become. The realisation that he did not know his old friend as well as he thought made him question his judgement, while the knowledge that he had, really, only himself to rely on introduced a new cynicism.

He had also become aware of an undertow in Ireland – something old as Time, rooted in the landscape, whispered in the wind, the old Ireland whose nobility had flourished long ago. The great mansion that was Clonshule House seemed, to him, positioned on a fault line, a crack in the fabric of history. He had visited the French town of Albi once, where the triumphalist cathedral rose, fortress-like, in the middle of the town. It had been built in the thirteenth century to remind the Cathar heretics who was master, built to remind them that Holy Rome had conquered them. Clonshule was something the same.

He was maturing fast; his dreams for the future were increasingly absorbing. Although only a few months had passed since he had been overwhelmed by the first passion of his life, he knew he was changing. Certainties were replacing doubts, responsibilities were no longer fearsome, and best of all, like a blessing, confidence had come in his ability to succeed.

He wondered what Ellen had made of his letter. He meant what he had said – that he would wait for her, and he thrilled to the memory of her pure lips, her shy elfin beauty, her difference. Someday he would go back and claim her, he told himself, but in the meantime he had to admit that it was only fair to give the dear girl a breathing space, a chance to grow up.

# Chapter 8

*Kilcrannagh, June 1904*

Almost three years had passed. The calendar hanging in the kitchen was turned over to June, 1904. Ellen had sat the King's Scholarship and the results, for better or worse, were due today. She had said nothing about it at breakfast and now went to stand at the open kitchen window to wait for the post. She was only half-aware of the new blooms on the trellis, or the speckled starling that was shovelling his head into a pool of rainwater and fluffing out his feathers. From the orchard, she could hear Harry's voice and Franny's laughter. In the hall, the clock chimed eleven and then came the sound for which she had been straining her ears – Danny the Post's bicycle on the gravel and the slap of letters onto the mat in the hall.

Maggie emerged from the pantry and exclaimed, 'What ails you at all? You're as white as limewash!'

'My results,' Ellen croaked.

Her aunt came into the kitchen and, with a deadpan face, handed Ellen two stiff white envelopes.

Ellen just stared at them. 'Will you open them, Aunt?'

Her aunt took a knife from the drawer, slit one of the envelopes, perused the letter quickly and handed it to her niece. 'I think you'd better read it for yourself.'

Ellen saw the letter heading – Training College of Our Lady of Mercy, Carysfort Park, Blackrock, Co Dublin – and steeled herself. Of course I can't have done it, she told herself. How absurd to think I could.

*Dear Miss Healy,*

*With reference to your application for a scholarship we are, based on your performance in the King's Scholarship examinations, pleased to offer you such a place for the forthcoming two-year course commencing on the 2nd September. If you accept this place you will be one of two students admitted in open scholarship competition. Enclosed please find copies of the College Rules, the Prospectus and a list of the requisites you should bring with you. Perhaps you would confirm whether you are accepting this place by the 10th inst.*

*Yours sincerely,*

*Sister Maria Hogan*

The other letter contained her actual results, a row of honours. Ellen felt her aunt's arms around her, her warm voice in her ear and realised her stern guardian had tears in her eyes. 'Well done, my dearest, bravest girl.'

Ellen sank on the nearest chair and cried.

'How does the conquering heroine feel?' Franny demanded as they sat down to lunch.

Ellen laughed. She took from her pocket the list of Carysfort's first-year subjects, and with a wry face, handed it to her cousin. Franny read it aloud in a voice that began on a pragmatic note and rose to a shriek of laughter, 'Reading, Penmanship, Spelling and Punctuation, Grammar, Composition, Geography, English Literature, Arithmetic and Mensuration, Theory of Method, Practice of Teaching, Needlework, Music, Drawing, Bookkeeping, Cookery, Science Manual Instruction.' She looked at Ellen, sardonic eyebrows raised, 'Is that all?'

Harry murmured, 'Impressive! But with the usual notable omissions!'

'What omissions?'

'Irish and History. Identity itself!'

Franny sighed. She gave the list of subjects back to Ellen, swallowed a spoonful of soup and eyed Harry doubtfully. She felt the new certainty in him. The horizon now pulling back for Ellen had made him, she suspected, more aware of his own prospect of independence and manhood. It filled her with fear. Everything was changing, but she would not be part of it. 'You'll be off to Dublin next year too,' she said after a moment, 'and then I'll have no one.'

'Come on, Fran,' Harry replied cheerfully, 'you can go up to stay with Clare sometimes, and then we'll be all together again!' He looked at his aunt for confirmation.

'Clare has her hands full,' she said.

'But I could help her, Mother!'

'She has a maid dear, and very little extra space.'

'You're saying she doesn't want me,' Franny said tonelessly after a moment. 'I've never even seen her baby! She keeps threatening to invite me, but she never does.' She lowered her head and muttered to Harry under her breath, 'I should run away.'

Harry looked troubled and glanced at his aunt.

'It's not a question of not wanting you, darling,' her mother said.

'It's just that I would upset her nice, cosy domestic bliss. Isn't that it, Mother?'

'Don't be so tiresome, Frances!' Mrs Murphy said and turned to her niece. 'Ellen my clever girl, you must write and tell your father the wonderful news.'

When everything was cleared away, Ellen went to her room and shut the door. She looked at her books on the table where she had worked so hard and on which she had once scratched Guy Forrister's name. She rubbed her finger over the dent in the varnish and wondered what he was doing now. He seemed a long way off, no longer the focus of the violent passion that had possessed her. She had not seen him since that day, nearly three years earlier, when he had given her the ring and she had not received word from him since the clandestine note he had delivered in person at the school. He sent the family Christmas cards every year, polite festive greetings. Was he embarrassed, she wondered, when he remembered his declarations of undying love? Would they meet again someday and laugh over their childish infatuation? But would he think her very changed? Would he even recognise her?

She turned to examine her reflection in the cheval glass, a young woman in an ankle-length skirt and high-necked blouse, a different being from the girl in the blue dress, long since outgrown. She took up her pen.

> *Dear Father,*
>
> *I have good news – I have won a scholarship to Carysfort. I can hardly believe it, but I have a letter to prove it! Unfortunately there will be expenditure the scholarship does not cover – books, clothes, travel. I'm sorry to have to burden you with these.*

She sighed and sat back in her chair. She hated asking him for money. But her father's reply came within the week: '*Congratulations on your success. I am proud and happy to pay for whatever you need!*'

Franny was allowed to read this letter when she was alone with Ellen later that day.

'Well at least he's paying your expenses. But it's still rotten that he is prepared to fund Harry's fees, and not yours!'

'Fran, he's doing what he can! Boys have to acquire a profession. Women are expected to get married and be kept by their husbands.'

'So they hand us over – lock, stock and barrel – to someone else's power. When you think about it, men and their cheeky rules should all be blown up!'

Ellen laughed. 'All?'

'Except Harry,' Franny conceded hurriedly, 'and maybe one or two others,' she added with a grin and lowering her voice, 'like certain young Englishmen!'

'Oh Fran … that's all water under the bridge.'

Guy's former stepmother was now Ellen's own stepmother. Her father and Mrs Forrister had married in the spring of 1902. Aunt Harriet had gone to Dublin for the wedding and had returned a little taciturn. When pressed she said there had been a wedding breakfast for a few guests in the Gresham Hotel, and that the newlyweds had gone for a honeymoon to Dunmore East from whence they would go home to Tralee.

'That's the last we'll see of Father, Sis,' Harry had said. 'Queenie has him now and there's an end to it!'

But their father had brought his new bride to visit some two months later when the new Mrs Healy, with an air of conferring a special favour, had invited her stepchildren to call her Lilian. This invitation still remained difficult, even during their latest visit, which followed Ellen's acceptance of her place in Carysfort.

'Any word of Guy, Mrs F … I mean Lilian?' Harry had asked diffidently. 'I hope my stupid accident when we went fishing didn't put him off coming back.'

'I expect he's very busy. He has his Commission now you know …'

'I would expect nothing less,' Harry said with a grin. 'Does he still visit Clonshule?'

From the hesitation in Lilian's response Ellen was sure that

Guy did visit Clonshule, and a painful sense of rejection twisted inside her.

Lilian directed a coy glance at Ellen, 'He does ask for you all from time to time, you know, but he spends as much as he can of his holidays at his place in France. I shouldn't be surprised if he marries a little French girl in the end!'

Ellen was unprepared for the pain.

'Have you ever been there … Lilian? In Guy's place in France?' asked Harry.

'Good Lord, no! Such a long journey. I don't think I'd be able for it.'

He hasn't asked you, Ellen thought. In fact I wonder if he contacts you at all. Why should he, after all?

'Well …' John Healy said, glancing at his wife, 'we may take a notion one of these days. They say Paris is not to be missed.'

That evening, after Harry and Franny had gone to bed, Aunt Harriet said gently to her niece, 'Well, Ellen, you see Guy had other fish to fry after all. I mention it only to illustrate that what happened three years ago is part of the painful process of growing up. You were both little more than children.'

'What am I to do with his ring? Do you still have it?'

'Of course! But you should time its return with delicacy. You don't want to make an issue of a childish episode. You will have an opportunity sometime to pass it off in an easy manner.'

Ellen had to acknowledge that her aunt had been right about virtually everything. Guy's memory, as she had predicted, had begun to lose its edge. She was soon to be a student at Carysfort, en route for one of the few careers open to women, and no longer the young girl enthralled by an exciting stranger.

The days leading up to Ellen's departure for Dublin were full. There were trips to town for new clothes, underwear, towels and bed linen. Everything had to be marked with her name. A trunk lay open on the floor of her bedroom and into it, items were neatly folded and ticked off the list.

'Anyone would think you were emigrating!' Franny exclaimed, squatting on the floor to help with the packing, and suddenly turning away to wipe her eyes.

Ellen heard her desolation. Fran had been like this for days, weeping suddenly over trifles.

'Fran!' she whispered, kneeling beside her and hugging her. 'Don't be so down in the dumps! I have to go to Dublin, but I'll always be there for you!'

'It's all right for you,' Franny replied, angrily wiping her eyes. 'You'll be in Dublin and I'll be stuck here with Mother. Can you imagine it – just the two of us alone here? Forever?'

When Jimmy drove Ellen to town the next day, he congratulated her, 'It was wonderful work! A scholarship like that! You're a great little woman, Ellen Healy!'

'You never thought I'd do it, did you Jimmy? Tell the truth now!'

Jimmy glanced at her and then stared fixedly between the horse's ears, 'On the contrary,' he replied in a low voice. 'I knew you'd do it!'

Her knees touched his as the trap was jolted over a pothole, and she pulled her legs back. Jimmy noted her reaction and tried to ignore it. He wished with all his heart that he had not burned his boats three years ago by blathering his mouth off. They had been such friends, he and Ellen, until then. She had been the real reason for his toil in the Murphy establishment down the years, which he was well aware they had all taken for granted.

He was now a man of substance in his own right, having bought out his land from Wallace under the recent Act, and also the field from Mrs Murphy, in which he had grazing rights. He knew he was eyed by many of the young women in the parish as an eligible prospect. But he also knew he was a one-woman man. It was not something of his making; it was simply a fact. And, since the object of his worship had so little time for him, he felt it was a kind of curse.

'Jimmy,' Ellen whispered, glancing at the harsh melancholy in his face, 'is something wrong?'

'Sure the place won't be the same,' he replied gruffly, whacking the pony's rump with the reins, 'when you're gone'. He paused and added in a serious tone, 'You will take care of yourself, won't you, Ellen? Dublin is a big city.'

'Jimmy, I'll be with the *nuns*!'

He smiled but added after a moment in a tight voice, 'I hope you won't take too much heed of that ... English fellow ... if he turns up in Dublin.'

'English fellow? Ellen repeated. 'Oh Jimmy, if you mean Guy Forrister you needn't worry. He hasn't darkened the door for years, although he could have come easily, for I'm sure he visits the Wallaces – his friends at Clonshule.'

'Aye,' Jimmy said quietly. 'Do you know where they came from, Ellen, the so-called county Wallaces? Cromwellian planters who were paid for their murdering in Ireland with Irish land, while its hereditary owners were killed, expelled, or permitted to lick their boots. It's said that limestone mansion of theirs was built by forced labour.'

'That's hardly Guy Forrister's fault!'

Ellen looked at him, but he did not return her gaze. She saw how stern his profile was. She knew, because Harry had told her, that he belonged to the ancient aristocracy of Monaghan and she felt an instinctive admiration along with a strange dread. Their aunt always shushed Harry when he talked history, but Ellen sensed she did so not out of concern for the truth, but because she was afraid of it.

'It was all a long time ago, Jimmy, wasn't it?'

'So, if your crimes are old enough, you are entitled to the spoils?'

'I'm only saying that none of it has anything to do with Guy.'

'Who is decent,' Jimmy said, 'I've no doubt!' He glanced at her and added, 'There is an old Gaelic proverb, Ellen, you could bear in mind for when he turns up again … because turn up he will!'

'What proverb?' she demanded crossly.

Jimmy cleared his throat, 'Beware the horns of a bull, the hooves of a horse, and the smile of an Englishman.'

On Friday, 2 September 1904, Ellen took the train to Dublin and was met at Kingsbridge Station by Frank Ahern, Clare's husband. She hardly recognised the young man in the high wing collar and neat, waxed moustache, whom she had met only on the occasion of his and Clare's wedding; but he soon put her at ease, answering her questions about Clare and baby Matty. Clare was dying to see her, he said, and asked if she was free for lunch on Sunday?

She said she certainly was.

'Cab or tram to your destination, Madam?' Frank asked with a twinkle.

As her trunk would follow by arrangement, Ellen opted for the exciting new electric tram that ran on rails and was powered from overhead wires.

The gates of Carysfort Park were open. An avenue wound through parkland to the college, an immense three-storey red-brick building, with rooftop crosses stark against the sky. Ellen pointed to the fields where cows were grazing.

'Do the nuns have a farm?'

'The place is self-contained, Ellen. Sister Keenan, the foundress, wanted to make a statement about the importance of educating women.' Frank glanced at her with a grin. 'I can't think why!'

Ellen aimed a mock swipe at him and pointed to the Romanesque arch above the door with the coat of arms of the Mercy Order: '*Ad Majorem Dei Gloriam*. A.D. 1901'

'To the greater glory of God! That's why.'

Frank kissed her cheek. 'I'll be off. Will I call for you on Sunday?'

'No. I'll make my own way. I'm a big girl now.'

Ellen watched Frank's retreating back for a few seconds. When he turned to wave she waved back at him and then she crossed the threshold into her future.

The scent of polish, sheen of parquet, bloom of flowers before the statue of Our Lady, light flooding from tall windows, were Ellen's first awareness of her new home. There were other students in the spacious hallway, dressed, like her, in the regulation black dresses and white collars, chatting and laughing or copying timetables from a notice board.

When her trunk arrived, she took her things to the dormitory, surveyed with delight her little cubicle with its narrow iron bed, chest of drawers with basin and ewer, and its tiny wardrobe – her private domain for the next two years. She heard sounds from the adjoining cubicle and put her head around the partition to introduce herself.

Her neighbour was folding blouses. She had an abundance of chestnut hair and, when she turned, Ellen saw that her eyes were blue and fringed with long lashes. Around her collar was a black ribbon with a cameo brooch. Her cheeks dimpled as she held out her hand. 'Deirdre Callaghan,' she said in a lilting Cork accent.

'Ellen Healy.'

'Have a sweet, Ellen!' She gestured to a tin of Oatfields toffees lying open on her bed. 'Where are you from?'

'Monaghan. And you?'

'Clonakilty.' She glanced into Ellen's cubicle and added, 'Let's get your bed made, before the drill sergeant comes around!'

The bed made, the unpacking completed, the timetable studied, Deirdre went off to find out what was next in store for them. Ellen went to a window to view Carysfort Park. Beyond it she could see the row of white stucco Victorian houses on Carysfort Avenue, where two policemen were on the beat. Members of the

DMP – the Dublin Metropolitan Police – they had black uniforms and helmets like the English 'Bobbies', very different to the green uniform of the Royal Irish Constabulary worn by her father. She took out his photograph. He was wearing his cap with its crowned harp, the RIC emblem. How was he now? Was he happy?

'They'll feed us after prayers!' Deirdre suddenly announced behind her and looked over her shoulder at the photograph. 'Who's the Peeler for God's sake?'

'My father?'

'I'm sorry!'

But Ellen had seen the contempt in her eyes and said coldly, 'He is a good man.'

'I'm sure he is, if he's your dad! It's just that we had dealings recently with the RIC back home. An eviction …' She paused when she saw the effect this had on Ellen. 'Evictions are never pretty, Ellen. They take the roof off, you know, and throw the family – the hereditary owners of the land – into the ditch. In this particular case, one of the policemen was shot.'

'My father never mentions evictions. He is stationed in Tralee.'

'They have evictions in Kerry too.'

Conversation died. The bell rang for prayers.

The students filed in silence to the chapel for Benediction. The organ sprang into life. The voices of the nuns rose in the *Tantum Ergo;* incense wafted to the vaulted roof. The priest raised the gold monstrance over the small congregation and a white-veiled novice rang the bell from the steps of the sanctuary. Ellen bent her head and tried to pray, but all she could think of was her father. Please protect him, dear Lord. But her turmoil ebbed before the sublime music, the resplendent stained glass and the magnificent flowers on the marble altar. It was replaced by gratitude.

Thank you, Jesus, for letting me come here. Keep Father in Thy Holy keeping and Harry and Franny and Aunt Harriet, and Jimmy too. She remembered Jimmy's words when last she had seen him and thought of Guy, wincing at how silly she had been, and wondering where he was now. But she sighed inwardly with the knowledge that she would give almost anything to see him again.

At that very moment Guy Forrister was sipping sherry with Bertie Wallace at Clonshule.

# Chapter 9

Franny cursed her brakes as she negotiated the hill by Aviemore House, the eighteenth-century mansion that still lorded it over the town despite the more recent cathedral putting up its spire in the distance. She had just turned into Mill Street when she heard an urgent call from the pavement.

'Miss Murphy … I say … Franny!'

Fran put a foot onto the wet road and skidded to a halt, spraying horse manure over her skirt. She had already registered that the voice was English and recognised its owner as soon as she laid eyes on him. He was accompanied by a friend. Both young men were in fashionable jackets, incongruous among the farmers who thronged the street on market day.

'Guy Forrister!' she exclaimed, annoyed that she was cutting such a sorry figure, 'Older and wiser though you may be, you have just ruined my best skirt.'

She dragged the bike against the pavement and looked at him severely, fully aware that this was the youth in whose cause she had once resorted to subterfuge. Already she was wondering if she would be called upon to do so again. 'And even though you've acquired a military bearing,' she added, 'I refuse to be intimidated by peremptory instructions.'

'I'm very sorry Franny,' Guy said laughing, 'but you should get your brakes mended. Allow me to introduce my friend Bertram Wallace,' he added turning to the sleek young man at his side. 'Bertie, Miss Murphy.'

'I have heard much about Miss Murphy,' Bertram said laconically, rocking back on his heels and regarding the girl before him with a combination of licence and hauteur. Franny felt the condescension and reddened.

'As I have heard nothing at all about you, Mr Wallace,' she replied crisply, 'you have the advantage of me. But I will nonetheless assume of you only the best.'

'Don't dream of bandying words with Franny,' a laughing Guy warned his friend. Turning back to her he asked nonchalantly, 'I trust everyone at home is well; your mother, Harry, Ellen?'

'Yes thank you. But Ellen is not at home anymore. She's in Dublin.'

'So, she … got her scholarship?'

'But of course!'

'Well done, Ellen,' Guy exclaimed with a subdued whistle. 'But may I drive you home, Franny? You could leave that rattletrap into Kavanagh's and get the brakes mended.'

He glanced interrogatively at his friend as he said this, adding, 'You don't mind if I borrow the trap, Bertie, to bring Miss Murphy home?' and Bertram Wallace, saying he had business with his land agent, tipped his hat and wished Franny good day. He told Guy he would see him at the Westenra for luncheon and left.

Accompanied by Guy, Franny walked the bike to Kavanagh's bicycle shop, where they said it would be ready for collection tomorrow.

'You can always send your manservant for it,' Guy said, turning to Franny in the greasy shop that smelled of machine parts and lubricating oil. The shop became suddenly silent and the other customers directed covert glances at him.

'Jimmy MacMahon is not anyone's manservant,' Franny said, mortified, aware that everyone in the shop knew who Jimmy was, just as they knew her. 'He is a family friend without whom we would be lost.'

'I beg your pardon, Franny. I did not intend to be in the least disparaging.'

When they had left the shop she said to him, 'In Ireland you must not make assumptions about social status. We have had a very dislocating history.'

He gave her an apologetic smile, 'I know next to nothing about it. Will you educate me?'

'If you are really interested you must do it for yourself, or ask Harry, who will be more than happy to oblige.'

Guy recalled Harry's outburst at the dinner table several years ago and felt that further raillery was out of place. He accompanied Franny while she carried out her mother's errands – to the Hibernian Bank in Church Square where she stood in a queue while he waited by the door, and then to W. S. Blake's, the chemist. He walked around outside, listening to the urban bustle, northern voices, rolling of carts and ring of iron-shod hooves. This is really a handsome town, he thought, admiring the church, the courthouse and the monument to Colonel Vesey Dawson who had died in the Battle of Inkerman in 1854. So much was in cut stone, well planned and well laid out. He said as much to Franny when she emerged from the chemist's, but she only shrugged.

'It's a planters' town,' she said. 'What was destroyed to enable its creation is now beyond our reach.' She turned to Guy with a frown and a half laugh, 'Like so much of Ireland. Which leaves us with a hole in our souls I suppose.'

'Oh, Fran,' Guy exclaimed with an exasperated laugh. 'You are far too young and vital to have a hole in your soul!'

Mrs Murphy greeted her niece's aspiring lover with as much politeness as though she had never written a warning letter to him. Franny went to change her skirt and Harry came running downstairs. He clapped Guy on the shoulder.

'I'd been wondering about where you'd got to. If you still want to go fishing I promise I won't get drowned this time!'

Guy saw how Harry had grown. The newly broken voice of last time had deepened, and now a moustache shadowed his upper lip. The instinctive liking he had taken to him three years ago filled him with its warmth. 'I have a luncheon appointment, but there will be another occasion. The fish will not escape me forever!'

Guy glanced around the room in search of recent photographs. There was the upright piano with its two brass sconces where he had accompanied Ellen's singing. What did she look like now? Would she still brighten when she saw him? He felt uncertain about many things that had been his heart's desire just three years ago. He had changed, but to what extent he hardly knew.

Mrs Murphy excused herself, saying she would organise some tea, and when she was gone Guy said to Harry, 'Franny tells me that Ellen got her scholarship.'

'That's right! She left for Dublin just over a week ago. There was a letter from her today.' Harry reached to the mantelpiece where Ellen's missive was propped behind a candlestick and handed it to him. 'Read it if you like. I don't think anyone would mind!'

Guy opened out the pages. They had come from her hands! He loved her writing – tidy, organised, with uprights slanting towards the future, the way she directed her courage he thought suddenly, against the odds.

*Dearest Aunt Harriet, Harry, Franny,*

*I can't believe I'm here. I have even made a new friend – Deirdre Callaghan from Clonakilty! Frank collected me at the station and I am to have lunch with him and Clare on Sunday and I'm so looking forward to it!*

*Carysfort exceeds my expectations – it's colossal, with classrooms, lecture rooms and dormitories, a recreation hall and a chapel with splendid stained glass where Mass is celebrated every morning on an altar ablaze with flowers from the nuns' conservatory.*

*Our seventeen subjects fill every hour of the working week until 6 p.m. English Lit. is my favourite, of course (no surprises there). We have a wonderful choir and I practise piano in one of the music rooms almost every day.*

*Harry, you'd love Elementary Science. We are doing experiments to show the specific heat of iron tacks and how to find the relative weight of different kinds of wood. I'm not sure how this will benefit the nation's children but we have to write it up in our science notebooks and do precise drawings of the experiments. The notebooks will be inspected by someone from the Board in due course.*

*I'm very happy and would like to thank each of you for putting up with me these past few years when I was all work and no fun.*

*Do write and tell me all the news.*
*All my love,*
*Ellen.*

Guy handed the letter back. 'She seems to be settling in well,' he said politely.

Before Harry could reply, his aunt came back into the room, and Franny, changed and smiling, was behind her with a tea tray.

That evening, in the smoking room of Clonshule House, Guy looked back on his day and cursed himself for an idiot. He should not have gone back to Kilcrannagh, not while Mrs Murphy was there. She had engineered a few minutes alone with him and politely intimated that Ellen was working for a career in teaching, and that the last thing she needed was for him to contact her.

'I am protective of her, Guy. She lost her mother at a tender age and hardly ever sees her father. She is at an impressionable stage in her life, and unless you have the most honourable intentions, please do not try to renew your acquaintance. You would not like to have it on your conscience that you were the cause of a major upset in her life.'

Guy accepted a cheroot from Bertie Wallace.

'You're very quiet this evening Forrister. Thinking of the little piece we met this morning, eh?'

The remark was typical of Bertie, but it offended. He was referring to Franny, whom Guy had found oddly changed. It was not just that she had become a pretty sixteen-year-old, or that her wit was sharper than ever, but he had sensed in her a reflection and vulnerability bordering on desperation. On the journey back to her home in Wallace's trap, she had confided that, next year, *both* her cousins would be at college in Dublin. And then she had laughed, but her laughter had been tight and bruised. It had suddenly occurred to him that what really bothered her was not so much Ellen's absence, or her own circumscribed life, but the prospect of losing Harry to the world. She loves him, he thought with sudden shocked insight. And is afraid she's about to lose him.

'I'm a bit tired,' he told Bertie. 'Think I'll have an early night.'

'I'd have one myself, if I could have it with Mary McKenna,' Bertie replied with a guffaw. 'But she's gone home to that squalid cottage and I'll have to wait until tomorrow.'

He was referring to one of the dairymaids he had boasted of having conquered. 'It's great to be master here at last, Forrister!' he added expansively, pouring himself a brandy. 'The old man became very fussy in his latter years. Although by all accounts he had a different view of things when he was young … up every skirt in the house.'

Bertie brayed again, but Guy made no reply. He already knew about Mary McKenna, because, two days ago, he had met the distraught girl looking for somewhere to hide.

'You can hide in my room,' he had told her, and remembered her look of tired contempt.

When Guy had stubbed out his cheroot he went upstairs, sliding his hand along the flowing mahogany balustrade, aware of the elegance of this house, with its high ceilings, Turkey carpets, Georgian furniture, bronzes, vases and ornaments from all over the world. Sometimes he compared it with his gentle French retreat, Fontebelle, which was so different in atmosphere. But tonight he was exercised by something else, an unease he could not identify, although he knew it had to do with his interview with Mrs Murphy.

For the past two years he had tried to put Ellen Healy out of his head. This was not just because his feelings had altered, but because he had begun to doubt them. Other distractions had intruded on the romantic space in his soul. He was not a boy anymore. As well as providing military training, Sandhurst had opened a fast, smart world to him. He was now part of a set only too delighted to be entertained in his sandstone manor in France and to entertain him, in turn, in town and country houses, where one night last December, after a drunken orgy, he had lost his virginity. The experience had made him wary of the wild creature that lurked just under his skin. From his new, more mature, vantage point his pursuit of Ellen seemed infantile. Sometimes he wondered why he had made such a fool of himself over the girl. He hoped that she had lost that damn ring and forgotten the whole silly episode. Her aunt had been right to have warned him off then, but today's conversation had deeply offended him: 'Unless your intentions are of the most honourable …'

He wondered what Ellen had represented that had so enthralled him. He felt it again today as he had crossed the threshold of her home and had seen a photograph of her on the mantelpiece in that room where she had once given vent to a fury of tears in her father's arms. Her fragility had mirrored his own at that period in his life. However much he might have projected self-sufficiency, he had been just eighteen, parentless and hungry to belong. He had been charmed by that small family. Even Harry's near drowning had drawn him in further. Only he would ever know the risk he had taken with his own life that day.

His thoughts returned with renewed annoyance to Bertie's vulgar comment. Since his father had died, Bertie's penchant for self-indulgence had been liberated, and his proclaimed intention of enjoying his youth had become a religion. His readiness to put down anyone he perceived as not being of his own class, Guy found unnecessary, especially as it was so particularly marked in Ireland where so few were of his class. Nor had they any wish to be, he suspected, remembering the sullen disdain in the faces of some of the servants. But Franny Murphy, he thought, smiling at the remembrance, had put Bertie smartly in his place. She was a vivacious girl, even if she did not possess the reserve or the strength of her cousin. And Ellen was so unaware of her own attributes that they shone all the brighter, now that he knew something about the crassness of the world.

He got up and paced around the room, glanced at some oriental prints and a painting of some place in Kerry. Yes, of course, Ireland was part of his unease, and Franny had unwittingly provoked it. From his first visit he had found it disturbingly and profoundly different to England. He wondered what his brother Nigel would have made of it, if he had visited as intended last year. But Sophie had preferred France – the weather was more certain – so they had taken their son James to Fontebelle instead.

But what was to be done about Ellen? Part of him longed to re-establish contact. He could presumably call on her in that college in Dublin and take her out to tea. He imagined her with pleasure, her hair upswept, her skirts sweeping the floor. Did she still possess that contained passion? Would there still be the same effortless complicity between them?

'But everything has become so damn serious!' he muttered aloud, thinking of Mrs Murphy again. 'Why can't a man go to see a girl without having to take her on for life? I know I asked her to wait for me, but at eighteen I might be forgiven.'

He stood at the window, gazed out at the dusk and the gravelled Clonshule driveway that curved out of sight between rows of copper beeches. I suppose everything is serious for her because she has no margin for error. Poor girl. I don't want to mess up her life or tie her down, and I don't want to be tied down myself. Not yet! There's the army after all … service abroad … Maybe when I get back … She's Irish, of course, Catholic … everything would be so damn complicated anyway.

He undressed, climbed into bed and listened to the night-time sounds of the household – the creaking floor above his head where the housekeeper had her room, several clocks striking 10 p.m. more or less in unison, the querulous voice of Mrs Wallace, Bertie's mother, as she was helped upstairs by her maid. The last thing he noticed before he slept was the mix of camphor and beeswax that seemed to permeate everything. But when he finally slipped into sleep it wasn't Ellen, but Franny, troubled and distraught, who invaded his dreams.

# *Chapter 10*

On Sunday, Ellen set out to keep her lunch appointment with Clare and Frank. She had to make the journey to Sackville Street and there change trams. The route to the city centre, lined with Victorian and Georgian houses, gave her a view right across Dublin Bay. The tram clanked past desultory horse-drawn traffic, cyclists and a few motor cars bearing important-looking men. She stared at the motors with avid interest. But they were so expensive – £150 plus – and were bound to remain a curiosity.

The terminus was at Nelson's Pillar in the middle of Sackville Street, Dublin's nucleus and its meeting place. Northside and southside tramways converged here. Ellen alighted. She saw to her left the classical portico of the General Post Office and on the other side of the cobbled street, the posh Imperial Hotel and Clery's department store where her aunt always shopped when in Dublin. The Pillar soared beside her, a tall, Doric granite pedestal. She craned her neck, but could only glimpse a bit of Trafalgar's hero who stared across the rooftops of what had once been the second city of the Empire.

'There's a stairs inside, Miss. You can walk up to the top,' a voice said in her ear. 'Great view!'

Ellen turned and found herself looking at an untidy individual with rounded shoulders, an unkempt moustache and a grubby winged collar.

'I don't have the time.'

'Where are you off to?'

'South Circular Road,' Ellen said, and was immediately furious with herself.

'A country girl?' he said with a grin. 'First time in Dublin too?'

Uncertain how to deal with him, Ellen turned away.

'Sure the tram will get you there in a few minutes,' he said behind her. 'Why don't you let me show you around?'

Ellen saw her tram and made for it, stepped on board and went upstairs to the open deck. But her new acquaintance came up the stairs behind her.

'What a coincidence that I'm going in the same direction, Miss!'

He sat beside her, leaned across her to indicate the shiny yellow motor purring sedately in front of the Post Office. 'That's the future for you! All the horses will be gone!' He squeezed a little closer. 'Won't that be queer?'

He smelled of danger. She said in a cold voice that she was a student teacher and tried not to show fear. 'If you will excuse me …'

But he would not let her out. His knee met hers and his arm coiled companionably around the back of the seat. From the tram stairs came the sound of footsteps and in a moment a middle-aged couple sat down on the other side of the aisle. Ellen took the opportunity of thrusting aside the restraining knee and stood up.

'Excuse me!' she said in a voice so loud that the couple stared at her. The man had no option now but to let her pass, and she fled down the little stairs and into the street. She would pick up a tram somewhere else, she thought, as she headed in the direction of O'Connell Bridge.

When Clare and Frank returned home from Mass, Matty, their

darling, was standing at the sitting-room window waiting for them, his head just above the level of the sill and his eyes full of tears.

He welcomed their return with upraised arms and cries of 'Muddy, Daddy, uppity daisy.' Doris, the maid, who had just put a white cloth on the dining-room table, muttered, 'I suppose yez will be wantin' toast, ma'am?' and Clare said that of course they would. 'We'll breakfast in the kitchen this morning, Doris. And you can set the dining table for lunch. We're having a guest!'

Frank put his son on his shoulder, brought him into the little back garden and played with him until Clare summoned them with a quiet imperiousness. 'Frank! Breakfast.'

Frank obeyed the summons, reflecting that Clare had her mother's managerial streak, and that he was the beneficiary. Doris was terrified of her, but he loved her beauty and her bossiness with blind devotion. In the tightly laced grey dress that swept the ground, her hair piled on top of her head, she seemed more like a willowy model for a chocolate box than a young matron. He knew he was the envy of his male peers and for this he felt a dumb gratitude.

Clare had donned an apron and was dishing out scrambled eggs. Frank tucked in.

'Yum!' he said appreciatively.

'You sound like a six-year-old!' Clare said reprovingly. She was spooning egg into Matty who was sitting in his high chair and offering resistance. 'We'll be having chicken for lunch,' she went on. 'A treat for our clever Ellen!' She added after a moment, 'Isn't it such a shame Fran didn't emulate her? Where will she find a husband if she's going to be stuck at home with Mother?'

'Invite her to stay with us for a while?'

'Frank, we've no room! Anyway I couldn't be responsible for her. She'd be off chaining herself to railings first chance she got!'

'Aren't you exaggerating?'

Clare laughed. 'Of course I am! But she would still be a responsibility.'

'I hope Ellen succeeds in finding us,' Frank said.

'Of course she will! Ellen's very independent, and the trams make everything so simple.'

Ellen almost walked under a tram at the corner of Bachelor's Walk. It came screeching around the corner on the curved rails bedded in the cobbles. She stood aside to let it pass and glanced back but saw no sign of her tormentor. The five-storey building to her right was home to M. Kelly and Sons, who had a giant sign advertising Fishing Tackle, and this made her think of Harry, and then, reluctantly, Guy. To her left was O'Connell's monument with its mighty bronze angels. She was aware of the city's pulse – the clopping of hooves, the scraping of trams powered by their overhead web of wires. She crossed the bridge, looked down at the green river and headed for Westmorland Street where she could see the portico of the Bank of Ireland. She knew this was near Grafton Street, so beloved of Clare for its smart shops. As she had time to kill, it would be fun to do a bit of window shopping.

But this was Sunday and Grafton Street was almost deserted. She paused at Switzers' window to admire a white gown with a bodice and sleeves made entirely of Carrickmacross lace, the same lace the St Louis nuns had brought to Monaghan. Her reflection in the plate glass showed a young woman in long black skirt and tight jacket, white high-necked blouse and black straw hat. The reflection stared, immobile as a statue, at the glorious lace gown.

Ellen was imagining herself in that exquisite creation on Harry's arm, moving up a red-carpeted aisle while the organ music swelled and her groom waited for her at the steps of the altar. She imagined him turning to her, eyes alight with love.

But it was no bridegroom who was suddenly reflected beside her in the window.

'So here you are, Miss.'

Ellen jumped. It was the man from the tram.

'How dare you follow me!' she said and looked around desperately. But, except for a few women window shopping the street was empty.

'Frosty little piece!' he whispered indulgently, propelling her into a recessed doorway. He pressed her hungrily to him, his hand squeezing her breast.

Nothing in Ellen's life had prepared her for the unspoken assumption that she was designed for casual usage by whomsoever of the male sex was brazen enough. She froze with shock, but shock was quickly replaced by a wave of outrage that instinctively brought her knee up between the man's legs. He gasped as though hit with an axe and doubled over. She shoved past him into the street and took to her heels.

She was trembling and out of breath by the time she reached St Stephen's Green. Here, at least, were people going about their Sunday morning pursuits. Husband and wives strolled on the pavements as well-dressed children played in the park behind the railings. For a moment she thought she would hide there, but then she realised its shrubbery would only provide cover for her stalker. She wanted to weep and thought of Franny and how she had been going on for years about the position of women.

She stood uncertainly, scanning the street for a policeman and, when she could see none, approached a well-dressed woman and asked where was the nearest police station. The woman said she didn't know.

'A man assaulted me!' Ellen said, indicating Grafton Street. 'I'm afraid he will follow me.'

The woman looked suddenly haughty. She shook her head and moved away.

Ellen passed a young flower-seller and made for the cab stand outside the Shelbourne Hotel. Here a few hansom cabs waited in line, the horses drooping their heads and occasionally stamping their feet, the bored cabbies smoking cigarettes. The fare would be an unexpected expense, but at least she would be whisked to safety.

As she was about to cross the street she saw a young man emerge from the hotel. The walk, the carriage, the aura of easy privilege, struck her with visceral recognition. His head was bent as though in thought. He raised it and looked absently across the street. A tram advertising 'WHITE HEATHER LAUNDRY' slid between them, but when it passed the young man was still there, staring rigidly at her as though he had walked into a wall.

Guy Forrister collected himself and called her name while raising his hand in greeting. He dodged a dray, crossed the street and in a moment Ellen found herself face to face with her old love. He raised his hat politely and shook hands.

'I thought my eyes must be playing tricks! Is it really Ellen Healy?'

He was all poise and good fellowship, but also deliberate distance. Ellen was aware of it immediately, aware of his new military bearing, his admission to man's estate. Her desire to tell him about her misadventure disappeared. He would escort her to the police, of course, and then he would have to know that she had been touched by a lout and that she couldn't look after herself.

She saw his eyes examining her, the pupils dilating momentarily, a brief flash of the old hunger that was just as quickly gone. She knew that she was flushing.

'Is something wrong?' he asked gently. 'You're out of breath!'

'I've been hurrying,' she replied with a forced laugh, glancing towards Grafton Street. She caught her breath when she saw her assailant emerge at the top of the street, and had to prevent herself clutching at Guy's hand.

'What is it, Ellen?'

'I've a luncheon appointment!' she gasped. 'I was just about to take a cab.'

'That's easily arranged,' he said, and offered his arm.

She took it gratefully. Barely had she touched him when all her senses filled with his warmth. She felt the resilient muscle under her fingers, and the overpowering sense of belonging and understanding.

'I missed you in Kilcrannagh last week,' he said as they walked towards the line of cabs. 'I met Franny in the town and dropped in to see the family. Your aunt is as formidable as ever!'

'You stayed in Clonshule?'

He nodded. 'Ireland beckoned after I returned from France. So I took up my friend Bertie's standing invitation.'

'So you still have your house in France?'

'Fontebelle became legally mine a few months ago when I achieved my majority,' he replied with a smile. 'I spent part of the summer there with some friends.'

'Amid the lavender?'

'Ellen,' he said with a laugh, turning to look at her, 'what a one you always were for romance!'

'Was I?' Ellen replied in a low voice. 'I'm not sure I can be entirely blamed for it.'

His face became fixed. 'But where are you off to this fine September Sunday?'

'To my cousin Clare's … for lunch. I'm at Carysfort now.'

'Of course! They told me. May I congratulate you?'

'Thank you. Are you still at Sandhurst?'

'No. I've my commission now. Next stop India.'

'For a long time?'

'I don't know. Seven years … or thereabouts.'

He handed her into a cab, asked the driver to wait, dashed to the pavement flower girl and returned with a posy of violets.

'If you ever need me, Ellen,' he said as he handed them to her, 'write to me at Lindthorp, my brother's place in Yorkshire.' He looked at her, his eyes lingering on her face. He squeezed her hand. 'Remember me to Harry!' he added as he turned away. In a moment he was gone, striding by the railings of the Green. Ellen watched him, saw him turn and look after the cab before it rolled out of sight.

She sank back on the tired leather and let the cab take her to Lismore Street. She spent the short journey with her nose buried in the violets. India! she told herself, trying desperately to assuage her heart. The other side of the world.

The Ahern residence was in the middle of a red brick Victorian terrace with a tiny front garden and black, freshly painted railings. Ellen opened the gate, heard her footsteps on the short, tiled path and knocked at the door, which was almost immediately thrown open. Frank greeted her with brotherly arms outstretched.

'So you found us, Ellen my dear! Welcome to our humble abode!'

He closed the door behind her and Clare, beautiful as ever, swept downstairs.

'I knew you'd arrive on the dot,' she said in her precise, slightly breathless voice, as though she had seen Ellen only the day before. 'You were always reliable. I'm simply delighted at your success!' She kissed her cousin's cheek, while the maid craned a curious head from the kitchen.

'Doris, will you shut that door please!'

Ellen registered that here Clare was queen, lady of the linoleum hall, the mahogany coat stand, the wisp of a maid and the adoring husband.

'You look different,' Clare went on approvingly, 'with your hair up. Quite the young lady, and with that Healy air about you.'

Franny was about to reciprocate with her own compliments when Clare added gaily, 'How sweet of you to bring me violets! Frank darling, will you put them in water while I show Ellen the house?'

Ellen yielded up Guy's violets and Frank obediently took them to the kitchen.

Ellen followed her cousin around the house. Matty was in a cot in a room of his own, having been put down for his nap, but as soon as his mother peeped in he sprang up and rattled the bars of his cage. He had blonde curls and his mother's green eyes.

Clare picked him up. 'Oh you are a ton! This is your cousin Ellen.'

Matty did not seem impressed. He pouted his disapproval and clung to his parent.

But Ellen was impressed – by the love nest, all freshly papered, with two small interconnecting reception rooms downstairs, and the kitchen with its shining blacked range and red-and-black tiled floor. Outside in the tiny back garden was a sunny flagged area, surrounded by a wall smothered with clematis. Two cushioned cane chairs were positioned under the back window in a sun trap.

'Would you care for a sherry?'

'Thank you.'

Ellen sank among the cushions and sipped Oleroso as she listened to Clare talk first of Matty and then of Frank and his job with the *Irish Independent*. She felt she was a poor visitor. The events of the morning were like a dead weight, a reproof almost of her existence. That she could have been touched by an impertinent stranger! That she had been fool enough to speak to him! And that she should have met Guy out of the blue, a changed Guy whom she hardly knew who was soon to disappear to India. When she looked at Clare she thought how she was blessed, with a doting husband, a child and a home of her own.

'Poor Franny's a bit down in the dumps,' she said when the conversation turned to Kilcrannagh. 'With me gone, and Harry leaving, I think she's feeling very left out.'

Clare frowned. 'Frank was suggesting earlier that we could invite her to stay for a bit. But Ellen, there's nowhere for her to sleep. Doris has the box room, and Matty has the spare room. And you know what Fran is like.'

It is not for me to press her, Ellen thought, seeing the firm line around Clare's mouth. She felt sorry for Franny, and on the verge of being overwhelmed by her own sore heart.

She did not stay long after lunch. But before she left she surreptitiously lifted a few of Guy's violets from the little glass vase where Clare had arranged them, and put them into her pocket.

Ellen pressed the rescued violets between the pages of her missal and tried to convince herself that Guy would try to contact her before returning to England; he might even call to the college. But doubt overtook her later as she lay awake in the somnolent dormitory, hearing her new friend Deirdre mutter in her sleep. Why did I try to convince myself I had forgotten him? Why did I ever have to meet him at all?

But on Tuesday morning a letter arrived for her. She recognised the writing and delayed opening it until morning break, nursing it in her pocket as though it were some kind of secret scripture, wonderful to touch, more wonderful still to imagine. When she did open it she forced herself to read it slowly.

*My dear Ellen,*

*How delightful to bump into you like that and to see you looking so well. Although you were all grown up in a long dress, your hair up, meeting you made me feel like eighteen again.*

*I know how hard you worked and am so pleased for you that you achieved your dream. I wish all females had your brains and your application.*

*I hope you have forgiven my rather excessive conduct three years ago, which you may ascribe to my (very) callow youth. Your aunt was quite right to take a stern line with me. I would not upset your life for the world.*

*Yours very truly,*
*Guy.*

Ellen contained the pain. She thought of the ring, the serpent of wisdom, the loving boy who had once pressed it into her hand.

She closed her eyes at the memory of the eager pressure of his mouth and wondered what on earth her aunt had said to him when he had recently visited Kilcrannagh.

He asked me to wait for him. He said not to give up on him! And now he writes to say it was not him speaking at all, but his callow youth! Which, of course, it probably was.

She bit the end of her pen, dipped it in ink and wrote angrily, posted the letter before she could have second thoughts, addressing it to the Shelbourne Hotel.

*Dear Guy,*

*Thank you for your letter and congratulations on obtaining your commission. I'm sure you will have a great career and end up a Field Marshall.*

*There is a ring belonging to you which I should return. Shall I send it to your hotel?*

*I do want you to know that I did not ever find your conduct callow but, of course, as it is your conduct, you are best placed to summarise it.*

*With very best wishes for your future,*

*Ellen.*

The reply came within days.

*Dear Ellen,*
*Keep the ring. I don't want it back. Think of me kindly.*
*All the best my dear, dear, girl,*
*Guy.*

While Ellen was still smarting from this exchange, she received a letter from Franny in which she described her meeting with Guy in Monaghan and how he had come back to the house for tea.

*Mother had a chat with him. I tried to listen, Ellen, for your sake, but the door was firmly shut. You know how formidable she can be – more so this past year, to the point that I sometimes find her unbearable. I only hope she has not scared him off.*

So that was what happened, Ellen thought darkly. Aunt Harriet had had a 'chat' with him. It had all been too much. What had she said to him? Had she invited him to put his cards on the table, or something of that sort? She understood it now – what had begun in impetuous, spontaneous joy had been marred and overloaded. Letters from her aunt to begin with; chats with her aunt to end it. All well-meaning, while the principal chance of her life's happiness was banished beyond recall.

Oh let it go, she told herself. It's too humiliating. She thought about it all day and in the evening wrote a short note to her aunt.

*Dear Aunt,*

*Would you be kind enough to return to Guy Forrister the ring you have in safekeeping. I met him in Dublin (entirely by chance) while on my way to see Clare and Frank, and I feel strongly the impropriety of my retaining any keepsake from him. You should send it care of the Sandhurst Military Academy. I don't want to make a drama of it, so couch its return gently and politely and convey our best wishes, of course, for his future career.*

The year dragged on to Christmas. Ellen worked and tried not to think of the enigma called Guy anymore. Spring came all too soon, followed by summer, exams and holidays. In the autumn, Harry came back with her to Dublin to attend St Patrick's Teacher Training College on the northside of the city. He had taken fond leave of Franny, who had put a brave face on his departure, whispering that she'd be up in Dublin herself soon and they'd all be together again.

Ellen had arranged to meet Deirdre at Kingsbridge Station from where they would go to Carysfort together. But as there was half an hour in hand between her own and Harry's arrival in the capital, and Deirdre's train from Cork, the siblings arranged the dispatching of their trunks to their respective colleges and then repaired to the first-class waiting room, where Ellen had promised to meet her friend.

'You needn't stay, Harry. I'm sure you want to get to St Pats.'

'I'll wait until your friend comes, I want to meet this paragon!'

Deirdre strode into the waiting room ten minutes later and Ellen made the introductions.

'How do you do Miss Callaghan?'

Miss Callaghan laughed. 'So you're Ellen's brother!'

Her dimples dived into her cheeks. Ellen saw the arrested expression in Harry's eye as he followed them. 'I have three tickets for the theatre next Saturday,' he told them after he had exchanged pleasantries with his new acquaintance. '*Pélleas et Mélisande* at the Gaiety … Mrs Patrick Campbell and Madame Sarah Bernhardt!'

'How did you manage that from Kilcrannagh?' Ellenh demanded.

'Ever hear of the postal service, dear sister? Will you join us Miss Callaghan?'

Miss Callaghan said that if he was serious she would be delighted. Ellen was amused. She was sure he did not have the tickets and wondered if he would manage to procure them.

But he did.

The seats were in the gods. Harry had borrowed a pair of opera glasses and they were able to see on stage the two living legends. Seated beside her brother, Ellen's peripheral vision kept her informed of how often he turned his head to glance at her friend, half curiously, she realised, and entirely appreciatively, and her heart sank for lonely Franny whom she was perfectly well aware worshipped his shadow.

'We have to get back!' she said when the play was over. 'College curfew!'

'Lord save me from sensible women! How about a quick coffee?'

The coffees were hot and milky, served in a café in King Street by a tired waitress.

'I'm thinking of joining the Gaelic League.' Deirdre said suddenly, as she sipped the scalding brew. 'What do you think of it, Mr Healy?'

Harry put a second sugar lump in his cup. 'Depends on why you want to join, Miss Callaghan.'

'Because of a poor little coalman I read about the other day who was prosecuted for printing his name on his cart in Irish.'

'A Mr Pearse defended him,' Ellen murmured, 'but the poor divil still forfeited his coal and was fined ten shillings for "illegibility".'

'The Inspectors of Lunacy should hear an appeal,' Harry said, adding casually, 'I have already joined the Gaelic League.'

'Why?' Deirdre asked.

'I find myself fascinated by its political possibilities.'

Deirdre smiled at him across the small round table. 'Call me Deirdre, Mr Healy,' she said quietly.

'And I'm Harry!' he replied with a grin.

In that second year in Carysfort, time seemed to collapse with all the demands on it. Extracurricular classes at the Gaelic League introduced Ellen and Deirdre to a newly evolving political spectrum. They met people like Mr De Valera, the Countess Markievicz, the barrister, Mr Pearse who ran a school, and scores of others committed to the revival of all things Irish. College broke up for Christmas and the two siblings went home to find Franny unusually volatile, full of fun one minute and pensive the next, but listening avidly to their accounts of life in Dublin. Easter came and then the end of another academic year loomed with its final exams. It seemed incredible to Ellen and Deirdre that they were looking into the end of their college life. Just as they were getting into their stride, everything was about to change. Life would get serious and the blissful days in Carysfort would become a dream.

The friends left Carysfort College forever one morning in July 1906 and went out into the world as qualified national school teachers. They were to meet Harry at Kingsbridge from where he and Ellen would return to Monaghan, while Deirdre would take the train to Cork. In the cab, Ellen craned her head for a last look at the Alma Mater they had just lost. But all she could see was the rooftops.

'Well, at least we have jobs,' she said with a sigh. She had accepted the first job that had offered itself – a school in County Galway, near the town of Ballinasloe, while Deirdre had landed one in a private school in Dublin. She would be near Harry next year while he completed his course in St Pat's. They both planned to canvass for the new political party, an offshoot of the Gaelic League, called Sinn Féin. Translated with idiomatic emphasis, it meant 'Ourselves Alone' and its declared aim was national independence. Ellen had her own name for it.

'I suppose you'll be putting your energies into the Impossible Goal Party?'

'I wish you wouldn't call it that!' Deirdre replied crossly. 'Nothing is impossible until you are dead!'

'Don't talk like that, Dee! I couldn't bear it if anything were to happen to either you or Harry!'

'Ah come and spend August with me in Clonakilty,' Deirdre said, 'and don't be such a worrywart!'

'I can't. I should spend time at home. Franny's been alone all year. According to Aunt Harriet, she has her nails bitten to the quick and is like a half-dormant volcano.'

'She misses Harry,' Deirdre said in a subdued voice. 'And who can blame her?'

'Are you in love with him, Dee?' Ellen asked after a moment, glancing at her friend.

Deirdre turned in the jolting cab. Her eyes darkened and she looked her friend in the face.

'Of course I am in love with him!'

The cab rattled along the Blackrock Road. Across the bay, Howth was visible in a blue haze. The tide was out and the miles of wet sand glistened in the morning sunlight. Ellen thought anxiously of Franny who had intimated in her recent letter that, one way or the other, she intended to run away to Dublin.

# Chapter 11

Franny sat on the edge of the big brass bed she had shared with Ellen when they were children, gnawed her nails and stared out the window. The sun was blazing. She saw the flowerbeds at the side of the house, where her mother, busily weeding, was waiting for her. She stared at the trees bordering the road. Through the gaps between them she could see anyone who passed. A few minutes earlier the Heffernans' trap had rolled smartly by and she had caught a glimpse of Veronica whom she had known at school. But the Heffernans didn't call. She had lost touch with Veronica, who had always liked to crow that her family was related to the Wallaces.

After Ellen had gone to Carysfort, Franny had considered asking for her room just so she could have a better view of the local comings and goings. But it would only have given rise to complications when Ellen returned. Anyway, she was attached to her own space, in which she knew every crack in the ceiling and every chip in the cream-coloured paintwork.

Her bookshelves were full of volumes inherited from her sister and cousins, as well as current ones from the public library. The selection included most of the Brönte sisters, *Little Women*, *What Katie Did*, *The Black Tulip*, *Treasure Island*, *Robinson Crusoe*, *Lorna Doone* and A.M. Sullivan's *The Story of Ireland*, which she reminded herself she must return to Jimmy. Leaning against it was the volume covered in brown paper, *On War*, that Harry had once claimed was a maths textbook.

On her mantelpiece, beside a statue of Our Lady of Lourdes, was an array of schoolbooks, some of which she loathed, such as geography, arithmetic, geometry, and some she loved, like *The Oxford Book of English Verse* and various readers with extracts from works of literature. In addition there were Latin and French primers, and books on drawing and watercolouring.

But what had recently kept her reading in her room for days on end was the latest novel borrowed from the library, *Anna Karenina*, which she found riveting and deeply troubling, for it was about a woman who had lost control of her life.

Sometimes she regretted that she had not apologised to Sister Anselm at the convent and done what they wanted. They would have kept her – after all she had only refused to go to Mass one weekday morning in winter when the chapel was so cold she found it unbearable. She had stubbornly stayed in bed and, although enjoined to rise and obey, had remained there until breakfast. She had been thirteen then. She had refused to back down, saying that she saw no reason why she should have to go to Mass every day of the week. But Mother Superior held to the view that Franny was not only insubordinate, but spiritually mutinous.

'Frances will not be instructed,' she informed her mother. 'She thinks her own strength is sufficient for her life. She will always rush in where angels fear to tread.'

In the end, her mother, jaundiced by the catalogue of her daughter's imperfections, had told them she would take her from the school and educate her herself. But she had been grim-faced about the whole episode, telling Franny that no other educational establishment would take her now and that the nuns had been running a school, not a hotel.

'You think it's a school, Mother. It's really a penitentiary where young girls are trained to be good little ciphers without an original thought. And where they have to get up at blooming 6.30 every single morning!'

For two weeks Franny had been euphoric at being rid of her educational establishment. After that she began to miss her old friends, boarders all and out of reach. When they did not try to contact her, she sensed that she was a reject from ordinary girlhood, thrown back for company on her two cousins whose lives she watched expand as they worked for their futures, while her own contracted. She had compensated by voracious reading and provocative arguments, but now she was facing growing despair.

She felt she didn't have a future. True, she would not starve, her mother had some capital, which she and Clare would share. And, now that the latter was married and in good circumstances, Mother would probably leave Kilcrannagh to her. All this, of course, was predicated on her mother's continued love and goodwill, normal in ordinary circumstances, but not so easily assured when your mother was your exacting teacher and when you had to spend your whole life in her pocket.

Of course she might get married – her mother told her confidently that someday she would – but she could not imagine ever finding anyone she loved as much as she loved Harry. Franny felt her very existence had become an insoluble dilemma: the prospect of having a life of her own was no longer an option; it was something she needed like air and water. She felt like a badly potted plant, artificially confined and doomed to grow stunted. Like most women's lives, she reminded herself when almost overwhelmed by self-pity she wrote down an angry list of the disabilities under which they laboured. Top of the list were the three most important:

1. They were not represented in Parliament.
2. They were a dispossessed people.
3. They were deliberately kept dependent on men.

The list was capable of extension and she kept it to one side, ready for additions. She knew she could not blame her mother for these and other perceived ills. But, much as she loved her, her resentment of her authority grew stronger by the day. The only light in this bleak scenario was that Harry and Ellen were coming home that very evening for the summer.

She had laundered her best summer frock in anticipation, and it hung waiting on a padded hanger. It was blue, a softer shade than Ellen's dress of five years ago. She had washed her hair and brushed it until the glints in it shone like gold thread. She felt butterflies in her tummy at the thought of her reunion with Harry whom she had not seen since Christmas. Would he have changed? Would he find her changed? For the better? Grown up at last? Could he, by any quirk of fate, come to love her as a woman?

She moved to the window, and her mother, her straw hat askew, looked up. Franny registered the silent summons, the imperious movement of the hand that was so typically her mother. She nodded, moved back from the window muttering, 'Blast, blast, blast,' and flounced downstairs. She picked up her old straw hat and went into the garden.

'You spent a long time getting your sun hat,' said her mother.

Franny jammed the hat on her head and took up a hoe. 'It's hot today, Mother! Too hot for gardening.'

'I know, dear, but with Ellen and Harry due back I want the place looking its best.'

Franny whacked at a dandelion root. 'Isn't it funny how important people become when they're no longer around.'

Mrs Murphy glanced at her daughter and frowned. Franny had been exceptionally difficult for days. 'Ellen is finished in Carysfort now,' she said mildly. 'She will be with us for just a few weeks and after that we will only see her during the school holidays.'

Franny groaned, 'I know. Why did she opt for a job in blooming Ballinasloe?'

'She has to get on with her life,' her mother replied, dismayed at her daughter's persistent petulance and unwilling to be drawn into challenge. 'But we will certainly miss her here!'

'She's special, Mother, isn't she? Quiet, deep and honest. Not like me.'

'What is the matter with you, Franny?'

'I've something on my conscience.'

Her mother leaned back on her hunkers and looked up at her with a startled expression.

'You remember a few years ago,' Franny went on, 'when Guy Forrister came to visit and he gave Ellen a ring?'

'So she told you about that?'

'I overheard you talking. Her door was open. When you took it away from her I retrieved it for her.'

Mrs Murphy put down her hoe and stood up. 'Are you telling me,' she demanded, looking down at her daughter, 'that is was you who took that ring from my drawer?'

Franny nodded. 'It was wrong of me, but I could not bear to see Ellen so distraught. I know I should have told you before now.'

'You certainly should, Frances. It was dishonourable of you to let her take the blame.'

'She wanted it that way. After all, she did take the ring back when I recovered it, which wasn't very honourable either. But I should have owned up all the same. May I ask you, Mother,' she added, lowering her voice, 'if you still have it?'

'Franny, I don't know what has got into you these days. I'm not sure it's any of your concern, but for your information, I have sent the ring back to Guy Forrister. At your cousin's explicit request.'

'Oh Mother. You have ruined everything. They love each other.'

'Are you not concerning yourself with something that is none of your business?'

Before Franny could make a caustic response, the two women heard the sound of bowling wheels. They glanced towards the gate. Franny registered the muted male command – 'Whoa', and the grinding of iron-shod feet. She jumped up and smoothed her skirts. They couldn't have arrived early, could they? Her heart leaped at the prospect. They might have got an early train and hired a trap at the station. But that voice came again and she knew it was not Harry's.

'It's a young man,' Mrs Murphy said, moving towards the gate. 'I wonder what he wants?'

Frances recognised him as soon as she saw him. It was Mr Wallace, Guy Forrister's friend.

Bertram Wallace tied the reins, stood at the gate and looked at the scene before him. There were two women among the roses and the lupins; one was obviously the mother and the other, although her face was shadowed by her hat, he was sure was the frisky little filly he had met with Forrister in Monaghan. He raised his boater in cheery greeting.

'Good day to you ladies,' he called. 'Is it possible that I might beg a drink of water? Driving is such thirsty work in this weather!'

Frances watched as her mother opened the squeaking gate and invited the visitor in. He exclaimed in surprise as she came forward, 'Well, well, if it isn't Miss Murphy! How delightful it is to see you again, and on such a wonderful day!'

Franny extended her hand politely.

'I trust you got your brakes mended?' he added cheerfully as he mopped his brow.

'Mother, this is Mr Wallace. I met him more than a year ago when I was coming from the library. He kindly lent his trap to Guy so he could drive me home.'

A few minutes later the trio were seated in the shade of a lilac, quaffing Maggie's homemade lemonade. Franny was keenly aware that her straw hat was tattered and that her sprigged cotton dress had seen better days, but pretended she didn't care. She didn't like Bertram Wallace: his laugh was too loud, and his eyes strayed repeatedly to her bosom, where she knew one of the buttons was loose. In addition, his accent was extraordinary, as though he were rolling a red hot marble in his mouth – the result no doubt of his

English education. But Guy was English, and he didn't sound like that.

'Been doing a spot of recce,' he told Mrs Murphy. 'Never bothered much before ... old man looked after things ... Seems we still have a thousand acres this side of the town! But since the last Act the tenants are buying out, you know. Eager to borrow, poor monkeys ... the ones who can manage it.'

Franny glanced at her mother, but her face was deadpan. She said quietly, 'The ones who are left, you mean, Mr Wallace? Were not many of them forced to emigrate during the Famine, and afterwards?'

'True, very true.'

'Your family have been at Clonshule for a long time?'

'By Jove, yes. Since 1656!'

'Shortly after Cromwell paid us a visit? When your ancestors came over ... from England. They must have been terribly rich to have bought so much land,' she added, widening her eyes.

Bertie Wallace pursed his mouth and then laughed easily. 'Bought? But you are ribbing me Miss Murphy! Right of conquest would be more apt, my dear young lady. Right of conquest!'

'The word "right" keeps poor company with the word "conquest",' Franny said sweetly. 'Does it not trouble you at all, Mr Wallace, that for two hundred and fifty years, the people hereabouts have regarded your family as nothing better than armed brigands?'

'Franny!'

But Fran had the bit between her teeth. She did not look at her mother and continued.

'People don't forget, you know, Mr Wallace. This is an ancient land with as long a memory.'

Oh God, she thought, why can't I stay cool and collected? He is a guest after all, and it was ages ago. She smiled archly to take the sting from her comment. But Bertie Wallace was only momentarily taken aback.

'You've been listening to sour grapes, eh! You have a Fenian here!' he said to Mrs Murphy, with a loud laugh. 'A girl with spirit!'

Frances saw his eyes size her up and return to her bosom.

He smacked his lips and, declaring the lemonade to have been the best he had ever tasted, rose to leave.

As Franny and her mother walked their guest to the gate, he paused to examine a shrub.

'I say, what an interesting shrub! These lower leaves seem iridescent.'

'It's a camellia. It flowers early,' Mrs Murphy said. 'Are you interested in gardening, Mr Wallace?'

Bertram Wallace shook his head. 'Dear lady, I am ignorant of all such matters. But do you think you could let me have a cutting … for my mother … keenly interested …' and when his hostess left them to attend to his request he turned to Franny and whispered with a soft smile, 'You are a delicious little firebrand!' and his hand brushed, with blithe assurance, against her breast.

# Chapter 12

Franny caught her breath as two things happened at once: the first was blind outrage, a desire to slap Bertram Wallace's face with all her might. The other was an unexpected, leaping sensuality, that sent thrills through her whole body and left her breathless.

She moved back, stiff with confusion. Her mother returned with the cuttings in wet newspaper, commenting that they were struck and hoping they would take nicely.

Their visitor thanked her. 'You must come to visit us at Clonshule … and Miss Murphy of course … more than happy to return the compliment.'

Mrs Murphy murmured politely that they would be delighted.

'Shall we set a date then?' he demanded expansively. 'What about Saturday?'

'I'm afraid my niece and nephew will be back from Dublin …'

'Bring them too. The more the merrier. I'll send the trap. Three o'clock?' In a moment he had the reins in his hand, said 'H'up' to the pony and was gone.

'That performance about armed brigands was not well done!' Mrs Murphy said sternly to her daughter as the sound of the trap receded, 'He was our guest!'

'It was water off a duck's back, Mother. You saw that yourself.'

'He seemed quite taken with you, notwithstanding.'

'You are thinking, Mother, that he is the heir to Clonshule. But I don't care if he's the heir to Kingdom Come. And I will not be going to take tea with him next Saturday!'

Her mother sighed. 'Why do you ascribe ulterior motives to me, dear? You have taken the sun,' she added. 'You are very flushed.'

Franny was spared the necessity of making a rejoinder. They heard the footsteps behind them and turned to see Jimmy striding across the gravel. He tipped his cap.

'Just wondering ma'am, will I go straight to the train this evening, or is anyone coming with me to meet the returning scholars?' His face was glowing with perspiration. 'It'll be grand to see them! I wonder will his first year in Dublin have changed Harry much? And of course, Ellen is now qualified.'

'Oh, I'll go with you,' Franny said eagerly.

'And you must join us for supper, Jimmy,' her mother added, gathering up the lemonade jug and glasses, and heading for the house.

'Thank you ma'am.'

When Mrs Murphy had moved out of earshot, he leaned towards Franny.

'Was that himself from Clonshule I saw leaving just now?'

'Yes, Mr Wallace.'

'He wasn't trying to squeeze money out of your mother?'

'Jimmy, the man just called for a drink of water! We're not his tenants!'

'A good thing too!' he said grimly. 'His steward has just served eviction notices on three families above at Clegarrbh.'

Franny put a hand to her mouth. She knew as well as anyone that only the emigrant boat awaited the evicted. 'Poor things! What will they do?'

'What the Irish have had to do ever since the Sassanach got a grip on this country – emigrate or die!' He looked at her and added, 'Mr Wallace is a sporting gentleman, but this time he may meet more sport than he bargained for!'

'What do you mean, Jimmy?'

But he did not answer.

That evening Mrs Murphy opened a bottle of wine to toast her two returned family members who did not look at all the worse for their train journey, although Ellen was quiet, and Harry jubilant that he had 'miraculously' passed his first year. In fact he was particularly garrulous this evening – evidently excited by the restoration of the familial, and the Bordeaux he swallowed so appreciatively.

Jimmy, who never drank, needed a little encouragement to taste the wine.

'My first ever glass of wine, ma'am!'

'Someone brought us a case of Bordeaux a few years ago,' Mrs Murphy said. 'It ages well.'

'Yes, Guy brought it,' Franny said pointedly. 'It was very kind of him!'

She glanced at Ellen and saw that her face had tightened.

'Tell us everything about Dublin,' she demanded cheerfully. 'I especially want to hear about you, Harry, for poor Ellen had been stuck in a convent, while you have had the run of the town.'

'St Pat's has rules too, you know.'

But he told them about his lecture schedule, his trips into the city, the Georgian streets graced by magnificent houses, the slums he had walked through where barefoot, ragged children played hopscotch and begged for pennies.

'What about the Gaelic League?' Jimmy asked, looking at Ellen. 'You must meet plenty of interesting people there!'

'All the intelligentsia!' Ellen said. 'Like Mr Pearse who was mentioned in the paper, and Mr de Valera who will be teaching in Carysfort next year.'

'De Valera is a complex character,' Harry said. 'Difficult

to read. Pearse is a driven man intent on running a bilingual school. But of course,' he went on, 'the real excitement is the new political party …'

'And what about women?' Franny interrupted. 'When are *we* going to get the vote or must we found our own party?'

Harry's face assumed a whimsical softness. 'You sound like Ellen's friend Deirdre! She's the most amusing girl you could meet … brilliant too … and pretty! You'd like her, Fran.'

'She's in this organisation?'

'To be sure. She's got a job lined up in Dublin for next year, so she'll be canvassing with me for the Municipal Elections.' His face glowed. 'In fact,' he added, 'I was thinking of inviting her down sometime so that she could meet you all.'

Franny retreated into silence, picked at her meal, her heart plummeting sickeningly.

I've lost, she thought. It was slipping from me while I was blind. And now I've lost.

Ellen tried to think of something light to deflect the subtly changed atmosphere. Harry shifted uncomfortably, aware of the sudden tension, but unsure what had caused it.

'Well now,' his aunt said, 'we've our own bit of news. Mr Wallace of Clonshule House paid us a visit today, and is sending his trap for us to take tea with him and his mother on Saturday. We're all invited.'

Jimmy looked meditative. 'Are you going?'

'Why not? It will be a diversion, and interesting too to see Clonshule House.'

'I could draw it for you,' Jimmy replied. 'A big square block of a place, with every elegance you can think of, built,' he added mildly, 'on expropriation and murder.'

Harry looked at him and there passed between some silent intelligence. 'Well, I think I'll go anyway,' he said with his quirky grin. He turned to his cousin, 'What about you Fran?'

'Bluebeard's castle?' she replied with a brittle giggle. Her mother looked at her with surprise when she added, 'Wouldn't miss it for the world!'

Clonshule House was, as Jimmy had pointed out, a square limestone pile, built with Georgian elegance with tall windows, a basement and a short flight of granite steps to the front door. They could glimpse it from the road but when they turned in at the gate lodge, the beeches lining the avenue blotted it from view. Sitting beside her cousin in Bertram Wallace's trap, Ellen reflected on the irony of visiting Guy Forrister's friend. But there was no point in thinking about Guy anymore. He was out of her life, gone to India; he would not be back for years.

On either side of the long avenue stretched acres of parkland. As the trap turned a bend in the driveway, the house rose before them. It was built on a natural incline of the land, so that parkland and pasture, avenue, woodland and gate lodge, fell away from it, and it remained on its promontory, lording it over its thousands of acres as far the eye could see.

Behind the house was what appeared to be a walled garden, and to one side a sweep of woodland of oak and birch and hazel that stretched down the incline.

'It's beautiful!' Ellen said. So it was here that Guy had been staying when he had come to pay court to her, where he had written a note to tell her she was the only girl in the world.

'God, the arrogance!' Franny muttered with a giggle.

'Never underestimate arrogance,' Harry replied. 'It's the principal weapon of war.'

The driver, who had barely spoken when he had collected them, turned and threw at Harry a swift, appraising look from narrowed eyes.

'Shall we leave history alone for today, Harry?' his aunt said.

As soon as the trap drew up in the forecourt, Bertie Wallace came down the steps to greet his guests. The little filly was there, he saw at a glance, in a fetching blue number too by Jove. With her were her mother and two other people he had not met, but knew by repute – Forrister's stepsister and brother – in a manner of speaking. He knew that Forrister had once been stuck on the Healy girl. In fact, despite preaching sense to him, he had seemed hell-bent on her. He studied Ellen for a few moment before deciding she was a proud little crystal angel, brittle and untouchable. Whereas the other girl … now that was a filly of another colour altogether. He remembered with pleasure the soft resilience of her breast when he had caressed it, the way the nipple had hardened, the sheen of perspiration on her neck. Even as she had sprung back he had seen the crimson stain her face and throat. He would put any wager you liked on it – there would be pleasure there for the taking.

He watched while MacKenna, the coachman, let down the step and opened the trap door. The women braced themselves, Miss Murphy put a hand to fix her waistband and he moved forward to hand them down.

'Mrs Murphy, Miss Murphy. How delightful to see you. So glad you could come.'

Tea was a crucifixion, Franny thought. Served in the drawing room with a silver service and lots of tiny cucumber sandwiches and small cakes, while Mrs Wallace, who was a little deaf, thanked Mrs Murphy loudly for the cuttings she had sent her and, after strained pleasantries, invited her guests to see the garden.

'I would love to see it!' Mrs Murphy said. 'We glimpsed it from the trap. I believe only Father O'Dowd has one to compare.'

'Who? Oh, you mean the little parish priest.'

Mrs Wallace recollected herself, put a finger to her lips, and when the maid had left the room, added, 'You have to be so careful, you know. They tell their priests everything!'

'Really Mother,' Bertie said with a cheerful laugh, 'must remember our company'.

'What's that you said, dear?'

Ellen, amused by their host's attempts to shush his mother, looked around her. She saw the crystal chandelier, the marble fireplace, the gilt overmantel, the antique furniture, and through the open windows, the view over the countryside. Was Guy's French house, Fontebelle, like this? It would have shutters of course – Guy had said they were essential in summer. But it would belong in its setting, a French house in a French countryside. It wasn't a planter's castle, built on suffering. She was pulled from her reverie by Franny's voice.

'Not everyone rushes off to confession, Mrs Wallace. I don't! There are some of us who don't tell our priests anything.'

'Really, Franny!' her mother murmured. 'This is hardly the …'

'You don't say, Miss Murphy!' Bertie Wallace interjected. 'But then a young lady like you would have nothing to confess.'

'Unless she made it up,' Harry added, grinning at his cousin, 'which of course is a sin against the Holy Ghost!'

'Harry!' his aunt exclaimed. 'Really!'

There was a moment's silence, broken by Mrs Wallace who said she was so sorry … she hadn't realised … Of course many Roman Catholics were …

Her son interrupted her, chivvied everyone to come outdoors and see the garden that was almost as good as the parish priest's. He laughed as he said this and pushed up the lower sash of a tall Georgian window and opened the wooden doors that were located under it.

Ellen saw the heat in Bertram Wallace's glance at Franny, and suddenly suspected why they had been invited to tea at Clonshule.

# Chapter 13

It was only a short walk through the gate in the walled garden to the woodland, and Franny took it. She wanted to be away from everyone. The glances from Bertram Wallace when no one was looking, the way his eyes wandered over her, made her feel naked. In any case, she could not pretend to her usual vivacity. Harry was in love with a girl called Deirdre he had met in Dublin. He spoke of her constantly and every time he did, his face lit up.

She felt as though nothing much mattered anymore. She had always known she loved Harry. Were they not soul mates, 'friends forever' as he said himself? She needed him the way a plant needed sunlight and the prospect of losing him to another woman, to a different life, was a bereavement, a misery beyond anything she had ever known.

She saw the dog roses, sprays of them deeper in the woods by a clearing, and she directed her way towards them, glad to leave behind her mother and Mrs Wallace who were talking flowers, and Ellen and Harry who were being shown the wonders of the garden by the overpowering Mr Wallace who had so insulted her on Monday. Ellen had seemed almost in a trance; but it was not the Wallaces that mesmerised her, Franny knew, it was the beauty of Clonshule and the knowledge that Guy Forrister had visited here and walked in the same garden.

She looked back at the massive elegance of the house and let her eyes rise to the servants-quarters high up, where the windows were ovals, the so-called ox eyes. At one of them there seemed to be a statue. Or was it a face? She leaned back against a tree, confident of her own invisibility in the woodland. Yes, there it was, the white face of a young woman, gazing fixedly at the garden below. There was something unnatural in her immobility, as though she were indeed the statue she had first mistaken her for, like some discarded piece of decorative lumber. Then the girl moved, turned her head and was gone.

Franny heard footsteps in the undergrowth and, glancing back towards the garden gate, saw that Bertram Wallace had left the garden. He was looking to the right and left and was mincing along carefully. She suspected at once that he was looking for her.

She crept from one tree to the next and flattered herself against the trunk of an oak at the edge of the clearing. But to little avail. Wallace saw the blue flash of her skirt and with a subdued whoop of delight he was with her almost immediately.

'Playing hide and seek, you naughty puss?' he said breathlessly, and put his hand on her arm. Franny felt as though his fingers burned her flesh. She smelled his breath; it was warm, like new-mown hay.

'Mr Wallace,' she said, snatching her arm away, 'I think you forget yourself!'

'Forgetting oneself, Miss Murphy, is the principal pleasure known to man … and woman too! But why don't you call me Bertie? After all, we are going to be so well acquainted!'

As he said this he pushed her back against the bole and covered her mouth with his. Franny felt the wet greed of his lips and heard her heart hammering. She did not move as his hand roved over her breast. The pleasure took her breath away. Her hat came adrift and fell into the bracken.

What does it matter? she asked herself angrily, when a shocked reminder surfaced in her brain. What does anything matter if I cannot have Harry, if I must become an old maid, a slave to my mother until I die?

It was an excuse, and she knew it. The truth was that she was virtually powerless, overwhelmed by a desire that was the more powerful for being forbidden, and for having as object a man she loathed.

Delighted with her passivity, Bertie laid her on the ground, lifted the hem of her skirt in one practised movement, slid his hand upwards until it was probing inside her drawers. He was panting now, but so was she. She tried to push him away, suddenly frightened at the speed and the irrevocable nature of what was happening. She had only a sketchy knowledge of the facts of life; but now she felt the male organ, as the books called it, something she had never seen but knew existed, bulging through Bertie Wallace's trousers.

Bertie began to tear with one hand at the buttons of his flies. Desire deserted Franny and was replaced by panic. She tried to spring up, but his weight was on her, his hand under her skirt and, struggle as she might, she could not budge him. She was about to scream when she heard Harry's voice calling her, then footsteps behind them in the wood.

Bertie Wallace jumped up, straightened his clothes and said in a pragmatic voice, 'Stay here and tidy up. I'll lead them in the other direction. We'll finish this another day, Miss Murphy!'

Then he was gone. She heard his voice, normal enough, as he addressed Harry, his breathlessness ostensibly attributable to rushing through woodland on a warm day.

'I've been looking for your cousin … bit worried about her leaving us … there's an old ice house that's not too safe … over here … an old well also.'

Franny heard Harry's alarmed response as the footsteps moved away. She stood up, smoothed her skirts, rearranged her hair and restored her hat. Her mind was numb. She plucked a few ferns, put them against her hot face and called out to Ellen whom she could see following her brother.

'Where did you get to?' Ellen cried, coming towards her through the wood. 'I was worried about you, but the others thought you had gone back to the house.' She added in a low voice, 'Fran, you look so … is everything all right?'

Franny was unable to meet her cousin's eyes.

'It was so lovely out here!' She held out the ferns by way of an alibi. 'I sat down … must have dozed … I didn't get much sleep last night.'

Franny saw that Ellen was regarding her strangely and hated herself.

Half an hour later, Bertram Wallace was all urbanity as he handed the ladies back into the trap and, with barely a glance at Franny, suggested that he entertain them all at Clonshule again. 'In a week or two, Mrs Murphy. I have to go away for a short while, but I'll be back then.'

That night, while the house slept, Franny washed herself repeatedly at her basin and afterwards knelt for hours before the statue of Our Lady on her mantelpiece. The floor was hard, bare shellacked boards and after a while her knees began to hurt, but she took the pain and discomfort as her due. She prayed for forgiveness, for strength to ensure that such an occurrence would never take place again. She offered thanks for her deliverance before it had been too late. She wept that Bertram Wallace's hands had invaded her.

The nuns were right, she thought. I am headstrong, and I have walked in where angels fear to tread. Oh God, why did I never realise the Devil is real, and lives in me!

She thought of Ellen, who had been taciturn on the way home, glancing at her occasionally in frowning perplexity. How horrified she would have been if she had been told the truth. Ice-cool Ellen, who had loved someone, but who had had the strength to give him up! Franny had forced herself to make conversation, avoiding her mother's eye and schooling her voice. She told them of the girl she had seen at one of the high windows and how she had mistaken her for a statue.

'You've been reading too much Brontë,' Ellen said. 'You're thinking of the mad woman in the attic!'

'Mad is right!' MacKenna, Wallace's coachman had muttered and, leaning over the edge of the trap, he had hawked and spat, leaving a gobbet of yellow sputum on the road.

'Begging your pardon ma'am,' he said to Mrs Murphy. He glanced at Harry, but the latter seemed far away.

A week went by. Franny kept to the house and did not venture into Monaghan except in Ellen's company. Harry had taken to staying out late with Jimmy. Once or twice she saw him returning in the small hours, watched him from behind her curtains as he moved quietly around the side of the house just as the cock began his salute to the day.

Where had he been? He was so lucky to be a man and master of his night time, instead of lying awake hour after hour as she did, or pacing her room barefoot and longing for the dawn.

'Where were you?' she asked him when they were alone together in the drawing room one day after lunch and Harry was examining the bookshelves. 'Last night,' she added as he looked at her with raised eyebrows, 'and almost every night since you came home?'

She watched his reaction, wondering if he could have been drinking. But Harry showed no signs of liquor, neither on his breath nor in his eyes; nor did he even sleep so late into the day that it would have alarmed her mother.

'I was with Jimmy,' he replied patiently, 'and one or two of his friends.'

'Drinking?'

Harry gave a small exasperated grunt. 'Don't interrogate me, Franny. We were talking, if you must know!'

'You could stay at home and talk to me! I can never get to sleep until the small hours anyway!'

Harry's irritation vanished. 'Dear little Fran,' he said, turning to her with a winning smile, 'I'm not much fun, am I? And we haven't seen each other for months! I'll make it up to you.' Then he continued his scrutiny of the bookshelves. 'You didn't see any of Jimmy's books, did you?'

'I have the history book upstairs, and another one also – the one covered in brown paper.'

Harry turned to her, looked at her carefully. 'What were you doing with that?'

'Studying maths,' Franny replied with a straight face.

'I just want to restore them to Jimmy,' Harry said. 'Will you get them for me?'

Franny went upstairs directly, taking the steps two at a time, meeting Maggie with her arms full of sheets.

'Glory be to God!' the latter exclaimed, 'but will you go easy. You nearly broke me poor neck!'

'Sorry, Maggie!' Franny was feeling elated. There was some kind of mystery here. She knew, and Harry knew that she knew, what that book covered in brown paper was all about. So why did he make a secret of it? It was hardly a crime, after all, to study the waging of war. She brought the books down and handed them to him without a word. Her mother came into the room looking troubled.

'I have received some worrying news,' she said. 'It seems that Mr Wallace's agent was fired on last evening. Luckily he only sustained minor injuries.'

'But what would have provoked that, Mother? A nice inoffensive gentleman like him.'

'I gather there was another unfortunate eviction.'

Harry turned, looked out of the window and asked, 'Did they apprehend the culprit?'

'It seems not, but the constabulary will be scouring the parish.'

That evening Sergeant Finnegan from the barracks called and asked if anyone had seen anything suspicious. He chatted to Aunt

Harriet in the drawing room, accepted a small tot of whiskey and said that things in the country were going to blazes. And when Jimmy came around the following morning he told them almost casually that his home had been searched by the police the night before.

Mrs Murphy looked horrified. 'That was very distressing for you, Jimmy!'

'Sure they were only doing their job, ma'am!'

As the days passed and they saw no more of Bertram Wallace, Franny's panic began to subside. He had presumably gone away for a while, as he had indicated, but she did not ever want to see or hear from him again. Her mother had sent a polite note of thanks for having entertained them for the afternoon. Given the circumstances of what had occurred, the irony, even the impropriety, of a thank-you note was not lost on Franny, but what could she have said that would have prevented it? She could hardly say, 'Dear Mother, Mr Wallace assaulted me and put his hand up my skirt. If Harry had not disturbed him he would have had his way with me.'

Franny desperately wanted to share her turmoil with someone. She needed to discuss the dreadful episode with a sympathetic ear, needed to understand why she had not screamed at the outset and perhaps prevented the outrage. But in whom could she confide? Not in her mother; the very thought made her shudder. Not in Harry; she would die first. Not in graceful Ellen.

That left Jimmy, or confession. But Father O'Dowd would be shocked too, would enjoin purity on her, as though she needed to hear it, would counsel prayer, which she now resorted to on a nightly basis in a fever of new-found piety. She could not tell Jimmy either. But as long as she could tell no one it continued to consume her, so much so that her mother commented on how thin she was getting and told her not to take Ellen's leaving home so much to heart.

# *Chapter 14*

A few days later, while Ellen was at the drawing-room window working on a watercolour of the garden, she saw Jimmy, in his old waterproof and rubber boots, come through the gate. She watched him as he closed it behind him, struck by his perennial aura of purpose. Whether he was discussing books, driving the trap or digging a ditch there was the impression that he had mapped his life, was headed towards some pre-determined objective and that all the iron in his soul was focused on it.

Recently she had been haunted by spectres of mediocrity. It was something to become a teacher, but where would that lead her? Where would it lead Harry? They might persuade the children they taught to stuff their heads with knowledge. But, given the span of a lifetime, was that enough for personal fulfilment?

She thought of Guy because she could not help it. How had he felt when his ring was returned? The whole thing had been so clumsily handled. If I ever again have something important in my life, she told herself, I will grapple it to my soul with hoops of steel!

She sighed as she looked at her canvas. She did not regard herself as much of an artist, but she had rendered a fairly colourful account of the hollyhocks, the roses and herbaceous borders.

And yet they lacked something – daring perhaps. Yes they needed daring, because, ultimately, daring was life.

Jimmy saw her and came to the window. She pushed up the sash.

'Harry's gone to Monaghan since early morning,' she said. 'He'll be back soon.'

Jimmy did not seem surprised. 'Can I see the magnum opus?'

'Flatterer!' She turned the easel around so he could get a view. 'It's not finished yet. It needs contrast. And, above all, boldness.'

Jimmy considered the picture for a moment and pronounced it to be a masterpiece.

'Jimmy, you should stand for Parliament! You'd out-fib the lot of them!'

'The Irish Parliamentary Party would be a bit tame for my liking,' he replied with a laugh. 'I will miss you Ellen,' he said after a moment's silence, adding with painful diffidence, 'I would like to visit you in your new place.'

Ellen saw the hope in his eyes and the mist pearling on his tweed cap. A private panic filled her. She did not want to hurt Jimmy's feelings, but she did not want him visiting her, with all it would imply.

'You'll get your death, standing there,' she said as lightly as she could. 'Ballinasloe is a long way off.'

Jimmy's eyes dulled. 'It's him, isn't it?' he said. 'You're eating your heart out for him still – the Englishman?' When she bridled at his he added, 'Always remember – he's a friend of Wallaces'.'

'What have you got against Mr Wallace, Jimmy? We had tea with him recently!'

He looked as though he had something to tell her, but he shrugged instead and moved away, his wellingtons squelching through puddles.

Jimmy went to the haggard to get fodder for the manger. Franny was there. She had moulded herself a place in the hay rick and was curled like a cat in the fragrant gloom, her eyes closed.

Beside her the hay knife, a giant cleaver was stuck into the rick.

'Franny!' Jimmy exclaimed with a start. 'What on earth are you doing here?'

Franny sat up and looked at him calmly. 'I had to get out of the house. Mother is driving me crazy. Ellen is painting. Harry is never here. Jimmy, I am going to run away! I've been thinking about it for ages and my mind is made up.'

Jimmy leaned against the rick. 'To what?'

'Does it matter?'

'It does! If you are running to something worthwhile, fine! If you are running away from something, that's another matter. And I think you are running away from something!'

Franny was silent.

'Perhaps your recent encounter with Mr Wallace had something to do with it?'

When she did not respond, Jimmy added, 'It did not go unnoticed from the servants' windows of Clonshule House.'

Franny flushed crimson. She heard the scorn in his voice and shame seared through her. 'They couldn't have seen us!'

'One of the dairymaids, Mary MacKenna, saw you among the trees. She is expecting Wallace's child and is sensitive to his sexual adventures.' He considered her horrified face for a moment before adding in a low voice, 'She told me to warn you, if it's not too late, that he will not take no for an answer.'

Franny covered her burning cheeks with her hands and burst into tears.

'I hope it's not too late!' Jimmy added brutally.

'Oh Jimmy. What do you take me for? I didn't want any of it.'

There were footsteps in the yard, Harry's voice calling.

'For God sake, go out to him!' Franny said, drying her eyes. 'I don't want him to see me in this state. And don't tell him anything.'

'Of course I won't!'

Jimmy went to the yard. Franny sighed and wiped her nose on her sodden hanky. One of the servants at Clonshule had seen her with Mr Wallace, a girl who was already pregnant by him. So it would soon be all over the town! And what a monster he was, fathering children on his servants, who had little option but to yield to him. Disgust filled her that she had ever thrilled, however unwillingly, to his touch.

She leaned over and touched the blade of the hay knife, wishing she could do something to get out of the world. She pressed harder and the blade sliced her finger. Watching the drops of blood fall into the hay, she struggled with the fierce prompt to put her wrist against the same lethal edge. How long would it take? But what if Jimmy found her before all was over? She would be dragged back to consciousness, subjected to endless preaching and the concerned contempt reserved for the unsuccessful suicide.

She sat for a while trying to collect herself, sucking the wound, idly noting the implements stacked along the edge of the shed – fork and hoe and spade. She struggled for some kind of equanimity. Then she saw something that was making an unnatural outline in the rick. She stood up, walked around the side of the haggard and cleared away hay with her left hand. Something hard and long was wedged deep into the compacted hay, something wrapped in oil cloth. She tugged at the corner of the wrapping and stifled her exclamation at what she found. She was looking at the stocks of two rifles.

Ellen tired of her watercolour. It was almost finished, bright and colourful with carefully added panache, but it needed shadows and these would have to await the next fine day.

She washed her brush, put her paints away and left the picture to dry on the easel. She went upstairs, walking softly so as not to disturb her aunt who had retired to bed with a headache after fraught words with Franny at lunchtime. She was glad of the sanctuary that was still her room and wondering at the unease she felt, put it down to the earlier domestic contretemps and her impending departure. There was also poor Jimmy, who had evidently not given up hope of her. She hated the disappointment she had seen in his eyes. But she could not have pretended to something she did not feel in order to spare his feelings.

He had been right about Guy, or almost right. It was true he was never far from her mind. She did not doubt that she would never see him again, but she wondered if she would ever again encounter anyone with whom she would feel so excited, so known, so at peace. She was ruefully aware that she was now at an age when, if they had waited for each other, as they had once so innocently envisaged, they might be celebrating their engagement. Instead she was heading for County Galway alone and he was embarked on a life that would take him halfway around the world.

The old leather suitcase she was bringing with her was open on the floor. Better leave it to air for a while, she said to herself and opened the window. From below she heard voices, and glancing down saw Harry and Jimmy coming around the corner of the house. As usual they were deep in conversation. She was struck, as she so frequently was, by their entente, and by how low their kept their voices.

She went back to the suitcase, began to fill it with folded clothes including warm skirts for the winter ahead, boots and two woollen jackets. She took down her mother's journal and fingered it lovingly. It was too precious to take with her, but she opened it and was soon engrossed, absorbed by references to herself and her siblings when they were infants. She was terribly moved by the loving words of a young woman who had not known how short a time she had to live. The sloping writing in faded ink, expressed the anxieties of having a policeman husband in a country governed by Coercion Acts, and contained intermittent reflections on the country's future after the death of Parnell.

And to think her father – who had had such a woman with whom to share his life – had subsequently married a Lilian Forrister! Well, they were presumably happy. She heard Franny's light step on the stairs and half expected her to come looking for her, but Franny went into her bedroom and closed the door. Ellen was very concerned about her. It was distinctly possible, she thought, that Mr Wallace had made some kind of advances to her cousin in the wood two weeks ago. She had seen how Franny had paled and flushed alternatively on the way home and how brittle her voice had been, as though innocent gaiety had deserted her. But it was probably attributable to the strain she was under, what with Harry harping constantly on Deirdre and his looming return to Dublin. He was obviously looking forward to it, going back to the girl of his heart, his political activities and his second year at college. While Franny, the fiery, funny, clever friend of their childhood, was doomed to remain behind. Even Clare, who might have invited her to stay, had failed to do so; but then Clare's allure and competence had never interfered with her selfishness.

She heard Franny's door open again, heard her descend the stairs, a slower tread than usual. Ellen thought she had better follow her and prepare supper. It was Maggie's day off – she had gone to visit her mother in Cavan and would not be back until tomorrow – so they were fending for themselves.

The last thing Ellen touched before she closed and locked her mother's journal was the card that had accompanied Guy's ring: *For the only girl in the world. All my love forever.* She had kept it hidden among the pages of the diary, and she brushed her fingers over it now as though bidding him, and her youth, farewell.

Franny bandaged her injured finger and began setting the supper table. She had gone out to hide her bike in the hedge near the gate and now she finalised her plan of campaign. She was going to run away. Her savings of £7 12s. 4d., were enough to keep her going until she found work. She would go to Dublin. She didn't care if she had to wait at table or scrub floors; she had to get away from home, from the fraught loneliness of it and the certain knowledge that Bertram Wallace would soon be back, would call no doubt, and she would be expected to entertain him while he sent her mother off for more cuttings.

It was intolerable. But she would give him the slip, would stay with Clare in Dublin until she could find a room of her own. Clare might not be pleased, but she could hardly throw her into the street.

Meanwhile the only thing to do was pretend everything was normal. She would slip away after supper when everyone thought she had gone up to bed, cycle to Monaghan, stay overnight at the Westenra and take the Dublin train in the morning. She would not be missed until lunchtime; they would assume she was sleeping late, as she so often did after reading half the night.

When Ellen came downstairs she found Fran in the kitchen and suggested they have a simple supper – a salad with hard-boiled eggs and tomatoes.

Franny agreed cheerily, and when her cousin demanded suddenly, 'Fran, what on earth have you done to your finger?' she replied truthfully that she had cut it on a knife.

'Let me see it? You might need a doctor.'

'It's barely a scratch!'

Harry, when he came in, was equally solicitous of her injury, but Franny made light of it. She could see how both her cousins were relieved at her good humour, and she even summoned the courage to go upstairs, knock on her mother's door and ask if she would be coming down for supper or would she prefer to have a tray in her room.

'I'll take some tea and toast, Franny. Would you ask Ellen to bring it up?'

'I'm sorry for being so impossible, Mother,' Franny blurted, half desperate with the knowledge that she was really saying goodbye.

'Yes, it is rather a pity,' her mother replied. 'It's making life impossible. You're creating a draught,' she added irritably as

Franny stood indecisively at the open door.

Franny went downstairs, tried unsuccessfully to eat a supper and make normal conversation with her cousins. But although Ellen commented on how little she ate, reminding her she had eaten nothing either at lunch, she and Harry seemed to have a lot on their minds.

Franny wanted to confront Harry about her find in the haggard. There had always been a shotgun in the house – a Greener – kept in her mother's study. It was still there, so what did they want more guns for? Perhaps they belonged to someone else and Jimmy was just keeping them in a safe place? Did Harry even know about them? Could they, by any stroke of the imagination, have been used in the recent shooting at the Clegarrbh eviction? She was afraid, however, to ask these questions in front of Ellen.

After supper the three young people tidied things away without any of their normal banter, and then Franny said she was going to bed.

'I'll have an early night too,' Ellen said. She went upstairs almost immediately and left Franny and Harry alone in the kitchen.

Now that she was alone with Harry, Franny's sore heart overflowed. But she contained the challenge that rose to her lips. She did not want to part in anger. She had so many things to say to him, so many questions, but she could not trust herself to put them to him. She knew he would get upset, would distance himself, and then she might give her plans away. He would do his best to dissuade her, would even feel obliged to tell her mother. So she gave him a forced smile, expecting him to say he had to go out, but he did not. Instead, he straddled a chair by the range and looked at her with a smile.

'Don't go to bed yet, Fran! We've hardly had a chance to talk since I came home.'

Franny sat at the table. 'That's because you've always got better things to do.'

'Well, they're important things,' he replied tersely, evidently stung. 'You wouldn't understand.'

'Wouldn't I? Why is that? Because I'm a woman? Anyway if you won't confide in me, how can I understand? You've changed Harry.'

'Fran, don't be like this! You've not been your old self recently. What's got into you?'

'Not as much as has evidently got into you. I'm not the one who secretes rifles in the haggard!'

Harry stared at her in horror.

'I found them earlier,' she went on, sure now that he was fully aware of their existence, and their purpose. 'If you really want to hide them you should make a better job of it!' But Harry had already sprung to his feet. 'Don't just walk out, Harry! Please tell me what is going on. I'm not a child!'

When Harry didn't reply she added, 'You needn't answer. It's written across your face. You and Jimmy had some hand in the Clegarrbh shooting. The two of you are hell-bent on life in English jails.'

Harry was silent for a moment, his face dark and hard. 'All right. I'll tell you, Fran. It's just two old rifles but it's a start. We are taking back our country no matter what the cost.'

Franny gasped. 'Are you mad? The two of you? Wresting Ireland from the British Empire? When Home Rule is bound to come one of these days.'

'Don't be stupid, Fran! They'll never give us Home Rule, and even if they do, it will suck us all the more permanently into the Empire. Don't look like that!' he added irritably. 'It's a long process, and England will have to concede eventually.'

Franny stared at the cousin she no longer knew. 'I do not think the government will make any concessions,' she said. 'They are in a position of total power so why should they?'

'They've left just enough of us alive to give them a reason! Now if you will forgive me, Fran, I will attend to the better concealment of our arms. I need hardly tell you to keep your mouth firmly shut on what I have just told you. My life, Jimmy's life, depends on it.'

He went out. Franny went upstairs, lay down on her bed and put a pillow over her head. His life, she thought. His *life*!

When the clock struck nine she rose, went to the window and surveyed the garden and the road, waited for a few minutes after the last chime had died to ascertain what movement there was in the house. But nothing seemed to be stirring. Ellen was probably reading; she had lent her *Anna Karenina*, although it was overdue at the library. She felt sure that Harry had gone to see Jimmy again. He would soon be back in Dublin. If she were there too she would force him to involve her in whatever secret activities he was involved in.

She donned a skirt and blouse and arranged her hair carefully so that it would withstand the cycle ride to Monaghan. Her heart was thumping, but her hands were steady as she took up her savings, turned her brass doorknob and crept downstairs.

# Chapter 15

Bertram Wallace, fresh off the evening train from Dublin, was dining in the Westenra Hotel. He was thinking about his visit to his friend, Captain Hamilton, in Dublin Castle to whom he had passed on his suspicions. And how right he had been too! After just three days in the capital he had received a wire about an abortive eviction where his steward had been shot and wounded. Of course the perpetrator had not been located. You couldn't expect any better from the country police. The only ones you could trust were the Dublin Metropolitan.

He had come to Dublin to seek police help because he was convinced that the woods around Clonshule were being used for illegal activity. His now recuperating steward had reported a couple of weeks ago that clearings had been trampled by dozens of boots, but that although he had staked out several areas, he had not been able to surprise the poachers. Reckoning that it was not poaching that was afoot, Bertie had inspected the clearings himself and been satisfied that the compacted earth and the serried boot prints spoke of military drilling. In a small silly way of course, and nothing to worry about provided prompt action was taken. A whiff of grape would soon send the peasants scurrying. But now, after the wounding of his steward, the first priority was to find the gunman and deal with him summarily. There was a certain pleasure in the prospect of forceful reimposition of law and order.

Movement in the hotel foyer, which he could see clearly through the open door of the dining room, drew his attention. He looked up and could scarcely believe his eyes. Crossing the foyer was the Murphy filly, and she seemed to be alone. Not only that, but she was carrying a small suitcase. He suppressed the desire to get up at once and greet her. But better to watch the quarry, see what the little puss was up to. He raised his wine glass, took a sip, observed a tired Franny going to the desk and laid down his fork in amazement as she signed the register. By Jove, she was staying the night. Did that mean she was accompanied after all? Was her mother, or one of her cousins, with her?

He waited and chewed his sirloin without tasting it. There was no sign of any escort. The girl took the key, looked around nervously and headed for the stairs. What was it all about? Had she an assignation? He thought about that possibility for a while, remembered the virginal state of which he had partially disencumbered her, and dismissed it. Excitement gathered in him. She had family in the capital; she was probably on her way to Dublin.

Well now … he thought, leaning back in his chair and charged with the prospect of delights to come. He rose from the table, approached the reception desk and asked about the young lady who had just registered.

The receptionist looked at him with a frown. 'You mean Miss Murphy?'

'She looked quite famished,' Bertie said. 'Would you send her up some of that chicken pie you have on the menu? Tell her it's compliments of the house. Oh, and a bottle of champagne. Well chilled!'

The receptionist looked at him questioningly, but Bertie knew how to silence doubt. He slid a pound note to her across the counter.

Franny had taken off her hat and coat, her boots and her

stockings. She was about to take off her blouse and skirt and get into bed when the knock came to the door. She froze, wondering if she had already been discovered, if her mother had sent Harry after her, or if she had followed her herself. The knock came again, polite but insistent. Franny went to the door and called out, 'Who is it?'

'Room service, Miss,' a young male voice replied.

She opened the door a chink, saw a boy in a white apron with a trolley bearing china and cutlery, a wine glass, a wine cooler with a bottle and a covered dish from which rose an appetising aroma, reminding her that she had scarcely eaten all day. A glance along the corridor confirmed it to be empty.

'You've made a mistake. I didn't order anything!'

'Compliments of the management, Miss!' the boy replied with a grin and made to push the trolley through the door.

'I can't afford to pay anything extra!'

'No Miss. It's all taken care of.'

Franny, wondering what she should do, stood back to let him enter. Perhaps supper was included automatically in hotel tariffs. She had never stayed in a hotel before and didn't know.

The boy set the small table, positioned the trolley beside it, lingered for a tip and when he did not receive one, turned in disappointment to the door. Bertram Wallace, however, was waiting outside to reward the boy with a shilling.

'Don't be alarmed Miss Murphy,' Bertie said, closing the door after the departing waiter, suddenly afraid from the appalled face before him that the girl would scream. 'I saw you in the foyer and I thought I'd just come up and apologise.' He waited for this to sink in, stood lugubriously like a naughty boy expecting castigation.

'Please leave the room, Mr Wallace.'

'I do beg your pardon, Miss Murphy. I was a bit carried away last time and I wanted to make amends. Thought a bite of supper and a glass of champagne … what?' and he indicated the supper on the table and smiled affably, indicating that bygones should be bygones.

Franny tried to remain calm, but was acutely aware of her predicament. She was alone in a hotel bedroom with Mr Wallace, with her stockings over the bed end and his champagne supper on the table. If she screamed someone would come, but that would be the end of her reputation. I have to handle this properly, she thought. I must stay cool. But she remembered what had already happened to her at this man's hands, remembered what Jimmy had told her about the servant girl and she knew that she was already compromised. The glint in his eye was like that of a cat with a mouse, anticipatory, hungry, determined.

Even if she ran screaming for the police, the officers of the law would probably just find it amusing. The man before her was immensely rich, proprietor of a great house and thousands of acres. She was a young woman, virtually penniless. In the eyes of every man alive, except her own kin, she was fair game. And she knew, looking at him, that he saw her as precisely that.

Fear flooded her. Black spots swam before her eyes and her knees began to shake. The day's excitements, the lack of food, the discovery of the guns, the intelligence she had learned from Harry, the terror of what she had done and the horror of what now presented itself, were taking their toll.

'Please,' she said, in a voice that wept with full cognizance of their relative positions. 'Please.' The room began to sway. I will not faint, she told herself. I will not faint! But, despite her desperate injunctions, the world around her tipped crazily. She clutched at the end of the brass bed and Bertie Wallace moved forward to help her.

'Dear young lady,' he murmured, 'you're quite done in! Here, let me help you.'

He took her hands, pulled her into his arms and pushed her back onto the bed.

'Good girl,' he whispered urgently. 'Good girl, good girl.'

*

When Franny came to herself she was lying on the bed with Bertram Wallace on top of her. He was stroking and kissing her face, rubbing his hands over her bosom, grunting a little and moving rhythmically. Between her legs was pain, spearing upwards, as though she were being split in two. She tried to free herself, tried to scream, but his hand was clamped over her mouth. He arched suddenly and cried out, then collapsed on top of her.

'Quite wonderful, Miss Murphy!' he said breathlessly after a moment, removing his hand from her face. 'I am sorry if I hurt you!'

He was still panting, but he chucked her gently under the chin while she tried to turn away her head. 'It's not the end of the world, you know, young lady,' he added, easing himself up and assuming a seated position on the edge of the bed where he regarded her whimsically. 'You will grow to like it you know … with practice.' He added jovially, 'Isn't that right … eh?'

When Franny neither looked at him nor spoke, he restored his clothing and left almost immediately, putting a ten-pound note on the table where the supper was going cold. She heard the door close behind him and lay quietly, aware of the lamplight, the silent curtained room. She was in a state where she did not know whether she had dreamed it all. It was too preposterous to be true, too terrible for rational thought. She had run away from home; she was in a room in the Westenra Hotel, and Mr Wallace had just …

She put a hand to her breast, found her buttons intact, but realised all was not well elsewhere. Her skirts were rumpled, pulled up around her thighs. There was a throbbing soreness between her legs. She moved and realising she was wet, sat up in alarm. She saw her drawers on the floor by the bed, white and innocent with the broderie anglaise she had stitched herself. Suddenly, like a child after a nightmare, she was weeping for her mother. But she could not go back to her mother and tell her. She was now on the other side of a divide, one high as Heaven, one she would never be able to cross.

She lay there in conflicting emotions, while her tears dribbled into her ears. After a little time, a cold determination, unlike anything she had ever experienced, was born in her. It was the absolute necessity of revenge.

# Chapter 16

Franny never remembered leaving the hotel early next morning or the train journey to Dublin. Her arrival on Clare's doorstep, however, left its mark.

'Why didn't you write?' Clare drew herself up with typical hauteur. 'I like to know when people are coming.'

Franny whimpered from the cavernous distance that seemed to separate her from every living thing. 'I'm sorry, I'm sorry … sorry.'

Clare's expression of exasperation changed to one of alarm. 'What's happened to you, Franny? Were you in an accident?'

'Nothing happened to me! What makes you think something happened to me?'

'You're so white … and your eyes. Fran … for God's sake.' Clare took her sister's hand and drew her into the house. Franny dropped her bag and retched. Gobbets of bile landed on the polished linoleum and streaked the front of her blouse. Clare uttered a small, untypical scream and Doris came running.

'I'm sorry … I'm sorry …'

Doris wiped up the mess, dabbed at Franny's clothes with a wet towel. 'It'll be all right Miss. It won't stain.'

'It will!' Franny replied, weeping. 'It will … it will.'

Clare brought her sister to her sitting room. 'Fran, I must know what has happened?' She paused and added in a very quiet voice, 'Is it Mother …? Has something …?'

Franny shook her head. She saw a welcoming sofa, a safe harbour, sat down, rested against the cushions and closed her eyes. The taste of bile was in her mouth. Her hands were shaking. She was shivering. She felt like a small woodland creature that had just escaped a tiger's den. The world was terrible; she wanted to scream its horror aloud. But there could be no release here, and no discreet ear. Clare would summon her mother. Harry would know. And Ellen.

'Mother's fine,' she murmured, trying to stop her voice from quivering. 'It's that journey!'

Clare took a bottle of brandy from a cabinet. She poured a tot, handed it to her sister with a frown. 'I've never known you to be travel sick. But then you haven't travelled much! Drink that down. Mother knows you were coming here, I suppose?'

'No, no one knows …' She coughed on the fiery spirit and repeated, 'No one.'

Clare had been afraid for some time that Franny would arrive on her doorstep, especially as her alter ego, Harry, was now at college in Dublin. In a way she was surprised that she had not done so already. She had her excuses lined up. It was true that she did not have a spare bedroom; it was also true that she felt her opinionated sister to be a potential embarrassment. She watched Franny as she sipped the brandy and wondered more at her distraught state than at her sudden appearance. Of course! She's had a row with Mother. And poor Mother is up to high doh, no doubt, wondering where she is. I'll have to send her a telegram. She sighed, sat beside Franny and took her hand, noting that it was as cold as ice.

'You shouldn't let your feelings run away with you, dear. Now, we must wire Mother that you are safe!' She went to the davenport in the corner, casting a glance at herself as she passed the mirror above the mantelpiece, scribbled a few words on a sheet of paper, signalled Doris and handed her the draft with instructions to send the wire immediately. She turned back to her sister and added, 'We'll have to decide what is the best thing.'

Franny, hearing 'we' and 'best thing', opened her eyes and sat bolt upright.

'We?' she intoned hysterically. 'I am here to find a job. I am going to stay in Dublin! No *we* is going to decide my life anymore!'

'But you can't rush into things, you know, dear! Major decisions in life need careful thought.'

'I've been thinking about it for months, Clare,' Franny said in a calmer voice. 'I can't go on in Kilcrannagh.'

'But darling, where will you live in Dublin? What will you live on? I'd love to have you here, of course, but we simply do not have the room!'

Franny stared at her sister. 'You will either put me up until I can manage, or I will sleep outside in the gutter,' she said with a hard little laugh. 'It is, after all, just the place for me.'

Clare started. 'Really Fran, have you gone mad?'

Clare made room for her sister by shifting Matty's cot into the matrimonial chamber, but Franny found that she could not so easily reassume the mantle of innocent young womanhood. Hour on hour, day on day, she was haunted by what had happened to her. How could I have been so *stupid*? she asked herself in bursts of self-hatred. She loathed the ease with which Bertram Wallace had trapped her, re-ran over and over the occurrences that had brought her to that pass – the sly touch on her breast in her garden, the embrace in the Clonshule woods, the hotel room when he had raped her and left money on the table. He had used her as though he had a right, as though she were some rag on which he could blow his nose … and then left money! She had torn his ten pounds into pieces and dumped it in the chamber pot on top of her vomit. But if only something had intervened, some angel with a fiery sword. If only she had not run away from home …

She felt her head would explode; she vacillated between self-destructiveness and boiling rage. She could not eat, and although Clare had, with bad grace, made room for her, she barely slept, but dozed fitfully in her room during the day, afraid to go out.

But she did scour the Situations Vacant advertisements in the paper Frank brought home each evening. There were few jobs for females, other than the menial, and she was not qualified to be a governess or stenographer. The only other possibility was shop assistant, or lady's companion. But that demanded that she go out for interview, and as day followed day she was more and more terrified of the outdoors and what might lurk there. She tortured herself with self-recrimination: I should have avoided him from the first. If only I had not …

And all the while, she dared not consider the potential consequences.

After a week Clare spoke to her. 'You're driving Frank crazy. Matty is nervous around you. Doris walks on eggs and quite honestly, I don't need to have my home invaded any longer. Harry is coming back to college on Saturday and Mother is coming with him to bring you home.'

'Traitor!' Franny screamed and ran upstairs. She donned her coat and a hat with a veil and stormed out, her blood too high for apprehension. But, once outside the door, she froze, backing against the railings and staring around her suspiciously. The street, however, was peaceful. A few women stood chatting at a corner and a horse-drawn baker's van moved from door to door. All was normal.

Reassured, she caught a tram to Nelson's Pillar, gazing out at ordinary womanhood on the streets. How many of them were hiding secrets similar to her own? But, if so, how could they smile and laugh? How could they bear to live?

She alighted near O'Connell Bridge, leaned on the parapet and stared down into the pea-green Liffey, trying to summon the resolve that would take her out of the world. Jump! a voice in her head said. Go on, be done with it! Have that much backbone! She gripped the stone balustrade, daring herself. Go on. There can be no life now!

An old woman in a black shawl leaned beside her on the parapet and indicated the smelly Liffey with a dismissive nod, 'Sure yeh wouldn't know what does be in it!'

'*I* could be in it!' Franny blurted, turning to look at the shawlie. 'Washed out into the bay.'

'Yeh might end up in Wales an' all!' the old woman agreed thoughtfully, nodding her head as though everything had its compensations. 'But why would you be thinkin' such thoughts, a *stóir*? An' you wid yer life ahead of yeh?'

Franny looked into the old face beside her and saw rheumy eyes in folds of wrinkles.

'Because a man … raped me!'

It was out! The relief was extraordinary. The sky did not fall, nor the whole city turn to stare at her.

'Sure, what else!' the woman replied in the same mournful tones, as though she were discussing the price of carrots. 'An' thim – wid their airs and their importance! No, look out for yer own life, luv. They took a poor girl outta that oul' river this mornin' … but her face …' she added, nodding at Franny meaningfully and lowering her voice. 'Rats!'

Franny shuddered and fled, hardly aware of the tram sliding towards her as she dodged across the street, or the distracted howl of the tram driver, 'Young wan, will yeh mind where yer goin' for the love of Jaysus!'

The tram clattered on its way, and Franny leaned dizzily against a lamp post in the centre of O'Connell Bridge. The world was a whirl. It moved by her with frightening purpose – powerful horses drawing Guinness drays, humble coal carts with blackened drivers, trams rattling, ragged newspaper urchins in broken boots or bare feet, cyclists in peaked caps, tightly laced women with trailing dresses. And the clatter and hum! She felt like a minnow in a roaring sea.

Afraid of drawing attention to herself, she crossed to D'Olier Street and walked around by Trinity College. In a few minutes she found herself in Grafton Street, which was supposed to have the nicest shops in the city. Striped awnings shaded the windows. The street was being washed, pungent horse manure sluiced into the gutters. Ladies crossed the street carefully, lifting their hems. Two young boys in sailor suits passed by with their father. One of them reminded her of Harry. He would soon be back in Dublin. But how could she ever look him in the face again!

Lured by the smell of roasting coffee and desperate to sit down and think, she went into Bewley's Oriental Café and ordered a coffee and a bun. She sat on a bentwood chair and considered her options while she picked at the currants in the bun and sipped the scalding, milky coffee. Her aborted design on her own life had left her shaken and exhausted. '*Look out for yer life, luv …*'

I have a choice, Franny thought after a while. I can either let what has happened destroy me, turn me into a fugitive, or a suicide … Or I can somehow prevail over it and live.

When she left the café her attention was caught by a small card taped to the window of a nearby milliner's shop. Under the blue-and-white awning was the name of the establishment – Le Chapeau. *Assistant wanted*, the card said. *Apply within.*

Franny stared into the shop. It was full of wonderful hats festooned with feathers, tulle, flowers, ribbons, even artificial fruit. A couple of fashionable ladies were seated before mirrors, trying on one creation after another with total concentration, tilting their heads and studying their profiles with hand mirrors supplied by bobbing assistants.

Franny plucked up her courage and entered the shop.

'The position in the window … is it still available?'

The manageress gave Fran a swift appraisal and took her into her office.

# *Chapter 17*

The manageress of Le Chapeau was laced almost to asphyxiation, her ample bosom curving formidably and unnaturally forward courtesy of her S-Bend corset. But her eyes were sharp and shrewd.

'Will you put your veil up, please!'

'Of course. I'm sorry.'

The manageress inspected her. 'You seem a respectable young person. Have you any experience in this business?'

'I've never worked. But I would like to. I have no references, but I'm … honest.' Franny looked the woman in the eye. 'I've recently come to Dublin and I'm hoping to find a position.'

The manageress considered her prospective employee. She liked her girls to have had some kind of experience in the trade, and she liked to have references. But this young person had a certain class, and class was good for business.

'We give a good training to our staff. We have a boarding house where we expect them to live, run by a respectable woman. You would have to share a room. The rules about callers are extremely strict. So, if you have a young man …'

'Oh no!' Franny gulped. 'Not at all!'

The manageress smiled thin approval. 'My name is Mrs Wright,' she said. 'I can offer you a probationary six-month period at two shillings per week and your board and lodging in Mrs MacLoughlin's establishment in Bachelor's Walk.'

Franny returned exultantly to Lismore Street. Clare was out, so she hurriedly packed her bag and left a note on her dressing table.

*Dear Clare,*

*I've got a job and lodgings, so I'm out of your hair! Hurrah for both of us!*

*Franny*

She thanked Doris as she left and, feeling rich, gave her a sixpence.

Franny rejoiced in her change of fortune. The challenge of becoming a trainee milliner, her decision to survive against the odds, pushed her recent terrible history from the forefront of her mind. She sent a postcard showing Nelson's Pillar to her mother. 'I'm fine,' she wrote. 'I've got a job and you need not worry about me.'

But she did not give the address of her new lodgings, the Dickensian establishment overlooking the river. Instead she tried to palliate her guilt at her mother's certain anxiety by fantasies of how she would surprise her. Her new quarters were almost next door to Butler's musical shop whose window advertised Trench gramophones. Franny saw herself being able to buy one of these wonders, which her mother had always wanted. She imagined bringing it back to Kilcrannagh and listening with her mother of an evening to the brass lily pouring forth its melodies.

The boarding house was clean and spartan. Occupying three floors above a boot emporium, it was within an easy walk of Le Chapeau. The proprietor, Mrs MacLoughlin, was a middle-aged widow with a twenty-one-year-old daughter, Noreen, with whom Fran was to share a room. Tall and slender, with a rope of bright red hair worn in a plait, Noreen's face was completely covered in freckles, but they only seemed to enhance her unusual looks.

'I hope you don't mind sharing,' Noreen said as she showed her the room with the two narrow beds and the statue of St Martin de Porres on the mantelpiece. 'We're a bit stuck for space, and Mother is a terrible skinflint.'

This made Franny laugh. The sound of her own merriment was strange in her ears.

'I don't mind, but it must be awful for you though, having to share with strangers!'

'It depends on the stranger. I think you and I will get on. We're talking, you see. The acid test. Shy people are so boring!' Noreen went on to tell her she was a student in the School of Art and that she dreamed of leaving home.

'Pulling up stumps doesn't always work out the way you plan,' Franny replied in a low voice, 'particularly if you're a girl!'

Noreen looked at her curiously. 'You can say that again. Women are the eternal underclass. But things are changing. Just look at what women are doing in England.' She added a little fiercely, 'There's a new suffrage organisation here in Ireland. Are you interested?'

'Am I *interested*?' Franny echoed. She could hardly believe her ears.

Franny's life as a milliner began the following morning. She learned little about hats and their manufacture, and a great deal about deference to customers. She listened to what her colleagues told her, but fended off their curiosity. One of girls, Mary Foy, whispered a little rhyme in her ear during their shared break:

Mrs Wright
Is not so bright
And poor Mrs Mac

When not downing sack
Makes dubious dinners
To sink us poor sinners.

Franny congratulated her, 'You should go into the poetry business,' she said.

'It doesn't pay,' Mary said modestly, 'but neither does selling hats.'

Franny thought with sudden longing of her books in Kilcrannagh, of the real poetry that seared the soul.

Le Chapeau closed for lunch hour when everyone was expected back in the steamy dining room of the house at Bachelor's Walk for potatoes, veg and two ounces of indeterminate meat served in thick, farinaceous gravy. Franny could not bear this meal and instead began to meet Noreen for a bun in Bewley's, when it rained or an apple in St Stephen's Green when the weather was clement, luxuriating in her new friendship with a kindred spirit. It went a long way towards salving her isolation and loneliness and the terrible vulnerability she now felt before the world.

Franny soon realised how easily wide-brimmed hats in straw or felt could, with relatively inexpensive additions, be turned into elaborate creations with elaborate prices. The basic shapes, made by a technique called blocking, were finished with wire and petersham, and trimmed with the feathers and tulle that gave the finished article its flamboyance.

'You buy your stock fully finished,' she said to Mrs Wright one morning as she was putting new models on display. 'But we could just as easily add the trimmings ourselves,' and she took a plain straw model and wound a ribbon around the brim. 'Now with a few flowers or tulle, it becomes a different kettle of fish! Anyone good with their hands could do it.'

Mrs Wright took a haughty, disapproving breath. 'Miss Murphy, we have neither the time nor the expertise to finish hats here! And, as one of the most fashionable milliners in Dublin, none of our merchandise is a kettle of fish.'

Franny nodded meekly. 'Of course not. I'm sorry.'

I forgot about power. she told herself ruefully. Don't rock the hat boat! But she threw herself enthusiastically into her new métier.

'That is you exactly, Madam!' she told an old dowager who was angling her head to view the umpteenth hat she had tried on.

'I think you are right, young woman,' the customer replied. She examined her beaked profile in a hand mirror. 'You have the eye. Not everyone does! And you have charm, which not everyone does either!'

'Thank you, Madam.'

'You were a bit forward, Miss Murphy.' Mrs Wright told her afterwards. 'But as the customer bought the hat I will overlook it. I would remind you that, as you have only recently joined us, it is a little soon for knowledgeable airs.'

Franny apologised. Keep your mouth shut, she told herself. You were always your own worst enemy. Someday you might have your own emporium! She imagined her own shop – chic hats finished by her own hands. She saw herself for one yearning moment as rich and successful, the past safely behind her, safely out of reach.

Mrs MacLoughlin seemed miffed at first when both her daughter and her latest lodger began to avoid her dinners but, as full board was still being paid, economic considerations prevailed. She was glad her daughter had taken to the new lodger, who seemed a respectable young person. It meant she had no complaints about the shared accommodation from either of them. She might have had more reservations had she overhead their conversations.

'I've told Alma Mulhall about you!' Noreen told her new friend. 'She's a friend of Mrs Sheehy-Skeffington, the driving force in the fight for female suffrage.'

'I've read about her in the paper, Noreen. I'd love to meet her.'

The following Monday Noreen arrived at their rendezvous in

Bewley's accompanied by a preoccupied-looking young woman who wore round spectacles and had her brown hair parted in the middle and pulled back into a chignon.

'Franny, this is Alma,' Noreen said. 'Alma, if you want a new warrior, Frances here is your woman. And now my friends, I must be off. I have to see a man about a dog.'

Noreen disappeared. Alma seated herself and said with a rueful smile, 'I fear the dog is fictional!'

Franny laughed. Alma studied her for a moment. Her face became serious.

'I understand you are interested in the franchise struggle.'

'Interested? I spent years ranting at home, but do you think anyone would listen?'

Alma gave a dry laugh. 'Because something is right does not guarantee it an audience. It takes time, loosening a pebble here, a stone there, before you will have an avalanche. Now, in the new organisation we need all the intelligent people we can get.'

The talk went on. Married women had the same legal status as children, criminals and lunatics, and if they did not force change themselves, they would remain in that bizarre company indefinitely. Spinsters were society's ghosts, despised and discriminated against unless they were left in possession of a fortune.

'You're preaching to the converted.' Franny said.

'There's a meeting in Molesworth Hall on Friday. Mrs Sheehy-Skeffington will be speaking.'

'I'll be there!'

Alma smiled. 'And will you come to my At Home on Sunday, Frances? I live in Howth.'

Her voice trailed off. Someone had come to stand behind Franny's chair. Alma raised her face to him with polite enquiry and Franny turned to look up at him. For a split second, she did not know him; it seemed too impossible that he should have found her. He might as well have come from Hades, home of the damned. But his voice was as light and coaxing as though he had never violated her, as though he had never shattered her world, never made her bleed and weep.

'My dear Miss Murphy. What a fortuitous encounter!'

# Chapter 18

Afterwards Franny wrote it down, as she wrote down so many things in the thick notebook Alma gave her. She wrote although her wrist tired in her efforts at exorcism, wrote night after night until her hand grew stiff.

*The reaction was not of my conscious making. I began to shake. I picked up the knife, but Alma plucked it from my hand and then I fled, knocking over the chair, hating my cowardice. Alma had some words with him and followed me.*

*'Calm down Frances,' she said when she had my arm in a fierce grip and was marching me down Grafton Street. 'You can tell me everything later if you want to, but just calm down.'*

*I needed someone to tell me what to do. She steered me; I went with her. I had no idea where we were going. I had started to weep, with uncontrollable, violent shuddering. I remember the stares of passers-by, a big black door opening, a cool tiled hall, the smell of polish and disinfectant and a bearded man in a pinstripe suit.*

*'Alma!' he exclaimed. But he was looking at me. 'What on earth …'*

*'A friend! In shock, Father!'*

*Oh how warm that blanket was in which he wrapped me, placed me like a child in the armchair before his fire!*

*'My father is a doctor,' Alma said in my ear in the same quiet, soothing*

*voice. 'Don't be afraid. These are his consulting rooms.'*

*They whispered together and he left the room, went next door, for I could hear his steps in the hall and another door opening, and then he came with a cup of warm milk and after that left us alone.*

*Of course she got the story from me. It is not easy to hide anything from Alma; she is so quiet and grave and has the gift of empathy. So she knows why I ran from Bertram Wallace; and she knows that I am not the strong person she needs for the new organisation. She gave me this note book. She took it from her father's surgery. It was intended for medical records.*

*'Write in it every day,' she ordered. 'Write what happened. Write the pain until it goes.'*

'I particularly want you to come to my At Home next Sunday.' Alma said as they parted on that dreadful Monday when Franny, although late, insisted on returning to work. 'Meeting interesting people, becoming involved in what is happening, is the way forward, the best way to forget.'

Noreen had been invited also. So the following Sunday the two young women took the Howth tram, which ran along the northside of Dublin Bay. Franny gazed out at the wide blue vista and the screaming gulls and thought how wonderful was the sea. It could take you away from everything.

'You're very quiet today,' Noreen said. 'Is something wrong?'

'I'm just nervous.'

Fran had not divulged her recent history to Noreen and she knew that Alma would never divulge it either. It was private and shameful and the fewer who knew about it the quicker it might fade, the quicker she might recover some vestige of the person she had been.

When they got to Howth they had a long walk up a steep incline before they came to open gates that bore the name Rathcormac and found, at the end of short avenue, a big house overlooking the sea.

Alma's drawing room had the relaxed conversational buzz of people who knew each other well. A coal fire burned in the hearth; tea and sandwiches were served by a maid in a white cap and apron. The view through the window was breathtaking – Dublin in the distance, nestled against mountains as blue as the bay. Overwhelmed with diffidence, Fran stood uncertainly as Noreen disappeared to speak to someone she knew. But Alma saw her and was with her in a moment.

'How are you now, Frances?' she asked, bending towards her solicitously and taking both her hands. 'Are you better?'

'I'm so sorry, Alma, about Monday.'

'Don't be! You had reason. I told that fellow I'd get the police if he ever came within a mile of you again.'

Franny shook her head. She didn't want to speak about Bertram Wallace and was glad when Alma began introducing her to her guests. Shyly, she shook hands with Mrs Sheehy-Skeffington and her husband Francis. Mrs Skeffington was clever-looking with round spectacles and a serious face, and her bearded husband was gentle and unassuming.

'The husband's quite a character – a pacifist and a feminist.' Noreen whispered a few minutes later. 'Everyone calls him Skeffy!'

Then a poet called Austin Clarke came to talk to her and also a beautiful woman called Estella Solomons whom Noreen said was another artist. Across the room, a stately lady was deep in conversation with a tall man with a squint. They radiated such purpose and intensity that Franny's eyes returned to them again and again.

'Who is she?' she whispered to Noreen.

'Countess Markievicz of course!'

'My cousins used to mention her!' Franny said breathlessly. 'Isn't she in the Gaelic League?'

'She's in everything! The man she's talking to is also in the League. He is Mr Pearse.'

My God, Fran said to herself. I'm in the same room with one

of Harry's icons! She watched Mr Pearse covertly for a moment, wishing she had the courage to speak to him. But the lovely countess frightened her. She reminded her of a plate in one of her history books – Athena, goddess of war and wisdom. Her musing was interrupted by a young man with dark eyes, dark hair and darker moustache.

'Delightful to see you, Noreen! And who, may I ask, is your lovely friend?'

'Liam! I thought you were supposed to be in Paris. My lovely friend is Frances Murphy, my new room-mate?' She turned to Franny with a laugh. 'This is Liam, Alma's young and gifted brother. A portrait painter of burgeoning renown.'

Liam took Franny's hand.

'More burgeon than renown,' he said with a grin. 'Are you an art student too?'

'No, unfortunately. I've never even been in an artist's studio. But I'd like to, sometime.'

'Well, now's your chance. Mine is right here in the house.'

'Go on!' Noreen said. 'Have a look at Liam's studio. You'll get an idea of our métier,' and Liam conducted her into the hall and down to the back of the house.

Liam's studio was a big, bright room with two high windows. Reeking of paint, linseed oil and turps, it contained a forest of brushes, tubes of paint, rags, canvases in various stages of completion and was permeated by a powerful sense of personal pilgrimage. A half-finished canvas sat on an easel – a woman in three-quarter profile, part in monochrome, part already painted. It seemed to a fascinated Franny that the artist had caught his subject off guard, revealing the striving soul beneath the skin.

'How do you catch the essence of the sitter?'

'I suspect you're being kind, Miss Murphy. In fact everything depends on how open the sitter is, how much of herself she gives. Would you sit for me sometime?' He looked at her intently. 'Your face is so pale and expressive. I've been asked to do an allegorical work and you would make a lovely Melancholy ... or Innocence?'

Franny flushed. 'I could not presume to personify either the one or the other!'

'Then I will paint you for what you are,' he said gravely. 'A young woman in search of her destiny.'

'I'd rather create it than search for it. The outcome might be surer!'

He laughed and looked at her with interest. 'What do you do?' he asked.

'I work in a milliner's in Grafton Street.'

'But you would prefer to be an art student?'

'I certainly would, if I had the talent. I'm good with my hands, but it's not the same thing as genius.'

He chuckled. 'My dear girl, nothing is! But I think you could be anything you wanted,' he replied gallantly and conducted her back to the drawing room where she discovered that Noreen had already left.

'She said to tell you she's spending the night with a friend,' Alma said, 'and asked that you inform her mother she'll be home first thing in the morning'.

'I'd better go,' Franny said. 'I have to catch the tram. Goodbye Alma. Thank you very much for inviting me.'

'The pleasure was mine!' Alma looked pointedly at Liam and some silent intelligence seemed to pass between them.

'May I drive you home?' he asked.

In a few minutes Fran had her first drive in a motor. And, although it was also her first time alone with a strange man since her recent history with Bertram Wallace, she felt no fear. Liam was gentle in his handling of the car, gentle in the way he spoke to her. He talked of his own life, his plans for the future – he was soon to leave Dublin for a year's study in Paris. Franny began to relax. She thought of the extraordinary people she had met and the possibilities opening before her, of being involved with what was stirring in Ireland.

When she got back to Bachelor's Walk the other girls from Le Chapeau were all out; they had gone on an outing to Greystones. Mrs Mac said, poor little souls – the sea air would do them good. So Franny had tea alone with her landlady who seemed concerned about Noreen and wanted to know the identity of the friend with whom she was staying the night.

'I do not know, Mrs MacLoughlin.'

'Does my daughter have a young man?'

Franny said truthfully that she did not know that either.

After tea, the landlady produced from the sideboard a bottle of gin and poured a measure into a glass. She took a cigarette from a drawer, lit up and settled back in her easy chair with a rustle of poplin skirts.

'My little Sunday indulgence,' she said. 'At my age one must be allowed a few pleasures!' She inhaled with a little groan, sipped her gin and raised her eyebrows at Franny. 'You're a quiet little thing. Which part of the country are you from?'

'Monaghan.'

'Pretty girl like you will have no trouble catching a husband.'

She indicated the yellowing photograph of a young man in uniform that sat on the mantelpiece. 'Noreen's father. But didn't he die of appendicitis, God help him, when she was still very young. He was in the Dublin Fusiliers.'

Fran glanced at the uniformed young man in the photograph and suddenly thought of Guy, also in uniform … somewhere … and everything that once had been changed beyond recall.

'And do you have a young man at home?' Mrs Mac was asking.

'No.'

Desperate to evade her landlady's curiosity, she excused herself, saying she had her chores to do. She went to the kitchen and ironed her blouses in readiness for the week ahead, carefully starching the high-boned collars. When her work was finished she went to bed.

Her head was full of the afternoon, the people she had met,

the interesting conversations. Female suffrage had been discussed, but not as much as something Harry would have empathised with – the future of the country. The words in every mouth had been Home Rule. She thought of Liam and his studio where he could be alone with his art. She thought of his kindness in leaving her home. She worried that Alma must think she was unhinged and cursed the way she had gone to pieces last Monday.

I might be able to cope if only my period would come. She had been keeping that particular fear at bay, but it frightened her more than anything. It might mean nothing, she told herself, and offered up a small, desperate prayer.

Noreen returned the following morning and had a row with her mother that resounded through the household.

'Mother wants to control my entire life!' she informed Franny when they were alone in their room.

'She was wondering if you had a young man.'

'Of course I have! But I'm not sleeping with him. I'm not a fool! Are you all right, Fran?' Noreen added, 'You're looking a bit grim!'

'My period is late,' Franny said dully.

'Happens to me all the time. Mother says that if you don't feed, you don't bleed! Bit crass, isn't she?' Noreen looked at her friend sharply and added, 'But you don't have any reason to … worry? Do you Fran?'

'Of course not.'

'Well then all you need is building up. You'll have to start coming home for Mother's dinners,' she added with a laugh.

Harry appeared in the shop the following morning at precisely 12.30. Franny would always remember the time because the clock in Mrs Wright's office had just chimed the half hour.

He strolled into the shop, the epitome of the young man about town, and grinned at his cousin as though he had known all along exactly where to find her. She was serving a customer and although she gasped, she concealed her shock. Harry looked lugubriously at a display of hats, picked one up, put it on his head and inspected himself thoughtfully in the mirror. Staff and customers suppressed their hilarity and Mrs Wright approached him carefully.

'Can I help you, sir?' she demanded in a no-nonsense voice.

'I wish to purchase a hat for a charming young cousin of mine,' Harry said in voice that carried. 'I think this one would be very becoming.'

'Surely the young lady should try it on first, sir!' the manageress said. 'It will look quite different on her!'

'We will ask her as soon as she is free,' Harry replied, indicating Franny with a movement of his head.

'Miss Murphy is your cousin?'

'She is indeed. And today is her birthday!'

Franny heard it all. She felt like exploding with joy. But she also felt her employer's eyes on her, so she put her customer's purchase into a hat box, secured the lid, bade her a polite good day, then turned to her cousin with as much aplomb as she could muster.

'Hello, Harry! What a surprise!'

'I was just telling this good lady that as it's your birthday I am taking you out to lunch.'

'This young gentleman is your cousin, Miss Murphy?'

'Yes, Mr Harry Healy! Harry, this is Mrs Wright, the manageress.'

Harry bowed. 'Delighted to make your acquaintance, Madam. And now Fran, will you please try on this hat?'

Franny felt she would do anything to escape the suspicion she saw in her employer's eyes, the sidelong curiosity in those of her colleagues, or the amusement on the faces of the two customers who had paused to watch. But she obliged. The hat was in pale straw with a wreath of ribbons. It was lovely and not out of place with her grey and white dress. It had a price tag of two pounds, nineteen shillings and eleven pence.

'Is there a staff reduction?' Harry asked Mrs Wright, as he produced his wallet.

'I'm afraid not,' she replied stiffly. 'My staff do not normally purchase the models in my shop.'

'What a pity! There is a further purchase I would like to make. You had a hat in your window last Friday – with a pale blue ribbon around the crown and a particularly flamboyant brim.' He directed his gaze across the shop and indicated a stand. 'There it is! I will take that one too.'

Franny looked on in astonishment.

'Now,' Harry told Mrs Wright firmly, 'with your kind permission I would like to take my young cousin here out for an early luncheon. I have not seen her for some time and we have a lot to catch up on.'

He smiled winningly and Mrs Wright seemed at a loss.

'She must be back by 2 p.m. Sharp! Last week she was very late on one occasion.'

'Of course!'

Franny put the second hat in a box, fetched her coat and gloves, put on her new hat and left the shop with Harry, wondering how it was that some people could walk on water. As soon as they were out of sight of Le Chapeau's window, Franny stopped in the street and turned to her cousin.

'Just what do you think you're playing at, Harry Healy?'

'I'm buying you a hat and I'm taking you to lunch,' he replied reasonably.

'How did you know where to find me?'

Harry took her hand. 'Come on Fran, Dublin is a small place. I was walking in Grafton Street with Deirdre last Friday evening when she got all misty-eyed about a hat in the window of your establishment. The shop was closed, but I inspected the lusted-after bonnet. And lo! Whom did I see in the dim interior, but my long-lost cousin.'

'I generally try to ensure I am hidden from the window.'

'I wasn't sure it was you. Your redoubtable employer was totting up receipts, and you were tidying things away. I was about to tap on the window, but Miss Callaghan suggested it would attract the ire of the receipt totter. So I came today instead.'

Franny's heart plummeted at the ring of permanence surrounding Deirdre Callaghan's name. She let go of Harry's arm and walked beside him in silence until she realised he was steering her through the door of Jammet's Restaurant at the corner of Andrew Lane.

'We can't lunch here, Harry,' she hissed. 'It costs the earth. And you've just bought two expensive hats!'

'Stop fussing! I'm flush. I had a bit of luck with the gee-gees. A tip from one of the lads. It's not a habit,' he added severely, 'so you can take that look off your face.'

'You are spending your windfall on me!' Franny exclaimed. 'You are kinder than I deserve, Harry.'

'But what else are windfalls for? You have given us all a dreadful fright, *a cushla*,' he added, lowering his voice, 'and I want to find out why.'

Jammet's was the best restaurant in the city. French and elegant, with deep carpets and wall paintings, it was a world away from the life of the average Dubliner and the teeming slums just across the river. The cousins were quickly seated and the maître d' handed them menus and a wine list.

'I'll have the *Poulet Rôti aux Fines Herbes*,' Fran murmured with one of her old giggles as she did her best with the French.

Harry ordered the *Sole Bonne Femme* for himself and a bottle of Sancerre. 'It's your birthday, remember! And "a little wine gladdeneth the heart"!'

'Birthday indeed!' Franny snorted. 'Do you remember Ellen's fifteenth, when Guy Forrister came with that case of wine?' Harry nodded and she added, 'You told Mrs Wright a whopper!'

'I would tell her forty whoppers to get talking to you. Don't you realise we've been looking for you everywhere?'

'I hope you haven't informed Mother where I am?'

'That's your decision, old thing. But I will tell her you're safe and in respectable employment.'

Franny sighed and looked around at the carpeted restaurant – the damask and silver, the flowers on the tables, the quiet service, the ambience of plenty. She felt she would give her immortal soul to be back in her lost world, with no sword of Damocles hovering over her, no dreadful, shameful stain. What had she to say to Harry? That she intended to stay in Dublin? That she was never going home? That the sight of him was too painful to bear?

The wine was brought. Harry tasted it, nodded as urbanely as though he drank it every day. When the waiter had poured it and departed, Harry knit his brows and leaned across the table.

'What is it, little cousin? Why did you run away? Why have you circles under your eyes? You can tell me.'

'I'm not going home!'

'But you left without a word. And you left Clare's house without a forwarding address.'

'Oh Harry, Clare wanted rid of me. And Mother would hardly talk to me anyway. If I'd told her what I intended she'd have locked me in my room. I suppose I should have written to her, but I need to prove I can have a life on my own terms. And then I can visit her … and all will be forgiven.'

After a moment's silence Harry said casually, 'You may be overestimating your mother. She is very angry. I hope you haven't told anyone?' he added almost as an afterthought.

'Told anyone? What?' Franny whispered, her face suddenly white.

'You know, the … items … you found in the haggard?'

She sat back in relief and laughed mockingly. 'So that's why you were so desperate to talk to me? That's the real reason for the hat … for the lunch?'

'No!' Harry said emphatically. 'But it is important!'

'Your secret is safe. I don't know what you are doing, Harry, you and Jimmy, but I hope you will be careful!'

'I was a bit … dramatic … in what I told you that evening. We were simply minding the … items. It's not something for you to worry about. They're old anyway.'

'Guns can still work when they're old, Harry. Or so I hear. To where did you move them?'

He smiled and shook his head.

'Harry,' she said after a moment in a low voice, 'is there somewhere I could borrow a small pistol?'

Harry's expression wavered between alarm and hilarity. 'What would you want it for? To dispatch your employer? I wouldn't blame you, but it tends to be frowned upon.'

'Self-protection?'

'Dublin is hardly that dangerous!' He leaned towards her, 'Fran, exactly what am I to tell your mother before she has someone on your tail? She's asked my father to find you through his contacts in the DMP.'

Franny groaned. The Dublin Metropolitan Police arriving at the shop would finish her prospects.

'Can I tell her I met you and that you are all right?' Harry pressed on. 'She's quite frantic, you know.'

'Oh yes. Tell your father too – that you know where I am and that I'm grand, and that I'll go home to visit as soon as I can.'

'All right. That should keep them quiet for a while.' He swallowed and moaned ecstatically. 'God the pleasure! How do the Frenchies do it, with a bit of oul' fish? By the way,' he added suddenly, raising his voice and looking at his cousin with speculation, 'in case it's of any interest to you – Mr Wallace called not long after your precipitous departure to inquire after you. He said he would try to find you in Dublin.'

Franny put down her knife and fork, picked up her bag and rose from the table.

'Thank you for the lunch, for the hat. But do not come and see me again. Do not tell my mother or Clare where I am! I do not want to see *anyone*! If you manage to keep your mouth shut I will not divulge to anyone that you and Jimmy have guns hidden for the purpose of overthrowing the British Empire.'

She did not wait to register his consternation. She left the restaurant, hurried back to Le Chapeau but found it locked. She waited, walked around, unhappy, bereft, until two o'clock when Mrs Wright appeared and re-admitted her.

Harry remained sitting at the table, shocked at Franny's sudden and vitriolic outburst. He resisted the urge to follow her. He knew Franny and decided it would be better to let her cool off. He thought of what Deirdre had said when they had looked through the window of that hat shop the preceding Friday, 'Your cousin looks poorly and deeply troubled.' He remembered the haunted look in Franny's eyes just now as she had stared back at him across the table, and wondered what had happened to her vivacity. I'll have to keep tabs on Fran, he told himself.

The bottle of Sancerre was still half full. He would ask them to put a cork in it so he could take it with him. Jimmy might appreciate it, although he generally drank only water. He was arriving later at Kingsbridge Station. There was a meeting tomorrow.

As the days passed Franny waited, with ever-increasing apprehension, for her next period.

But it did not come. Two periods missed. Tender breasts. Intermittent nausea. She could no longer stave off the cold fear that filled her chest and strangled her guts.

One morning Noreen reminded her of a meeting to be held that evening in Molesworth Hall.

'Can I cry off?'

'But Fran, you know we need everyone we can get. Don't let us down. Alma was so delighted to have an articulate new recruit!'

Franny could not bear that Alma's impression of her would be of a hysteric. So she went to the meeting. It lasted two hours and when she tried to slink away afterwards, Alma pounced on her.

'How are you, darling? Would you be up to a leaflet delivery? We thought you and Noreen could do the Pembroke Ward.'

'Of course.'

'Liam will drop the leaflets off at your lodgings tonight. Our printing press is on its last legs, but he knows how to coax it.'

At 9 p.m. the maid in Bachelor's Walk came up to say there was a young gentleman to see Miss Murphy.

'You'll have to talk to him in the hall, dear,' Mrs MacLoughlin told her. 'You know the rules! And as this is a respectable house, please make it brief!'

Liam was standing patiently in the narrow hall. He had a box under his arm. She put it on the hallstand, opened the top flap and looked in. It contained two hundred leaflets, he said, and Alma's written instructions for their delivery. He added with a grin, 'I'm off to Paris tomorrow.'

'Lucky, lucky Liam!'

'I do feel privileged. The French State School of Art … for a whole year!' He smiled. 'But I did enjoy our conversation the other evening. I do hope I will see you when I come home?'

'I'm sure you will,' Franny said. 'I'm not going anywhere.'

She saw him to the door. It had begun to rain and he lingered on the threshold.

'I have not given up hope that you will allow me to paint you,' he said. 'There's so much in your face. Innocence … passion.'

'Oh Liam, it's my gorgeous sister Clare, you should paint. Or my cousin Ellen, who looks just like an angel.'

'But I want to paint *you*, Franny. Passion is life!'

A policeman passing by the open door glanced at them from under his black helmet, wished them good night and then directed his interest at something huddled by a horse trough further down the quay. The form got up, shrank from the law and shambled away.

'I'll nip after that poor oul' divil,' Liam said, 'give him the price of a doss house.'

Franny watched as, with long strides, he crossed the quay and followed the tramp. She saw him hand the man a coin, heard the woozy shout, 'May God and his Holy Mother bless you sir!' What a wonderful man Liam is, she thought. He is kind to the bone.

Liam found his motor, which he had left across the street, cranked it and jumped in as it spluttered to life. He waved as he moved off. Franny waved back and shut the door. She felt raw. Before her was the gulf between a life of dignity and the living death of the outcast. Just a few yards across the street, the river was at low tide. Tomorrow morning it would yield up this night's harvest of despair. Her period was now seriously overdue. And every passing day made the situation more and more insoluble. What am I going to do? she wondered. What am I going to do?

On her way to breakfast next morning, she suddenly rushed for the lavatory. Noreen heard her retching and followed her.

'You poor ol' thing! What's brought this on?'

Franny was white and shaking. The acrid puke was in her nose, its taint in her mouth.

'Headache,' she gasped.

'You'd better go back to bed. I'll get one of the girls to tell Mrs Wright.'

'She'll dismiss me.'

'No she won't!' Mrs Mac said, coming on the scene. 'You can work overtime during stocktaking. Only thing for a sick headache is a quiet, darkened room. I'll tell Mrs Wright I made you stay in bed.'

Noreen went off to college, promising Franny that she would bring back some oranges.

When the girls had all gone to the shop and Mrs MacLoughlin had gone to the market and the house was empty, Franny knelt down beside her bed. She directed her eyes to the statue on the mantelpiece and asked the saint to help her, to forgive her. If her whole life were not to contain destruction and disgrace there was only one thing to be done. She wondered if Mr Wallace spared a thought for his victims. Or was he too busy crowing to other cruel little cockerels like himself? She got up from her knees. Prayer had not helped. Heaven was either deaf or uninterested.

With a wall of desperation urging her on, she went downstairs and, when she had ascertained that the maid was in the kitchen, she nipped into the dining room and removed the bottle of gin from its hiding place. She needed something, anything, to deaden the horror. She would repay the landlady, tell her it was for the headache.

She brought the gin back to her room, and sip by sip, glass by glass, she sought its counsel. When she had finished the bottle she unsteadily folded several towels and put them on the bed. Then she crawled to Noreen's workbox, and searched with trembling hands among the knitting needles.

# Chapter 19

When Franny surfaced she felt at peace. She moved, realised she was in an iron bed in a small white room. The curtains – a lattice design in green – were drawn. A carafe of water and a tumbler stood on the bedside locker. For a moment she had no memory, but as soon as she struggled it came back, like lamplight flooding a shuttered room.

She groaned. Dear God … what had she done? Had she succeeded? Where was she now? She tried to sit up, but pain knifed up her spine. She wanted to get out of bed but found she was attached to a thin tube that was delivering a solution to her vein. The door opened, admitting a tall man in a white coat. It took her a moment to recognise Dr Mulhall, Alma's father.

'You are in Mercer's Hospital, young woman,' he said matter-of-factly. 'You were brought here in an ambulance.' Then he added coldly, 'You tried to abort your unborn child.'

Franny averted her gaze. She saw a kidney dish and steel instruments on a trolley.

'You have lost a good deal of blood,' he went on. 'But you have not lost the baby. Your action, quite apart from destroying your child, might have cost you your life.'

Franny did not look the doctor in the eye. She stared at his portly waistcoat. His fob watch stared back at her haughtily.

What do I care about my life? she thought.

'You will have to rest up for some time,' the doctor continued, 'so you will need someone to take care of you. Where is your family?'

'I cannot contact them,' Franny said dully. 'They would not want me, not like this.'

'How do you know until you ask? Perhaps you have friends who will take you in?'

Franny shook her head. She could not go back to Bachelor's Walk now.

'There is a young woman outside who found you and called the ambulance. Perhaps she can talk sense to you.'

Noreen came in looking frightened. 'Why didn't you say something, Fran? You must have been frantic. I'm sure we could have found you someone to … do the job … properly.'

'It's a criminal offence,' Franny whispered. 'Dr Mulhall has left me in no doubt!'

'Every single thing to do with the rights of women is a criminal offence!' Noreen said fiercely. 'But you can't do it yourself. You wouldn't even know where you were sticking it! Oh God! It's a lucky thing I came home during a free class. I thought you would bleed to death. Mother is like a lunatic. The other girls know something terrible happened, but I warned Mother to tell them you had a burst appendix. You know what this town is like.'

A shadow darkened the doorway.

'May I come in?' Jimmy said.

Franny introduced them, but Noreen looked suspiciously at Jimmy and left after a few moments, saying she would come back tomorrow. Jimmy awkwardly deposited a paper bag of sweets on the bedside locker and took Franny's hand. Harry had told him where she worked, he said. One the girls in Le Chapeau had given her address and Mrs MacLoughlin had done the rest.

'A burst appendix? Fran, you're lucky to be alive!'

'An attempted abortion,' Franny said dully looking through the window to an outside brick wall. 'You'll probably find out anyway.'

She felt his shock.

'Fran,' he whispered, 'has it got to do with Wallace?'

Franny moaned. 'Of course it has! I know you warned me, Jimmy … but the evening I left home he cornered me in the Westenra. He sent up supper and champagne. He tricked his way into my room.'

'With or without your consent?' Jimmy demanded brutally.

Fran turned burning eyes on him. She saw his clenched jaw and the thin line to his mouth.

'What do you think?' she demanded angrily. 'Why do you imagine I wanted to get away to Dublin? Why do men always assume the worst of women and the best of themselves?'

Jimmy considered her for a moment. 'Someday, Fran,' he said in a cold, quiet voice, 'we will dispatch his likes, bag and baggage, out of Ireland.'

'Don't do anything stupid on my account and don't tell Harry.'

Jimmy's face softened. 'How you love that charmer! Of course I will not tell him. He has enough to occupy him with his mighty hopes.'

'I suppose he told you what I found in the haggard!'

There was a sudden flash of humour. 'Of course! They were there for sporting purposes, Fran. I never doubted that you would keep your mouth shut!'

Months later Franny wrote in her notebook:

*Alma saved me from the curious. She took me from the hospital and brought me home. She told me I must stay at Rathcormac until I had the baby, and that her father was in agreement.*

*'He is not overly fond of rapists!' she said. 'Anyway he spends most of his time in his consulting rooms. Liam's in Paris, as you know, so we'll have the house, more or less, to ourselves.'*

*When I said it would have saved all this fuss if only I had gone to someone who knew how to do things properly, Alma looked at me with her pained, myopic exasperation and said there were several backstreet abortionists in Dublin who took your money and when things went wrong you ended up in the Alexandra Basin.*

*My daughter was born in Rathcormac, and delivered by Dr Mulhall. She hardly cried when she was born. I could not look at her. But when she was taken away she began to wail. And I heard it, and knew it – the cry of abandonment.*

*'She is very small, your daughter,' Alma said when she come in to see me, 'barely six pounds, but she is so beautiful. Should you not see her, just once? Before you banish her?'*

*The truth was that my daughter's cry had gone to my soul and I suddenly wanted to hold her, to search her face for my own, for my mother's, for Harry's, for anyone's except her father's.*

*When Alma put her into my arms the child stopped crying, nuzzled blindly against me, as though she knew who I was. She did not look like anyone I had ever known, but she was exquisite. Alma left us alone and, clumsily, I put the rosebud mouth to my breast.*

*It wasn't a question of forgiving her father – that I will never do. It was a matter of simple justice. It was none of her doing, and I was suddenly overwhelmed by a need to be just. How else could I hope to be avenged?*

*If I desert you who will love you? I whispered, while my baby nursed ecstatically, pulling urgently at my swollen breast, and various demons struggled in me for mastery. Remembering Oliver Twist, I saw the cold flags of the orphanage, the stone walls, the child asking for more, and yearning with all the passionate love of childhood for the mother who had abandoned her.*

*'I will be your champion!' I eventually told my tiny mite. 'What happened was not your fault! Are we agreed?' She closed surprisingly strong fingers around my thumb.*

Alma was delighted at her decision and Liam, when he returned from Paris, behaved as though it were the most natural thing in the world to find her in his home with a baby. Alma had told him the full story.

'What are you going to call her?' he asked, bending so tenderly over the cradle that Franny felt her heart swell. When she said 'Hannah' he murmured that he understood the choice – the same Christian name as Mrs Skeffington who was doing so much for women.

'But I think you should write and tell your mother,' he said. 'She has a right to know she is a grandmother.'

The following day Franny wrote the hardest letter of her life.

*My dearest Mother,*

*I hope you are well and I am very sorry to have given you anxiety and worry, but my news will be most unwelcome. I have given birth to a daughter. Her name is Hannah and she is beautiful. I remain unwed and have no contact with her father.*

*Try to forgive me, dearest Mother.*

*Your loving daughter, Franny.*

She received a reply almost by return of post.

*No man of any station will look at you now, nor will any man with even modest pretensions to respectability. Mr Wallace no longer calls to inquire after you, and has left for England. (He was injured a few months ago, attacked as he left his Dublin club. I hear he intends to quit Ireland.)*

*I do not know why you have brought this disgrace on your family. I will not tell Clare, Harry or Ellen of your shame. You are no longer my daughter.*

*Your desolated Mother.*

Franny thought of Clare and Ellen and Harry. They would never know her circumstances. But it doesn't matter now, she told herself. I am on my own.

# *Part 2*

# Chapter 20

*Ireland, August 1912*

Guy drove to Kilcrannagh from Clonshule. He was driving a Humber, one of two motors Bertie kept at the house, and he drove carefully. The roads were potholed, the countryside sunny and the meadows dotted with haycocks. Some people working in the fields stopped to stare at the vehicle that nosed along their roads. A few raised a hand in friendly salute.

The grouse season had started a week ago and Bertie had invited Guy and two old friends – Dan Sutherland and Ambrose Crothers, whom they had known at Harrow – to stay at Clonshule. Guy found the big house changed from his last visit eight years earlier; there were fewer servants and there was no longer the sense of it being the hub of a lively Irish country house society. Old Mrs Wallace kept to her room, and Bertie, whom he had not seen since 1906, was altered. Already balding, he had put on weight; but he had acquired an aura of immense solvency, along with a limp.

'Fellow attacked me at night in Dublin,' he explained when Guy asked him what had happened. 'Coming out of the club! Broke two ribs, damaged my knee. Doubt it'll ever mend!'

'Good Lord! When was this?'

'In '06, two years after you left for India.' Bertie laughed mirthlessly. 'I gave a good account of myself,' he said with a flash of his dark eyes, 'otherwise I wouldn't be telling the tale. Country's gone to hell, you know. All this business about Home Rule gives the green light to every lunatic.'

'But it will never become a reality, Bertie? After all, Ulster won't wear it!'

'Short-term thinking, dear boy. Just look at the state of the world. Trouble in every breeze. Even women are out smashing windows. Things are going to get worse and therefore clever Bertie has made a decision.'

'What decision, Wallace?' Sutherland demanded. 'You're too damn crafty for ordinary mortals.'

Bertie laughed. 'Your old pal has sold the estate to his tenants for a great heap of money, courtesy of the last Land Act – all except the demesne and the house.' He added ruefully, 'Poor old Mater didn't like it and can't be budged. Nowadays I only come here for the shooting and then head back to London.'

'You still have your place in Belgravia?' Guy asked, remembering the house in Eaton Square where he had once met Bertie after the Easter school break.

His host nodded. 'Of course, old bean. Come and visit!'

After dinner, as he had handed around cigars, Bertie asked, glancing conspiratorially at Sutherland and Crothers, 'I say, Forrister, are you planning to renew acquaintance with that little piece of fluff you were so taken with a few years ago?'

'If you are referring to Miss Healy, I shall certainly try,' Guy replied stiffly. 'Her family were my friends.'

Bertie winked at his other guests. 'You sly dog! But they were not as friendly as the fair Miss Murphy.'

'What do you mean?'

'Just that I had her, old boy,' Bertie replied with a loud guffaw. 'Paid her well too by Jove! So no complaints on either side.'

He waited for congratulations. Sutherland and Crothers looked at him with grins of open admiration. Neither of them knew Miss Murphy, but they knew Bertie very well indeed.

Guy did not hide his disgust. Anything more unlikely he could not imagine than Bertie Wallace *having* Franny Murphy. He remembered his boast about the little housemaid, Mary McKenna, now no longer in evidence. Where women were concerned Bertie had always been a windbag.

'Oh stop disapproving, Forrister,' Bertie said. 'It's too ageing! Tell us about India.'

At this point, Guy had behind him nearly eight years in the subcontinent. His years of secondment as a subaltern at the North West Frontier had left him lean, tanned and fit, with the rank of captain. But the experience itself had been a revelation. India's savage beauty – its smells and colours, absurd wealth and abject poverty, teeming peoples, fervour of monotheist and pagan religions in one great melting pot – had been a jolt. The complexity of cultures had generated in him an impression of cosmic mystery, so much so that, with the passage of time, the army had ceased to fulfil his sense of purpose. Instead he found himself questioning the meaning of authority and its responsibilities. Military life was by now reflex anyway, and it left him free to think. He'd hoped, as he'd looked at the panorama of the great subcontinent England claimed as her own, as he'd examined the claims of Buddhist, Hindu, Moslem, Sikh and Farsi as to the purpose of existence, that Britain had given these people something in exchange for all she had taken – such as centralised government and the rule of law.

At first he'd been very lonely. There were no single Englishwomen at his outpost, and although the leave he spent at Delhi, and at miraculously beautiful Srinagar, had provided space for flirtations, they had never gone very deep. Although sexual mores were loose enough, the social scene was ossified, obsessed with place, rigid with taboos. And even though Ellen had disappeared into the past, she still represented a kind of iconic femininity. The little ring he had given her had been returned to him by her aunt, half apologetically it must be said. And that had been that.

Until the day when, emerging from a visit to a courtesan, he'd seen a weeping Indian girl–child being led away by a middle-aged man. At the time he had assumed the man was her father; only later did he learn that the child had been sold.

Ellen Healy's tearful fifteen-year-old face had surfaced in the midst of his outrage and, from then on, she had come back to haunt him. Set against the burning backdrop of India, the dusty loneliness of his frontier outpost, the stilted nature of what social life there was, she stood out in her courage and fragility in the Irish rain.

His period of service over, he'd come home with accumulated leave to a lazy summer at Lindthorp, to be spoilt by Nigel and Sophie and showered with affection by his young nephew, James. He'd intended to go to France; his house there was in the care of the Fargues, old retainers, but he found he needed to fill himself first with England. It was necessary to his life, like slaking a thirst.

And Lindthorp was certainly seductive in its sedate progression of summer days, which he had spent fishing with his nephew and making up numbers at croquet and tea parties. Order, quietude, parkland reminiscent of the one in France and the sense of family had been a haven. He liked the young women Sophie invited to parties, although they did not inspire in him anything more than liking. Then, one day, Sophie, with an apologetic air, had put into his hands a small under-addressed envelope.

'I forgot all about this, darling,' she said with a rueful moue. It came at Christmas. I hope it's not important.'

It was a Christmas card – birds on wintry branches, a snowscape with holly, a tiny blue satin bow and a few words in a feminine hand.

'To Guy, Happy Christmas. Ellen.'

Nothing more. Of course he had told her approximately when he would be coming home, he reminded himself as he puzzled it over. And she had evidently remembered.

From that point on, he had to fight the lure of Ireland. He conceded that meeting Ellen again was the only way to get her out of his system, establish whether or not he was suffering from some kind of idiotic sentiment brought on by his years of exile. She would be nearly twenty-six now, old enough to make her own decisions without her aunt interfering. If he did not move quickly, life would almost certainly carry her into another man's arms.

So he had told his hosts that he was taking up an invitation from his old friend Bertie Wallace to shoot grouse at Clonshule.

Nine-year-old James had been particularly miffed at his departure. 'Why do you want to go to Ireland, Uncle? I thought you liked it here.'

'Of course I like it here!' he replied, ruffling the boy's brown hair. 'Why wouldn't I, with a nephew like you? But I have friends in Ireland whom I haven't seen for years.'

On the day of his departure his brother had winded him with one of his hearty claps on the shoulder. 'Do write, old chap, won't you? Come back to us when you can.'

Dark-haired Sophie, elegant in her fashionable V-necked tennis dress, had said that she suspected there was *Someone* in Ireland. And he had smiled back and said maybe there was. The family had waved him off, James standing beside his parents on the steps of the redbrick manor house as the motor left with him for the station. He would remember the tableau in years to come.

Now he turned the bend in the Irish country road where he had once escorted Ellen to the school. Kilcrannagh came into view. The modest cut-stone house was the same: laurel hedge, Virginia creeper, green-painted windows. He had half expected it to be gone and was amused at his own fatuity – only a fool imagined things sank of existence when he was no longer around to look at them. He wondered who would be there – the redoubtable Mrs Murphy? Harry? And bubbly Franny so defamed by that idiot Bertie? And … Ellen?

He wished it were raining and that she were approaching on a bicycle. He imagined her face when he called to her, 'May I offer you a lift, Miss Healy?' Eight years ago he had put her into a cab outside the Shelbourne. But eight years was not that long in the overall scheme of things. And even if she were employed at the far side of the country, she was likely to be at home for the summer holidays.

Guy parked on the side of the road, got out of the car and approached the gate. The gate squeaked, prompting a terrier he had never seen before to come barking around the side of the house. This, in turn, prompted the appearance of a young man at the drawing-room window who started and then waved. In a moment the front door was open and Harry was standing there.

'My dear old fellow!' Harry exclaimed, vigorously shaking his hand. 'What a wonderful surprise! We all thought you had been eaten by tigers long ago!'

Harry was still slight, but several inches taller than when Guy had last seen him. His face had filled a little, his body lean, his moustache clipped.

Guy grasped the outstretched hand. 'I'm staying in Clonshule for the grouse. Thought I'd drop by to see you all.'

'You look so fit and well! Come in. Come in. Aunt will be glad to see you.'

Guy crossed the threshold, registering the same old scent of baking bread.

# Chapter 21

The drawing room was almost unchanged – the chesterfield suite sported the same chintz covers, very worn now in places. There was the upright piano where he had accompanied Ellen's singing that first evening, and there was the window where he had stood when she had rushed into her father's arms. A roll-top desk now took up the far corner of the room; the bookcase was stuffed with new tomes and a slender volume was lying open on the armrest of one of the chairs. Roses arranged in two large glass vases filled the room with perfume.

'I trust the family is in good health?'

'My aunt is resting right now. She'll be down as soon as she knows you're here. But the two girls are not at home any more. Fran's in Dublin, and dear old Ellen has left us.'

'Oh?' Guy said, and his heart executed a small, sickening drop.

'Gone to the west.' Harry went on. 'A place called Balcarragh, County Galway. She got married last Easter. Chap by the name of Brendan Kennedy.'

The silence that followed this remark was, Guy thought, a well, deep and dark. Into it, trying to hide his bitter disappointment, he murmured, 'Married! I see ... I hope she'll be very happy.'

Harry took a bottle from a desk drawer. 'Can I offer you a Jameson? There's sherry too, if you'd prefer.'

Guy accepted the whiskey and let its astringency warm his guts. All he could think of was that Ellen was gone, that he was too late.

'Her husband … decent sort, is he?'

'Very. A schoolmaster, and a farmer too … lots older than her though.' Harry dropped his voice and added as though by way of explanation, 'My father died last year. But perhaps you heard?'

Guy shook his head. 'I'm sorry, I didn't know. I've lost touch with my stepmother.'

'*Our* stepmother!' Harry said with a chuckle, 'The poor woman must have felt very let down. No dazzling tribute for her services. None of my uncle's American gold!'

Guy vaguely recalled mention of this gentleman and had doubted the claims made for him. 'I remember she spoke of him. Did you know him?'

'Never saw him. He died in Washington two years ago.' Harry sighed and added, 'With his kind of wealth he must have been damned with importuning relatives, so I'm very glad we were not a part of the begging brigade. Do sit down, Guy!'

Guy sat on the couch and glanced at the book on the armrest. The title was in a strange script. 'What are you reading?' he asked.

Harry picked up the book and handed it to him. 'It's poetry. Irish. Some of it nearly fifteen hundred years old! I'm aiming at proficiency in my native tongue.'

'Good for you!'

Harry started trying to interest him in the occasional similarity between Irish and French when there was movement upstairs. Mrs Murphy would, no doubt, be joining them in a matter of minutes, Guy realised, and then he would not be able to escape without tea and embarrassing small talk. He had no wish to see her, now that Ellen was gone.

So he turned to Harry and suggested with a strained laugh, 'Would you be up to trying Duff's Pool again? I hate being bested!'

'Today?'

'Why not? At least it's not raining!'

There was another creak from the ceiling. Harry glanced up and said with a chuckle,

'I'll get the rods and the wellies.'

Guy followed Harry into the hall and Maggie came from the kitchen, a plumper Maggie than formerly, with a chin to match her expanded waistline.

'How are you at all, Sir?' she cried. 'Sure 'tis years since we laid eyes on you! I've just told the missus you're here and she'll be down in a minute!'

Guy said he was fine and was glad to find her looking so well. Harry produced the rods and the wellingtons as Mrs Murphy came downstairs. Guy was shocked at how she had aged. Her hair was white, her face lined and her eyes haunted. She was thin, where formerly she had been stout, but her carriage was upright as of old. He shook hands with her politely.

'I'm glad to see you, Guy,' she said, 'looking so dashing. You must come back for tea. Harry, don't fall in the river this time!' she added with attempted jocularity.

Guy thanked her and said he would like to accept her invitation but that they were expecting him back early at Clonshule.

'Have you heard how well our young man here has done for himself?' she asked, with a proud glance at her nephew.

'He is very modest, Mrs Murphy. He has told me nothing about himself!'

'Not only did he graduate from St Patrick's, but when they set up the new National University four years ago he enrolled for a BA and obtained his degree this summer'

'Congratulations!' Guy exclaimed, turning to Harry. 'Will you teach?'

Harry nodded. 'I have accepted a post at a school near Dublin. It's an interesting scholastic experiment, run by a passionate educationalist.'

'Yes,' Mrs Murphy said, nodding. 'A Mr Pearse.'

At Duff's Pool the water was limpid, the river as placid as though it had never torn along with murderous force.

'Sometimes I still think of the day you pulled me out.'

'Least I could do, Harry! Couldn't have them finding your corpse downstream, could I? Can you imagine what it would have done to your sister?'

Harry arranged the rug under a beech. The only sounds were birdsong, swirling water and the breeze lazing among the leaves.

'Tell me what you've been doing with yourself,' he said, as he baited his rod. 'Ellen told us you went to India?'

'I was there for nearly eight years.'

'What was it like?'

'Hot!'

Harry grinned and cast his line out into the river with a practised flick.

'You must have thought occasionally of cooler climes!'

Guy laughed.

'My dear fellow, I used to fantasise about the chilled rosé we drink in Fontebelle in summer! Especially when we were on long and dusty manoeuvres. But you get used to things. Look,' he whispered, gesturing at the tug on Harry's float, 'you already have a customer.'

Harry began to play the fish and slowly wound in a brown trout.

'What about Franny?' Guy asked when Harry had put the fish in his canvas bag. 'Is she married too?'

There was long silence, broken when Harry said with a sigh, 'No. There's a story there, Guy. And none of us are over it, especially my aunt, although she is too far stiff-necked to do anything to resolve it. Fran hightailed it to Dublin six years ago. She ran away.'

'But why?'

Harry shrugged. 'Maybe she felt life here was pointless. No one took her seriously, so she went to find people who would. At least that's my reading of it. I met her in Dublin shortly afterwards.

Tried to talk sense to her, but we ended up having a row. She said she was involved with the women's suffrage movement and happy at last. Although she looked anything but …' He stared at the swirling brown water and added, 'Then there was some kind of a letter she sent to Aunt Harriet, which we were never allowed to see. All every mysterious, but Aunt is made of granite and won't forgive Fran for deserting us. Personally, I think we failed her.'

Guy compared this account against the one provided by Bertie. I knew Bertie was lying, he told himself. He really is a consummate scoundrel to so defame a poor young lady.

'But how is she managing?'

'I gather she's gone into business.'

'Doing what?'

'She has a hat shop of all things … in Chatham Street.'

'What fun! I will call to see her.'

'I doubt you would be welcome.' Harry paused and looked apologetically at his old friend. 'It's nothing personal, Guy. She has expressly broken with her past, declared that she does not want any of us to darken her door, or words to that effect.'

'I suppose you will have to await a change of heart,' Guy murmured after a moment. 'Time heals everything, does it not?'

'That is what I'm hoping.'

Guy waited for a bite, but his line seemed fixed in eternity. He was aware of the torpid countryside, the swooping cloud shadows, the lowing of a cow in the distance, the barking of a dog and the bumble bees busy in the clover. He secured his rod and lay back on the bank, looking through the dappled foliage above him.

Everything changes, he thought. We grow, we move into other chapters. I will go back to England tomorrow. I will forget Ellen. I have more to do than waste my time mooning after what is lost. A fat trout impaled itself on his hook and in a moment he was alive again, playing out the line and hauling in the booty.

An hour later, he said he had to be getting back to Clonshule. Harry asked as they gathered up the rods, 'And what now? Will you return to India?'

'The subcontinent has exhausted its allure for the present,' Guy replied. 'My CO put my name down for a vacant post at Catterick. Yorkshire and home has its appeal, especially as I will be on hand if there is to be a scrap in Europe.'

Harry looked taken aback. 'You think there will be a war?'

'Just a feeling. Look at the rumblings in the Balkans. Old grievances … I wouldn't like to miss the fray if there is one.'

Harry was silent. A terrible thought had occurred to him and he looked at his old friend with foreboding. 'Guy,' he said quietly, 'you will probably think this a silly question, but what do you know of Ireland?'

'Enough to love it!' Guy looked at him with a smile. 'I have been here many times, after all. Why do you ask?'

'Just that … if there were a war … I would want to fight for Ireland.'

'Of course you would!' Guy replied. 'We would all be fighting for our empire – which includes Ireland.'

'I'm afraid it doesn't!'

'Oh come on, Harry!' Guy said laughing. 'We have a magnificent empire – one on which the sun never sets – and we are justly proud of it.'

'You don't know what happened here,' Harry murmured, waving his hand at some midges. 'If you did. If it had happened in your England …' He shrugged, adding, 'Never mind, how could you know?'

'Whatever it was, it's all a bit long ago now, isn't it?' Guy replied gently. 'And a young chap like you has all of life ahead of him. You haven't told me if there is a lady in your life.'

Harry smiled. 'You're an old fox, Forrister! There is someone. Her name is Deirdre. We're engaged, but God knows when we'll be able to tie the knot.'

They got into the car. Guy drove Harry home, passing the MacMahon farmhouse. Jimmy appeared at the top of the boreen and turned his head to look after them.

'There's your old friend,' Guy said drily as he dropped him at the gate.

'Jim's the salt of the earth,' Harry said. 'Better read than I am. Given the chance, he could be anything.'

'Such men are dangerous!'

Harry recognised Shakespeare and laughed. He thrust at Guy the canvas bag containing their catch. 'You keep them, Guy. They might like them at Clonshule. My aunt doesn't care much for fish.'

Guy drove away in a cloud of exhaust and dust. He passed the spot where he had waylaid Ellen coming back from school. He could still see that long hair in loose waves, the flush of her translucent skin, all the more potent in memory because she was lost to him.

'She's married.' he repeated to himself aloud. 'She's bloody married!'

# Chapter 22

*County Galway, November 1913*

The black kettle hung from a blackened crane. Ellen positioned it over the fire, fed in fresh sods while squinting against the puffs of smoke. Brendan would be home soon, hungry and cold. She looked around her whitewashed kitchen, the scrubbed deal table, the old dresser and its row of plates. Set in walls three feet thick, the small windows were gay with yellow curtains. She had made them, along with a bedspread for their bed, on the new Singer sewing machine with the foot trestle that Brendan had bought her. Above her head, through the rafters, was the new thatch he had commissioned in honour of their marriage. He had had the house whitewashed both inside and out and told her he was the luckiest man alive.

'Are you happy, Ellen, *a stóirín*?'

He always used the diminutive of the Irish endearment, as though she were a child.

She told herself she should be happy, and counted her blessings: she had a caring husband; she had a home; she had a profession. Kilcrannagh already seemed another life, and yet, fifteen months into her marriage she had begun to feel that, in some fundamental way, her life there and here were the same, as though nothing had really changed after all, or ever would.

She glanced through the window to her garden and beyond it to the avenue, where the naked beeches awaited spring. No sign of Brendan yet. He had stayed behind at the school and she had cycled home to get the supper on. She heard the sleet against the window and the wind moan in the chimney with its spine-tingling loneliness. The west had ghosts in every blast of winter. The Famine had been terrible here and its shadow lingered. The land, she thought, remembered the corpses, the weary processions to the coffin ships, the desolated countryside where the banshee wailed through bog and glen.

Once the stew was simmering, she opened her letter from Deirdre. It had been waiting for her when she returned, and she had deliberately put it aside to prolong its pleasure.

*Dearest Ellen,*

*Many thanks for your invitation to spend Christmas. Harry and I would love to come. He is working so hard at St Enda's that it is nearly impossible to prise him out of its clutches, but by then he should be ready for a well-earned rest.*

The letter continued with small snippets of news. Ellen put it down. Just wait until they hear what I have to tell them, she thought.

She went into the parlour, trimmed the wick, lit the lamp and set the fire. Brendan liked to read the paper here, or sometimes recite poetry to her of an evening – Tennyson, Longfellow, Wordsworth. She would sit, knitting, listening, aware that he loved poetry. It was the only time she saw him touched to the marrow, the only time he really let down his guard.

She put the turf ash into the galvanised bucket and a small cloud drifted into the room, dirtying the hearth and leaving a fine deposit on the furniture. Next week, thank God, her new maid would arrive and take the chores from her. The girl was coming from Inishmore, one of the Aran islands to the west, and wouldn't have a word of English.

She folded the newspapers – yesterday's *Irish Independent* and the periodical to which Brendan subscribed called *Irish Freedom*. She swept the hearth and took a duster from her apron pocket. She ran it over the sideboard and table, over their wedding portrait, herself in her cream silk dress and wide hat, he seated stiffly on the studio chair, unsmiling, intent on the camera and posterity. Finally, she wiped the wall clock that he wound so ceremoniously every Saturday. Like the one in Kilcrannagh, the clock was the voice of the house. It chimed now, and five mellow strokes trembled under the wood casing. What, she wondered, could have delayed him?

Brendan Kennedy was 'a spoiled priest'. He had divulged this to his wife as his personal secret after their marriage. After just three years in Maynooth, he had left the seminary. But however much courage it had taken to leave, it still carried a stigma, and no one in the parish, apart from Father Devlin, the parish priest, knew the secret of his past.

Ellen didn't care about it one way or the other. What she did care about was that Brendan was forty-seven years old and often fell asleep by the fire of an evening. She was only beginning to realise how set he was in his ways, how nothing must be allowed to interfere with the order of his day, with his reading, or, of late, his camera – her extravagant wedding present.

Their first meeting had been accidental. She had noticed him immediately at the teachers' social where she had seen him for the first time – the grey, distinguished-looking man who held himself apart.

'I'm the Master out at Balcarragh,' he had informed her as he helped her to ham salad. 'I need an assistant.' Quizzical eyes met hers. 'Would you be interested?'

It had not been her intention, once installed in the job, to also become the Master's wife. But a number of factors had conspired to persuade her. Quite apart from her respect and liking for Brendan, and her loneliness, the death of her father had aroused old insecurities. She seldom saw Harry. Fran never contacted her. her cousin had given up on them for reasons of her own and had warned them all off. Only Deirdre wrote with any regularity. She and Harry had become engaged as soon as he got his degree and this had prompted Ellen's own yearning for security.

'You should marry Mr Kennedy,' Deirdre had written. '*Carpe diem* and all that! How many eligible suitors will you find in the bogs?'

Ellen was full of conflicting yearnings. She longed for security because it had always escaped her, but she also yearned for enduring love. She knew that the one person who loved her in this way was Jimmy McMahon. He had summoned up the courage to show his heart when she returned to Kilcrannagh on the Christmas following her departure for her new job.

'For God's sake, Ellen,' he'd blurted when he had her alone for a moment, 'what is a beautiful lady like you doing in the wilds? Why don't you come home and throw your lot in with me?'

'Balcarragh is not in the wilds!' she'd laughed and fobbed him off. Quite apart from the fact that she did not love him as he loved her, there was something disquieting about Jimmy, something fiercely principled, and just as fiercely obdurate.

The last Christmas before her marriage, she had, on a nostalgic impulse, sent a card to Guy. She had been intermittently haunted by a longing for him – for the sight of his face, his gentlemanly bearing, his aura of grave, personal responsibility, and above all, for his lost love. She had addressed the Christmas card to his brother's home, Lindthorp, in Yorkshire. She knew her father would have been able to give the full address, but she did not want to ask him and have Lilian make something out of it. Guy might be coming home from India soon. He *might* get it. He might reply.

But she had heard nothing from him.

So, when Brendan Kennedy had asked her, with diffidence and admiration, if she would honour him by becoming Mrs Kennedy, she'd told herself he would make a kind husband, a good father and that it was time for her to settle down.

'He's a fine, decent man,' one of her colleagues said to her. 'And in the end, what else is needed?'

Harry had escorted her down the isle of the local church and her aunt had hosted a small wedding breakfast in the Westenra Hotel. Jimmy had knelt at the back of the church during the ceremony but had declined the invitation to the wedding reception. Deirdre had been there, and Clare and Frank had also come from Dublin. Clare looked wonderful in an eau de nil dress, with a hat that set off her lovely face and glorious hair. But Fran had not come, although Ellen had defied her aunt and sent an invitation.

'Will someone tell me?' Ellen demanded when she got Clare alone. 'Why didn't Franny come to my wedding? I miss her so much!'

'Mother is too proud for her own good,' Clare replied. 'She fell out with Fran over her leaving home and won't speak to her.'

'But surely Fran has tried to heal the rift?'

'I saw her once in that little shop of hers,' Clare replied. 'She told me quite baldly to go away.'

'You must have done something to upset her.'

Clare bridled. 'I couldn't have her living with us, if that's what you mean. But it doesn't mean I don't worry about her. It doesn't mean I don't care about her!'

The conversation had ended there. Mrs Murphy had appeared and Clare had drifted away to talk to someone else.

'I hope you will be very happy, my dear child,' her aunt said.

'Are you happy with my choice, Aunt Harriet?'

'That is hardly the criterion! Your romantic skirmish with young Mr Forrister was youthful folly and it was my duty to warn you! But Brendan is a good man and you will be safe with him.'

I would have been safe with Guy too, Ellen thought. I would

have been much more than safe.

'I was just talking to Clare about Franny,' she'd said, to change the subject and to confront her aunt with the mystery of her cousin's disappearance.

But her aunt's reaction had shocked her, 'Do not speak to me of that girl! She is no longer my daughter.'

Before leaving on honeymoon, Ellen had scribbled a note to Franny and asked Deirdre to post it. It said simply:

> *Darling Fran,*
>
> *I missed you at my wedding today more than I can say. I do not know why your mother is so unforgiving, but I love you. Could you visit us in Balcarragh? It'll probably be years before I get to Dublin again!*

The reply, brutal in its import, was waiting for her in Balcarragh when she returned from honeymoon.

> *Dear Ellen,*
>
> *I know you mean well, but the only thing I ask from my family is that they stay out of my life.*
>
> *Franny*

Ellen and Brendan's honeymoon was spent in Clifden, Connemara. On their wedding night Ellen went up to bed alone, leaving her husband downstairs with his newspaper. Although he projected relaxed *savoir faire*, she knew he was half-paralysed with diffidence, like a man who had undertaken to leap the Shannon and now wasn't sure if his legs were long enough.

Upstairs, she'd changed nervously into her nightgown, let down her hair and brushed it in the lamplight before the mirror, bending her head so that the long tresses almost touched the carpet. She'd had a fantasy once, of her wedding night, in which her new husband would uncoil her hair. She shivered at what that thought had always conjured, the slow smoothing under the bristles, the touch of his hand at her neck … at her breast … She closed her eyes and it was as though Guy stood behind her, watching in the mirror.

Brendan's arrival, heralded by a discreet knock on the door, had made her jump.

'Are you decent *a stóirín*?'

She'd climbed quickly into bed while Brendan tiptoed to the bathroom, returning in his nightshirt. He blew out the lamp and eagerly reached for her. But her senses were fixed on a dog-eared longing and she closed her eyes and imagined it was Guy's hands … Guy's body …

Afterwards he said shyly, triumphantly, 'I hope I wasn't clumsy, Ellen … I've never done this before, you know.'

'I've never done it before either!'

'I know that! But it was good … it pleased you?'

'Of course it did!'

What have I done? Ellen asked herself. On my wedding night I have lain with another man, albeit a phantom.

The moonlight seeping through the curtains had outlined her husband's profile, the resolute chin, high bridge of his nose. His breathing was deepening; he was nodding off with small snores, secure in his conjugality, in his wife's love. I will make it up to you, she promised him silently. *You* are real, while Guy belongs to childhood, a bedtime story of princes and spells.

Brought back to the mundane present by Fingal's barking, she glanced at herself in the mirror above the parlour mantelpiece, a preoccupied and tired young woman, with a smut on her face and wisps of hair adrift. She wiped the smut, tidied her hair, took off her apron and went to the door. In the distance she heard the trap coming, wheels turning on the stony road. Paddy Brannigan, the wiry bachelor who lived in a labourer's cottage nearby and ran the farm, appeared at the stable and raised his arm to the Master in greeting. In a moment Brendan arrived in the trap, walking the pony down the avenue, throwing the reins to Paddy.

Ellen felt the slow burn of excitement. She had something to tell her husband this evening which would seal their life together, something for which she knew he longed.

Brendan came in, tired as always after school, bending his head to get through the low door.

'You're cold!' she said, taking his hands. 'Come to the fire.'

She wanted to tell him her secret, but even as it was on the tip of her tongue a new shyness prevented her. It was so momentous a disclosure that it seemed once those words were spoken life would never be the same.

'Would you like to eat now?'

'To tell the truth, Ellen *a ghrá*, I'm more than ready.'

He sat down, unlaced his boots and put on his slippers. Then he added gently and enquiringly, 'Ellen, is something bothering you?'

'What makes you ask that?'

'You're fidgeting. Tell me what it is.'

'I just wanted to ask you, Brendan,' she said slowly, watching his face, 'how would you feel if, in June of next year, you were to become a father?'

He looked at her in silence, rose from his chair and took her in his arms.

'You are so dainty,' he whispered into her hair, 'so fragile in my arms! How can you possess so miraculous a power!'

# Chapter 23

*County Galway, December 1913*

With the approach of Christmas, Ellen became excited at the prospect of Harry and Deirdre's visit. She went to a lot of trouble decorating the house with the red-berried holly that grew along the avenue and Máire Ní Suibhne, the girl from Inishmore, polished every stick of furniture. Harry was coming a day in advance of Deirdre, who was delayed by a teachers' meeting at her school. Two Christmas cakes had been made, as had two plum puddings, generously laced with whiskey.

When the day came at last, Brendan set off in the trap to collect Harry at the station. There was little traffic – a trap coming from the direction of Athenry, a donkey and cart, a lone cyclist. He crossed the road, proceeded down a rutted boreen to the small flag station at Cloncappal, which was situated in the middle of the bog. It was a cold evening with a grey mist over the land; smells of dank vegetation mixed with the smell of turf smoke.

Brendan was eager to see his brother-in-law. Deirdre would not be coming until tomorrow and this suited him. It would give him a chance to talk to young Harry whom he thought far too easily influenced by the radical elements in Dublin. So much had happened in the last eighteen months – the giant demonstration in Dublin for Home Rule, the signing of the Ulster Covenant by Loyalists who vowed to defeat it, the setting up of the Ulster Volunteer Force, the attempt to break the trade unions, the massive Lockout in Dublin lasting months and, more recently, the formation of the Irish Volunteers in the south, a counterweight to those in the north.

Sabre rattling? Perhaps. But posturing tended to acquire its own momentum and career out of control.

He watched the train approach, fiery sparks peppering the darkness. The station master, Joe Brophy, waved his red flag. The iron dragon slowed with a metallic screech and ground to a halt with the hiss of braking steam. Harry, in a belted tweed ulster, a Gladstone bag in one hand and a Switzers shopping bag in the other, jumped from the train, saw Brendan and strode towards him along the platform.

'Colder than Dublin,' he said. 'And I thought you were nearer the Gulf Stream!'

Brendan laughed, shook hands and looked at him closely. 'You're wearing spectacles!' he exclaimed. 'Since when?'

'Couple of months. I was beginning to peer at everything.'

Brendan escorted his guest to the waiting trap and in a couple of moments they were moving along the empty, dark boreen. The pony knew the way well and Brendan relaxed the reins and let him choose his pace. But he kept his voice low.

'How fares the new organisation?'

'The Volunteers? Every red-blooded man in Dublin is in it!'

'And you?'

'Of course! And my redoubtable headmaster too, and his brother. And everyone worth a damn.'

Brendan's reply was muted. 'Even from here I can see the momentum growing. But you should avoid the rabid elements, Harry. I read an article by your headmaster recently.'

'He's a visionary!'

'Dreamers live dangerously. He may drag you into a head-on confrontation. Remember, it cannot be won. Cunning, caution, is the way to proceed … *Festina lente*.'

Harry contained a sigh of exasperation. 'We can't afford another seven hundred years. There'll be nothing left that is Irish, least of all people!'

Don't be so damned safe, Brendan, he thought irritably. Don't be so damn *prudent*! He was aware of the scent of the firs in the crisp night air, the steady walk of the pony, the rattle of the bit, the strangeness of being en route to his sister's new home. How odd was life. It promised so much to comfort the heart, and some, like Brendan, had it – love and domesticity. And caution. Above all caution. But, for others, life drove you with a cause not of your making.

'Do you remember the story of the Pass of Thermopylae, Brendan?' he asked after a moment. 'Ancient Greece? Three men holding the pass against three hundred?'

'Of course!'

'Do you recall what Leonidas said?'

'What are you driving at, Harry?'

'He said, "We are not here for safety".'

His brother-in-law turned to him in the gloom. 'I know that, Harry,' he said quietly. 'I am more aware of it than you imagine.'

Ellen embraced the brother she had not seen since her wedding.

'You look every inch the schoolmaster with those specs! I want to hear every detail of your life. No item too small!'

'You sound like a collecting charity!'

Ellen laughed and added shyly, 'Did Brendan tell you our news?'

'I thought you'd like to tell him yourself,' Brendan said with a proud smile.

'What news?'

'Well, we're promoting you to uncle – next June!'

Harry gasped. 'That is wonderful! I wish much joy to you

both!' Then he added, 'Make sure he looks just a bit like me, El. Keep your priorities right.'

Ellen gave an exasperated sigh and said, 'It might be a girl.'

'Could still look like me,' he replied, raising his eyebrows and posing with one leg in front of the other, 'On a good day.'

After a lamplit supper, they relaxed around the fire in the flagged kitchen. Máire had tidied things away and gone to her little room behind the kitchen, bidding them goodnight – '*Oíche mhaith*' – and Harry had replied to her in Irish, '*Codladh sámh, a Mháire*', to wish her sweet dreams.

'Tell me about Dublin,' Ellen said.

'There's tension everywhere. The Lockout has left a bitter taste, as has that bad business in August when the police broke up a meeting being addressed by Larkin.'

'The trade union leader? Were you there?'

Harry nodded. 'The crowd was quiet, listening to Larkin speaking from the balcony of the Imperial Hotel. Most people were just curious, with nothing better to do on a Sunday. The police charged with batons and sabres. There was blood on the street, on the pavement, spattered on the walls.'

Ellen clapped a hand to her mouth.

'Great God!' Brendan exclaimed. 'Were you hurt?'

'A bruise or two,' Harry said with a shrug. 'But we won't have a recurrence. James Connolly, the Belfast labour leader, has helped organise a citizen army to face down the police. And the new Volunteer force will counter the Unionists.'

Ellen asked as evenly as she could, 'Do they have much support!'

'The Volunteers? Yes … growing! And the likelihood of a branch for women in the months to come!'

In the hearth the sods settled suddenly with a shower of sparks and a burning brand smoked its way onto the floor. Brendan jumped up and kicked it back to the fire.

'If everyone will be confronting everyone,' Ellen whispered, 'how will it all end?'

Harry shrugged. 'It will end when we are free.'

'What about arms?' Brendan asked, frowning at his wife as though to silence her.

'We've managed to get some.'

'You will need safekeeping for them.'

'Of course. But since the King proclaimed the entire country, it's illegal to import them.'

'Martial law won't stop them in the North,' Brendan said.

'No. And it won't stop us in the South either!'

Ellen shivered. But something in her own blood stirred and her heart beat faster.

'Would you involve yourself with violence, Harry?' she asked quietly, ignoring her husband's eye.

He waited for a moment before replying. 'We have momentum now, Ellen. If we do not act soon we will lose it, possibly forever. We will be merged inextricably with Britain, become a nation of imitators. Thousands of years of a unique and distinguished culture – our own spirituality if you want to put it that way – will be obliterated forever. It is a terrible prospect,' he added, staring fixedly at his sister, 'to allow your country to lose its soul.'

'Would you join the new Volunteers, Brendan?' Ellen whispered, turning to her husband.

'I am not in a position to do so, Ellen. Anyway, they have no teeth.'

Harry smiled at his sister. 'What about you, Sis?' he asked teasingly. 'Would you join the new women's force?'

Ellen avoided her husband's eye. She gave a small hysterical laugh. 'I would if I could!'

'Well you cannot!' her husband said sternly.

'I know that!' Ellen replied and left the room.

The next day was 23 December. Ellen went with Harry to collect Deirdre at the station, hoping for a drive full of the relaxed banter of the old days.

'Oh, for a motor car!' she cried. 'It has to be warmer.'

Harry gave a derisive whinny. 'Quite apart from a price tag of two hundred pounds, the cost of running them is quite interesting. Petrol one shilling and nine pence a gallon. Now compare that with keeping a pony.'

He had his hat well down on his head and a woollen scarf around his neck. Occasionally he handed her the reins, removed his spectacles and wiped the mist from them.

'I suppose your headmaster has a motor?' asked Ellen.

'Pearse? Of course. His family – his mother and sisters – live in the school. The atmosphere is extraordinary. Everything is taught through Irish. The games are all Gaelic. Discipline is based on honour – no caning. The boys will not break their word to Pearse.'

'So you have a scholastic Utopia?'

'An experiment if you like, but it works.'

He was like a coiled spring, she thought. He had left her behind. She had somehow assumed the world marched at her pace, but a fierce purpose was growing in Harry and it moved and involved her whether she liked it or not.

'Do you ever see Franny?' she asked, to change the subject and to find out what he knew about their cousin, whose absence from her life still filled her with pain.

He shook his head. 'Not for a long time. I dropped in to see her once in that shop of hers, but she was cold and distant and unlike her old self.'

'Why has she turned her back on us?'

'Perhaps she imagines we failed her … and we did, when you think of it. We assumed she was a child, a fixture at home, not a living, breathing human being with needs. But she seems all right … successful even, with her fine hats on display. She was always a clever little thing with her hands.'

'Good at everything!' Ellen said shortly. 'And brave!'

*And very hurt*, she wanted to add. *By you.*

But she was impressed that her brother saw women not only

as people, but as people with legitimate needs. This struck her as unusual in a man, and her heart warmed to him.

'When were you last in Kilcrannagh?' she asked him, wondering how her aunt was coping.

'August. I went there after the fracas in Dublin, to lick my wounds. Aunt Harriet is getting neither mellower nor younger. Oh, and Guy Forrister came while I was there.' Harry slapped the pony's rump with the reins. 'He was looking very fit. We went fishing. Without mishap this time, you'll be glad to hear!'

Ellen caught her breath and a hollowness opened in the pit of her being.

'So … he's back,' she said as casually as she could. 'Is he well?'

'Very, as far as I could see. Brown as a berry, with that taut fitness you see in military men. He's opted for a new home posting. Catterick I think he said. He wants to be on hand if there's a scrap in Europe. At least that was how he put it.'

'Did he … ask for me?'

Harry glanced at her, but she was looking rigidly ahead and she knew he could not see her face in the gloom.

'To tell you the truth, El, I think it was the reason he came. He seemed very disappointed not to see you. I think he was sweet on you in the old days, without anyone knowing.'

The silence was broken by the sonorous hooting of the little train approaching across the bogland.

Deirdre leaned out the window to open the door of her compartment. Harry saw her and ran down the platform. She stepped out, an elegant silhouette, hatted and gloved, her long woollen coat buttoned to the chin, her hair swept up under a hat with a short brim. Ellen stayed back while her brother took his fiancée in his arms, and then she came forward to embrace her friend.

'It's wonderful to get a good oul' hoult of you again. You might as well be living on the moon for all I see of you!' she said with tears in her eyes.

The stationmaster waved his green flag and the train chugged from the station leaving a cloud of sparks to enliven the dusk. The three young people left the station arm in arm, full of the joy of reunion.

'I'm glad this house has three bedrooms, Dee,' Ellen joked later as she sat at the foot of Deirdre's bed. 'Otherwise the two of us would have had to share a room and the two darlin' lads share the other one!'

She was warm and cosy in the combined light of fire and candle, delighting in the company of her old friend. Deirdre, hairbrush in hand, was bending over and dragging the bristles through her curls.

'I can't wait for your and Harry's wedding,' she added. 'Have you named a day?'

Deirdre righted herself and laughed. 'Too much to do, Ellen dear! If Harry and I had to wait until we could get married we'd be dried up old sticks! So don't be surprised if there's a pattering of not-so-little feet during the night!' She looked at her with a half grin, 'Are you very shocked?'

Ellen gulped, 'I hope you're … careful!'

'Too bloomin' careful! I think of our wedding all the time … but Ireland comes first.'

'Next thing you'll tell me is you're ready to shed your blood,' Ellen said lightly.

'I am,' Deirdre replied cheerfully. 'Having said that, I'd much rather hold onto it.'

'You're as bad as Harry!' Ellen exclaimed. 'Brendan says he's bewitched. I told him it started while he was still a boy, but he blames that headmaster of his.'

Deirdre's eyes returned to the fire. 'Pearse? And well he might. You know he's a poet?' She cleared her throat:

> O wise man riddle me this: what if the dream came
> true?

What if the dream came true? and if millions unborn
shall dwell
In the house I have shaped in my heart

She fixed her eyes on Ellen and said, 'Or listen to this.'

I have turned my face
To the road before me
To the work that I see
And the death I shall die

Ellen's stomach lurched. She put her hand on it, thinking of the life within. What can *I* do? she wondered and answered the question. Nothing. I can only look on, like a ghost at the edge of my own life.

'How will it all end if it isn't stopped?' she asked.

'It can't be stopped. The whole problem now is to raise funds.'

'For arms?'

Dee turned to her with a shrug of her shoulders. 'What else, Ellen darling?'

'But Harry might be hurt … ' Her voice trailed away as she recalled how Brendan had dismissed her yesterday evening. I wish I could be with you both, she thought. I am too young for this imprisonment.

Deirdre averted her gaze. Do you think you love him more than I do? she thought. But I would rather be near him in the thick of it, than anything else I can think of.

Bidding her friend goodnight, Ellen went to the kitchen for a hot jar to warm her sheets. Through the closed door came the low voices of her brother and her husband. Hesitating on the threshold, she heard names – Pearse, Plunkett, MacDonagh, MacDiarmada. She opened the door. She was struck by their postures: her grey-haired husband, leaning back and listening, his right hand cupping his pipe; Harry leaning forward, intensity in the set of his shoulders and his outspread hands. They fell silent as she entered.

'Don't go silent on my account,' she said.

'It wasn't on your account, dear,' Brendan replied. He spoke gently, but his voice had a ring of husbandly authority, just the right degree to show Harry, she thought, who was in charge here.

Suppressing an impromptu tide of anger, she filled her hot jar and went to her bedroom. She lit her candle and sat on the bed, tired to her soul, piqued and hurt. The visit to which she had so looked forward had brought not warmth but chagrin, a sense of things being out of joint, a sense of her own powerlessness and a visceral fear of the future.

She pulled back the curtain and looked out at the moonlit night and the quiet countryside. Tomorrow was Wednesday, Christmas Eve; she would put a lighted candle in the window and pray for a peaceful world into which she would bring her first child. She poured some water into the basin and washed her hands and face, noticing that her fingers had swollen and that her wedding ring was imbedded in her flesh.

Already pregnancy had thickened her waist and was swelling her breasts. In a burst of irritation she tried to get the ring off, rubbing in soap, and eventually, with some effort, it slid down her finger. She looked at it in the palm of her hand, the thin gold band. Was it a symbol of fidelity and love? Or something else? After all, they used to put rings on slaves long ago.

She knew she did not love Brendan. It was bitter knowledge. She respected him certainly; but her blood never answered his caresses and part of her eternally resisted his self-satisfied authority. He would come to bed soon, half-embarrassed as he sought his rights as a husband. He would get them, of course. He had everything she had to give; he had the industry of her life – her income was paid to him; her body was his when he wanted. She had looked forward to a good chat with Deirdre, but Dee had moved into a place where she could not follow. She felt like a railway car shunted into a siding.

She wished she could see Franny. Why had she shut her out? What had she ever done that she should treat her like this? And poor Aunt Harriet was ageing in empty Kilcrannagh, where she had once ruled over a busy household. Thank God Jimmy was still keeping an eye on things for her. Was he in this movement too? One of the new Volunteers?

And, finally, she gave in and thought of Guy. She rose and went to her chest of drawers, carefully drew out her mother's old journal and found in the fly leaf, where she had left them, the few violets she had rescued from his bouquet, the small, gilt-edged card that sent his love, and his photograph. She stared at his young face for a few moments and ran a gentle finger over the fragile violets, remembering fondly the ring with the ruby eyes, the symbol of that first love, so powerful, so innocent. He had it back now, returned by her aunt at her own request. Had he given it to someone else?

But oh! To think that he had come to find her. Come to find her at last, when she had gone.

# *Chapter 24*

*County Galway, June 1914*

Mrs Kiely, the midwife, bathed Ellen and slipped a fresh nightgown over her head. 'You did well. The first one is never easy. I'll get the master now.'

She gathered up the blood-stained sheets and went out to the kitchen. The baby, a boy, lay in Ellen's arms, sucking his knuckle and peering at the world. Brendan came into the room with the nervous gait of someone entering a sanctum. He looked down at his wife and child, bent and kissed his wife's brow.

'Dear Ellen,' he said, studying the tiny face of his newborn. He put his hand on the baby's head and looked at his wife with tears in his eyes. 'His hair is dark gold,' he said.

'It's in the family … my mother.'

'And his name will be as we agreed?'

'Oh yes,' Ellen replied. 'Hugh. Let's have another one next year,' she added with a giddy laugh. 'Maybe this time it will be a girl … for me. If they are close in age they will be friends!'

Brendan was staring at her with a strange expression.

'Why are you looking at me like that?'

'Many things in this world I may know and understand,' her

husband replied. 'But I will never understand women!'

Mrs Kiely put the baby in the cradle, pulled the curtains and mother and child slipped into an exhausted sleep. Brendan stayed in the room looking at his son, the continuation of his line, flesh of his flesh, part of some great weft of meaning woven by God.

Máire Ní Suibhne knocked. 'Father Devlin does be at the gate, *a Mháistir*!'

Brendan went to the kitchen door, saw the parish priest's trap in the avenue and went out to welcome him. The evening was glorious; the meadows were high and the young swallows soared with the promise of summer.

Father Bernard Devlin was something of a friend. As manager of the school he was also Brendan's boss.

'I thought I'd pay a visit, Brendan, but young Máire tells me you've just become a father. So I'll just congratulate you and be on my way.'

'Come in and we'll wet the baby's head!'

The priest smiled at the idiom, tied the pony's reins to a tree, stepped down from the trap and followed his host. He was led to the parlour where Brendan, with unsteady hands, poured him a generous tot of whiskey and then one for himself. Mrs Kiely brought the baby, wrapped and sleeping, into the parlour for inspection.

'This is Hugh, my son!' Brendan said, his voice tight with pride. At the back of his mind was a sense that he had upstaged the clergy. The 'spoiled priest' had become a father after all, but a real one. 'Match that!' his gesture said. You may be a titular father, but I'm the real thing, the parent of a living child.

The priest peered into the newborn's face and raised his hand in automatic benediction.

'Any thought yet of a christening date?'

'Soon, I suppose. But it's up to herself.'

Mrs Kiely took her burden away and Máire knocked at the door. 'There was post the mornin', *a Mháistir*!' she said shyly, handing over two white envelopes. She bobbed respectfully at the priest.

'*Tá an Bearla go han mhaith agat anois, a Mháire!*' Father Devlin said expansively, telling her how good her English was. But complimenting her in Irish, only provoked a flood of the old language in response.

'I never knew you were fluent, Bernard!' Brendan exclaimed, when the maid had left the room.

'I've spent time on it. The oldest documented language north of the Alps – our language – the vernacular here when Christ was a child, is going to die an unnatural death if we don't get off our proverbials! But why don't you open your letters?'

Brendan would have preferred to read them in private, but he slipped his finger under the flaps of both envelopes. One letter was from Greene's bookshop in Dublin to tell him that they now had a copy, in translation, of *The Annals of the Four Masters* – a compendium of Irish history assembled in the seventeenth century to pass on the records of a civilisation facing final destruction. Would he send them a cheque?

He had opened the second letter before he realised it was addressed to Ellen. He cast his eye down the page and started, then frowned.

'Bad news?'

'This is extraordinary, Bernie. It's addressed to my wife, but she is not, I think, in a fit condition to deal with it.'

He held it out. The priest took the letter.

*Dearest Ellen,*

*I bumped into Harry in College Green the other day. It was wonderful to see him and to know that you spent last Christmas together, and above all to hear you are soon to give birth. I want you to know that my thoughts are with you and my prayers for a happy outcome.*

*I have not been a good friend or cousin for a long time and you must think I have forsaken you, Ellen, but there was a reason. I have a daughter – Hannah – now seven years old. She is quite wonderful; but she has no father. I am unwed, Ellen. Whether or not this is something you can stomach is up to you. If it is, I would love to see you. I have my own little hat shop in Chatham Street – 'Du Barry' – set up with the help of a good friend. It is doing well and I have an assistant, so I could get away and stay with you for a while to help with your new arrival, and meet your husband.*

*It would mean a lot. Do say yes, dear El, and forgive me if you can.*

*All my love forever,*

*Franny*

Father Devlin re-read the letter while the clock on the mantelpiece ticked out reproaches, and Brendan watched him with a frown.

'I had no idea Ellen had a cousin in this dreadful situation. The poor creature has evidently even kept the child. And, you will note, not one word of remorse!' He looked at Brendan. 'You can hardly have this hussy here. You have a position in the community.'

Brendan sighed. 'But does anyone need to know? I think Ellen is quite fond of her. She mentions her so wistfully sometimes.'

'These things have a habit of getting out! Do you want your son tended, your wife befriended, by a woman of … liberal virtue?'

Brendan gasped.

'No,' the priest added after a moment, 'your position would be untenable, especially as regards your position in the school.'

A threat? Brendan wondered. He nodded, took back the letter

and consigned it the fire. But first he jotted the Chatham Street address onto the back of an envelope, wondering at the odd name of the shop. Hadn't there been some French hussy of that name? Both men watched as the letter crinkled at the edges and burst into flame.

'In Ellen's fatigued state it is better so,' Father Devlin said. 'Why should she be burdened with someone like that?'

Brendan nodded. 'I will reply to this person myself.'

'Women nowadays,' the priest said with a sigh. 'God knows where it will end. If they're not breaking windows or harassing the House of Commons, they're burning churches. Did you see that outrage yesterday at Henley?'

Brendan said he had not had time to read the paper.

'Of course, today is a special day for you! But the world goes on – the Home Rule Bill has had its third reading, and we shall yet have peace and hope in Ireland.' The priest smoothed his moustache and added, 'But the Balkans are another matter … still simmering.'

He went on to discuss parish matters. But Brendan's heart was not in it and he was glad when the priest left.

When his visitor had gone, Brendan sat down to pen his reply to Franny. He suspected how dear this woman was to his wife, but he dreaded her influence. No matter how much Ellen liked to paint her as a loving, strong-minded individual, there was no gainsaying what she had become – a loose creature who had had an illegitimate child, carried on her own business, and had the temerity to think she could invade a respectable household. No doubt she intended to bring the little bastard daughter with her! And how long would they stay? Everyone in the parish would soon know who they were. The men would size her up, the women shun her.

He began to feel angry at how his virtuous home might have been compromised and his reputation, and his wife's, diminished. But he would not reply in the vein that fired him. He would be polite, but he would be firm.

He took out a pad of writing paper and his fountain pen.

*Dear Madam,*

*I refer to your recent letter. My wife is unwell and has asked me to reply on her behalf. A visit from you at this juncture would, regrettably, not be possible as we are not in a position to welcome guests.*

*I wish you well,*
*Yours very truly,*

*Brendan Kennedy*

He put the note into an envelope, addressed it, looked in on his sleeping family before changing into his boots and seeking his bicycle. He would bring the letter immediately to the post. God alone knew whether that Jezebel was already girt for travel.

When he came home he felt relieved, but oddly guilty, like a man who had done something mean and underhand. It's for the best, he told himself, looking in again on the sleeping mother and child. In my position I can't be expected to run the gauntlet of that kind of notoriety. And Bernie Devlin made my position very clear.

When he regained the parlour and was alone, Brendan knelt by the fire, closed his eyes and offered thanks to the Almighty for his wife's safe deliverance and the blessing of a child. Then he picked up his paper, sat in his usual fireside chair and stretched his legs, staring into the grate and the whispering sods.

'I have a son,' he said aloud with a deep sigh of contentment, and the word 'son' lingered on his tongue and flavoured the air. 'I have a son!' He repeated it in Irish, '*Tá mac agam*!'

He opened the *Irish Independent* and was soon immersed. Bernie

Devlin had been right, he thought as he read. There was hope for Ireland. Home Rule within the Empire was almost certain now, but the ongoing trouble in the Balkans might spill over. People just didn't want to be ruled by other people and the Ottoman Empire needed to accept that as much as did the British. He thought of Harry and how he had wound them up last Christmas, and how Deirdre was every bit as radical as he was. They were good young people, both of them, and he hoped to the bottom of his soul that Ireland would be allowed the decency of her own parliament, and that further trouble would be averted. He also sent a fervent prayer to God that Europe would escape the bloody curse of war.

# Chapter 25

*Catterick, Yorkshire, August 1914*

Guy looked out at the barracks and at the green Dales beyond, aware of the new frisson in the air and his own contained excitement. So it had come after all. A major conflict. The assassination of the Archduke seemed an almost flimsy pretext. Tragic though the loss of individual life might be, the life and death of the Austrian dynasty was neither here nor there in a British context. It was a pretext of course; Germany had been getting too big for her boots for a long time and Britain would have to show who ruled the global empires of might and pelf.

He smiled at his private joke. But dear God – anything was better than cooling his heels in Catterick. If it weren't for Lindthorp … But Lindthorp was forty-five miles away.

The scrap would all be over by Christmas anyway, according to Field Marshall Sir John French. Personally he doubted the estimate. In his experience, everything in life took twice as long as predicted and cost twice as much, and military forecasts were more fragile than most. No, it would last at least a year, but Germany would be licked and there would be peace and the Empire would triumph.

And the cost? Well, like all wars, full accounting would be left to history and the bill to the next generation.

Empire and all that went with it did not excite him as much as once it had, but real war had a lure of gallantry and purpose. Where would he be posted? To the thick of the fight, he hoped. His life lacked excitement, lacked direction. He had somehow missed the boat; it had slipped its moorings while he was not looking.

But war required a united front, and that included Ireland, the part of the Empire that until recently, had taken up most cabinet time. Home Rule, no doubt, would now be rushed through its remaining stages.

He thought of the only real Irish people he knew, the Murphys and Ellen and Harry. The latter would be called up if they introduced conscription, or he might join anyway. It would be rather rum to run into him.

His batman put his head around the door. 'The CO wants to see you, Sir!'

Guy rose immediately but he had to wait outside his CO's office for five minutes before his secretary showed him in. He saluted smartly.

'Well, Forrister,' his bewhiskered Commanding Officer said, glancing up from his desk. 'It's what you've been waiting for.' He looked at some papers before him. 'You're off to Belgium. British Expeditionary Force. Pleased?'

'Yes Sir!'

'Teach the Hun a thing or two?'

Guy smiled. 'Of course, Sir!'

In Culgreine, a month later, Jimmy was sitting by the fire. He'd returned from the fields in a downpour and was warming his legs by the hearth. Steam rose from his saturated corduroys as he read the *Irish Independent* in the dying light. It was Machiavellian certainly, but it was good, sound, cynical politics, and only to be expected, he told himself as he finished the article. Blackie, his sheepdog, stretched by the ashy hearth, head on paws, eyed his master plaintively.

'Dinner in a minute,' Jimmy informed him, 'so you can stop looking like I'd just robbed the poor box.'

He shook out the paper, folded it and stared into the flames. So Home Rule would not be implemented until the cessation of hostilities. Get as many Irish as possible to fight in England's war, use Home Rule as a carrot, and with a bit of luck the Irish would all be killed and you could keep the carrot. And the Volunteers, he thought, snorting and shaking his head in disgust, were flocking to join up. Redmond, the leader of the Irish party in Westminster, was encouraging Irishmen to go out to fight for the Freedom of Small Nations. Jimmy had seen the recruiting posters himself, an exhorting female figure with a harp – Ireland telling her sons 'Go!'

He sighed and viciously poked the fire. He heard the rain against the window and the wind in the chimney. The Volunteers, now numbering almost 200,000 men, the same organisation that, just two months earlier, had acquired arms for patriotic purposes, were falling for the bait. Of course their arms were a small fraction of the arms already in the hands of the northern Unionists, but they were weapons nonetheless – 1,500 rifles and 45,000 rounds of ammunition. They had been run into Howth Harbour on board a yacht owned by that most singular of beings – a passionate Irish Nationalist who just happened to be an Englishman. His name was Erskine Childers. If only there were only more like him. A handful of just men could rewrite history, change the world!

He threw the paper down and turned to his dusty cupboard. A hunk of cold fat bacon sat on a greasy plate. He cut a thick slice, threw it to Blackie who leaped to catch it and wolf it down. Then Jimmy took a few potatoes from a sack, washed them and put them down to boil in the black pot hanging from the crane. He located his two remaining eggs and put them aside. He would scramble them when the potatoes were done.

He had work this evening if the rain cleared – drilling in the Clonshule woods. It was easy now that Wallace was in England and his bailiffs redundant. He thought about Wallace bitterly, the planter thug who had raped his friend. He had wanted to kill him that night in Dublin when he had waylaid him, but had pulled back at the last moment in fear for his own soul. He knew he would never be able to justify it in confession. Without remorse – and there would be none – he would never receive absolution.

Priests would shrive you for killing in war, but never for revenge. The result was that the bugger Wallace was lame and would be out of the war. He had inadvertently done him a mighty service.

'You have a convoluted sense of humour!' he told the picture of the Sacred Heart on the opposite wall.

Outside the rain was drumming on the galvanised roof of his turf shed and gushing down the drainpipe to the overflowing rainwater barrel. Winter was coming. He looked up through the rafter at his thatch; it was still sound, would last another season. He had a rifle there, wrapped in oilcloth.

'Divil a drilling we'll be doing tonight,' he conceded aloud. He wondered how many of the men would turn up anyway, now that war fever had gripped them and they were going into the British army to fight for a shibboleth.

He looked around for his book of Blake's poetry to assuage his anguish and found it on the windowsill by the churn. He resumed his seat by the hearth, checked that the spuds were boiling and opened the book. He had marked his place with a small snap of Ellen, one he had 'borrowed' from her aunt's collection one day when the old lady was not looking.

It was half profile, a delicate young girl with her hair down her back.

'God bless you, my darling love,' he whispered and his calloused hand gently touched the portrait, lingering on her hair.

# Chapter 26

*Dublin, 1916*

The war was eighteen months old, and already so many of the young lads Ellen had taught had gone away. The conflict had touched even Balcarragh in more ways than one, reminding her that they were not, in fact, cut off from the wider world. Because of the war, the price of food had risen steeply, making the farm more lucrative. But the Germans had not invaded Ireland, as was rumoured to have been their intent after the Zeppelin raid on Norfolk in January the previous year. They were sufficiently occupied on the Western Front, the horror of which had come home to Ireland as hospital ships with Irish casualties had begun arriving at Kingstown. In fact, the reality of the conflict had been brutally apparent for the first time when the transatlantic liner, *Lusitania*, had been torpedoed off Kinsale, with the loss of more than 1,500 passengers. The newspapers had filled with pathetic pictures of survivors, and the inquest had condemned Germany for 'wholesale murder before the tribunal of the civilised world'.

'Wouldn't surprise me if that ship was carrying munitions,' Brendan had mused at the time. 'Look at the scale of the explosion!'

Brendan said that nothing would surprise him anymore. The waste of heroism in Gallipoli, the hell of Verdun, the young lives lost in their millions. How could Europe ever recover? No. This war was a blunder of the first magnitude, a crime on the young.

He's a kind of pocket Cassandra, Ellen thought. He sees things and he's powerless. But he cannot see me.

Tonight Brendan was having a bridge party. Father Devlin, the dentist, John Curry and the doctor, Des MacGrath, were all due at eight. Ellen had made a batch of scones in case they wanted tea, but Brendan knew they would only be interested in *uisce beatha* – the water of life. He checked the sideboard and found he still had two bottles of Jameson.

The doctor and dentist arrived in a motor; the parish priest came in his trap. Although she was not to be involved in the evening's entertainment, Ellen greeted her guests. Hers was the woman's domain – the kitchen and the baby. She would have loved to have been a part of tonight's lively, witty company, and when the men were installed and mellow with laughter, she listened outside the parlour door, wondering what conversation so enthralled them. Máire Ní Suibhne caught her at it and muttered with a laugh, '*Tá siad go léir cosúil le paistí*!' – 'they're all like children' – and then looked stricken because she knew that her mistress had overheard.

She means that *I'm* like a child, Ellen thought, a lonely child listening at doors. If Brendan had caught her eavesdropping, she asked herself bitterly, would he have sent her to bed early? But she refused the usual sense of exclusion. She had something special to look forward to. They were going on holiday soon, she and Brendan, for the Easter break, to wonderful Dublin which she had not seen for years.

In the warm lamplit parlour, Brendan poured whiskey for his guests and the talk turned to the war.

'God moves in mysterious ways,' the doctor said, shaking his head. 'Who will believe in the old class structure after this? The self-serving frailties of authority are being stripped bare!'

'Is that why the Church condemns war?' the dentist asked innocently and bid two no trump.

Brendan was partnering the parish priest and contained his smile.

But Bernie Devlin ignored the bait. 'Off to Dublin for Easter, Brendan?' he said, raising his eyes from his cards.

'Yes. Ellen wants to celebrate my birthday with a bit of a holiday.'

'Good idea. You're a young man yet, so make the most of it!'

'Fifty years young on Easter Sunday!' Brendan replied lugubriously.

In fact it had taken a fair amount of work on Ellen's part to get Brendan to agree to an Easter break. 'How often will you turn fifty?' she had demanded. And when did we last have some time together?' Ellen longed for anything that would take her away from Balcarragh for a while, that would take her to Dublin.

'A second honeymoon?' he said sentimentally. 'We can wander around like young sweethearts.'

Ellen wondered at this. She and Brendan had never been 'sweethearts' in its conventional sense and it seemed rather late now to create something between them that should have been there from the beginning. But still, he had mentioned it. So perhaps he wanted it too, however covertly – the intimacy and tenderness for which she hungered. She was more than her function of wife, mother, homemaker and teacher – however comprehensive these functions might be. I was Ellen Healy long before I ever became Mrs Brendan Kennedy, she thought. And somewhere, beneath all that exterior of unyielding self-sufficiency, Brendan must be human; he must want love.

And to her delight, her persuasion had worked.

'If you're so keen on it, *a stóirín*, sure why not? Hughie is a big boy now and Máire is competent.'

*

A few days later saw Ellen seated in a first-class compartment, watching the stationmaster raise his flag. Except for Paddy, the Cloncappal platform was empty. Paddy had driven them to the train and was now taking last-minute instructions from his employer through the open window. The engine gave a sudden cough and belched smoke. Paddy stepped back and Brendan raised his hand in farewell.

'There'll be smuts on everything, Brendan!' Ellen cried as the train lurched. 'Close the window!'

Her husband reached for the leather strap and pulled up the pane. He dislodged a black speck from his cuff, sat down and regarded his wife.

'Well, here we are, Ellen, off to Dublin's fair city! Just the two of us!'

His mouth twitched a little whimsically. He took out his book, *Essex in Ireland*, an account of Queen Elizabeth's unlucky favourite and his disastrous campaign in Ireland. Elegant and stern, he did not look at all like a man in search of romance. Ellen looked at the wiry hairs on the back of his hands, the cuffs of his white shirt, so carefully ironed by Máire and now besmirched by smuts, the sheen of gold cuff links. She caught her own dim reflection in the glazed picture of Glendalough opposite – a young woman in a cream, tailor-made costume, with a matching hat in which two feathers slanted at a fashionable angle. No one would ever think to look at me, she thought, that I am racked by increasingly violent emotions. She had gone to a great deal of trouble to look stylish for this trip. But Brendan had barely noticed, although he had looked sideways at her in the trap as though conscious of her suddenly as a separate being.

'You're looking very smart. I hope we can keep the rain off that nice outfit!' Then he had opened his book and was absorbed.

The train was gathering speed, laborious puffs replaced by rhythmic pounding. Raindrops hit the windows and dribbled down the glass. Ellen pressed her nose against the pane. Through the trees she caught a glimpse of Paddy driving the trap home along the boreen that led to the main road. In a moment he was out of sight among the trees. What age was Paddy? Forty, fifty? Older? He was coy on the subject of his age. The county was full of bachelors who lived out their lives alone, who worked for a pittance and spent their evenings at the pub. There was no industry and few jobs. Emigration had continued since the Famine and Ireland was emptying.

The green countryside, the fields and stone walls, the grazing sheep and cattle, the whitewashed thatched cottages, all flew by to staccato thunder.

She took from her bag her novel by Mr Wells, *The War of the Worlds*, currently on loan from the library, but her mind was not on the text; she was thinking of little Hughie and hoping he would not fret. She was also wondering when she might broach to Brendan the question of money. She had none and needed some for shopping. But even though it was her own money – she had earned it after all – she hated having to ask for it. She would mention it later, she decided, and turned her thoughts to the capital.

How much would Dublin have changed? The world had rattled on without her now for years; even the war, although nearly two years old, had left them relatively untouched. She and Brendan looked on from a distance, avidly devouring newspapers. Deirdre's letters from Dublin painted the picture of a city ill at ease with itself.

*Some of our friends have received police notices under the Defence of the Realm Act, requiring them to leave Ireland, and live in Britain where their activities can be more easily monitored. They have refused, and are now in prison.*

*There is a feeling of almost religious fervour among those of the Volunteers who have declined to enlist. The authorities treat them as a joke, as overgrown boy scouts and let them march and drill. They are afraid of drying up enlistings, and like to believe the Volunteers' only purpose is the defence of the country in the event of invasion. Your brother is like a cat on hot bricks. We hope to marry in October, but I am wary of making too many plans just yet.*

*Various London Irish have come home, escaping conscription, to join the Volunteers. Count Plunkett is providing them with lodgings at his place in Kimmage. Among them is a young post office worker from Clonakilty called Mick Collins. It's good to have someone to talk to about home. There'll be a parade of the Volunteers on Easter Sunday. You can watch it if you like and after that the day will be ours.*

Brendan looked up at his wife, saw her book in her lap and her eyes fixed dreamily on the countryside.

'Does Mr Wells bore you?'

'No. But I get a headache if I read while the train is moving. I prefer to think.'

'Weighty thoughts?' he asked whimsically, lifting his grey eyebrows.

She smiled automatically, shook her head and reached for the string bag in which she had her knitting. It was a pullover for Brendan, and as it needed only a little more work she had brought it with her to finish on the journey. She purled the last few rows, knotted the yarn and smoothed out the completed piece on her lap.

'There!' she said. 'I just have to make it up and you'll be able to wear it in Dublin.'

Brendan looked up from his book.

'It's kind of you, *a stóir*.' He twitched his nose as he sometimes did when he joked and added slyly, 'I'll knit you one for your birthday in September. You'll be thirty, after all, and in need of woollies!'

Ellen really laughed this time. But the word 'birthday' suddenly conjured another birthday – already almost half her lifetime ago. It surfaced of its own accord, fresh as yesterday, images of a blue dress and a young Englishman who had kissed her hand. Brendan chuckled, went back to his reading and left her to the past.

Ellen caught her breath at the intensity of the person she had been then, a girl-woman on the threshold of life. Oh Lord, what romance did I not invest in Guy's little ring. Silly child that I was! Silly child that I still am … She knew a secret part of her thrilled to it yet, despite all the trouble it had brought in its wake, and wondered had her aunt really been right. Would it never have worked?

But what it was to have felt so deeply. It was as though she had touched the quick of existence, the meaning of everything. Where was Guy now? Presumably at the war. Where? France? Belgium? The thought of him lying injured in some filthy trench brought such desolation that she had to blink back the tears. She looked at her husband and went back to completing the pullover.

Dublin came in a few hours. Ellen felt the old excitement as the train chugged into Kingsbridge. In the hiss of breaking steam, the station was alive with arrivals and departures, busy people with their minds on the Easter weekend, uniformed soldiers heading off to enjoy themselves, indifferent to the acrid smoke that clung to everything.

Brendan alighted first with their suitcase and helped her down. She craned her neck to see if there was any sign of Deirdre and Harry who were supposed to be meeting them.

'There's Deirdre!' Ellen cried. 'I don't see Harry yet, but Dee is waving.'

She ran down the platform, embraced her old friend, aware as she put her arms around her that Deirdre was thinner, and that her face was strangely grave.

'Harry sends his excuses, Ellen. Something came up.'

In a few minutes the three were in a hansom cab, clopping through the rainy quays, Brendan commenting on the great gates of the Guinness brewery and the massive green dome of the Four Courts. Ellen was silent, remembering this city from her two precious years here, when everything lay ahead. It seemed to her now that too much had happened in too short a time. Then she reminded herself that she was getting on, that her life was too full for nostalgia and that she should be grateful. She had a little darling at home and a good husband. She was a lucky woman.

She compared her lot with Deirdre's, who was still unmarried, and who now sat beside her in sporadic bursts of conversation – How was Hughie? How was school? How was the farm? – followed by lapses into apparent preoccupation. She was still teaching in that private school, which paid so badly, and still waiting for Harry whom she so desperately loved. But at least they were aiming at an October wedding.

Ellen squeezed her friend's hand, 'It's wonderful to see you. I can't believe it's more than two years.'

She realised with astonishment that Deirdre's hand was heavily calloused. 'What have you been doing, Dee? Scrubbing floors?' she asked with a laugh, holding up one of her friend's hands and inspecting it.

'It's just a bit of wear and tear from consorting with firearms,' Deirdre said, withdrawing her hand and looking at her levelly. '*Cumann na mBan*, which as you know is the women's branch of the Volunteers, is officially unarmed, but many of us train in firearms nonetheless.'

Ellen gasped and Brendan looked appalled.

'Unsuitable business for women!' he said.

'Tomorrow's parade that you mentioned in your letter,' Ellen asked, 'will you be taking part as well as Harry?'

Deirdre nodded. 'He was sorry he couldn't come to the station and said to give you his love. He'll see you later if he can.'

'Well that shouldn't overtax him.' Ellen joked, 'seeing as we're staying in your lodgings.'

They were approaching Eden Quay. The newsboys were shouting their wares. A headline placard read *Arms Seized.* Brendan thumped on the roof for the cabbie to stop, let down the window and bought a copy of the *Dublin Evening Mail.* He scanned the paper quickly, before folding it so that he could read page 8.

'Arms from Germany?' he said in a disbelieving voice and looked at Deirdre as though she were personally responsible. 'If they were intended for the Volunteers, as I presume they were, I think you and Harry and the rest of your friends had all better look to your hideouts! You have pushed it too far too fast!'

Deirdre paled, a visible whitening that drained her face of life. She snatched the paper from Brendan's hands.

'Read it out loud!' Ellen demanded.

Deirdre bit her lip and obeyed.

*A sensation was caused in Tralee this evening by the announcement that a collapsible boat containing a large quantity of arms and ammunition was seized about 4 o'clock at Carrahane Strand by the Ardfert police. In close vicinity to the boat, a stranger of unknown nationality was arrested and is detained in custody.*

*Where the boat came from or for whom the arms were intended is at present unknown. The authorities, police, military and naval, have been communicated with and further sensational developments are expected.*

Deirdre handed the paper back to Brendan but did not meet his eyes.

'Well … Deirdre?' he said in a low voice, 'Are you going to enlighten us?'

'Enlighten you? I am as much in the dark as you are! Despite your rather flattering notions, I do not run the Volunteers. The Supreme Military Council does that, so you should address yourself to them. Anyway,' she added, 'the business in Kerry might be nothing to do with us.'

# Chapter 27

Captain Guy Forrister shut the door and looked around his borrowed Dublin rooms. One of his fellow officers, Frederick Duggan (Duggy), who had been at Neuve Chapelle with him, had offered his rooms to him for his Dublin stay. On his arrival, he had found the caretaker and been furnished with a set of keys.

Duggy, a Corkman, had been a medical student at the Royal College of Surgeons in Dublin at the outbreak of war. His old rooms were almost diagonally across the Green from the college doors, and his father – an eminent surgeon – had kept them on against his son's return. Or as a talisman against his return, Guy thought, aware of how much superstition informed everyone these days.

The drawing room, lined with bookcases, contained a chesterfield suite, a desk, a leather chair and a worn Turkey carpet. It had a white Adam fireplace of considerable elegance, complete with marble swags and Georgian brass firedogs.

The air in the bedroom was close and he pushed up the reluctant sash window. He took off his cap and greatcoat, lay gingerly on the bed and sighed with relief. He heard the sounds from the street – the scrape of trams, iron-shod hooves, turning of wheels, beep of a motor horn and cries of the newspaper urchins. I am back in Dublin, he thought; it is still here at any rate, more or less the same.

The wound he had sustained near Armentières was still tender; he had been lucky that it hadn't become infected, lucky too that he had not been affected by the mustard gas. His first wound had been at Mons, during the terrible retreat when the war had been barely four weeks old. The British Expeditionary Force had been heavily outnumbered – 6,000 badly trained young Germans against 1,600 British with Lee Enfield rifles that could deliver up to twenty-five aimed shots per minute, and Vickers submachine guns with an ammunition belt nine yards long. The British had been chased by a flood of Germans who had pushed all ahead of them by sheer force of numbers.

The men of the II Corps had seen a shining angel in the sky, which had halted the German Cavalry. But even Heaven seemed to have given up after that – no more angels, just the demons of suffering and death. His regiment – the Fourth Dragoon Guards – had been part of the 900-strong cavalry that had stopped the enemy advance and let the infantry get clear. They had done it despite the volumes of dust that made it impossible to see beyond the man in front, so that they had ridden with drawn sabres into carnage. He could still hear the screams of the horses and the cries of the men. He could still see the ground littered with corpses and feel the hot blood running into his boot. That had been his first wound, a thigh laceration, which had mercifully missed the femoral artery.

His second wound, taken at Neuve Chapelle, had missed his heart but smashed two ribs. It was deemed healed enough for him to go back to the fray in two weeks' time. While recuperating at Lindthorp, he thanked God every time he had looked at his nephew James – now nearly sixteen – that the boy was too still young to be swallowed by the madness. But what if it went on and on? It was bad enough for Sophie that Nigel was in Flanders. She was lucky to have a good manager in spry old Bill Gregory, and nearly all the work on the home farm was now done by women; there was even a woman farrier in the village! The world was changing fast and Guy did not know if he would recognise it when the war was done.

All he did know was that something indescribably evil was in progress; he could not distance himself from the sense of pointless calamity. The conflict into which he had so eagerly flung himself was nothing like the projection. Instead, Europe's young manhood was being systematically butchered. He had seen boys little older than James sent to die in their thousands in no man's land. He had seen lads of nineteen shot for cowardice, *pour encourager les autres*; although their comrades were only lads too, and their bravery in the main, was superhuman. As for the trenches, they had been propped up with sandbags and rows of rotting corpses that could not be moved, while the sated rats scuttled everywhere, and even sat on the men while they slept.

His own latest wounding was somewhat of a haze. He recalled the stench of death that morning, the smell of the latrines and the salty reek of blood. There had been a barrage the night before, but the dawn had been cold and silent, empty of birdsong, the new dead lying as though asleep. Making his way back from the latrine he had heard the crazed sounds of agony and realised that one of the men was up top, trapped. He peered above the parapet across the mudflat that had once been farmland, saw some blasted trees against the horizon and, a few yards from the trench, a private, curled up in a pool of congealed blood.

The round that opened up as he had stumbled across those few impossible yards had killed the boy, Private Fletcher from Hackney, who had only the day before been chuckling over a letter from home. He himself had heard nothing. There had been a cataclysmic sense of impact, then everything had stopped; the earth had tilted. He had felt himself as part of the wind, floating in a strange, universal hush, as though the war, the bloodshed and the suffering was only froth on Time's river, rolling by with serene indifference.

A week later they told him that the sentry had returned fire, providing cover under which they had managed to drag him back to relative safety. In the field hospital he had woken to find blue-grey eyes looking into his. As from a distance he heard something unintelligible about his wound and other hospital matters, mundane and uninteresting compared with the enigma before him, Ellen's face swimming in and out of focus, as though he were looking at her from under water.

'How beautiful you are, Ellen.'

'I'm not Ellen, dear.'

He had heard the smile in her English voice. The world had come into sharper focus: a young VAD in her grey uniform with white collar and cuffs. The pain in his chest had gripped him tighter and he had groaned.

'We'll give you something for that. You've had an operation, shrapnel in your lung, broken ribs. But you're lucky. They'll be sending you home to get better.'

So, he had gone home to Lindthorp. Sophie, missing Nigel who was in Belgium, had wept with relief when he had arrived, and had later confessed her terror for her husband whose letters came weekly, full of chat about everything except the war.

As Guy became stronger, his young nephew James, on mid-term break from school, had accompanied him on a country walk by the river, posing eager questions that Guy could not bear to answer.

'But you are not really describing anything, Uncle!' the boy exclaimed eventually in a disappointed voice. 'You keep changing the subject!'

It was then the first episode had happened. Someone in the nearby woods had fired a shotgun and had somehow opened up the German barrage across no man's land, conjuring the stench, the emptiness of any dimension that had to do with humanity.

Guy felt his body shake like a flag in a gale and had to sit down suddenly on the riverbank. James had stood beside him, staring at his shaking hands.

'It's only Burgess shooting rabbits, Uncle! It's all right …'

Guy had lain on the bank until normality returned, trying to pretend he was just tired. But his nephew was looking at him with a troubled gaze.

'Sorry old chap,' Guy whispered. 'I don't know what got into me.'

The boy had shrugged, but he had been quiet for the rest of the day, regarding his uncle from sombre, questioning eyes. Guy prayed it would not return, that altered state when all he heard was the shells, and all he knew was that it could be borne no longer.

'It's the war,' he had told James that evening when they were alone together after dinner, dismissing it as of no consequence.

'I think that says it all, Uncle.'

A powerful sense of bonding had been born in Guy. He had envied his brother his fine, compassionate son.

The nostalgic hankering to go back to Ireland had begun as his strength had returned. His youth was still there; he needed to taste it again, to rediscover a way of life removed from the hell that was destroying Europe. But he would not be going to Clonshule and had no inclination to do so. His friendship with Bertie Wallace had ended dramatically. Bertie, lame from mysterious injuries sustained some years before in Dublin, now had a desk job in the Admiralty. Guy had met him by chance at the RAC Club in Pall Mall where, over a drink, he had been made privy to the success of his old friend's investments. A tipsy Bertie had boasted of how the money from the sale of the Clonshule estate had been invested in armaments stocks well before the war.

'I saw it coming! Don't tell me I don't have a good nose, old boy!'

Guy had thought of the reek of Evil, the bloody dismembered limbs, the femurs that propped up the trenches and the youngsters who stared blindly at the sun. They only send the bravest and best, he thought bitterly, and they turn them into clods of earth.

Although Bertie had married the Honourable Clarissa Vaughan, and had a two-year-old son, his penchant for sexual dalliance had apparently remained unabated. He confided to Guy that he kept a mistress in Chelsea.

'Best bit of fluff since the Murphy Puss!'

'Don't refer to Miss Murphy like that, Wallace! She's a respectable lady with her own business.'

'Is she, by Jove? What kind of business? Probably owes it all to my ten pounds!'

The guffaw showed Bertie's gold fillings. It seemed to Guy to be a challenge, like a monkey raising his mane.

'How dare you speak of that lady like that!'

Anger, hot and careless, surged in him and, with a blow that winded him, he had knocked his old friend to the ground. Other club members had intervened to separate them.

But Guy, although enjoined to apologise, had not apologised. He did not particularly care if Bertie sought revenge. He did not much care about anything. The thousand-yard stare of famished men, the cursing of guns, had changed him. He had become old, he told himself, old and tired and intolerant of cruelty.

Now there was a knock on the sitting-room door. Guy raised himself on his elbow and called, 'Yes?'

The heavy mahogany door opened. A girl in a black dress came tentatively into the room. She had an armful of sheets and towels.

'The caretaker asked me to leave these with you, Sir.'

'Wait!' Guy said, levering himself from the bed and searching for a shilling. He went into the sitting room and handed her the tip.

'Thank you, Sir,' she replied in her rich brogue that was so full of yesterdays.

'What is your name?'

'Eileen, sir.'

'Thank you, Eileen.'

The girl withdrew. In his head Guy rearranged the spelling of Eileen. Slowly and carefully he added and subtracted. Ellen. He thought about her for while, got up and went to the window that overlooked St Stephen's Green. But the little flower-seller no longer plied her wares on the pavement. She had been swallowed by history. To think he had given Ellen a few violets and then walked away. We are offered what is ours, he thought after a moment, but either we fail to recognise the gift, or we think, like fools, that it will come again.

He looked at himself in the mirror, thin, pale, with a few premature grey hairs. Ellen was gone, like the flower-seller. Harry too? Had he made it thus far through the war? Had he joined up, the young man who had assured him with such covert intensity that he wanted to fight for Ireland? Was he too dissolved in the French mud?

'Enough sentiment, old boy,' he told himself aloud. 'You're in Dublin. Time to look up an old friend.'

He donned his jacket, buttoned it, put on his cap and straightened to a military bearing. Then he hurried down the flowing staircase of the Georgian house and let himself out into St Stephen's Green. He would take a walk. There was a hat shop he was determined to visit in Chatham Street.

# Chapter 28

Franny was attending to her window display prior to closing. Business was good; the war had restrained flamboyance, in hats as in everything, but had pumped money into the economy. No woman would be seen out of doors without a hat, and there were more and more women working outside the home. In addition, the pay sent home by soldiers on the Western Front was making a huge difference to the spending power of the ordinary Dubliner. In fact, business had become so good that Fran had been able to buy out the lease from Liam. Dear Liam, who had so kindly set her up after Hannah's birth, using his inheritance from his mother.

'A purely business arrangement!' he had insisted. 'I know a good opportunity when I see one.'

The opportunity in question had been the lease on a dusty little shop in Chatham Street with a big window.

'You have been talking of how you would like a chance to "finish" hats yourself,' he'd said. 'Now you can! Alma will teach you bookkeeping, and in no time you'll be a lady of substance.'

Franny could not refuse his offer. With the shop went a three-room apartment overhead.

The project had taken a huge amount of work, firstly in getting the shop into shape and then in stubbornly following her dream.

Alma had sent a nursemaid for the baby, insisting, 'I don't want to hear one word of objection. You can't run a shop and a baby!' She had also suggested the rather outlandish name for the stylish new venture – Du Barry.

'Wasn't she some kind of royal French mistress?' Fran had asked doubtfully.

'Sure let her,' Liam had advised. 'You won't be confused with her!'

When the shop had been given a chic French décor, it was almost unrecognisable. Advertisements had brought in the first customers; word of mouth had done the rest. Franny had put all her energy into it and the venture had finally paid off. She now employed a full-time assistant and had a liquid bank balance, even some left after paying Liam back. But how long would the bonanza last? The blessed peace would come, but with it demobilisation and, perhaps, recession.

Liam said he was glad to be out of the business. 'Money grubbing gives me a headache. Paint and canvas is all I ever want from life!'

But paint and canvas had been sidelined by the war, for Liam had enlisted in the first fever of enthusiasm, to the great chagrin of his father and sister and Franny's own anxiety.

As the war had progressed Franny's business had begun to run itself. She had sent Hannah to a private school in Donnybrook. Mother and daughter spent their weekends at Rathcormac, keeping Alma company and helping with her now sporadic At Homes, but these ended abruptly with her father's sudden death. In any case, the war had stymied the thrust towards women's suffrage. In England it had been shelved for the duration.

One year into the war, Liam had been discharged because of chronic asthma, a condition he had had as a child, which had returned savagely in the trenches. The doctors had not been optimistic about his condition, forecasting a shortened life.

Once home, however, Howth, the sea air and familiar

surroundings had eased his tortured struggle for breath; and Hannah had begun her enchantment of him. The little girl would watch as he worked, stretching herself on the floor of his studio among the canvases, the brush he had given her in her hand, the watercolours ready for the bright splashes on paper.

'This is Mother!' she would sing, as a pink head was painted above an amorphous blue body. 'And this is Liam, and this is Auntie Alma … and this is Pixie … and these are Pixie's kittens … and this is water beetle.' This last she had met in the garden and kept in a milk bottle half-filled with water.

'One day, young lady,' Liam told her, inspecting her work and realising with a sense of shock that it had life, 'you will be the toast of Dublin's art world. You must work!'

'Painting is fun …' Hannah sang back. 'Is not *work*!'

Liam was refining his own technique. He was now exhibiting, and his portraits had begun to achieve something approaching notoriety. It might not be always flattering to be painted by Liam Mulhall, but it was always you. But Fran would not let him paint her. If he did, she thought, he would really see me. I would not be able to hide from him anymore.

Nowadays Franny imagined her life as a journey towards self-sufficiency. She dared not dream of marriage. She loved Hannah and was going to make a future for her, leave her in a position that she would never have to depend on anyone. It was working so far, and it had to continue working. She had no safe haven to which she could return; she had broken all ties with her family and although she had written to Ellen two years ago almost begging to be let back into her life, the answer from her husband had been painfully categorical.

And lovely Clare, who had tried to send her packing, and who had come to the shop one day to seek forgiveness, was dead. Her second baby, another son, had killed her, and had died with her. Frank, flying from his grief, had joined up at the beginning of the war, leaving little Matty in the care of his married sister.

Her sister's death had shocked Franny and tortured her with remorse. She had written to her mother on hearing of it, angry that she had not been notified, but desperate to heal the breach between them before mortality made that too impossible. Her mother, however, had remained silent, the deadly accusing silence of the estranged and outraged parent. How did it come to this? Fran often asked herself.

She had never imagined that Harry could disappear from her life, but he had taken her at her word and did not darken her door. All she knew about him was that he was teaching at St Enda's School. She had met him only once since their lunch in Jammet's, bumping into him at College Green, when he had told her Ellen was pregnant. She still saw him sometimes, but from a distance. She would watch the Volunteers when they were on parade, lose herself in the small crowd that gathered in Sackville Street, her heart swelling as he marched past in military formation – green uniform, slouch hat, rifle at the ready.

There would presumably be a parade tomorrow. But tomorrow was Easter Sunday and she had promised Liam and Alma that she and Hannah would spend the weekend in Rathcormac.

She was suddenly aware of a shadow outside on the pavement. It was a British officer, and he seemed to be looking for something because he craned his neck to look at the sign above the door. When he gazed in the window the light was behind him and she could not see his face. The bell tinkled as the door opened. She came from the window. Perhaps he was looking for directions; it was unusual for a man to come alone into a milliner's.

'May I help you, sir?'

Guy looked at Franny with a whimsical smile. He was thinking how strange it was to find her in this bright little shop filled with ladies' headgear, wedged between a pawnbrokers and a chemist, and decorated like his tragic great-aunt's boudoir at Fontebelle.

Franny stared back at him, drew herself up coldly as his gaze intensified.

'My dear Franny, it is a delight to see you again.'

She put out her hand and colour flooded her face.

'Guy Forrister! You shouldn't go around wearing military caps if you want to be recognised!'

How pale and thin, he's got, she thought, her heart filling with pity. How dreadfully haggard. 'Would you like some tea?' she asked, 'I was just about to close up the shop.'

In Franny's sitting room above the shop, Guy removed his cap and sat down at one end of a capacious settee covered in cushions and childish drawings. A doll with a plump porcelain face, ringlets, a satin dress with lace and flounces, sat at the other end and stared at him vacantly, her hat askew.

'Here, let me clear those out of your way!' Franny said. She hastily picked up the drawings and the doll, put them on the sideboard, then reached for the scuttle and threw coal on the fire.

'And to think I was afraid you had changed,' he said.

But she had changed. The mischief was gone. Instead she was a sombre young woman in a dark brown dress with a white collar, attractive certainly, although her large eyes were smudged with shadows. This person was the Murphy Puss, if Bertie was to be believed.

'There's sherry somewhere if you prefer.'

'Tea would be perfect.'

She disappeared into the adjoining kitchen and Guy was left to examine his surroundings.

His eyes returned to the doll, who sat examining him from the sideboard, then his gaze moved to the walls and ceiling. The room had evidently been divided in two for a partition ran the length of it, slicing into the cornicing. The walls were painted white, but the pictures filling every available space gave the place a Bohemian ambience. He was delighted to see that one of them was a watercolour of the garden at Kilcrannagh; he recognised the pergola, although the two women in straw hats picking flowers were anonymous.

'You have talent, Franny!' he said when she returned with a tray.

'Flatterer! I have a small accomplishment. Talent is a horse of another colour.' She looked at him, 'Milk, sugar? I should remember I suppose, but I haven't taken tea with you for quite some time.' She handed him the cup and saucer, saw that he winced as he stretched for it.

'Were you hurt?' she whispered.

'Just a scratch.' He gestured back to the water colours. 'But seriously, I never realised you were such an artist.'

Franny accepted the diversion. She followed his gaze to the display on the wall and laughed. 'Only one is mine. The one of the garden. The female figures are supposed to be Ellen and my mother.'

'I see.'

'You know Ellen is married?'

He nodded.

'She is a mother now. Her son must be nearly two.'

Of course she would be a mother by now, Guy told himself, suppressing a pang. What did you expect?

'He is hardly the naïf artist. Her husband?' he asked with a smile, gesturing to the pages of drawings she had left on the sideboard. Franny saw the pain in him, and his avid curiosity.

'Of course not. The drawings were done by a nine-year-old.'

'Indeed! They have a certain panache.' What nine year old? he wondered.

Franny measured him for a moment, but vouchsafed no further information. She pointed to a landscape in exquisite watercolours and added, 'Now that artist has real talent. He captures the elemental nature of things. He does mostly portraits ... He's a friend of mine.'

Guy nodded. He knew all about the elemental nature of things. He could tell her about the crashing shells that obliterated the senses, the relentless boom of death; he could tell her about the mud slicked with human guts; he could tell her that he was going back to it and that the madness would go on and on and on until not one single young man was left to walk the earth.

Franny bent to the hearth to poke the fire. Flames licked the coals. She dropped the tongs and it clattered to the hearth.

A cold sweat broke out on Guy. His hands began to shake. He dropped the tea cup. It rolled onto the carpet, spilling its contents. He hunkered into his shoulders, hearing the barking of the guns, the cries of his men, and he saw the white face of Private Fletcher, his eyes filled with blood. His whole body trembled; his legs jerked to a rhythm of their own as though they were on strings.

Franny sat beside him and took his hands.

'I'm … sorry,' he said, spitting the words through chattering teeth, 'so … so … sorry.' And he jerked on. Franny's eyes were bright with tears.

'It's all right, dear Guy,' she whispered. 'It takes other people like this too.' She wept suddenly; her tears dripped onto his hands.

Guy knew he was cursed. His shaking subsided. He thanked Franny, apologising again. He was very tired, he said. He should go. He thought of his bed in Duggy's rooms. He wondered bitterly if he would make the short distance without something else setting him off. He reached into his pocket, took out his pristine handkerchief and handed it to Franny.

'Who gave you my address?' she asked, as she blew her nose.

'Harry. Before the war. But I shouldn't have come, Franny. I'm a wreck.'

'What else would you be?' she cried, handing him back his handkerchief. 'After what you've been through? What else could you be and stay human?' She dropped her voice and added in a whisper, 'This is what happens to people when they are raped!'

He looked at her white face in silence. A terrible thought came to him.

'Raped?' he whispered.

She bent her head. He did not need to question her. In the

old days they used to hang them, he thought. Nowadays they give them desk jobs and safe passage through the most terrible conflict the world has ever seen.

'I'm so sorry he got away with it,' he said.

'He met with a misfortune,' Franny whispered. ' I don't know of course that it had anything to do with me.'

'A misfortune? Oh Fran, it is his lameness that is saving his life!'

They heard the voices outside on the pavement – a child's piping voice and a man's – the sound of a key in the door and steps on the stairs. A little girl in a brown coat, button boots and velvet tam o'shanter rushed into the room and, seeing Guy, drew back uncertainly. A young man with a dark moustache appeared behind her. He seemed out of breath.

'You win, young lady …'

Guy rose to his feet.

'Guy, this is Liam Mulhall, the artist whose work you have been admiring,' Franny said. 'And this,' she added, in a low, proud voice, gesturing to the child and raising her chin, 'is my daughter, Hannah.'

She looked at Liam and her daughter. 'This is Captain Guy Forrister … an old friend.'

# Chapter 29

'Captain Forrister?' Liam echoed, looking curiously at Franny when Guy was gone. 'You never mentioned him before?'

'He used to visit us in Kilcrannagh. Years ago.' She lowered her voice, 'Unfortunate man has a touch of the shakes. He went wobbly when I dropped the tongs.'

'Poor bloke! Was he the friend of …' he added, frowning as his voice petered away when he saw Hannah staring at him.

'Is there a secret?' she asked, widening her big brown eyes. 'Who is he a friend of?'

'No one darling.'

Hannah frowned. 'Can I go to stay with Cissie? She said I could stay the night.'

Cissie was Hannah's friend from school.

'No darling.'

'That's two no's!' Hannah said gravely. 'But it is Easter!'

'You are going to Rathcormac with your mother and me,' Liam said with a smile.

Hannah's lips parted expectantly. Her mother nodded and added, 'For Sunday and Monday!'

'That's great!' Hannah whooped.

The child looked angelic above the black velvet of her collar, her laughing dark eyes vivid in her pale face. Her mother thought how easy it was to please her. But how long would it be, she wondered, before she insisted on answers to her questions? Hannah had been told her father was dead, and that he and her mother had never married.

'Poor Mother!' Hannah sometimes muttered to herself, imagining how her young love had died before her wedding. 'Poor Mother …'

But whenever Hannah tried to engage her mother in remembrance of this romantic tragedy, whenever she fished for the details, she was always left with the sense that there was something dreadful associated with it. The absence of any picture of her father, any spontaneous mention of his name, reinforced the sense of some terrible shame. And she also knew by now how her mother's unwed status made both of them outsiders.

'Don't you want to watch the Volunteers parading tomorrow, Mother?' she said suddenly.

Franny shook her head. 'No darling.'

'We could go to Howth later if you like, give you time to see some of the parade,' Liam said.

Franny's heart filled with gratitude. Liam knew perfectly well why she liked to watch the Volunteers' parade, yet he never attempted to dissuade her. He had been her friend for many years. She knew he loved her and she wondered at his infinite patience.

'Sunday is ours,' she said. 'Easter Monday too.'

Hannah hung up her hat and coat, then went to rescue Daisy, her doll, from the sideboard, straightened her hat and smoothed out her satin dress. Daisy had been a birthday present from Liam. Franny poured Liam a sherry and he perched on the end of the sofa recently vacated by Guy.

'Isn't it extraordinary,' he said, 'that these parades are tolerated. Even though the Volunteers shipped guns in at Howth two years ago they still have not been banned.'

'It suits the government to pretend it's all pantomime,' Franny said. 'They're afraid that if they ban them it will stop the men enlisting.'

Liam sighed. 'Maybe. But I can assure you that panto is better than war.'

Franny, remembering the old rifle stocks she had seen in the haggard all those years ago, remembering the fire in Harry's eyes, shook her head.

'It was never panto.'

'So you think it's building into something? You're worried for your cousin?' He said it gently, glancing at Hannah. But Hannah was absorbed in Daisy.

Franny hardly trusted herself to reply. The fatigue of the day's work, the emotionally charged meeting with Guy, the headache she had not managed to stave off, the thought of Harry involved in something covert and dangerous, were draining her. The silence was broken by Hannah's quiet, tentative voice.

'We could have a picnic tomorrow in Howth, Mamma? With Alma? And I could bring Daisy?'

Liam met Franny's eye. He laughed. 'Why not? If the weather is fine. And if it isn't, young lady, you are going to paint me a splendid picture!'

Hannah seemed pleased with these arrangements.

Franny looked at Liam. 'I need to lie down for a while,' she said. 'Do you mind?'

'I'll make some tea,' Liam said. 'What would you say to some well-turned toast? My supervisor here will help me. You have a nice nap and we'll wake you when everything's ready.'

Franny's bedroom was just off the sitting room and beside her small workroom where she trimmed her hats. She shared the room with Hannah. Once, when Hannah had been at school, and the shop had been closed for lunch, Liam had arrived with a bottle of wine, crusty fresh bread and pâté and, after lunch, had kissed her passionately and tried to carry her to bed. Franny's resistance had been so frantic that he had backed away, got up and walked around the room.

'I cannot tell you Fran, how much I wish you wouldn't shrink from me. I hate the presence of this Wallace fellow in our lives!' He paused and looked at her angrily. 'Flush him down the jakes, for the love of Jesus.'

'I'm not good enough for you,' Franny whispered. 'I'm damaged goods.'

Looking up she had met his angry glare.

'Christ woman, what is the matter with you? Don't ever, ever, let me hear you describe yourself as merchandise again!'

She lay back now, eyes closed, listening to the sounds from the street. Outside her protective walls, beloved dirty Dublin went about its Easter Saturday evening. Inside were the sounds of Liam's and Hannah's voices in the kitchen, and Hannah's sudden laugh.

There was a knock and Liam's head appeared around the door.

'*Madame est servie*! And when she hath supped her tay she might condescend to be driven to Rathcormac!'

'You should be an actor,' she said, and slid her feet off the bed.

The cab bringing Ellen, Brendan and Deirdre from Kingsbridge Station, stopped at the Victorian villa in Sandymount where Deirdre lived, and where she had procured lodgings for them for the Easter weekend. The house had heavy lace curtains and a flight of granite steps to a glossy black door. A neat border contained a drill of faded, desiccated daffs. Inside the gate, a ladies' bicycle was propped against the railings. The air smelled of the sea.

'So this is your home?'

Deirdre nodded. 'For the past four years. I have a small front bedroom. You will have a back room overlooking the garden – comfortable and quiet. The landlady is a Mrs Coughlan who lives next door. She's away this weekend, but you can pay Dehlia, who really runs the place.'

She put her key in the lock and opened the door. The hall had shellacked boards covered with a red runner, which continued up the stairs. A business-like maid in a white apron, linen over her arm, turned at the back of the hallway and came forward.

'Dehlia, these are my friends, Mr and Mrs Kennedy.' Deirdre turned to Ellen. 'This is Dehlia, who makes my life comfortable.'

Dehlia reddened. 'There's a note for you Miss … delivered an hour ago.' She went to the hall table, handed Dee a sealed envelope and produced a room key, which she handed to Brendan. 'Room number six. Would you like some tea, sir?'

'At the moment I'd much prefer forty winks,' Brendan replied. 'If the ladies don't mind.'

'Tea for two, Dehlia! Thank you!' Deirdre said briskly. She rapidly perused the note and thrust it into her pocket, adding, 'Bring the tray to my room. I don't have much time.'

Brendan and Ellen found their room. Brendan sat on the bed with a tired sigh. Ellen stood at the window and looked out at the back garden. It had lawn, shrubs and a brick path leading to a door that gave onto a laneway. She took off her hat, poured water into the porcelain basin and washed her face and hands.

'I'm going to Deirdre's room,' she said as she extricated from their luggage the small gifts she had brought with her – eggs carefully wrapped in a cardboard box, a cake of soda bread and a pound of country butter. Máire had insulated the latter in several sheets of greaseproof paper tied around with string. 'You have your snooze.' She crossed the landing and knocked on Deirdre's door.

Deirdre's room was indeed small. A brass bed took up one wall; against the other was a bow-fronted chest of drawers, on top of which a small vase sported a few tired daffs, a bookcase and a wardrobe. Books and periodicals were piled everywhere. The middle of the floor was filled by a small round table and two chairs. On the table were three neat piles of school copybooks.

'Don't mind the mess!' Deirdre said from behind a screen. 'Dehlia has strict instructions not to disturb anything. I'll be with you in a moment.'

She emerged from the screen and Ellen gasped. Deirdre was wearing an olive green military uniform, long jacket with some kind of brooch on the lapel, long skirt, striped tie and pale green shirt. Her face was still pale, but her whole demeanour reeked of purpose.

'This is my *Cumann* uniform.'

Ellen gulped. 'It's very … military! I brought you these, Dee,' she added lamely, holding out her gifts.

'You're a darling!'

The maid appeared with the tea tray. She evinced no surprise at the sight of Deirdre in military garb. Dee told her to take Ellen's gifts to the kitchen, with a warning not to let Mr Touhy gobble them up. Dehlia laughed and left.

'Who's Mr Touhy?'

'Another lodger! Greedy as sin!'

Deirdre cleared a space on the table, poured tea and handed the cup to Ellen. 'Milk, no sugar? Like the old days?' she asked.

'I'm speechless!' Ellen replied, taking the cup.

'By what?'

'By your air of masculine independence and competence. I knew you were in *Cumann na mBan*, but I never imagined you in uniform!'

'Doesn't it suit me?' Deirdre asked with a grin. 'Do I not personify the spirit of the age?'

She poured tea for herself, perched on the edge of the table and looked down at her friend. 'Ellen, if you had stayed in Dublin you would have joined the *Cumann* too and we would be sisters in arms.'

'You would convince a saint!' Ellen murmured, while inside her there suddenly whispered a longing for such freedom. 'But do you ever get time to go home?'

'No, girl!' She drank some tea and glanced at the clock. 'I have to go! I must present myself at headquarters – Liberty Hall. Sorry Ellen. That note I just got ...'

'Another of these famous meetings?'

Deirdre nodded. 'There's several today.' She sighed. 'I know you've only just got here. You'll have to forgive me. When you made your plans I didn't know something important would blow up.'

Ellen watched in consternation as Deirdre took a pistol from a drawer.

'What's that for?'

'It's a Browning automatic,' Deirdre replied in a pragmatic voice as she slipped it into her pocket. 'The women are not supposed to be armed, but some of us have our own pistols.'

'Deirdre!' Ellen cried. 'Where is Harry in all of this?'

Deirdre cast an eye on the door and whispered, 'I cannot explain. Ellen, I know you will not understand, but your coming this weekend has turned out to be a bad idea ... from everyone's perspective. You and Brendan ... really ... should go home.'

'Go home? We've just got here!'

'Yes I know. But I didn't realise ... I may not be back this evening, so don't wait up for me.' She hesitated and added in a whisper, 'Listen carefully ... on no account should either of you venture into the city tomorrow! On *no* account!'

'But it's Easter Sunday, Dee! Whyever not?'

Dee shook her head. She took a green slouch hat from her wardrobe shelf, put it on, fixed a hat pin and then she was gone. Ellen heard the front door close. She went to the window and watched Dee wheel her bicycle out the front gate, mount it and pedal away. She remained there for a few minutes after Deirdre had disappeared, staring into the street. Then she thought she might as well bring down the tea tray and save her friend that much bother. When she lifted it she saw a poem in Dee's writing among the papers on the table. She put the tray on a chair and picked up the piece of paper.

*I come of the seed of the people, the people that*
*sorrow,*
*That have no treasure but hope,*
*No riches laid up but a memory*
*Of an ancient glory.*

*I say to my people that they are holy, that they are*
*august despite their chains,*
*That they are greater than those that hold them, and*
*stronger and purer,*
*And I say to my people's masters: Beware,*
*Beware of the thing that is coming …*

Was Dee the author of this? She turned the page over and saw written on the other side – Mr. Pearse.

Ellen went back to Brendan and found him asleep, soft snores lifting his moustache. 'Brendan!' she whispered, repeating it urgently until he grunted and opened his eyes.

'I'm sorry, dear. Have I been dozing for long? Did you want to go out?' He pulled himself to a sitting position and added, 'Why are you looking like that?'

'Deirdre says we must not go into the city tomorrow!'

He gave a dry laugh, reached out and patted her hand. 'What an alarmist young friend you have! What has she been telling you?'

'Nothing specific … but a warning nonetheless.'

'Ellen,' he said, pulling himself off the bed, 'that little friend of yours is just looking for drama. You saw the way she was quick to claim she had trained in firearms!' He shook his head.

'Now I happen to *know* that the women's corps of the Volunteers is purely auxiliary. *No* firearms!'

Ellen bridled. She turned her face away. 'She would never accept it was "auxiliary",' she said in a low voice. 'She has a Browning automatic! I saw it myself. Why do you think women are fools?'

The question was angry and spontaneous. Even as she said it she knew that Brendan assumed female inferiority and drew stature from it. And, at that moment, she hated him for it.

'Fools? No! Gullible? Yes!' he replied reasonably, tapping his foot as he did when he thought he was being challenged. 'You shouldn't listen to nonsense!'

'Tomorrow will tell whether it's nonsense or not!' she replied angrily. 'But right now this gullible woman is going out for a walk and, as she is penniless, she would like some money!'

Brendan started visibly. 'What do you want money for? And you are not going out walking on your own. I absolutely forbid it!'

Ellen picked up her hat, and fixed it fiercely to her head before the mirror with two long hatpins. Then she reached for Brendan's jacket, which was draped over the back of a chair. She extracted his wallet, took out a fiver and put it into her pocket.

'*My* money,' she told him quietly, fixing him with a level gaze. 'I earned it, and as slavery was abolished early in the last century, I am going to have it. I am fully aware, even if you are not, how you like to keep me powerless!'

She put the fiver into her pocket, marched downstairs, picked up an umbrella in the hall, left the house and walked in a fury through Sandymount until she came to the sea. Then she leaned on the sea wall until her heart resumed its normal rhythm. 'I'm tired of bondage,' she muttered. 'I'm sick to death of having to watch what I say and what I do!'

She sighed. The weekend would not be a romantic idyll after all. Brendan might subscribe to sentiment, but he did not subscribe to romance. In fact, she told herself, he actively hated anything predicated on emotion. It was how he lived, safe from the stuff that drove humanity.

You could leave him, an internal voice prompted. You could pack your bags and come to Dublin. You would find work here; you could find Franny. You could join the *Cumann* and be with Deirdre …

It would mean I failed, she thought. And I can't leave my baby. If I tried to take him with me his father would recover him through the law. What rights, after all, does the law give me, compared to him? I am only his mother!

She felt the chill stone wall against her hands, the spitting rain driven against her umbrella so that she had to tighten her grip. The tide was out and the huge expanse of strand glistened in the evening light, marked here and there where lugworms had left sandy spirals. Sand pipers hopped and seagulls swooped, their wild screams echoing across the bay. In the distance she could make out the spires of Kingstown and, away against the horizon, the masts of a few ships. The wind blustered and knocked the breath from her. She held onto her hat.

Her mind reverted to what Deirdre had told her. Her anger abated and was replaced by questioning fear. She hoped they knew what they were doing. But then she reflected that Deirdre's life was fully lived; she had a profession, she was involved in the politics of the day, meeting the people who stirred the brew, in love with a man who loved her back. She would not have dished out a trenchant warning without reason, would not have indulged in empty dramatics. Brendan had dismissed her from habit; he was used to his word being the order of the day. But this time he didn't know what he was talking about. He hadn't seen the Browning automatic, or the pale intensity of Deirdre's face, or the poem: *Beware the thing that is coming.*

The fear clawed at her. Her brother and her friend, were involved in this. But what was it exactly? Some kind of demonstration with a patriotic message? Or something more, something desperate, something foolhardy? Didn't they know they were nothing to an imperial power which had never brooked the love of the Irish for their homeland, and which would not hesitate, if they went too far, to flush them away?

I need to see Harry. I need to find out what is going on. I will find this Liberty Hall and stop him before it is too late!

# Chapter 30

When he left Franny's shop, Guy retraced his steps to Grafton Street. Although still shaken and ashamed, he found himself wondering at the atmosphere in the city. His mind was racing and he decided to treat himself to a brandy and an early supper.

The street was being washed; the gutters overflowed. Last-minute shoppers were making their way home. He gave a sixpence to a begging urchin, bought the *Evening Mail* from a paper boy hoarse from shouting. A couple of officers passed him; like him, they were wearing field boots and jodhpurs. They exchanged crisp salutes. He hid his turmoil, his fear that he could no longer rely on the discipline of his body that years of military life had honed and toughened.

But it was the outrage Franny had endured that made him feel sick. He did not doubt for one moment that Wallace had forced himself on her, had fathered the little girl.

I have been a Jonah to that family! First I drag Harry on a fishing expedition where he nearly drowns, then I damn Ellen with my adolescent ardour and, as the *coup de grâce*, I introduce to little Franny the most unprincipled scoundrel I have ever met. No wonder Mrs Murphy kept me at arm's length! Women can smell peril. How wretched she must be at the way things have turned out.

Across the street he saw three young privates, home on leave, just a few of the 100,000 Irishmen who had gone out to fight for England. How long had they left to live? And he would be going back to it too. Would it ever end? Would quietude ever return? Ordinary mornings, ordinary evenings, sunlight without horror, birdsong in concert? Would he ever get back to Fontebelle?

When he reached O'Connell Bridge he stopped to look at the river. Upstream, the Halfpenny Bridge arched above the water and in the distance was the green dome of the Four Courts. Downstream was the beautiful Customs House which he had always admired, but what arrested his eye today was the building near it with a banner across its upper floor, which was sporting some kind of legend. Trying to make it out, he walked down the quay and in a couple of minutes found himself outside the large Georgian building. 'Head Office, Irish Transport And General Workers' Union' was written right across its front, but it was the words on the banner that made him stare: 'WE SERVE NEITHER KING NOR KAISER – BUT IRELAND!'

'That is Liberty Hall, Sir!'

A passing policeman was addressing him. The man wore the typical black London helmet and might have been confused for a bobby.

Guy gestured to the people entering and leaving the building, most of them in some sort of green uniforms, but not any uniforms he recognised. He could not help wondering what was happening on a quiet Easter Saturday that required so many uniformed people with such a naked sense of purpose.

'Who are these people?'

'Home Guard defence, y' know,' the bobby replied. 'They call themselves Citizens Army or Volunteers. Preparing for tomorrow's parade, Sir … while so many of our boys die at the Front!'

The policeman moved away and Guy made to follow, thinking

he would patronise the Butt Bar at the corner and buy that brandy. Obviously the authorities were au fait with this place and its activities. But still it left a sense of things being out of joint to see a nationalist banner over a door used by so many people in uniforms that were not British. He glanced around and saw a young woman striding purposefully on the opposite pavement. Suddenly troubled, he watched her for a few seconds. Before he had even seen her face he had dodged across the street and put his hand on her arm.

Ellen caught her breath. She saw the brown British uniform, the officer's dark eyes, haggard face, the waxed ends of his moustache. A second's incomprehension and alarm and she knew him, Guy, grave and exhausted, a ghost of the youth he had been but, like that youth of long ago, he was now raising her hand to his lips. Something ballooned in her chest. Her breath was pain.

'Are you real?'

'I never thought I would see you again, Ellen! May I escort you to wherever you're going?'

She gestured. 'I'm going to Liberty Hall. I'm trying to find Harry.'

'But I thought you lived in the west!'

'I do, but my husband and I are in Dublin for the Easter weekend!'

Guy smiled. 'I am in luck today, Ellen. I saw Franny an hour ago and now I bump into you!'

Ellen looked around as though expecting to see Fran coming down the quays. 'Franny? Where did you see her.'

'Chatham Street. Her hat shop!'

He tucked her hand under his arm. They crossed the quay together as though they walked out like this every day of their lives.

As well as being the headquarters of the Irish Transport and

General Workers' Union, Liberty Hall was the headquarters of the Irish Citizen Army, formed nearly three years earlier by James Connolly to prevent police harassment of workers. It was also home to what was left of the Irish Volunteer Corps, after the bulk of that organisation had taken the King's shilling and gone away to the war.

The sentry challenged them, looked at Guy suspiciously and denied them entry.

'I'm looking for Harry Healy,' Ellen said in the tone she used to recalcitrant students. 'I'm his sister. I've important news for him.'

A youth, who couldn't have been more than sixteen, was abruptly ordered, 'Tell Lieutenant Healy his sister is here!' and in a matter of minutes a young man in the Volunteers' uniform had joined them on the steps.

Ellen had not seen Harry in more than two years. He had changed, but it was not a physical transformation. What was different was his air of fierce introspection, as though, behind his round spectacles, he were engaged in momentous private stocktaking. He looked at her with startled recognition, kissed her cheek and turned with a frown to Guy. Then his face lit up.

'For a moment I didn't know you, old chap. But I'm very glad you're still above ground.'

Guy grinned and shook the outstretched hand. 'So am I!'

Harry glanced at the pips on Guy's epaulettes. 'A captain, no less! What has you here?'

'Sick leave. I got a scratch. Due back in France in ten days.'

Ellen felt nauseated. Wounded? No wonder he looks like a ghost.

'We bumped into each other,' she said. 'On the quay just this moment. I was coming to find you.'

Harry sighed. 'Oh Ellen, I know you must be very cross with me. I did so want to meet you and Brendan but something has come up.' He looked around. 'Where is he, by the way?'

'In Sandymount. Deirdre went off on her bike and I got a bit anxious about you.'

'What a little worrier you are!' He tweaked her lapel. 'And all dressed up to kill.'

And although he smiled and joked, his old spontaneity was gone. She knew he was just making noises, that he wanted rid of them. Aware of the bustle, the men and women in uniform, the messengers coming and going, the questioning frowns directed at the English officer, Ellen was filled with questions she could not ask in front of Guy. A bicycle clattered against the railings behind them and Harry said laconically, 'Ah, here's my delicious landmine!'

Deirdre was mounting the steps. She had an envelope in her hand and was out of breath. She did not seem pleased at the sight of her friend and stared at Guy.

'My darling girl,' Harry said, 'allow me to introduce Captain Forrister, an old friend who once saved my bacon. Guy, this is Deirdre Callaghan, my fiancée.'

'How do you do, Miss Callaghan?'

Guy shook Deirdre's hand. He felt her suspicious scrutiny; his own was thoroughly whetted. What on earth was afoot? Even if this place were really providing for home defence, it had all the atmosphere of serious and immediate military manoeuvres. He found himself wondering what ordnance these Volunteers had, and in what quantity. What might it represent if their nationalist ranting was not just guff? The government obviously treated them with contempt, but the country was no longer fully garrisoned because of the war, and anything was possible. He glanced at Ellen. What did she know?

'Will you watch the parade tomorrow, Guy?'

He met her ingenuous gaze and wondered if his imaginings were absurd.

'I doubt it.' He looked from her to Deirdre to Harry. 'But perhaps you could all have luncheon with me afterwards?'

He could not read the glance that passed from Harry to Deirdre. The latter shook her head and murmured, flushing, 'I'm afraid we're already bespoken.'

He turned to Ellen. 'And you Ellen, and your husband? I know it's very short notice. Will you both lunch with me tomorrow?'

He saw her hesitate. He saw the colour rise in her face.

'I would be delighted, Guy. I'm sure my husband would love to meet you.'

'Excellent! Shall we say one o'clock? Royal Hibernian?'

He bowed to Deirdre. 'Miss Callaghan.' He clapped a hand on Harry's shoulder. 'Goodbye my old friend until we meet again, hopefully above ground!'

Harry nodded. 'Look after yourself, Guy. I hope the bloody war ends soon.'

'Until tomorrow then.'

Ellen excused herself and hurried after him. 'Guy … I just want to say I'm looking forward to tomorrow, but if my husband has already made other plans I hope you will understand?'

'Of course!' He leaned back a little on his heels, regarding her whimsically. Then he added, his voice very low, 'We live in troubled times, Ellen. Because we do, I want you to know that I have never, for a moment, stopped loving you.'

He turned and was gone.

Ellen's breath caught in her chest. She stood quite still and watched Guy stride along the quay. Then she went back to take her leave of Deirdre and Harry, but the latter had already melted into the maw of the building.

'What possessed you to bring the British army here?' Deirdre demanded.

'He is an old friend, Dee.'

Deirdre suddenly sprang to attention. Two men in overcoats and slouch hats were coming up the steps. They nodded at her and passed into the hall.

'Who was that?'

'Pearse's brother Willy, and Seán Mac Diarmada. I'm really sorry El if I seem rude and peremptory, but I have to go now. What will you do tomorrow? Will you take up your English friend's offer of lunch?'

'Depends on Brendan.'

'You'd best go home. Will I get you a cab?'

'Stop making me feel like it's children's bedtime. I'm perfectly able to get myself home. And it's you, and Harry, who are the children. Dee … I don't know what you're up to, and I wonder if you know yourselves! I *beg* you to stop it now!'

Deirdre smiled, patted her hand as if to say there was nothing to worry about, and turned away. Ellen walked swiftly back to O'Connell Bridge feeling like someone who had slept for years, only to awaken to a different world. But she hugged to herself an extraordinary moment, delicious in its validation of the past: *I never, for a moment, stopped loving you.*

When she reached the bridge, she stood and looked into the river. I am nearly thirty and I have always played life by the book. Perhaps I should not have played by the book. She leaned over the parapet, saw the green water swirling at the stone arches. Maybe the book was for those without the courage to listen to their hearts. Courageous people, like Franny, wrote their own scripts, assumed their own destiny. What a nincompoop I have been, with my safe marriage, my safe little life! No wonder Fran broke with me! Well, her shop was in Chatham Street, a walk of some ten minutes. She would go there now and catch her before she closed. Visualising their reunion, tears sprang to her eyes. Surely they could thrash out whatever misunderstanding had come between them and never lose each other again.

She passed a barefoot urchin calling out his wares, a bundle of newspapers under his arm, his pinched white face streaked with dirt, his jacket tattered, the old lining exposed. She gave him a threepenny piece and waved away the paper.

Already the weekend was surreal. She had quarrelled with

Brendan and now she would have to apologise, restore his five pounds and tell him he was invited to lunch tomorrow by a British officer. That might pique his curiosity, or it might infuriate him that his wife could dream of accepting such an invitation without asking him first.

But I need to see Guy again. He is going back to the war and it may be my last chance. Oh *please* dear God …

# Chapter 31

When Ellen returned to the villa in Sandymount she found her husband gone.

'He left about an hour ago, Ma'am. He said he wouldn't be coming back.' The maid looked at Ellen curiously and Ellen reddened at the expression in the girl's eyes – an aborted clandestine affair, her look said; what else could explain the gentleman leaving alone? 'But he paid for the room. Until Tuesday, as arranged,' the maid went on sympathetically. 'Would you like a cup of tea, ma'am? The kettle is just after boiling. I could bring you a tray! And a few sandwiches?'

Ellen thanked Dehlia, took the room key and went upstairs. She was very tired. She had not been able to find Franny. She had found the hat shop all right, 'Du Barry' if you don't mind, but it was closed and the window display – minimal for the weekend – contained just three very elegant hats.

She looked around the room. The bed still bore the indentation of her husband's body; the towel was damp, the soap recently used. Propped against a vase on the mantelpiece was an envelope addressed to her. She took the letter from it, noting with self-disgust that her hand began to tremble. Covered in her husband's neat writing, was a page torn from the pocketbook he always carried with him and in which he noted the salient events of each day.

*My dear Ellen,*

*You will appreciate that your conduct has made it impossible for me to continue here for our little holiday. I have waited these past two hours for you to return from your regrettable tantrum, but it seems your husband does not rate even the most ordinary courtesy. Consequently I have decided to take the late train. I will overnight in Athlone and continue home tomorrow. You are already in possession of adequate funds ('slavery', by the way, is an ugly term for your privileged position of wife and mother) and the room is paid for until Tuesday, so you are in a position to spend the weekend with your friend and your brother as was presumably your intention all along.*

*I think the break would be good for both of us; for you because you need time to reflect on your conduct; for me because I find it insupportable. When you have returned to your senses it will be time enough to discuss your unfortunate lapse and to convince me it will not recur.*

*Your husband,*

*Brendan*

There was a knock on the door and Dehlia entered with a tea tray. When she was gone Ellen forced herself to drink some tea and eat a triangular egg sandwich, while her mind went over the contents of her husband's note. She reread it slowly.

He's always right, she thought. But why does he never, ever, wonder why I get upset? Why does he have to address me like a child? Why is everything about him? But no matter what she told herself, a new sense of abandonment and insecurity rose in her. He knew, and he knew she knew, that he held all the cards. He owned the house; he 'owned' their son and as school principal, he was even her boss.

She mentally replayed what had occurred. All right, it had been wrong of her to storm out. And she had said some horrible, hurtful things. But it wasn't just because of today, she told herself. It was a culmination of so many things, things too numerous to catalogue, some too petty to mention, but all tending towards a situation where he was king and she was vassal.

How furious was he really? What if he turned her out? The matrimonial home was his. What if he had her dismissed? No other school would employ her. Most importantly, and this thought made her feel ill, what if he arranged things so that her child was lost to her? He, not she, was Hughie's legal guardian.

A glance at the clock made her realise the last train had already left Kingsbridge. She struggled with her fury and her fear. She would go home as soon as possible … first thing tomorrow. Go home and eat humble pie. But he had more or less ordered her to remain in Dublin and reflect on her shortcomings. She felt angry at her powerlessness. Then it struck her that his letter had been calculated to intimidate. He does not love me! Why did I never see it? What he loves … what he needs from our relationship … is power.

Under his controlled exterior did he have any real regard for her? What if his love had never been more than kindness, the way you would reward a dog for learning pleasing tricks? He had never expressed the passion for which she had always hungered. Perhaps he did not possess it. Perhaps she did not inspire it?

Outside the day was fading, but she did not trouble to switch on the lamp. She stood up and went to the window, stared down into the darkening garden and saw a cat sneak through the shrubbery. It would indeed be better, she thought coldly, if I stayed where I am until Tuesday – or later. Right now I do not want to see Brendan. She had the perfect excuse – had he not ordered her to remain? In any case, she was filled with unease about Harry and Deirdre and wanted to see this Easter parade of theirs. She was also determined to see Franny as soon as her shop reopened next week. It was exciting to think that she would find her there among the fine hats she had seen through the window. She imagined Fran's 'Can I help you, Madam?', imagined her shock and hopefully her pleasure, imagined reconciliation and embracing her again. And then she thought of little Hughie waiting for her at home. But his father would be with him tonight and Máire was devoted to him.

So there were compensations for her present predicament. She would have time to revisit old haunts. And there would be nothing now to stop her having lunch with Guy tomorrow. The pleasure of that prospect filled her with tiny shivers as she pictured his grave face, his aura of personal responsibility and his new fragility. She felt again the surge of electricity when his lips had brushed her hand.

Ellen left her bedroom door slightly open and waited for Deirdre's return. She counted eleven resonant strokes from the clock in the hall before she heard a key turning in the hall door. She got out of bed and peered into the landing. She did not want to surprise a strange lodger in her nightgown, but she quickly saw that it was indeed Deirdre who was so wearily climbing the stairs.

'Dee …' she hissed.

Deirdre came hesitantly into the room, looking around expectantly for Brendan.

'Where's your husband?'

'Gone home!'

Deirdre closed the door and removed her green slouch hat. Wisps of her dark hair were undone and curled in tendrils at the back of her head. 'Gone home? Left you on your own?'

'We had a row.'

'Oh dear, I hope it isn't my fault. But it'll blow over, Ellen. He's a good man. I suppose you'll be following him tomorrow.'

Ellen looked at her friend in military uniform who had dark circles under her eyes and who was talking to her as though she were a child.

'The way I feel right now, Dee, I don't think I'd go back at all if it weren't for my son. I'm tired of being ordered about by a teacup tyrant!'

Deirdre laughed. 'Teacup tyrant! And I thought you two were such a devoted couple. You're putting me off the holy state of wedlock!'

'I suppose you couldn't come with me tomorrow afternoon to Carysfort?' Ellen said eagerly. 'After your parade? It would be nice to see our old Alma Mater.'

Deirdre shook her head. 'The parade has been cancelled. But the Volunteers and the *Cumann* are on standby ... so I'm stuck. Harry too. But I think you should still keep out of town.'

'Dee, what is there to be afraid of? I'm not scared by a little excitement! And I'll have Guy Forrister to protect me. I've decided to go ahead and lunch with him tomorrow.'

Deirdre frowned. 'Is that entirely wise?' she asked quietly.

'Don't get duenna-ish on me. I'm pushing thirty and he's an old friend. After all, to whom can I turn? My husband has decamped. And my best friend and my brother are playing soldiers!'

'Speaking of soldiers,' Dee said after a moment, 'Try to find out from him how many they have in the Castle. If you can do it subtly.'

'What on earth for?'

'Just useful ... in the event we are ... invaded.'

Ellen sighed. 'You should tell me the truth, Dee, if you expect me to spy for you.'

Deirdre gave her a tired smile. 'Spy is such an unpleasant word! I hardly know myself what's going on. But whatever you do, intimate nothing of what I've told you to Captain Forrister!'

'I'm not a fool. But I pray God that Harry and you and your band of hotheads have more sense than to challenge Britain. I have only one brother, one good friend and I love both of them.'

Deirdre's eyes filled with tears. She turned away.

'They are asking too much of you, Dee! They have you worn out.'

Deirdre turned back and looked at her with red eyes. 'Nothing is too much to ask. And now, dear Ellen, I am going to bed.'

When Guy got back to his rooms he threw his cap onto the table, loosened his tie and sank into an armchair. In a mirror across the room, he saw his reflection – an elegant officer in polished field boots and riding breeches. The uniform gave him the look of a man in command, part of the war machine that was grinding the youth of Europe into the fields of France and Belgium. But he knew he was not in command. The war was a sham, and his life not much better.

He was very troubled that he had had the shakes in Franny's sitting room. This was the second time. Was he to become another 'battle fatigue' statistic? A living casualty? He knew that such episodes were sometimes limited in number, sometimes they recurred indefinitely ... sometimes they got worse.

And then, even while he had been trying to get a grip on himself, he had bumped into Ellen – Ellen who had changed. Oh, she was elegant and lovely certainly, but there was such wistfulness there. She belonged to someone called Brendan, a man he might meet tomorrow. To have to look across the table at her *husband* ... make conversation ... Why did he have to invite them?

He rose and went to his bedroom, took a small felt purse from his bag and extracted the little ring Mrs Murphy had returned to him. He kept it with him nowadays as a talisman to help him through the war. And he had faith in it, because so far he was still alive. He clenched the ring in his hand, went back to the sitting room and the sofa, leaned his head back and stared at the ceiling. An electric light with amber glass hung from a central plaster rose. The clock chimed on the mantelpiece. Outside the day was almost gone. He could dine at the Shelbourne or the Royal Hibernian, both were only a stone's throw away; but he was not hungry. He rose, scanned the bookcase and saw the rows of medical textbooks. On the bottom shelf was *The Complete Works of Shakespeare*, *The*

*Lives of the Queens of England* in six volumes, and the *Rubaiyat of Omar Khayyam*. He unlocked the bookcase and reached for the Rubaiyat. It was only then that he saw, lying flat atop some books, a tome entitled *The Story of Ireland*. Wasn't this the book that had provoked Ellen's father all those years ago?

He took it out. A magazine called *An Claidheamh Soluis* immediately fell out onto the floor. It was a bilingual magazine, Gaelic printed opposite the English. I never knew old Duggy was a Hibernophile, he thought and then reminded himself impatiently that the man was Irish. He turned on the table lamp and sat down with his reading matter.

How old was the Gaelic script? It frustrated him that without the English translation he could not understand one word. He was filled with an extraordinary feeling of foreignness and uneasiness that this language, this script, was indigenous to Ireland, while his language was not, nor was his culture, nor had the Empire itself any roots in this land other than those it had transplanted in despite of its people. He put down the magazine and opened the book that Harry's father had once pronounced seditious.

Guy read well into the night. He learned of a venerable civilisation he had never known existed: rich, cultured, deliberately destroyed. He closed the book and put it on the floor. He hated history. He knew first-hand the greed that fuelled it, was fuelling it still. For this he had ordered droves of young lads over the top, sent them to die taking a hundred metres of hill, a hundred metres, which had been lost again the next day. So many of his 'men', who were really only boys, tremulous and heroic as they prepared for no man's land, had become in a matter of crimson seconds, just contours on the shell-blasted earth. Tears blinded him; he dashed them away. God damn war! he thought. God damn the whole infernal stupidity!

He switched off the lamp, leaving the street lights to illuminate his darkness. There was little traffic outside, just the sound of one or two horse-drawn cabs and a few motors. He wondered if he should let the medics know he had become another freak of the great adventure. But they might think he was malingering.

He turned his thoughts to gentle Fontebelle, to the great surrounding forests where once there had been moorland. He remembered the half-timbered farmhouses in sunlit clearings, the Armagnac grapes ripening in the late summer sun and the powerfully scented lavender with its feasting summer hordes of white butterflies and black bees. At least there was somewhere still untouched by this war. Thank God at least for that! Eventually he slept.

# Chapter 32

*Easter Sunday, 1916*

Franny loved Rathcormac. She loved the panoramic view across Dublin Bay, the lawns sloping to the neglected tennis court and the squeaking gate that gave onto the cliff walk. Dr Mulhall had died at the war's outbreak and had left the place to Liam, with the proviso that Alma had a right of residence until she married. So far, Alma had not married. Her At Homes had petered out with the advent of war, but she continued her work for the Irish Women's Franchise League, although that organisation, like its English counterpart, faced virtual paralysis. Just before the war, Mrs Sheehy-Skeffington had been imprisoned in Mountjoy Jail and had gone on hunger strike. But she had been released under the Cat and Mouse Act where they let you out until you recovered and then re-arrested you.

Liam, glad to be alive and glad to be home, spent most of his time in his studio where the two big windows made the most of the northern light and where he was sometimes joined by a precocious child who loved to paint.

Hannah knew she had been born in Rathcormac and treated it as her native soil. In her bedroom was a doll's house, which had once been Alma's – a small replica of a Georgian townhouse with rooms and furniture to scale, tiny 'marble' fireplaces and a kitchen with miniscule copper pans. The front of this curiosity opened on a hinge so that access was possible to every nook and cranny and Hannah could position the little dolls in whatever configuration suited her requirements. The little girl also loved an overgrown nook in the garden she called her Lair, from where she would stare out across the wild bay at the city and the Sugar Loaf mountains. But, most of all, she loved Liam's studio. Here she could paint as she liked and mess her pinafore and be smiled upon no matter what.

On Easter morning Alma, Liam, Franny and Hannah went to Mass in the rain and returned to a breakfast of toast and scrambled eggs. Hannah looked rebelliously at the helping handed her by Mrs Burke who did the cooking and ran the house.

'I hate eggs!'

'Pity!' Alma said. 'I have a big chocolate one for you! Now I'll have to give it away.' She opened a cupboard in the sideboard and extracted a large Easter egg wrapped in gold foil and tied with a pink ribbon, and asked Mrs Burke to bring it down to the kitchen.

'Can I change my mind?' asked Hannah.

The adults looked at each other and laughed.

'It's a lady's privilege!' Liam said.

Hannah attacked her scrambled eggs, keeping her eyes on the chocolate one, oblivious to the subdued merriment of everyone else at table. Alma handed over the prize when the child had cleared her plate.

'Happy Easter, darling Hannah!'

Hannah jumped up and kissed everyone. She opened her Easter egg, broke off a few pieces, offered it around but, except for Franny who nibbled a little bit, the adults declined.

'Your mother and I are going for a walk,' Liam informed the child when the breakfast things had been cleared away and the rain began to ease.

'Can I come?'

'No. I want you to finish that picture … the one of the boys and the donkey. And don't eat that chocolate monstrosity before lunch!'

He went to find Alma. She was at her desk, fountain pen in hand, working on an article for *Ban na hEireann* – Women of Ireland – a radical women's magazine.

'Fran and I are going out to air our lungs. Hannah's in the studio, so maybe you'd keep an eye on her?'

Alma nodded absently. 'Off you go. Be careful on the high path.'

When they were alone on the cliff walk, Liam pointed to the rise behind them and the drop where the growling sea was pelting the rocks with foam. Raindrops stung their faces, but he was in no hurry to find shelter.

'Our ancestors looked across this very bay,' he said. 'Thousands of years ago. They called this place *Binn Éadair* – Éadar's peak.'

He reached for her hand. 'Dearest, beloved Fran, I cannot wait any longer. I have brought you here this morning to beg you to marry me.'

Elegant in a pale-grey ensemble she had made herself and enveloped in a rain coat, Ellen shook out her umbrella and came through the door of the Royal Hibernian Hotel in Dawson Street. Guy was waiting in the foyer, reading the *Sunday Independent.* He looked pinched and tired, she thought, but distinguished. He saw her, smiled and sprang to his feet.

'So you were able to make it! I hardly dared hope.'

Ellen gave him her hand. 'Brendan couldn't come,' she explained, removing her wet coat with Guy's help. 'Something's come up and he had to go home.'

She had steeled herself for this meeting, forced herself when last-minute nerves had dictated retreat. Deirdre had left the house early without waking her and she had found her own way to Mass. In the Star of the Sea Church, she had prayed for wisdom and understanding, for her marriage, which right now was unendurable, for Harry and Kate, and for Guy whom she told God she would always love and who was soon going back to the war. I am drawn … held by him. He … knows who I am. I know him! He will be going back to France. Will I ever see him again? Dear God do not blame me.

Now the same Guy said politely, 'I am sorry he couldn't come.'

'I didn't want to miss our lunch so I hope you don't mind me coming on my own!'

'Ellen,' he said with a reproving laugh, 'I fear you are being disingenuous.'

Ellen felt herself reddening. Guy steered her to the dining room where well-dressed people were already at table and the air was full of English voices, evidently discussing the war, for Ellen heard, as she followed the waiter, several French-sounding place names alongside military titles.

When she and Guy were seated, she said, 'I hope the war hasn't touched your lovely Fontebelle.'

He shook his head. 'It's too far south. I'm surprised that you should even remember it!'

'I dreamed of it once. Funny isn't it? A house I have never seen! In my dreams it was pale pink, with white wrought-iron balconies.'

'It's actually a rather mellow sandstone,' Guy said. 'The colour of honey. And the wrought iron is black. If I had known we were meeting, I would have brought you photographs.'

'When were you there last?'

'Just before the war. But I have people looking after it – Monsieur and Madame Fargue. He keeps the grounds and she keeps the house. And yes,' he added with a smile, 'the lavender avenue is still extant. Pierre Fargue cuts it back every autumn and renews as necessary.'

'When the war is over will you go back?'

He nodded. 'I will go back and salve my soul.'

There was silence. He was studying the menu, but his face was sombre.

'Does your soul need salving, Guy?' she whispered.

'I'm afraid so, Ellen.'

'Mine does too. At least that's the way I felt this morning.'

She stared at the menu at though it held the answer. Why did I have to say that? she asked herself. She knew that Guy had glanced at her sharply. But she also knew he could see only her hat and its bit of veil over downcast eyes.

They both chose consommé to start, followed by rack of Wicklow lamb. Guy studied the wine list and ordered a Saint-Emilion Grand Cru.

'Is this wine from near your Fontebelle?'

'It's not far. North of Bordeaux. About three hours' drive in a motor.'

'The first time I had wine was when you came to visit us in Kilcrannagh. I have only tasted it three times since,' she added with a laugh, 'and not one bottle had an Irish label!'

'Well, I hope this one was worth the wait!'

She sipped and said it was, but in reality her mind was churning with all the questions she longed to ask. How badly had he been wounded? Was he married? Engaged? When was he due to return to the war? She knew, for it was written in his dilated pupils, how visible, how attractive, he found her.

Guy caught the scent of her cologne. How beautiful she is still, how fresh, how unique, he thought. It's as though no time has elapsed at all since that morning when I walked her to that miserable school. But she is someone else's wife now. And soon I will be a few bones in a French field.'

'You have children, Ellen?'

'I have a two-year-old boy. And you?'

'I am not married. Could never find the right girl!'

'I see.'

The colour mantled her face and slid below her collar.

Guy swallowed wine and willed it to slip down to wherever lurked his soul. I would like to get drunk, he thought. Later, when she is gone … Omar Khayyam would have approved …

Tomorrow's tangle to the winds resign
And lose your fingers in the tresses of
The cypress-slender Minister of Wine

If she were not here I would drink the whole bottle. And order two more, and bring them back to Duggy's, and, in honour of Old Khayyam, quaff my way to temporary oblivion.

Ellen was smiling at him. Her eyes were bright, the whites clear, the grey shot through with blue-green, like dawn in a forest.

'It's very strange, very wonderful to be having lunch together, Ellen. Tell me about your life.'

Ellen told him about Hughie, 'He's such a little bundle, so funny, so demanding … so bright.'

'And your husband?'

She met his eyes. 'Brendan is a good man. He is an excellent father.'

'I am glad that you are happy.'

A smile answered this oblique inquiry. Ah, she won't say she is. He was curious. Why do her eyes cloud at the mention of her husband? Why has the man gone home and left his young wife alone on Easter Sunday? Perhaps all is not rosy in the matrimonial garden; in his experience of married couples it hardly ever was.

'Did you think it very improper of me, Ellen, to speak to you as I did yesterday – when we were saying goodbye?'

He saw the blood bloom again under her skin. The waiter refilled their glasses.

'It was improper!' he answered for her. 'But these are not ordinary times. I meant what I said. I find it hard to forgive myself for having been such a puppy … years ago.' He swallowed some wine and added in a whisper, 'I still have the little ring your aunt returned to me … at your behest.' He stared into her eyes. They were wary, but proud. She loved me once. Perhaps she still does.

He was suddenly aware that he was bending halfway across the table and righted himself. 'Pity Harry couldn't join us. And his charming fiancée. Tell me, Ellen, does he have a lot to do with these Volunteer fellows?'

Ellen heard the curiosity and a warning bell jangled, dragging her back to reality. This was Captain Forrister, an officer of the Crown. Harry was her brother, involved with God alone knew what plans, what hopes, what hopelessness?

'A lot of young people are involved. It has to do with the defence of the country.'

'Ireland won't be invaded! The Hun is busy elsewhere. Harry must know that!'

Ellen averted her eyes and said, 'War brings unusual risks. Otherwise, I suppose, he would have enlisted.'

'Ellen, Ellen, you don't need to make any excuses! Last year alone saw more than 79,000 Irish Catholics in the British army. And already they had won seventeen Victoria Crosses! Not bad for a small nation fighting for its former foe.' He lowered his voice. 'Thing is, Ellen, I don't want to alarm you, but your brother could be involved in something potentially serious. Doesn't do to challenge Britain, you know, even if she is at war.'

He saw her pale.

'I can see his perspective, of course,' he went on. 'And in his shoes I would probably feel the same. But remember that all this stuff about Britain fighting for the freedom of small nations is just guff. Ireland is too near, too valuable, to be allowed independence.'

She stiffened, drew herself up a little. 'Indeed! Surely only the Irish should have a final say in that?'

'I am not talking morality here. I am talking political expediency. And political expediency is what drives the Empire.'

Ellen did not reply and Guy tried to imagine her as a teacher, she looked so reserved, even stern.

Then she said, almost idly, 'I'm sure Dublin Castle is too well garrisoned to fear anything from the Volunteers.'

Good girl, he thought. She was cool now, eyebrows raised. If she had to choose between Harry and the Empire she would choose Harry. Which begged the damn question: how many soldiers *did* they have in the Castle? Two? Three? Half a dozen? Hadn't they all gone off to some races caper somewhere?

'Of course it is! You don't think they would leave the nerve centre of British rule in Ireland unprotected?'

Guy felt he was over a barrel. He was with the only woman he had ever loved, and his old friend, her brother, was in more danger than she dreamed. He had learnt while breakfasting here that Sir Matthew Nathan, the Undersecretary for Ireland, was seeing the Viceroy to plan the arrest of the Volunteer leaders. The German ship intercepted off the Kerry coast had been carrying munitions for Sinn Féin. Sir Roger Casement, who had been on board the escorting U-boat, had been arrested. The authorities now knew that a rebellion had been planned and were about to move against the ringleaders. Oh Harry …

They ate their *Meringue Chantilly* and drank their coffee. He told her a few amusing anecdotes about the war, the ones pretending it was all a game.

'Would you like a liqueur?'

Her presence had become a torment. She had tried to pump him about the Castle, but this made her only more interesting. Was she also involved in whatever doomed nonsense was being concocted? How much did she really know?

'I have never tasted a liqueur, Guy.'

'Well then, why not try a good Catholic Benedictine? It's Easter after all. Something to celebrate.'

It came in a tulip-shaped glass. She said it was liquid fire. He picked up the *Sunday Independent* he had left by his chair on the floor.

'By the way, that parade of Harry's has been cancelled. It's in the paper.'

He handed it to her and watched as she read it. *Owing to the very critical position, all orders given to Irish Volunteers for Easter Sunday, are hereby rescinded, and no parades, marches or other movements of Irish Volunteers will take place.*

It was signed by Professor Eoin MacNeill, the Commander in Chief of the Volunteers.

'Perhaps there's a split of some kind among the leaders?' Guy suggested. He fixed her with his eyes and added in a rush, 'For God's sake, Ellen, get Harry to opt out of the whole damn business. You know I am talking sense. The Volunteers are serious! They are *not* playing at being soldiers.'

'What do you mean?'

'What I saw yesterday convinced me. Trust me, Ellen. The trenches give one a nose for Death!'

She gasped, put a hand to her mouth and took it away as though she did not know where it belonged.

'I shouldn't be worrying you. Just tell him to get out!'

'I have no influence with him! None whatever!' She rose. 'I must go.'

He signalled for the bill. The waiter helped her into her coat. In the lobby she said, 'Thank you, Guy, for the wonderful lunch.'

'My pleasure! May I escort you back to your hotel?'

'No need. I'll get the tram. I'm staying in Sandymount, in the same lodging house as Deirdre.'

They descended the steps to the street. 'I'm just around the corner from here – St Stephen's Green, No. 11 – rooms belonging to an Irish fellow officer who's in France at the moment.'

Ellen nodded. 'Does your wound still hurt?' she whispered suddenly.

He turned to look into her face. 'Not really. I get a bit tired sometimes, that's all.'

A car went by, slowed as it came to the junction with St Stephen's Green and moved off smartly with a loud backfire. Ellen nearly jumped out of her skin. Guy clutched the railings and slid jerkily to the pavement.

'Guy!'

He heard her cry, but he could make no reply. He knew his face was set, his eyes staring, knew his limbs had begun to shake. Some people came forward to help. They stared down at him compassionately as he jerked and twitched on the pavement.

'Where does he live, Miss?'

# Chapter 33

The guttering in the eaves woke Harry early on Easter Sunday. He groaned and turned over in his iron bed, springs crunching as he reached to pull back the curtains. There was a deluge outside but he wanted to keep an eye on The Hermitage, which was just down the road from his lodgings, keep an eye on it in case of raids … or miracles …

The Hermitage was the nucleus of *Scoil Éanna,* St Enda's School. It was an eighteenth-century mansion, which contained the boys' dormitories and living quarters for the headmaster's family. The Pearses had mortgaged their former home, Cullenswood House, to acquire a lease on this beautiful place for their educational experiment. They numbered five: the headmaster Padraic, his brother Willie – a sculptor who had studied at the Sorbonne and who taught Art – their mother and two sisters.

It had been raining for two weeks and could rain until the Day of Judgement for all Harry cared. Everything was over, indefinitely postponed, all the training, the hope and faith. He had geared himself for action today, had been to confession and put his affairs in order, leaving his few possessions and savings to Deirdre, and a memento each to his sister and his cousin. He knew the parade this morning was to have been but a mask for the Rising, but since last night's cancellation there would be no mobilisation. MacNeill, the Commander in Chief, had good reason for his decision. Now that the arms shipment to Kerry had turned into a farce, he had warned that a conflict could not be won, that it would entail pointless bloodshed. The northerner, Sir Roger Casement, who had orchestrated the arms shipment, had been arrested. The German ship with the consignment of munitions had been scuttled. The Castle, alerted now, would presumably arrest everyone. But MacNeill is not a member of the Military Council any more than I am, Harry thought. And *they* are the real revolutionaries. After all this time, all this planning, are *they* ready to accept a postponement?

He would be meeting Deirdre for lunch, but he wished she were here beside him; he wanted to drown his frustration between her breasts. Their blissful tryst in the Waverly Hotel last St Patrick's Day came back to torment him. But his passionate partner had been ambivalent afterwards, reminding him with reproach that they were still unmarried.

'Do you expect me to wait forever, Harry?'

They had been a bit careless that St Patrick's Day, both of them carried away. But Dee had made no reference to it since, so presumably all was well. Poor Dee! She worked so hard, attending classes in First Aid, carrying messages in the hollow bars of her bike, learning how to fire a Browning automatic and even becoming something of a markswoman.

The drizzle eased, dripping rhythmically like it used to from branches overhanging the turf shed in Kilcrannagh, in the days when he and Franny would fill the creel. He could still smell the turf, feel the coarse hairiness of the sods. Dismay at his cousin's disappearance from his life had given way to a private resentment. Until he had discovered the reason.

His aunt had come out with it last New Year's Eve. After partaking liberally of the port wine he had brought from Dublin, she had broken down when he had mentioned Franny, bent her head and wept as though her heart would burst, while he had tried to comfort her and to understand the words jerked out between her sobs.

'My child … is ruined … a fallen woman! Oh Harry, Harry, Frances is an unwed mother …'

'Of course she isn't, Aunt.'

'She sent me a letter!' His aunt indicated a drawer in the dresser. 'It's there, somewhere … Her daughter must be eight years old now. But Ellen is not to know of her disgrace … That such a thing could have happened … And my dear Clare, passed away … Oh, life is hard.'

'Who else knows?'

'Only Jimmy.'

'Does he now! He never said a word to me. Who is the father?'

Aunt Harriet had sighed, shrugged, dried her eyes. 'A French sailor for all I know.'

Harry went to the dresser and found in a drawer the letter in its dog-eared envelope. Stunned and breathless, he had let himself out and taken the boreen to Jimmy's where the light was still burning.

Jimmy answered as soon as Harry banged on the door, muttering loudly about *amadáns* who should be in their beds. Harry crossed the threshold and looked angrily around him, noting the light before the picture of the Sacred Heart and the presence on the wall of yet another holy picture – the Bleeding Heart of Mary. An open book lay on the table beside a mound of newspapers, a small snapshot beside it.

'So you've come to wish me Happy New Year?' Jimmy said caustically.

'I've just heard about Fran. But Aunt Harriet says you knew all the time!'

'I promised I'd keep my gob shut.'

'So you know who the father is?'

Jimmy looked at him in exasperation. 'I do.'

'Well?'

'Oh, who do you think it was? Who was the fucker had every pretty girl in the county damned?' He studied Harry for a moment and added contemptuously, 'And who was the eejit who brought his family to take tea with the like of that?'

Harry thought for a second. 'Wallace? I don't believe you,' He clenched his fists. 'I'll kill the bastard!'

'Unless you can hunt him down in London you'll have to forego the pleasure. He's never in Clonshule now.' Jimmy reached into the back of his cupboard and extracted a bottle of whiskey. 'I keep this in case I have distraught visitors.' He found a glass, poured a tot and handed it to Harry. 'Anyway, calculated murder is not your style.'

'Why didn't you deal with him?' Harry demanded, waving away the whiskey. 'You must have had plenty of chances!'

'Because I don't want to end up in Hell, you stupid bollix! But I had him that close,' he added, holding out his big calloused hands as though throttling someone. 'I waited for him one night in Dublin.'

'So, it was *you*!' Harry whispered, remembering what Guy said about an assault on Wallace. '*You* banjaxed his knee,' he whispered. 'You Machiavellian dark horse!'

Jimmy shrugged and turned to the hearth. Harry picked up the whiskey. His hand was shaking and some of the spirit spattered from the glass. He quickly wiped a droplet from the small photograph lying beside Jimmy's book, downed the spirit with a gulp and restored the glass to the table. Jimmy hurriedly removed the snap, but not before an astonished Harry had realised that its subject was Ellen.

A female voice on the floor below brought Harry back to the present. His landlady, Mrs Flood, was singing in Gaelic, a song about the flight of the Wild Geese, the Irishmen who, more than two centuries earlier, had left their shattered country to join the

Irish Brigade in the French army. The old language brought a queer comfort as its poetic nuance rose through the floor. From outside came the barking of the dog and then the swish of motors approaching on the wet road. He saw them slow and stop at Hermitage gate.

He jumped out of bed. Crown forces? A raiding party? He watched from the edge of the curtain while he pulled on his trousers and saw the cars turning into the gateway to the school. Pearse was there, he knew, furious no doubt, at the cancellation. His headmaster continued to fascinate him – half-Irish, half-English, a passionate educationalist, a barrister, a poet, a playwright, a public speaker of national stature:

'I hold it a Christian thing to hate evil,' he had said during his oration at the funeral last year of the old Fenian, O'Donovan Rossa, 'to hate oppression; and, hating them, to strive to overthrow them.'

Harry knew the speech by heart. Coming from so upstanding a source, delivered with a passion that had held the crowd mesmerised, it had had a powerful effect on him. Jimmy, who had travelled to Dublin for the funeral, had whispered in his ear, 'By Jaysus, but that headmaster of yours is mighty!'

'Shush … Jimmy … Listen!'

'They think they have pacified Ireland. They think they have purchased half of us and intimidated the other half … But the fools, the fools, the fools …'

Harry watched as the gardener came from the gate lodge and waved the cars through. It gave him a chance to identify some of the passengers. This was no raiding party. He recognised MacDiarmada, Ceannt, Connolly, Clarke, Plunkett – all members of the committed and impenetrable Military Council, the driving force behind the projected insurrection.

Franny and Liam came back to Rathcormac arm in arm. Lunch

was ready – vegetable soup, roast chicken, potatoes and peas. Hannah brought her painting of the morning for inspection and Liam propped it carefully where the light was right.

'It's good.' he said. 'You've caught the innocence of childhood and the patience of donkeyhood.'

The child looked pleased. Franny and Liam smiled at each other. Alma, ladling soup, looked from one of them to the other.

'What are you two so conspiratorial about? Out with it!'

'Fran and I have had a talk,' Liam said with a slow smile, 'and the upshot ,' he added, leaning over to take Franny's hand, 'is that Miss Murphy has finally consented to become my wife!'

'At last!' Alma exclaimed. 'You were taking so long about that, that I was thinking of giving you a push!'

But Hannah dropped her knife and fork and burst into tears.

'I thought you would be glad!' Franny cried, leaving her chair and coming around to hug her daughter. 'Is it so terrible?'

Hannah buried her face in her mother's breast.

'I was hoping!' She grinned through her tears at Liam. 'You see, now I have a father! I will pray to my own daddy in Heaven tonight and ask him not to mind.'

Liam looked at Franny and saw the tension in her face. She'll have to forget that bastard, he told himself.

'We'll have a celebratory dinner tonight,' Alma cried. 'At last, there's a use for Father's vintage champagne!'

# Chapter 34

When the passers-by had helped Guy up the stairs to his rooms, they deposited him on the sofa and left him and Ellen alone together. Guy was still trembling, but the spasms had passed.

Ellen sat down in the armchair opposite the sofa, uncertain whether or not she should try to find a doctor. Guy was quiet now. In Galway she had once seen another sufferer of battle fatigue at close quarters, a young fellow returned from France, dribbling and dragging his feet, jumping at every loud noise.

'Ellen …'

She rose and knelt beside him.

'I didn't want you to see me like this. You are very kind to come back with me. '

'Do you need a doctor?'

'There's little they can do. I really am all right now you know.'

'Can I get you anything?'

'I'd love some water. There's a kitchen of sorts through there.'

Ellen found the little kitchen and brought back a glass of water. She loosened Guy's collar and tie and helped him take off his tunic. Her breast, as she bent over him, touched his shoulder. Guy groaned. Ellen thought he was in pain. His eyes were closed. She saw the pulse beat in his throat.

'Why don't you take off your hat? I would love to see your hair,' he whispered.

She raised her arms, removed her hatpins and placed her hat upon the table. Her coiffure was still in place, although a few strands of hair curled at the nape of her neck.

'You used to wear it down.'

Ellen put her fingers through her mane and pulled. An array of hairpins fell onto the carpet. Her hair followed in long coils and when she leaned towards him, they touched his neck.

'Take off your coat.'

Ellen obeyed. She dared not acknowledge what she was doing.

'Your jacket, Ellen.'

She undid the buttons of her jacket and shrugged it off. Under it she was wearing a white lace blouse and a thin gold chain with an aquamarine pendant, a gift from Brendan.

Guy saw that her breasts were rounded, but her waist seemed impossibly small behind the wide, tight waistband of her skirt. She looked like the archetypal feminine – fragile and uncertain – although the tumbling of her hair and the brightness of her eyes made her look abandoned.

Alive now with desire, he was already imagining this scene to its conclusion. But he still made no move to touch her, afraid the spell would break.

'Darling Ellen, your blouse.'

Slowly, button by button, Ellen undid her lace blouse, exposing her beautiful shoulders and the cleavage of her bosom behind her white chemise.

'Come here, my one and only love.'

Guy pushed aside the straps of her chemise until it suddenly slid to her waist and her torso and breasts, dark nipples erect, were exposed. He rose from the sofa, grasped her wrists and pulled her towards the bedroom.

'Come and lie beside me. Ellen, just lie beside me …'

*

Harry met Deirdre for Easter Sunday lunch at a small restaurant in Baggot Street. He had important news and, because he was early, had managed to get the window table. He watched her arrive on her bicycle. He admired her grace as she dismounted, her curling, upswept hair, the rain on her hat and the slender wrists above her gloves. She looked tired and glum.

He stood up as she entered.

'You're early!' she said.

'With reason!'

She thought it was a compliment and smiled. He held her chair. She sat down, began to remove her gloves and said with a sigh, 'We could trot down to the Royal Hibernian. Take that Captain Forrister up on his lunch offer … as we're not doing anything better today and they haven't arrested us yet … and the food in the Hibernian is apparently edible.'

'Guy's invitation? It would be a bit incongruous, wouldn't it?'

'Your sister doesn't seem to think so. She has agreed to meet him.'

Harry raised his eyebrows. 'Really? I'm glad. I didn't want him to think he was being snubbed!'

'I asked her to find out from him how many men they have in the Castle. Not that it matters now!'

Harry stared at her, aghast. 'You asked her to spy? To use an unsuspecting old friendship?'

'I certainly did, Harry! Are we about to wage war or are we playing games?'

'War, but honourable war! Oh Dee, I have the most momentous news!' He watched her pupils dilate and added, 'The Military Council met this morning at St Enda's …'

'And?' she interrupted eagerly, sitting bolt upright.

Harry glanced over his shoulder, lowering his voice so that it was barely audible.

'All plans, as far as possible, go ahead tomorrow!'

'In spite of MacNeill's cancellation?'

He nodded. Deirdre gave a hard excited laugh laced with fear. 'That will leave us with just a handful. Volunteers, countrywide, cannot be advised in time of the second change in plan.'

'No matter. They will rise when they hear what is happening in Dublin.' Harry reached for Deirdre's hand. 'Mobilisation orders will be issued in the morning. I will be with Pearse!'

'And what about me?'

'Your unit of the *Cumann* will be with us! Live or die, my Deirdre, we go together!'

The afternoon shadows crept into the room in St Stephen's Green. The sounds from the street below, the voices of Sunday strollers, turned into the noises of evening. But the two lovers were conscious of nothing except their need.

It was nearly seven o'clock when Ellen woke to find Guy gazing at her like someone stunned. He had his fingers in her hair. Ellen felt the sheet against her naked limbs and his bare legs against hers. What have I done? But through every fibre of her being she felt only exhilaration.

'Ellen! Tell me you love me.'

She looked into his eyes and said, 'Then. Now. Always.' She added with a small laugh, 'Oh always!'

The room was full of magic. The prints on the walls were exquisite, the design of the curtain fabric wonderful in its delicacy. She no longer felt outside of everything, like a winter waif looking in at warmth. She was within the enchanted circle at last.

He was smiling. 'How do you feel?' he asked.

'New!'

'You are not angry?'

She shook her head. I have a child and a husband, she told herself. I am a teacher. What I have done, if known, will brand me forever. So why has this been the single most authentic happiness of my life? But she would not think today. Not today. She would deal with everything tomorrow.

Guy nuzzled into her neck. 'When the war is over I am going to take you away,' he whispered. 'We will be married and go to Fontebelle.'

'How?'

'We'll work out the details. Did I tell you there is a small lake there, with water lilies the French call *Nymphaea,* and golden carp that will almost eat out of your hand? Every morning in spring and summer the heron comes … And the frogs have their babies there … Oh Ellen, I have seen a tiny green bullfrog that would fit in your palm, sitting on a water-lily pad and croaking his heart out, a racket you would not believe. And the dragonflies lay their eggs there and fly above the water in a shimmer of blues and greens. And there are magnolia trees in the park with the most heavenly scent. And the deer come, lovely young stags in spring with their does, and the wild boar in winter.'

Ellen listened, eyes closed.

'Can you stay the night?' he asked eagerly. 'We could have supper somewhere. There's a little place in Ballsbridge.'

The temptation was terrible. But Deirdre would be frantic. She might even contact the police, and God knew where that would end.

'Darling, I can't. But we have tomorrow.'

'I'll make you some tea.'

Guy got out of bed. As he walked across the room, Ellen looked at the muscles ripple in his legs and buttocks, the wiry hair that spread up his spine and the pink scar on his back that told its own story. She had discovered it earlier with her lips.

# Chapter 35

*Easter Monday, 1916*

Franny woke at nine, turned over and lay torpid. She could hear the morning chorus through the open window and the sea sighing. I am engaged to be married … to the best and kindest of men, she thought. The room was alive. Joyous sunlight poured through a gap in the curtains and was reflected in the small cut-glass jars on the French dressing table and the bevelled mirror. In it she could see the foot of the brass bed and her own toes protruding from beneath the eiderdown. From downstairs came the sound of Mrs Burke riddling the ashes in the range. She heard the kitchen door close with its peculiar rattle, and then Hannah's voice in the garden, sweet as a serenade:

*Just a song at twilight when the lights are low,*
*And the flickering shadows softly come and go.*
*Though the heart be weary, sad the day and long*
*Still to us at twilight comes Love's old song*
*Comes Love's old sweet song.*

It was the song Ellen had sung in Kilcrannagh on the evening of her fifteenth birthday. Closing her eyes, Franny saw the young girl in the new blue dress and the elegant young man at the piano. She had met the same young man on Saturday, but now he was the haggard soldier of a terrible war.

Alma had taught Hannah this song. The child's voice was true; she had dreamed of being in the Special Choir at school, but this prize had so far eluded her and Franny suspected she was being punished for her illegitimacy.

There was a gentle tapping on her door. She wiped her eyes and called, 'Come in!'

'Top o' the mornin' to me darlin.'

Liam pushed the door open. Franny sat up, pulled the long plait of her hair from where it was caught under the pillow and regarded with pleasure the elegant tray – small silver tea pot, toast in a silver rack, boiled egg in a porcelain egg cup, blue-and-white china, all set out on an embroidered cloth. Liam deposited the tray on her knees and she put up her face for his kiss.

'Shure begob, didn't I set it meself?'

Franny compressed her lips and shook her head at the stage Irishness.

'It's very kind of you to spoil me …'

'I'm not spoiling you.' He shook out the napkin. 'I'm giving my fiancée a chance to rest. While some of us just daub a bit of paint on canvas all week, others of us have to work very hard at making a real living?'

He sat at the end of the bed while she ate her breakfast. She flushed and laughed under his intent gaze, offered him a finger of toast dipped in egg yolk.

'I've eaten. I had breakfast with Hannah an hour ago?'

'I heard her singing in the garden?'

'She's happy for us! She paid me a nice compliment. She said that if she had a choice of all the fathers in the whole world, she would still choose me!'

Franny put down the cup, pushed away the tray. 'She's very

wrapped up in this father business, isn't she? She prayed last night to her own, no doubt, to give us his blessing.'

'Oh Fran! Let Wallace go from our lives! She's a child! She'll forget as she grows older. She'll have a new dad, remember …'

The bed creaked as he kissed her, caressed her face and added, 'I love you and I don't want anything ever to come between us. Don't let it, Fran.'

Franny felt it was extraordinary that she could be loved. Nothing in her life, except Hannah, mattered in comparison. Liam moved closer. She felt his fingers touch her neck, probe gently under her nightgown for the swell of her breast.

'Your skin is wonderful!'

The panic came the moment he touched her. It wasn't as though she didn't love him; it was something with its own will. She said as lightly as she could. 'If you stay here any longer Mrs Burke will think my virtue is being compromised.' She was going to add, 'Again.' but thought better of it.

'Mrs B has more to occupy her.' But he straightened and added, 'Get dressed, my darling. Hannah has ordered a picnic lunch. It's a gorgeous day!'

He blew back a kiss from the door and was gone.

Franny donned her dressing gown and went to the bathroom. She ran hot water into the bath, added some of the lavender salts Alma favoured, pinned up her hair, got in and luxuriated in the hot, scented steam. But her mind was in turmoil. It was like having a disease, this pointless terror. What kind of a life would they have together if this went on? Lie in his arms with her teeth gritted? I thought I was over it! I thought I had exorcised him!

The face of her rapist rose like a genie in the steam.

Guy was also up early. Dizzy with happiness, he told himself that his damn shakes had been a blessing in disguise. It had brought him something he could not otherwise have dreamed. Pity Ellen hadn't been able to stay the night. But her friend would have been frantic if she had returned and found her absent, with her things still there and no word of explanation. So he had taken her back to Sandymount in a cab, kissing her hands and letting her down discreetly a few doors from her lodgings.

'What time tomorrow?'

'It will have to be the afternoon. I need some time with Harry … if I can get it!'

He'd prised the spare key from his key ring and handed it to her.

'Three o'clock, then. On the nail.'

'On the nail!'

Guy whistled as he shaved, running the cutthroat razor smoothly over his face and throat. He felt a different being almost to the shattered creature who had dragged himself up his stairs with the help of Ellen and two Good Samaritans only the day before. He did not know how he and Ellen would resolve the situation in which they now found themselves. He only knew he had never known bliss of this order. He was going to take her away, take her child too, make whatever arrangements were necessary so she could procure a divorce and marry him. The husband was a teacher and would surely act like a gentleman. He would discuss it with her this afternoon. And he would surprise her with the little ring, the symbol of the continuity between them.

He dressed, went downstairs and out into the morning. The trams in St Stephen's Green were crammed with people in holiday mood. The upper decks were full of laughing Dubliners heading to the seaside, the Phoenix Park or to the races. Guy wondered if he could interest Ellen in any of these possibilities for the afternoon. Personally, he dreamed of staying in, curtains drawn, continuing where they had left off. They could dine out in the evening, somewhere discreet.

He turned the corner into Dawson Street, retraced his steps of yesterday to the Royal Hibernian where he intended to breakfast.

He was inordinately hungry and envisaged a full breakfast of bacon and eggs with plenty of Irish brown bread and a pot of hot, strong tea. He had barely sat at table when Mrs Hamilton Norway entered the dining room. The wife of the Postmaster General for Ireland, she and her husband were among the people he had encountered yesterday morning in Dawson Street on his way to his luncheon appointment with Ellen. Captain Sid Richardson, whom he had known in Sandhurst, had been walking with them and had introduced them.

He rose as Mrs Norway found her way among the tables. She was followed by a youth still in his teens.

'Good morning Captain Forrister!' she said. 'I didn't realise you were staying here!'

Guy rose to his feet. 'I'm not. I have rooms locally.'

'This is my son Neville. He is on holiday from school.'

Guy shook hands. He knew the Norways had already lost their elder boy, Frederick, at Armentière, and he felt profoundly sorry for them. He had met the nineteen-year-old once, a bright and gallant boy with everything to live for.

'Captain Forrister is one of our heroes,' Mrs Norway told her young son. She added with a smile, 'Congratulations, Captain. I hear you are to have the Military Cross!'

Guy started. Evidently the wheels had turned behind the scenes.

'You know more than I do, Mrs Norway.'

'Hamilton could fill you in,' she replied. 'But he has gone to his desk in the Post Office.'

She moved on, followed by Neville, who glanced back and grinned.

Don't do that, Guy wanted to shout. Don't give me that look that says how much you admire me and how much you are longing to be part of it too, part of the bloody crime on the innocent, the heroic, the young! He calmed himself with thoughts of Ellen and resumed his breakfast.

*

Alma, Liam, Franny and Hannah took a midday walk to Howth summit. Liam carried the picnic hamper. It contained plates, glasses, the remains of yesterday's chicken, sliced ham, salad with lettuce, tomatoes and scallions. Mrs Burke had also added a lemon meringue pie and a jar of fresh, lightly whipped cream. Franny carried a blue tartan rug, Hannah a corked bottle of lemonade in a shopping bag. Alma carried her brother's sketch pad and pencils.

It was the best day for ages, bright sunshine, excellent visibility. The few clouds were high and threw violet shadows onto the sea. Below them the bay had never seemed so blue, the city in the distance more beautiful against its mountains. The ladies were wearing wide-brimmed straw hats; Liam sported a boater. He searched for a sheltered, shady spot in which to spread out the rug. The women helped him, gauging the direction of the sunlight.

'A girl has to watch her complexion!' Franny said.

'A boy has to watch her complexion too!' Liam replied.

Hannah laughed. 'Isn't he funny, Mother?'

'He's a flirtatious rascal,' Alma said, 'who thinks he's irresistible.'

Franny grinned at Liam and deposited herself on the rug with a sigh of delight. Alma joined her and the two women busied themselves setting out plates and cutlery. They heard the sound that came across the bay, the sharp, repeated crack of what sounded like gunfire. Alma straightened and stared across the water at the city, shading her eyes with her hand. The sound continued and Liam jumped to his feet.

'Good God!' he exclaimed, half under his breath.

'Volunteer manoeuvres, I expect,' Franny said, taking the salad out of the hamper. 'They must have decided to parade after all … and fire a few shots in the air.'

She thought of Harry and looked doubtfully across the bay at the city. Hannah, immobile as a statue, suddenly raised her hand, pointing to the city. 'Look, Mother. Look!'

Franny scrambled to her feet. Rising from the city were long wisps of smoke.

# Chapter 36

Guy had several hours to kill before his rendezvous with Ellen. He had breakfasted so well that he did not need lunch, so he took up the history book he had perused two nights earlier, lay on his bed, propped himself up on pillows and resumed where he had left off. He wanted to know more, not because he was a particular devotee of history, but because it was Irish history and therefore contained something of Ellen, her blood, her culture. But the contents were increasingly disturbing and he doubted their accuracy. When he had read the section on the Great Famine he threw down the book.

'Can it be true?' he muttered aloud. 'That, at a time when Ireland's staple food crop had failed, all the other food in the country was taken under armed guard to England? That sixty years ago the Government of Great Britain, the world's greatest and richest power, ensured that more than a million of the queen's subjects starved to death? That it took a nation's food, emptied it of its people and even sneered at their anguish?'

He tried to feel it was a calumny; but he was powerless against the sick, cynical sense of déjà vu. Of course it was true! An agriculturally rich, strategically important country, emptied of its indigenous people, would be an irresistible prize for an imperial power. An excuse like a potato famine had been heaven sent. Was not the present administration exterminating their own manhood right now on the fields of France and Flanders, for ends that had nothing to do with high moral objective?

He thought of young Neville Norway whom he had met that morning, and then of James, his nephew, almost the same age, and as eager for the fray, fired by prospects of glory and heroism. They could not know how quickly glory departed a corpse, nor how it stank after a week in the slime.

I will write to James he thought. I will warn him, tell him the truth. If I am killed next time around, the war may last beyond my death and he will come to it, poor boy, like a lamb to the butcher's block. There has to be someone in the family left alive.

He closed the book. He did not want to read further. He wanted to prepare for the afternoon and began by making his bed – military fashion. There was no batman here. He held Ellen's pillow to his face, searching for her scent and found a few ribs of her hair. He collected each rib carefully, ran them over his lips, wound them into a circlet, put them into an envelope and wrote her name on the outside. With a few more, he thought, I'll have enough for a locket, another talisman for the war. He put the envelope into his pocket. He looked for the ring. I must have put it down somewhere. God damn it, where did I leave it? He searched the sitting room and the bedroom and turned out his suitcase but to no avail. His attention was arrested by something going on outside, the sound of digging in the Green. He went to the window, saw some kind of activity beyond the railings of St Stephen's Green. His line of vision was impeded by the trees and he looked around for Duggy's field glasses, which he had seen in the bookcase. The trees leaped almost into the room. Beyond them he saw something that made him doubt his eyes. For a moment he thought they were gardeners, the men in the green uniforms digging in the shrubbery of the public parkland.

'Good Lord!' he muttered, 'Volunteer chappies are digging trenches?'

A few onlookers were suddenly ordered out of the park at bayonet point, and the gates padlocked.

'I say, these people are overstepping the mark with their war games,' Guy said aloud. 'Where are the police?'

He grabbed his cap and rushed downstairs. People were standing at the corner near Grafton Street, looking bewildered.

'The Volunteers are taking the city!' a dazed voice informed him.

'Sure the bowsies are in the GPO,' a woman added on a note of hysteria. 'Me poor husband's in Flanders. How will I get me Separation Allowance now?'

He heard the rattle of distant gunfire, heard it reverberate at other points in the city, turned and made his way down Grafton Street. His mind was feverish. How many troops did they have in Ireland? How many in Dublin Castle?

He looked around for a cab or a tram. But traffic was at a standstill. He strode to College Green, turned down Westmoreland Street and crossed O'Connell Bridge. En route he heard the crack of rifle fire again, nearer now. But it did not provoke his recent fragility; it was somehow too real, and the adrenalin surging in his veins was responding to genuine danger. Seeing his uniform, some people accosted him. The country had risen, some said. The Germans had come, others said. The Volunteers were in the Post Office and the Germans had invaded and would help them take the country. He saw, when he came to Sackville Street, that many of the shop windows had been smashed.

On the roof of the General Post Office fluttered a green flag and on it, in large white lettering, were the words 'Irish Republic'. Flying from another pole was a flag he had never seen before – a tricolour in green, white and orange. The building's parapet was lined with men with rifles. All the windows of the ground floor had been broken and barricaded with furniture; two men, rifles at the ready, stood at each of them. A placard fixed to the front of the building announced:

> *The Headquarters of The Provisional Government of The Irish Republic.*

On the wall was a printed proclamation.

But it was all pantomime to the small crowd of excited onlookers who stood in the shadow of Nelson's Pillar. They waited, talking and pointing, shouting abuse or encouragement.

'Where are the rest of yez?' a woman screamed at Guy. 'Are yez goin' to let the lousers get away wi' this?'

She thrust a sheet of paper at him. Guy pushed it automatically into his pocket. It would be a propaganda leaflet no doubt. The clatter of hooves on cobbles came from the north end of the street and a cry rose, 'Lancers! The Lancers are coming!' The small mob began to run. A voice he recognised was howling above the din, 'Guy … Guy!'

At one of the smashed and barricaded windows of the Post Office, he saw the glint of round spectacles and a face he knew. He saw the hand that knocked sideways the rifle aimed at him. Harry Healy was waving at him frantically, gesturing him to go away. Almost at the same moment, another bullet struck the cobbles beside Guy with a high-pitched whine. He ducked against a column fronting Clery's store. His revolver was already in his hand, his martial reflexes automatic. He looked back at the GPO but Harry had disappeared.

The sound of the approaching cavalry was now a thunder. For Guy it was like slow motion. The Lancers were already firing into the building and the Volunteers were returning fire. A bullet sang by Guy's ear, grazed the side of his skull and knocked his cap into the gutter. It was a sniper on the Post Office roof. Blood trickled down his neck. He returned fire, then ran, half-dazed, for the relative shelter of the Pillar's broad granite base. He heard a wounded horse scream as it plunged, the high-pitched crack of bullets striking stone and the cries of command. And all the time it rained gunfire from the GPO.

In the whirling senselessness it seemed to him that history was repeating itself. He was at Loos and the Germans were coming over the top, the Germans who, sick of bloodshed, had eventually stopped firing. He did not see the maddened, wounded animal that turned in the street and lashed out at him with its iron-shod feet.

Ellen took the tram into town. But it was stopped by police and the passengers advised to go home. 'Disturbances in the city!' the police said.

She thought of Deirdre and her warnings, Deirdre who had knocked on her door earlier to say goodbye, saying she had to muster at Liberty Hall.

'I thought I might see Harry today, Dee …'

'I don't think so.'

'It's Easter Monday! What will you be doing? Parading?'

'Something like that. Stay out of town!'

'Deirdre … you're driving me mad. When will you be back?'

'I don't know.'

Deirdre wrapped Ellen in a sudden fierce embrace. 'I'm terribly sorry everything's been messed up for you. But we will have time together when all this is over. Try to forgive us!' Then she was gone.

*Try to forgive us*? Ellen shook her head. She thought of Guy and what they had done and said and groaned with each remembrance, groaned with the fullness of it. She hardly knew who she was anymore. The prospect of the future Guy had outlined to her, divorce from Brendan, marriage to Guy and life after the war in lovely, secluded Fontebelle, far from the grinding ennui of being a woman in rural Ireland. And then she thought of Brendan and little Hughie, and tried to look at the facts.

If she went with Guy she would lose her child. Brendan would make sure of that. If she went with Guy, Brendan himself would be disgraced. He would have to leave the parish, leave his school. He would be marked – a spoiled priest whose wife had run away with an English officer. In provincial Ireland it would be hard to find a more damning indictment.

And he would never give her a divorce. Guy was so sure he would, but she knew he would not. No, he would be all rectitude, the best cover for revenge.

I would give half my life, she thought after a while, to go with Guy and say, 'Yes, I will marry you! To wait for you until the war is over, build a family with you and a home – where I could be myself, release myself … and love you. God, how I love you.' But, point by point, reason laid out before her the full price of joy. I cannot go with him at the expense of a forsaken child, an abandoned and humiliated Brendan. Nor could I endure my own ambiguous status. It would mock me to my grave. Of course you could be his … occasional mistress, came a gentle whisper. Whenever he's in Ireland. It would be better than nothing … and no one need ever know. You need each other … you have a right to some happiness. She wrestled with this, imagined it through to its finale of discovery and disgrace, and whispered her despair into the pillow. I must tell him today. But I must have one last evening … one last night in his arms.

And now the stupid tram was stopped and people were surmising as to the why the fine morning was reverberating with gunfire.

'Those Volunteer eejits,' someone said, 'a bunch of overgrown schoolboys.'

I'll walk, Ellen told herself. It's not that far.

When Ellen reached St Stephen's Green she found its southside impassable. Digging of some kind was going on inside the park. Looking down Dawson Street she could see there was a dead horse. The dray it had been pulling formed part of a barricade that also contained a sidecar, two motors and a big laundry van, out of which baskets had fallen, strewing laundry across the street. Four uniformed Volunteers were manning this barricade, commandeering any traffic that chanced to come, adding motor cars to the barricade and sending the owners away.

She hurried to Guy's rooms. She put the key in the unfamiliar lock and let herself into the hall, raced up the stairs and knocked on his door. When there was no answer she let herself in.

When Guy recovered consciousness he smelled chloral and thought he was having his wounds dressed in France. He lay for a moment staring at the ceiling. Hospital, he thought. I can rest for a while.

He stirred and tried to look around him. It was only then he realised his head was bandaged; the gauze was tight around his skull, its lumpiness against the pillow. He saw a shuttered window on one side of his bed; he saw the iron ends of other beds, the bump of other men's feet beneath blankets. He heard springs squeak as someone moved and moaned with escalating, all too familiar, anguish. A nurse came rushing, passed Guy's bed. After a moment the groans ceased.

A young nurse turned from the bed beside him, looked into his eyes and put a gentle hand on his shoulder. With her was a doctor in a white coat.

'Welcome back to us, Captain,' she said in a soft Irish brogue.

'Where am I?'

'Dublin Castle … temporary hospital. Can you tell me your name?'

Guy searched for his name; his head thumped. His whole life, all his knowledge and experience were like tangled dancers around a rickety maypole. But he was suddenly certain of one thing.

'I have to get up … Important appointment!'

'Not at this hour, I think,' she replied with a smile. 'Sure 'tis past midnight and whoever you had to meet is already away with the fairies!'

Ellen. he thought. Ellen is gone with the fairies.

The doctor shone a light in Guy's eyes and looked at him with bloodshot weariness.

'You were lucky. If the bullet had been …' he gestured with his thumb and index finger and shook his head. 'Sure you don't know your name?'

'You tell me. You must have my serial number.'

'Of course I know it. But it's not much use if you don't! It will come back … you must try to stay awake.'

'Where was I injured?'

'Sackville Street. The rebels are still in the Post Office.'

Guy had a momentary flash of a face he knew at a barricaded window. 'Harry Healy!' he said.

'That's not your name?'

But a door had opened in Guy's brain. 'No … a friend's! My name's Forrister. I'm on leave!'

'Well done, Captain! Looks like you'll be all right,' the doctor said. 'Is there anything you need?'

'I need to write a note to someone I was supposed to meet today,' Guy said slowly. 'I think I have the address in my pocket book.'

The nurse brought Guy his tunic after a couple of minutes, along with a cup of tea and a few biscuits. She propped him into a sitting position so he could eat and drink. When he was finished she put the cup on the bedside locker and searched his pockets.

'No pocket book,' she said.

I probably left it in Duggy's, Guy told himself. He was already feeling better. His headache had eased.

'Maybe you wrote the address on this?' the nurse said, handing Guy a crumpled sheet of paper she pulled from his pocket. 'Oh, it's one of those!' she added, half to herself, and made to put it aside. Guy glanced at the creased document and saw an underscored headline: 'Poblacht na hEireann'. It was the leaflet thrust at him that morning.

'What does it say? Read it. My eyes hurt.'

She whispered: '*The Provisional Government of the Irish Republic to the People of Ireland …*'

'Go on …'

Her voice lowered and she looked around carefully.

'*Irishmen and Irishwomen, in the name of God and of the dead generations from whom she receives her old traditions of nationhood, Ireland, through us, summons her children to her flag and strikes for her freedom …*'

She looked at him nervously and read on.

'*… We declare the right of the people of Ireland to the ownership of Ireland …*'

'Enough.' Guy said. 'I get the general drift!'

He took the paper from the nurse's hand, thanked her and leaned back on the pillows. He knew what would happen now. The rebels would be met with overwhelming force. Harry would be either executed or sent to jail in England to serve an indefinite sentence with hard labour. And his comrades also, and his fiery little fiancée. And Ellen's heart would break.

He heard voices outside and leaned gingerly out of bed to look through a crack in the shuttering. Below him in the Castle yard, he saw soldiers warming their hands around blazing fires. At least the castle had not fallen. Reinforcements had come from the Curragh camp of course. And there would soon be more. In a couple of days the Post Office would be a tomb.

The fools! he thought, letting the printed proclamation slip through his fingers to the floorboards. The fools, the fools, the fools …

# Chapter 37

Three o'clock came and went but there was no sign of Guy. Peering through the window, Ellen could see that the Volunteers had dug pits in St Stephen's Green and were manning them – three to a pit. The street was almost deserted. Firing went on intermittently; some of the shots seemed to go into the nearby Shelbourne Hotel . She heard the crash of breaking glass, saw a civilian slumped by the railings, blood trickling into the gutter. Where was the ambulance? Then came more shooting. She saw people running on the west side of the Green and firing from the College of Surgeons. She hid behind the curtains; snipers were not too particular. The clock chimed four. Where was Guy?

*Don't go into town!* Was Deirdre involved in this? Harry too? The military would now be summoned from the Curragh and from England. Was the insurrection nationwide? Was Brendan all right? Was Hughie?

*Try to forgive us.* She rushed to the bathroom and was sick. When she had washed her face she penned a note to Guy and propped it on the mantelpiece beside the clock. Then she let herself out and got to the corner of Grafton Street, dodging from doorway to doorway.

'You'll get yourself killed, Missus!' a man shouted at her from across the street.

There was another burst of gunfire.

'I have to get home. Are the trains running?'

'No. No trams either. And all the roads out of Dublin are held by the rebels.'

No trams? Flinching at the chatter of guns, she had no choice but to return to the shelter of Guy's rooms.

It was a night of gunfire. The morning dawned but still Guy did not return. Ellen ventured out during a lull, but found no shops open. Desperate for news of her brother and Deirdre, she approached the barricade in Dawson Street, but was told by a dishevelled man in a green uniform to go home.

'Can't you see there's a war on, Miss?'

Desultory firing recommenced. It was too dangerous to walk to Sandymount. She went back to Guy's rooms. In the afternoon she watched British troops arrive in armoured cars and rake St Stephen's Green with machine guns. They seemed to have accessed the roof of the Shelbourne Hotel and the United Services Club. The din was fearful. A bullet broke the window beside her and smashed into the shutter, making her cry out. There was an answering shot from the roof above her. So they were up there, snipers, over her head! She closed the heavy shutters and found herself in semi-darkness. Through chinks in the wood she could see raindrops on the window, oddly normal.

In the late afternoon it began to rain. She was faint; she had not eaten for almost twenty-four hours. Checking the kitchen, she found some tinned sardines and condensed milk. She opened the sardines and cut her finger on the tin. Blood dripped onto the counter and she sucked the wound. A few minutes later, she munched the sardines with a heel of stale bread.

After her meal she ventured into the landing, but except for the movement on the roof, there was no sense of human presence in the house; all away for the Easter weekend presumably, and unable to get back. In any case, she could not knock on other doors; her position was delicate – a married woman in an officer's rooms. She would have to sit it out, hold onto her sanity. Guy was out there in uniform, a target.

That night a machine-gun battle broke out nearby, lasting twenty minutes. She wept and prayed. Exhausted, she slept again in Guy's bed only to be woken by a noise like the end of the world – the boom of heavy guns. By the sound of it, they were demolishing the city. I should have taken Harry and Deirdre seriously long ago, she thought. They have brought about the destruction of Dublin!

She was amazed at the anger she felt towards people she had always loved. But, after a while, she had to acknowledge that, whatever they had done, this was no horseplay. As the bombardment continued, her imagination wrapped around them, holed up somewhere with their few firearms, fighting a hopeless battle and there gathered in her, a love beyond anything she had ever felt for them. How idiotically heroic to undertake a straight fight with a Colossus, to throw your life to the winds for a passionate belief!

When the shelling ceased the noise continued in her ears. And then the silence deafened. She closed her eyes and fixed the whole force of her mind on Guy. She put her arms around the pillow she had shared with him and whispered her love. Then she got out of bed and added a postscript to the note she had left him.

Guy stayed awake on Monday night. The little nurse would not let him sleep. Every time he slipped into a doze she woke him, asking him questions, his name, his regiment. 'With head injuries we have to keep the patient awake, in case of coma,' she informed him.

The noise in the city banished sleep anyway. By morning the turmoil in his mind had distilled into two questions: had Ellen made it home safely and what would become of Harry? He wrote a note to Ellen, addressed it, care of Miss Frances Murphy at Du Barry Milliner's, Chatham Street. He asked a nurse to post it, but she shook her head.

'The streets are too dangerous. Hundreds of civilians and military are dead. There are looters all over the place.'

On Wednesday morning the drubbing in Guy's skull eased and he could think more clearly. But then came the booming bass of a field gun, a sound he knew too well. The Front had come to Dublin. By nightfall the smell of a burning city reached into the ward. His old comrade, Sid Richardson, paid him a visit. Dressed in polished field boots and riding breeches he was the calm epitome of military command.

'Heard you were here, old chap! Bad luck. But we have the blighters pinned down now. A gunboat is on the river, armed with a three-footer. They've sent Maxwell you know. He'll flush the rebels out. Put an end to the nonsense.'

'Tell me, Sid,' Guy said, 'if the shoe were on the other foot, if Ireland were powerful and if she seized our country, destroyed its people, language, customs, culture, took all its wealth, and if demands for justice were ignored century on century, what would you do?'

Sid laughed. 'Dear boy, it happened to us. What do you think the Norman Conquest was all about? The rebels' cause was lost long ago, and like us, they'd better start to like it.'

'There's an old friend of mine in the Post Office. What are his chances?'

'Wouldn't be in his shoes!'

'When this is over … if he's hurt … can you see he's brought here?'

Sid pinched the end of his moustache between thumb and forefinger. 'Give me his name.'

In Howth, Franny, Liam, Hannah and Alma sat it out. Every day, as the drama played on, they watched the city from across the bay. On Wednesday and Thursday the boom of the field guns and the clatter of the machine guns came clearly across the water. Thick black columns of smoke were now rising from the city. By Thursday evening, it seemed as though the whole of Dublin was ablaze. The glare lit up the night sky, gouts of sudden incandescence, long tongues of fire and sudden explosions.

Franny hugged Hannah to her. In her mind's eye was Harry with his ridiculous old rifle. And the rest of them, their firearms bought with their own small savings, shooting it out with their last few rounds, while the world's great power pounded them to dust.

She saw the proclamation of the Republic; copies had been brought to Howth and distributed. She and Liam read it together: *We pray that no one who serves the cause shall dishonour it by cowardice, inhumanity or rapine.*

'Romantic idealism!' she cried. 'When did that ever win a battle?'

Later, when Hannah was asleep and Alma was foraging in the kitchen, she turned to Liam who had maintained a strange silence all day.

'There were other ways, Liam, surely? They could have gone about it peacefully … pressured Westminster?'

'Do you think it hasn't been tried, Fran? But heroism, even when vanquished, makes a noise that cannot be ignored.'

Franny thought about this. Women had died on hunger strike in England because the statement they had to make was more important than their lives. Emily Davison had killed herself under the hooves of the King's racehorse. But where were the votes for women?

'I am afraid my cousin is going to die,' she said dully. 'And I do not think it will make a difference.'

'Franny', he said gently, 'what you have seen this week is a watershed. It will certainly change Ireland. And, given time, it will also signal the end of an empire.'

# Chapter 38

*Dublin, Friday, 27 April, 1916*

The General Post Office was smashed, the windows broken and the men exhausted. Four days and nights, Deirdre thought, without sleep or rest. How many years of planning? How many messages and dispatches had she carried? How little time devoted to anything except the cause? But she knew the attempt was doomed. MacNeill's countermanding order had been obeyed in the provinces; the city insurgents were on their own.

Harry had two bullet wounds, one in the chest, one in the abdomen. He had trouble breathing and was in great pain. The whole of Sackville Street seemed to be in flames. The smoke stung Deirdre's eyes; the acrid stench made her gag. Around her was the roaring of flames, the noise of breaking glass and collapsing walls.

'The first time since Moscow,' Joe Plunkett said to her in his gentle voice. 'The first time a capital city has burned since 1812.' He put his monocle to his eye and looked at her quizzically. 'What do you say to that, Miss Callaghan?'

She loved Joe Plunkett; everyone did. Terminally ill with TB, he had come from his sickbed to help direct the Rising. His booted and spurred elegance amid the fury of war seemed to defy the reality taking place around them. And the reality was that the centre of Dublin was destroyed and the cause was lost.

'Courage!' he said. 'There's sap in us yet!'

'Is there?' Her gesture took in the ruins around her, the rattle of machine guns and the whine of bullets. 'How many men have we left?'

'Here? Maybe a hundred and twenty.'

'And how many have they?'

He raised his thin shoulders. 'Twenty, thirty thousand?' He smiled. 'You didn't expect us to win?'

'Of course I did!'

'Not this time, Deirdre. But remember that the race is not to the swift, nor the battle to the strong.'

Red crosses on their white pinafores, the members of the *Cumann* tended the wounded in the military hospital they had set up in one of the rooms in the GPO. They had spent the last four days feeding the men, nursing the wounded, rolling bandages and loading weapons. Many of them had carried dispatches and ferried food to the various manned stations around the city. Now they were summoned by Pearse who told them it was time for them to go. They were to leave the building under a Red Cross flag.

'No!' Deirdre cried, looking across to where Harry lay on a pallet. An incendiary exploded on the roof above them with a deafening roar and gouts of flame.

'Go!'

She shook her head.

'I'll be all right,' Harry whispered. 'You have to obey orders, Dee. Like a good soldier.'

'No!'

Most of the other women left; three remained. She had something important to say to Harry. But there were men everywhere and it was private.

The fire hoses were being deployed, but to little effect. Blazing timbers were crashing from the upper storeys. Harry looked around at the leaders – Connolly, writer and fiery socialist, lying near him on a stretcher, his ankle shattered; the dying poet Joe Plunkett, bandaged at the throat from his recent surgery for tuberculosis; Pearse, still feverish with purpose, although plainly done in with exhaustion; Tom Clarke, the fiery old Fenian, white and haggard, his clothes and face streaked with blood and dirt. And MacDermott, lame from polio, using his cane to cross the crazy amphitheatre. His personality was probably the most powerful of all; his charisma sparkled as though the day were won.

'We'll get you out, Harry! We're going to evacuate the building!'

'If Pearse orders surrender,' Harry said, 'the men will not obey.'

'They are soldiers and they will obey!' replied Mac Dermott.

'If you will give me back my rifle I will fight on!'

'Common sense, Harry, please! If we all die, we may as well throw our hat at it. You must live, you and the others … for another day.'

'You are not afraid … of what will happen on surrender?'

'Of one thing only. That the British will show mercy.'

Harry stifled a groan. The pain in his belly was a roar. MacDermott's voice was coming from far away.

'Mercy will make us a bunch of poltroons, idiotic enough to take on their might! But, with a bit of luck, Harry, they will execute us … the leaders.'

Harry closed his eyes. The burning in his chest echoed the burning around him, the stench of doom. The smoke was choking him and the pain was carrying him away.

The news filtered through to Kilcrannagh after days of wild rumour. There had been no newspapers since Sunday; no trains were running. But the police had been busy, assisting the British army, which had arrived in truckloads. Anyone suspected of being involved with the Volunteers was taken. They came to arrest Mrs

Murphy and bundled her into the back of a lorry.

'How dare you! Why are you doing this?'

But their faces were blank. Groups of people in Monaghan town turned out to watch the trucks leave. Some booed the occupants; they were mostly wives of men away at the war.

From his vantage point in the haggard where he was digging mangles, Jimmy MacMahon saw the Crossley Tender stop at the gate. He slipped through the sycamores that formed the perimeter and heard the shout ordering him to stop. He ignored it and ran. Something sliced into his thigh, knocking him into a ditch. Writhing, he gritted his teeth. Blood was running down his leg and into his boot. He probed at the wound gingerly. At least it wasn't spouting; the bullet had missed the artery. Thanks be to Jaysus the fuckers couldn't shoot straight!

He heard them coming, running through the potato field. The boreen dividing his farm from the Fahy's was to his right. The high hedgerow would provide cover and the Fahys would help him. But to what purpose? The army would be on them in no time and they would be rounded up as well.

He tore off his jacket, wrapped it around his waist to provide a buffer between his wound and the ground and forced himself along the length of the ditch. From there he slid into a culvert overgrown with briars. He tore his face and his hands, but desperation lent him indifference. He had been intending to clear this tangled patch; it was ironic that his failure to do so might save him. He lay under the carpet of thorns, heard the soldiers coming and tried not to breathe.

'He probably took the boreen,' one of the soldiers said after a cursory examination of the ditch. 'There's no sign of blood, although I was sure we hit the fecker.'

The soldier had an Irish accent and Jimmy damned him. He willed his heart to stop thumping; it was so loud he was sure they could hear it, and he thanked God they did not have dogs.

When they were gone he waited for what seemed an age, then eased himself from his hiding place and, rolling behind furze bushes and slithering along ditches, headed for the one place where he might be safe.

Once clear of the farm he kept to the side roads, keeping out of sight, uncertain who was friend or foe. Drenched with sweat and ditch water, lacerated by briars, in pain from his wound and weakened by loss of blood, he finally saw Clonshule House on its promontory. He crept through the demesne wall at a spot where the stones had crumbled. He knew from local intelligence that the great house was empty nowadays except for the housekeeper. Old Mrs Wallace had died last November.

But he was wary; the squireen and his wife might have returned from London for Easter. With his lameness the fucker was safe from the war.

There were no motors in the forecourt of Clonshule House, nor any sign of habitation. Shutters were closed. One window alone gave evidence of life – a window with pink geraniums between looped back curtains – the housekeeper, Mrs Roche's, room. The rest of the house looked forlorn with its leaking gutters, a sycamore sprouting from a chimney and a general air of decay. This place has run its course, he thought as he rested behind an oak, cursing his torn leg and wondering what was the latest from Dublin.

All anyone knew was that a handful of men had held five strategic points in the capital for five days. Harry had surely been in the thick of it! Jimmy burned with shame that he had not played the part ordained for his own unit, but the mobilisation orders had been cancelled and no one had known what to do or believe. He and his men had drilled assiduously in secret for months in all weathers. And at the last minute, all orders had been rescinded.

Would Ellen be proud of her brother? Her face rose in his mind with lingering regret. He would never be free of her, nor did he want to be. Once she had time for him, but that had been before the Englishman. His mind reverted to Harry. What would they do to him, assuming he had survived? The lack of news was enough to drive you mad.

Moving in the woodland around the side of the big house, he kept to the cover of the trees until he was near the gate to the walled garden. He tried it and found it locked. Everything looked deserted, but a sixth sense told him he was being observed. He glanced at the windows. Nothing stirred, but when he turned he saw a crouching figure watching him from the shaded woodland, a child with freckles and a cow's lick of red hair standing up on the crown of his head. He was perhaps eleven and looked like one of the McKennas.

'What do you want?' the boy demanded nervously. 'There's no one in the house except Mrs Roche.'

'I was just trying the gate. I was out for a walk.'

The boy looked him up and down, his eyes widening as he saw the congealed blood.

'Did the soldiers shoot you? They were around earlier.'

'Barbed wire. I was crossing a ditch!' He wondered if this youngster would be off like a hare and bring the army back with him. 'Why aren't you at school?'

'No school. Because of the Rising in Dublin! Everybody knows about it. The lock's useless! Look, it's rusted!' The child pushed against the gate and the lock gave way. 'But there's a better place to hide. I'll show you.'

A trap? It was life or death now. But the boy's eyes were ingenuous. 'There's a grand place in the grain loft. No one goes there. I play there sometimes. But better go around behind the garden.'

Jimmy limped behind his guide to the stable yard, where the loose boxes, green paint peeling, were shut up and bolted. They slipped into the coach house where dusty carriages stood in a row, their shafts resting on the ground, mute witnesses to another time.

It was with difficulty that Jimmy followed the barefoot boy up a rough wooden stairs to the loft. The floor was littered with hessian sacks and the place smelled of oats and the must of rotting wood.

'You'll be safe here. I'll come back later with food and water ... and somethin' to bandage your leg,' the boy said and turned to descend the rickety stairs.

'Thanks!' Jimmy called after him. 'What's your name?'

'Donal. Donal Byrne.'

'You look a bit like Mary McKenna who used to work in the big house!'

'Me ma. She doesn't work there anymore.'

Jimmy nodded. He knew who Donal was now and was not blind to the irony. But he was so tired he hardly cared any more if the youngster brought back the full force of the Empire.

The boy ran off and Jimmy lay down among the empty sacks. His leg was agony, but a dried crust of blood had staunched the flow and the trouser material had stuck into the wound. He was afraid to remove it. He wished he could bathe his injury and wondered if it would become infected. Maybe the boy would be able to find a drop of honey – the old women said it was good for wounds. He lay back, closed his eyes and drifted into sleep, hearing somewhere above him a rat scuttling in the roof.

Harry, eyes glazed, skin grey, raved and dreamed and slipped in and out of consciousness. In his lucid moments he knew it was all over. Pearse had surrendered; everyone had been arrested. He reached out for his rifle and met a human hand.

'Take it easy, Harry. You're in hospital!'

'Dee?' Harry's eyes opened. 'I thought I was dreaming.'

His voice rose as the pain crescendoed. The soldier in webbing and fixed bayonet doing duty in the ward nodded grimly and muttered, 'Poor bugger!'

A nurse came hurrying. Harry felt the prick of the blessed

needle, the rushing relief. He dozed. But the pain pulled him back.

'Darling.' It was Dee's voice, stressed and breaking.

He opened his eyes.

She's like an old woman, he thought. Why is she so hollow-eyed?

'You'll ruin your looks if you cry like that, Dee!'

The lights gleamed dimly in the ward. They had moved a screen around his bed. The pain had eased again; he felt a great peace now.

'What day is it?'

'Thursday … May 5th.' Deirdre sobbed and bit her lip.

'What happened to the others, Dee?'

'Connolly is still alive.'

She did not tell him that Padraic Pearse, his brother Willie and the poet Thomas McDonagh had already been executed and buried in quicklime. Harry seemed pacified.

'I have something important to tell you, Harry.' She bent her head and slowly murmured her private and incredible news into his ear. At first it did not seem to register. Then his face lit up.

'Time we were married, Dee,' he said. 'There's a priest around somewhere …'

Later, looking through the window at the scudding clouds, he smiled at her and whispered before he slipped away, 'I will be there, my Deirdre, wherever you are under the wild sky!'

Harry's was just one of many deaths. The country waited with bated breath as the secret court-martials continued, as one after the other the remaining leaders were executed, shot in the Stonebreakers Yard at Kilmainham Jail. Before his execution Sean MacDiarmada wrote: 'I feel happiness the like of which I have never experienced. I die that the Irish nation might live.'

The following week, the dying James Connolly, the last to face the firing squad, was carried to his execution on a stretcher. The rest of the insurgents were shipped off in cattle boats to English jails. Among them was Deirdre's friend from Clonakilty – one Michael

Collins. But although many Dubliners booed the departing rebels, some old men stood to attention on city pavements and saluted them as they were shuttled in trucks to the docks.

When he was released from hospital, Guy returned to his rooms in St Stephen's Green. He found Ellen's note on the mantelpiece by the clock.

> *My dearest,*
>
> *4.30 p.m. and no sign of you. I pray God you are all right.*
> *Firing is going on outside; the world is gone mad.*
> *I must go home. I am frantic about my child.*
> *I will always love you. But there can be no future for us, although*
> *I would give my soul for it.*
>
> *Ellen*
>
> *P.S. I love thee with the breath, smiles, tears of all my life.*
> *And, if God choose, I should but love thee better after death.*

He took out the envelope that contained the strands of her hair, kissed them, enclosed them in the little note and restored them to the envelope.

Back to the war, he thought wearily, returning the envelope to his breast pocket. The sooner the better.

# Chapter 39

*December 1918*

When the war was over, Guy went back to Fontebelle. It was an arduous journey. In northern France the railways had been bombed, the roads potholed from shelling; the countryside, blasted by four years of conflict, was forlorn. The atmosphere that hovered over every blood-drenched field and ditch was of visceral silence, a mourning beyond sadness that tainted the air and seeped into the soul.

He went to Fontebelle for Christmas. He returned alone, driving from Paris in an old Hispano-Suiza, bypassing Bordeaux and hurrying south to where the great forests of the Landes came to meet him. He slowed to savour the long straight roads between the great maritime pines, the stillness, the emptiness. It was a winter afternoon with long shafts of light among the trees. Here and there in forest clearings were the old half-timbered hamlets, surrounded by their flocks of hens and ducks. People in clogs and homespun clothes paused to gaze at the passing motor. You might assume they were untouched, he thought. Until you looked around for the young men.

He had sent a wire to the Fargues to prepare the house. The gates were open, the lavender avenue winter grey. He turned into the gateway and stopped. To left and right of him were trees separated by *allées* of wet grass, all dim with the approach of night.

A young stag shot suddenly from the wood and was lost again in the twilight.

He passed the little *maison de gardian*, empty and shuttered, and then the avenue broadened into a forecourt and the house was before him, the gentle Fontebelle manor. The front windows were bright. He had told the Fargues he wanted open shutters and candlelit windows for his homecoming, and in the gathering dusk the house looked as though it were awaiting guests. But many of the guests it had once entertained were now ghosts. He could see them, shadowy wraiths waiting for him by the worn sandstone steps to the hall door. There was Belling and Dickson and Henderson; old friends, laughing together, as they had on that last boar hunt before the war. The guilt seized him by the throat. Why them? Why not him?

The front door opened and Ginette's sturdy figure was framed against the lighted hall. She came onto the steps, followed by her husband. Guy stopped the car and alighted. Stiff and cold, he came towards them and took their hands.

They kissed him on both cheeks, pressed his hands as if to assure themselves he was real.

'*Bienvenue Monsieur.*' Ginette's eyes were wet.

'*Je suis ravi de vous revoir!*' Guy said, telling them how glad he was to see them and fighting the desire to weep.

'*Monsieur est fatigué!*' Ginette whispered wiping her eyes and asking him immediately if he was hungry with the eagerness of someone who had spent the day cooking. '*Vous devez avoir faim? Je vous ai préparé un petit dîner … quelques palombes.*'

Palombes! The migrating pigeons from the north that came every winter. Pierre was a good shot and Ginette a great cook. Guy realised he was hungry and thanked her. Pierre set about bringing in the bags and Guy followed his housekeeper indoors, crossing the tiles slowly, noting the *armoire Normande* – the cupboard used for coats – and the Aubusson tapestry that had always been there. They gave off the perfume of his youth.

'*Il y a un feu dans la bibliothèque*,' Ginette said.

Guy smiled at her. A fire in the library! Like old times …

'*Merci*.'

She bustled away to the kitchen and he went to the lamplit library where a log fire blazed in the old marble fireplace. The room was warm and close; the fire must have been going all day. He shivered in the heat and looked around at the books on their shelves. He had taken time to put them in order – literary books, military books, French books – long ago before the world had flipped.

He sat on a Louis XVI *canapé* before the fire, longing to sleep, but incapable of slumber. Belling, Dickson and Henderson hovered by the fire. They were joined by Harry Healy who looked at him with his old mischievous grin. Guy put his hands over his eyes. He began to sob. Pierre Fargue came to the door. He began to say the bags had been put in Monsieur's bedroom, but he heard the wrenching sounds as he crossed the threshold and withdrew soundlessly, wiping his eyes.

The morning came reluctantly. The night had been cold despite the embers glowing in the bedroom fireplace. Guy had hardly slept; his dreams had propelled him constantly into the relative calm of insomnia. He had been glad of the glow from the embers in the grate and the glimmer under his door of the lamp in the landing. But, nonetheless, the shadows of yesterday had thickened, clustering about him. The silence was the stillness of the Armistice: the eloquence of silenced guns.

At 8 a.m. he got out of bed, opened one of the two windows and threw back the shutters. The parkland around the house was covered by a freezing mist. A few birds chirped. Two deer grazed near the lake. Carpets of dead leaves brightened the ground with red and ochre. From the village came the tolling of the Mass bell. He went back to bed.

I will let in the peace. It will save me.

He reached for the locket around his neck in which he kept a thin twist of light brown hair. It had been his talisman during the last two years, replacing the little ring he had been unable to find in Duggy's room, although he had hunted for it high and low. When Ginette came to enquire if Monsieur would like a breakfast tray in his room, she found him fast asleep. She shut the window, quietly tended the fire and went away.

There was rejoicing in Dublin on Armistice Day, 11 November, 1918. Crowds walked the streets waving Union Jacks. Women, delighted that their men would soon be coming home, joined the celebrations. Scuffles broke out when groups waving the tricolour tried to burn the Union Jacks. Ambulances, bells jangling, dashed here and there to pick up the injured.

Jimmy was in Dublin. He watched the gaiety and the scuffles, distancing himself emotionally. He had come to the capital to see Michael Collins, who was now Commander-in-Chief of the Volunteers and the rising star of the underground national movement. Twenty-eight, tall, handsome, charismatic, his genius for organisation was becoming legendary.

Yesterday, after Mass, a stranger had whispered in Jimmy's ear that Mick Collins wanted to see him. He was to go up to Dublin immediately; a room had been booked for him in Moran's Hotel. Jimmy had thrown a change of clothes into a suitcase, taken the train on Monday morning and arrived in Dublin to Armistice disturbances. His contact, a nondescript man in a tweed cap, was waiting for him in Moran's crowded bar.

A touch on the arm, a nod, an address, a time – 5 p.m. Tuesday. 'Don't be late. He's a busy man.'

The following day Jimmy presented himself at the door of a modest Victorian red-brick. The woman who answered looked at him carefully, nodded when he gave his name, asked him a couple of seemingly fatuous questions before calling up the stairs, 'It's Mr MacMahon.'

When Jimmy looked up he saw a tall figure standing in the landing beneath a skylight.

'For a man who used to drill till he dropped you've a cautious class of a walk.' Michael Collins observed as Jimmy moved down the hall. He shook hands with him on the landing, ushered him into a back bedroom where a coal fire glowed and a desk was piled with papers. He pointed to a chair and flopped into his own behind the desk.

'I need cautious men. I've a job for you.'

Jimmy leaned forward eagerly. He had never met Collins and he found himself looking into the shrewdest eyes he had ever encountered in a young man.

'There's a limit to how much longer you can carry on in your area,' Collins went on. You're a known sympathiser. They'll lift you at the first sign of trouble.'

'So what's the new job?'

'I want you to train the lads in Mayo. What do you say to a change of identity as well as a change of scene? You could be an insurance salesman.' He grinned, 'Or, judging by your cheerful expression, an undertaker.'

Jimmy was thinking rapidly. He would have to get someone to run the farm.

'Sure, but what about the local boys I've been drilling?'

'They can have you until after Christmas. Then it's Mayo!'

'What about weapons?'

'Weapons?' Collins repeated, as though his visitor were insane. 'You can't have everything! Continue with wooden guns, hurley sticks, any oul' thing.'

'What made you pick me?'

'Weren't you hopping mad two years ago when MacNeill cancelled the mobilisations? Didn't you give them the slip after the Rising? Aren't you too good to waste?'

Jimmy smiled in spite of himself. 'You know a lot about me.'

Collins smiled back grimly. 'I have to know my people. I know you've spent years longing for a chance to change things. And change is the operative word.' Collins looked Jimmy in the eye. 'I'm not interested in the blood-and-guts heroes. Simple justice is what we want. Not revenge.'

Jimmy thought of Harry rotting in Glasnevin Cemetery and stared back at Collins. 'How long will the job last?'

Collins sighed. 'How the hell do I know? But I can tell you,' he added grimly 'what you can expect by way of wages … homelessness, hunger and cold. And worse to come. Now that the war is over there will be a general election. We will field candidates in every constituency. If they are returned they will refuse to sit in Westminster. We will form our own government right here in Dublin … and then, Boyo, the fireworks will begin again. But this time we won't be caught like rats in a trap. This time there'll be no highfalutin' blood sacrifice. Every man and every shot will count!'

Jimmy heard his heart pounding. 'There's to be a Peace Conference in Paris,' he said levelly, forcing himself to remain calm. 'It may persuade Britain to let Ireland go.'

Collins frowned and gave an exasperated grunt. '*Let* Ireland go? Of course they won't *let* Ireland go! But *go* Ireland will, all the same …'

Jimmy laughed and put out his hand.

Guy spent December in Fontebelle, a month with only the Fargues for company. He filled his days with walks; he read by his fireside; he talked to the local people and heard their catalogue of sorrow – sons and grandsons who would never came home, lost in Verdun, lost in the Somme.

Nigel, his brother, had died in Flanders. Sophie was a widow and James was fatherless. He thought of the pre-war excitement and the confident expectation of a quick resolution. Were they mad, the crowned heads, the politicians, the generals? Having loosed the dogs of wars, what made them think they could control them? They have ruined Europe.

He received separate letters from James along with a Christmas card featuring a deer in a snowscape.

*Dear Uncle,*

*I am sorry you are not spending Christmas with us, but Mother and I are glad you are safe in your Fontebelle.*

*We got three days, holiday from school for the Armistice. You should have seen the party in the village! Mother came, although she is very sad and talks a great deal about Father and old times.*

*There were long tables with trifles and cakes and bunting everywhere. I drank some fairly lethal fruit punch … It made one somewhat befuddled and Mother wasn't at all pleased!*

*The following day I forced myself to go out with the hunt, but it was frankly depressing. So many old faces missing. Farmer Perkins was there, of course, fat as ever, and Ivy (the daughter who laughs like a hyena), and solicitor Jones with his fluffy whiskers, and, of course, the Honourable Laetitia who must be at least eighty now, but is still spry as a greyhound. The fox of course (sensible animal) went to ground.*

*Next season, perhaps, will be better. You might be with us then? Rum to think I'll have gone up to Oxford in the interim. I think they must be glad of new blood (if one dare use that word); the place is half empty. But no point in being gloomy. It was a hard scrap, but at least we won.*

*Do write and let me know all your news from France. I've been working on my French, so next time I visit Fontebelle prepare to be amazed.*

*Your affectionate nephew,*

*James*

Touched by its covert yearning, Guy read this letter several times. Had he let James and Sophie down by not spending Christmas with them, particularly after their bereavement? But he would have been poor company. He needed this space. He had been afraid the gibbering, although it had not troubled him for two years, would return. Anyway, the social round in Lindthorp would have been unbearable – the young widows, the orphans, the vanished faces he would expect to see around every corner.

Little by little Fontebelle worked its magic. Rest, peace, good food and fine wine brought the return of some kind of equilibrium, if not *joie de vivre.*

Guy did not miss anyone. He was content just to 'be'. He spent his days reading and reflected on how much of a monk he was becoming. Occasionally he fingered the locket in which he kept Ellen's hair and dreamed of that rainy Easter Sunday. He hoped she had got safely home from the Dublin disturbances and was now raising the next Irish generation. How had she coped with poor Harry's death? And what a shame he had not been able to restore to her the little ring, the memento of their youth, something tangible by which to remember their crossed destinies.

As January wore on, he watched from a distance the events unfolding in Ireland. Nationalists had won an overwhelming majority of Irish seats in the general election and had refused to take their seats in Parliament, saying they were going to set up their own. That had put the cat squarely back among the pigeons. But why can't Westminster understand these people only seek what we take for granted: the right to live in freedom and the right not to be robbed?

And what of his future, now that the war was over? His accumulated leave would expire at the end of January. He could resign his commission, go to civvy street. And do what? Well, there was that book he wanted to write, and he had better write it while the madness and the heroism were still fresh. He had encountered first-hand the two extremes of the human spirit: brutality and cruelty on the one hand and transcendent nobility on the other.

That they co-existed in humanity was beyond his comprehension.

Then came the letter he had been expecting from his military masters in London. His new posting, it informed him, taking into account his knowledge of Ireland and his consequent usefulness in Intelligence, was Dublin Castle.

# Chapter 40

*Dublin, February 1919*

Guy heard the foghorns moaning and watched Dublin appear out of the mist. The Royal Mail boat pulled into the North Wall – the tongue of dockland on the north bank of the Liffey estuary. It was cold and bleak. Only the seagulls seemed carefree as they screamed and wheeled, white wings arched. Other sounds were muffled – the plashing of water against the quay, the shouts of the men securing hawsers to capstans, the rattle of horse-drawn carts. Droplets moistened the rails and seeped through Guy's gloves. The boat bumped against the quay and in a few moments he was moving down the gangway to the quayside where a waiting sergeant saluted smartly.

'Major Forrister, Sir?'

Guy nodded and returned the salute.

'I'm to take you to Dublin Castle, Sir. The car is waiting.'

'Very good. See to my luggage, will you?'

When they were both in the car Guy said, 'Take me around the city first. I haven't been here since the insurrection.'

'That must have been something, Sir!'

'Yes.'

'City's still rather a mess …'

The car slid along the docks. Guy looked across the river to the Grand Canal Basin, from where the gunboat, *Helga*, had fired on the city. He searched for a glimpse of Boland's Flour Mills, one of the hotspots during the Rising. A fellow by the name of De Valera had commanded a bunch of the rebels there. Although condemned to death, his American birth had secured his reprieve from the firing squad.

The car drove by the Customs House and came to Liberty Hall, ruined now, smashed by the *Helga's* guns.

'You can stop here for a moment.'

Guy got out and stood on the pavement. *Here* I met her! That Saturday. On this very spot. And in that building I saw Harry Healy as he prepared for his absurd war.

But all was calm now, all in ruins. It was seven on a Saturday morning, and Dublin was asleep in its blanket of mist. He got back into the car.

'How are things here now?'

'Fraught, Sir. You know they've set up their own parliament?'

Guy nodded. 'A bit ambitious, wouldn't you say? You can't run a country without money!'

'They're raising the money, Sir. Bloke by the name of Collins is floating a national loan from the back of a bicycle.' He laughed. 'We've been trying to catch him, but he's like the Scarlet Pimpernel. No one really knows what he looks like and he apparently cycles around town free as a bird.'

Guy looked around with interest as the car entered Sackville Street. The widest street in Europe resembled a graveyard, buildings like broken tombs, as bad as anything he had seen in France. He asked the driver to stop at the Pillar, where Lord Nelson, still impervious, stood on his lofty perch.

Here was the spot where a bullet had shaved the side of his head, here an iron-shod hoof had slashed at him. The once beautiful Post Office was gutted, its windows empty sockets now behind its massive Ionic portico. But at least there were no snipers on the roof today. In parts of the street reconstruction was underway, but the city still breathed the destruction and bitterness of war.

'Do you think we will ever be able to bring peace to Ireland?'

The driver shrugged. 'Not unless we give them back their country, Sir. Or kill them all. And I don't hold much with killing. Not since the Somme!' After a moment he added in a low voice, 'It's the … silence you see, Sir … afterwards …'

Guy knew only it only too well – the tumultuous silence of the dead.

Nigel was silent in a cemetery where the white crosses went on and on. And Harry Healy was hushed forever. And Ellen might as well have been a dream. Maybe she died too. Anything could have happened that week. Plenty of people had been caught in the crossfire. She had obviously been alive and well when she had penned the note to him. But the worst of the fighting had come afterwards.

I can find out, he reminded himself. Now that I'm back, I will visit Franny. But what work would they have for him at the Castle? Intelligence had a ring he did not care for.

In Balcarragh, the spring of 1919 was heralded with hail showers and sudden bursts of sunshine. Ellen, driving to school with little Hugh, who was now in Infants class, felt the sense of expectancy. Since the Rising, nothing was the same. People had been touched in some profound way. You saw it in their eyes, their carriage, their pride in the executed leaders and their overt resentment that they had been executed. Photographs of Pearse and the others leaders circulated. Ireland had new martyrs; patriot songs were sung again.

Sometimes Ellen tried to remember the ecstatic guilt of wakening on that Easter Monday morning. But the events of the day itself and those that followed were vague now, horror-bound. She had not been able to get home for a whole week and by then Brendan had been in such a state that he had welcomed her with tears and embraces. Detesting herself for a liar, she had made up a story he had readily believed, that she had spent all the time in Deirdre's lodgings, unable to travel.

She had not known Harry's fate until Deirdre's letter, almost a fortnight late, had come with the news of his death. The postman had apologised for its tardy delivery, as though events had somehow besmirched his professionalism. Recognising the writing, Ellen had taken the letter to her bedroom, sat on the bed and opened it with a pang of dread. It was dated Sunday, May 7 1916.

*My dearest Ellen,*

*I could not send a wire; communications are still down. In any case telegrams are brutal instruments when you must be simply frantic.*

*Harry was in the Post Office and I was there too. But he received two bad wounds, Ellen and, when the surrender came, his friend Captain Forrister, although hospitalised himself, managed to get him taken to the military hospital in Dublin Castle. They did their best for him there. I was allowed to be with him at the end.*

*I'm so sorry darling. I weep as I write – your brother's widow. We were married by a priest a few hours before he died. I used my mother's ring.*

*He is buried in Glasnevin. I enclose a sketch map of where to find his grave. Your cousin Frances was at the funeral and was a great comfort.*

*My grief is tempered, for Harry left me with something precious. God willing, I will become a mother next December. If the baby is a boy I am going to call him Fiach, an old Gaelic name, as his father wished. If she is a girl I will call her after you.*

*And in the Spring, Baby and I are pulling up stumps and going to America. I have kin in New York. I have never met them, but they have invited me to come and assure me of employment. So I should manage to survive. Which would be difficult here, as my school has refused to take me back, and other schools are not queueing up for the services of a female warrior.*

*I do not know if what we did had a point! I know now that it was doomed from the outset. But Pearse praised us on that last Thursday. He said that when the history of the fight would be written the foremost page should be given to the women of* Cumann na mBan. *So there!*

*I believe in Providence; I believe that God respects courage, that He understands passion, and has His own plans for nations as for people.*

*Your loving*

*Deirdre.*

The letter had slipped through Ellen's fingers and she had pushed her face into her pillows. She remained there in another world for a while, a world where she and Harry were children, a world she saw with death-defying clarity. She had to hold onto him now, consolidate memory now, before he slipped forever out of reach.

Brendan found her lying on their bed, staring blindly at the ceiling, her face smeared with tears. He picked up the letter from the bed, read it and moved to comfort her, taking her hand. 'My poor Ellen … But he is safe with God.'

She raised her head, leaned on her elbow and stared at him.

'I'm sick to my soul, Brendan Kennedy,' she cried, 'of castles in the air.'

Brendan looked shocked. 'No Ellen,' he said after a moment,

'it was not a castle in the air. It was a statement of love paid out with blood. Such statements live on!' He patted her hands. 'Take comfort in that. And Ellen … there are things I would like to say to you … You are a wonderful woman and very dear to me. I want you to know I'm sorry if I have ever hurt you, and I do readily forgive you for your overreacting when we were in Dublin.'

He is offering what he can, she thought, looking at his grave, lined face; he is a good man. His wife, on the other hand, is not good. She has injured him, broken her vow to him and may have injured him even more than she realised. She was waiting for something, which should have come that month and had not. A few weeks later she told him, to his joy, and her own guilt and rapture, that she was carrying a child. Mary had been born almost eight months later, in January 1917.

I have become a vessel full of secrets, Ellen thought now, letting five-year-old Hughie take the reins. How did I manage that? I intended my life to be above reproach, to be as perfect and honourable as it was possible for a woman to be? But I have Mary and I cannot regret her. Neither can I regret what I have done and so no absolution is possible.

Little Mary was at home right now in the tender care of Máire Ní Suibhne. Brendan was at home too. He was unwell these days, angry at finding himself breathless and sometimes weak. He had angina, the doctor said, and had to take things easy. So Ellen, on the days when he was off school, took his classes as well as her own. Father Devlin had been sympathetic at first but had pointed out that a new principal would have to be found. He made it clear she would not be considered. It would have to be a man.

'Life is strange,' she said to Hughie. 'Did you know that?'

Hughie nodded. He was concentrating on his driving, shaking the reins, annoyed that the pony continued plodding despite his efforts. He suddenly screeched, 'H'Up!' and the pony laid back startled ears and began to trot. The barefoot schoolchildren on the road smiled at them and she smiled back.

She was 'The Missus' now, a notable in the parish, something she found strange, like wearing a suit of clothes meant for someone else, someone older. Her whole world had changed. Harry was dead; Deirdre was living in America; Clare's husband, Frank, who had survived the war, was about to remarry – a Parisienne, the image of Clare, he said. And Aunt Harriet was fading.

Ellen, Brendan and the children had spent last Christmas at Kilcrannagh. They had found Aunt Harriet very thin and quiet. She had a new maid, Cait, who was terrified of her. Maggie was gone. She had married a local farmer, a seventy-year-old bachelor and was apparently bossing him around, for he was seen for the first time in twenty years with his boots polished and a new cap.

Father Devlin said the first Mass on Christmas morning. Looking over to the men's side of the church, Ellen had seen Jimmy near the front, apparently lost in prayer for he only rose from his knees for the Gospel.

Later, Brendan had commented on his military bearing. 'I thought you said that man was a fierce patriot. But where was he during the Rising? When the poor boys were left to die in their Dublin boltholes?' And then he had added bitterly, 'You might just as easily ask: Where was I?'

Ellen steered clear of this topic. She knew that Brendan now ardently wished he had played an active part in the struggle – 'the most inspired heroic gesture of the age' was how he now described it and part of her despised him for not being involved. She knew this was unfair, knew that she was lashing out because Harry was dead. And she suspected that Jimmy felt as Brendan did, felt that he and the rest of the lads had been betrayed. How his eyes had burned when he came by after Mass and found her alone in the kitchen.

'How are you at all, Ellen? And you with the two lovely children. Your husband tells me you were trapped in the capital during the Rising.'

'I just lay low, Jimmy. Unlike Harry, I am not the stuff of heroes.'

'God rest him!' Jimmy made the sign of the cross. And how's Captain Forrister? Did he survive the war?'

Ellen hated the slow flush that burned her face. 'I don't know.'

'I heard that he was instrumental in getting Harry to Dublin Castle hospital. But that he recovered …'

Ellen caught her breath. 'I didn't know he was injured. Did you hear anything else about him, Jimmy … afterwards?'

'No. He presumably carried out his duty and went back to the war.'

She turned her face away. Jimmy put a hand on her arm. 'Ellen, I came to say goodbye. I will soon be leaving here … but one of the Fahys' will look after things for your aunt.

'Oh Jimmy … Surely you're not emigrating?'

He shook his head. 'No. There's a job of work I have to do … I'll come back then. If I can.'

'Where are you going?'

He did not reply, but he offered his hand. She took it and he held it for a while, looking at her gravely, before he moved to the door. On the doorstep he said, 'Get Franny to visit her mother. She's married now you know, but your aunt won't talk about it. The woman's very ill, Ellen, but she won't talk about that either. The doctor says it's her lungs.'

She waited until he had reached the gate, when he stood for a moment, his glance lingering on her and on the house and the garden. Then he raised a hand and was gone. The following day she sent a wire to Franny and received hers almost by return: THANKS EL STOP GOING HOME IMMEDIATELY.

When another one came a few weeks later to say that Aunt Harriet had died, Ellen went alone to Kilcrannagh and in the bedroom where her aunt lay, white and cold, she found her cousin again.

It was after the funeral, when everyone had gone home, that she and Fran were able to catch up on the lost years. Sitting on the old settee in the drawing room, a room where the dirty cups and glasses awaited the morning, they had emptied a bottle of port wine between them and, into each other's keeping, had confided their lives.

Thinking of it, Ellen blinked away tears. Well Fran was back in Dublin now, but at least she wrote once a week. And Deirdre had kept in touch too, writing evocative letters from far-off America.

*Everything's built of wood here, Ellen – except of course the fine houses and tall buildings in the city. But despite the thrust towards modernity, America has an immense resonance of another time. In upper Manhattan are eighteenth-century buildings that might have graced London. An atmosphere of colonialism clings to them like a faded fragrance.*

*Your nephew Fiach is doing well. Already, he's thoroughly American. He looks like his father, but then of course I keep searching for resemblances in everything – the smile, the turn of the head ...*

*Dear Ellen, I wish you could join me here. But I know your wings are clipped. I wish you joy of the new baby. You have the perfect family now, a son and a daughter.*

*Give my best to your dear husband. I know he never approved of me, and I'm sure he'll approve of me even less when he knows I have forgiven him.*

*By the way, the enclosed poem is one I found in a notebook of Harry's. The author was the executed Thomas MacDonagh.*

*All my love,*

*Deirdre*

On a separate slip of paper she had printed three verses.

*His words were a little phrase*
*Of eternal song,*
*Lost in the chanting of lays*
*More loud and long.*

*His deed was a single word,*
*Called out alone*
*In a night when no echoes stirred*
*To laughter or moan.*

*But his songs new souls shall thrill,*
*The loud harp dumb,*
*And his deeds the echoes fill,*
*When the dawn is come.'*

The dawn? Ellen wondered and thought of the illegal parliament – the Dáil – convened last Janaury in Dublin's Mansion House. Deirdre's acquaintance, Michael Collins, had been appointed Minister for Home Affairs and Cathal Brugha, another of the surviving rebels, had addressed the waiting journalists with a salvo directed at the Imperial Parliament: 'We are done with England. Let the world know it.'

But was England done with Ireland? She watched the jouncing harness leave its imprint in the dusty sweat of the pony's coat, put her arm around her small son as the trap swayed over the worst of the potholes and took the reins from him. 'I think we're going fast enough, sweetheart! Don't you?'

'I want to go home to Dada.'

Brendan, very poorly these days, was increasingly agitated about the escalating unrest in the country. 'It's only a matter of time,' he told her, 'before England takes decisive action'. Lately he'd had some mysterious visitors while she was at school. He'd brushed aside her query as to who they were and Máire Ní Suibhne had not been able to satisfy her curiosity either. The Master, she said, had sent her up the road to the Lennons to return a bicycle light and when she'd come back the visitors had gone.

# Chapter 41

*Dublin, winter–spring, 1919–20*

Guy's new desk job in Dublin Castle did not lack fascination. Police reports passed in front of him, details of who went where and what was said at every meeting in every corner of the land. The country, he mused, was being governed through a spy network worthy of Kubla Khan. But the real fascination was the new parliament, illegal certainly, but one that had dared to hold its first session on 21 January. How much of the sensitive information on his desk, how much government strategy, was being spirited to it by the demure secretaries who scurried along the Castle corridors? How long could London pretend to rule a country where its own elected representatives had, by popular mandate, opted to govern themselves?

The winter of 1919 became for him a winter of discontent. He was isolated, by inclination as much as by circumstances. None of his former comrades was stationed in Dublin. Those few who had survived the war had been posted elsewhere. And many survivors of the global conflict had been hit by the Spanish Influenza, which had arrived like a latter-day Black Death. Bertie Wallace had also been a casualty, killed when a building in London, undermined in an air raid, had collapsed. He'd been with two companions, it seemed, but because of his lameness had been unable to escape.

Guy had tried to see Franny again, but had found that her shop was now a shoe shop. Miss Murphy, he was told, had married and was living in Howth. Did he want her address? He certainly did. He sent Fran a Christmas card, hoped for an invitation but heard nothing.

New Year 1920 found ruined Dublin taut with tension. But for Guy it nonetheless remained the romantic place where he had met Ellen on the quays, the place where they had spent an unforgettable Easter Sunday.

*There can be no future.* He would try to accept it. But if only he could be sure she had made it home safely. Given the disturbances, anything might have happened. And might still happen, he thought, given the new police sent from England to reinforce the RIC. A rough enough lot apparently, without even a proper uniform.

Wondering if Duggy had been demobbed, if he still had his rooms and was back at his studies, he set out to find him one evening in late April. He bought a bottle of Rémy Martin and directed his steps to St Stephen's Green.

He came to the square in the gathering dusk, glad of his greatcoat as the wind was very cold. The lights were on in the second-floor windows, the curtains drawn. He mounted the granite steps and rang Duggy's bell. A sash was pushed up somewhere above his head and a head appeared over the sill.

'Yes?' came Duggy's querulous Cork voice, adding when he saw the silent figure in the greatcoat below him on the steps, 'Who the hell are you?'

Guy raised his head and held up the bottle. 'Chap by the name of Rémy Martin!'

Duggy laughed. 'Can that be you, Forrister? Hang on old thing and I'll throw you down the keys. You know your way up.'

In a moment Guy had let himself into the house and had mounted the stairs. Duggy's sitting room was lamplit and a coal fire glowed. Books, notes and items of clothing were scattered here and there. A desk by the window was piled with textbooks. The man himself had put on weight and seemed a different person, in his tired pullover and corduroys, to the curt young officer he had known.

'I've disturbed you, Duggy!'

'Bloody obstetrics! But you can disturb me any time you like if you come accompanied by Monsieur Martin. Here, let me take your coat. Have a seat!'

Guy yielded up his greatcoat and sat into an armchair by the fire. Duggy found glasses and opened the bottle. He poured two tots, sniffed at the brandy with a little groan of pleasure, closed his eyes and swallowed.

'Jesus, wasn't this what we needed in the trenches. I still feel so damn guilty to have made it back! My mother claims full responsibility. She spent the entire war doing novenas.' He glanced at Guy. 'I hear you took a bit of a drubbing!'

'Lack of novenas! I'm fine now. But Duggy old chap, I never thanked you properly for the loan of your rooms.'

'You were most welcome, although you did choose your moment. God knows Easter 1916 was a rum time to take a break in Dublin!'

Guy nodded grim agreement. In this very room, Ellen had taken off her chemise. He could see her, there beside the settee; her scent was suddenly in his nostrils, her silken skin under his hands …

'Did you entertain a lady here by any chance?'

Guy started.

'An old friend. She came up for tea.'

Duggy did not smirk and Guy silently blessed him for it.

'She may have left a trinket behind,' Duggy said. He rose, went to a drawer in the overloaded desk and returned with something in his hand. 'Do you recognise it?'

Guy picked the snake ring from Duggy's palm. 'Where did you find it?'

'In the bookcase. I imagine the poor girl examining one of my textbooks in horror and then finding that she was under fire.'

'What do you mean. Under fire?'

Duggy drew back the heavy curtain and pointed to the splintered shutter where a bullet had torn the wood. 'But of course you were with her! It must have been quite a shock to have had an unexpected war outside your window.'

'I wasn't with her. I was in the damn hospital with a head wound! She was stuck here, on her own, unable to leave. And I do not know, Duggy, what became of her. I do not even know where she lives.'

Duggy looked troubled. 'There was a little stain, a blood stain, in the kitchen. Not that it necessarily means anything ...'

Guy put the ring into his pocket and finished his brandy.

'Don't rush off,' Duggy said. 'You can find out if she's all right, surely ... But not tonight?'

Guy pondered if he should write again to Franny, or if he could just call on her at her home in Howth. But a note arrived from her the following day.

*Dear Guy,*

*So nice to know you're back in the Emerald Isle. I've been unwell, otherwise I would have responded sooner to your Christmas card. I'm fine now, however, and would love to see you. How about afternoon tea next Saturday – say 4 p.m.? I'll expect you unless I hear to the contrary.*

*My husband – you met him when you called to the shop four years ago – is away at the moment and we can have a nice long natter about old times.'*

*Yours ever,*
*Franny*

*

The Howth tram was almost empty. Guy enjoyed the journey to the isthmus that formed the northern limit of the mist-covered bay. He alighted in the little fishing village, asked directions, and after an uphill walk of some twenty minutes, found himself at the gates of Rathcormac. But what a view the place had – the city across the bay looked so innocent against its mountains.

Franny opened the door. For second he didn't recognise her. Her hair was short and hugged the sides of her head. She had a new, matronly air, looked the picture of health and her face was alive with delight. She reached for his hand and pulled him into the house.

'Come in … so wonderful to see you!'

The tiled hall was divided in two by heavy tapestry curtains caught up with silken ropes. The walls were festooned with paintings. The house was warm and smelled of scones, beeswax and turps. A maid in a white apron came to take his coat.

'We'll have tea in the drawing room, Florrie.'

The maid disappeared and Franny ushered Guy into a spacious room with two large windows overlooking the sea. 'Next time you come we'll arrange fine weather! You will come, won't you, and meet Liam again? He's in Paris at present – some of his paintings will be exhibited.'

'Of course I'll come! I'd have come before now only I didn't want to intrude.'

'Guy, you couldn't intrude if you tried.'

The maid brought the tea tray and while Franny poured she chatted non-stop. Wasn't it wonderful he had come safely through the war! How long would he be in Ireland? She paused, cocked her head and smiled. Somewhere in the house a young girl was singing.

'That's Hannah. We have legally adopted her. She has a grand voice and is quite the little artist! Liam's encouraged her since she was knee-high. He thinks she has talent.'

'Does she ask about …?'

'Her father? Not any more … She knows he's dead. And I don't think about him any more either, Guy. I have learnt that life sweeps you along, opens new chapters, if only you will allow it … if only you do not brood. So I embrace the new, Guy … I hold it close, fix my eyes on the future and try to let the past go.'

'And the women's suffrage question? Is that all done and dusted?'

She laughed. 'Certainly not. That battle is only half-won! If Alma, Liam's sister, were here she would set you to rights on that. But she's in England now and won't be home until the end of the year.'

'But you are happy?'

She nodded. She put a hand on her stomach and looked at him shyly. 'The reason I didn't contact you earlier was because I was unwell. Don't look like that … it wasn't that awful influenza. It was just something called morning sickness.'

'Oh *Franny*. I wish you joy! May I ask when is the happy day?'

'End of July. When the summer is back to us. Liam is ecstatic, full of dreams for this wonderful new generation we're creating. He thinks we'll populate the isthmus! And Hannah knows of course and is just as excited. But Guy … I shouldn't rattle on … I have news for you, but first I want to know your plans. Are they going to send you back to India or will you stay in Ireland?'

"I'll be going back to France. I've decided to resign my commission.'

She sat up and stared at him.

'But I thought you loved the army! What will you do? Live the quiet life of a country gentleman in that lovely French place you once described for us all?'

'My *stepmother* once described to you all! But yes. Why not? I'll go back to Fontebelle. There's a book I want to write … And you'll also be glad to know that I can now be trusted with a teacup.'

She handed him his tea and offered fruitcake slices and macaroons set out on paper doilies and then asked quietly if he had been to see the city centre and the ruined Post Office. She put the teapot down suddenly and dashed away tears.

'I can't get used to it, you know!' she whispered. 'Every time I think about him …'

Guy dealt with the lump in his own throat.

'I saw Harry at a window in the Post Office … that Easter Monday,' he said tentatively, unwilling to stir up what he knew must be a painful memory but sure she would want to know.

Franny put her cup down. 'Oh did you, Guy? The poor boy gave his life for this country. Do you think it was all in vain?'

Guy shook his head. 'In vain? Not a chance. No modern power can indefinitely withstand the concerted will of a people. But what I was going to tell you, Fran, is that Harry saved my life on that Easter Monday. One of his comrades in the Post Office had me in his sights. I saw Harry push aside the rifle …'

Franny brightened. 'Of course he did! But Ellen would love to know it …'

He broke a piece of fruitcake and asked carefully, 'So she is well? You hear from her?'

Franny looked at him with a small smile. 'I do. She has two children now!'

'I see.' Guy tried to stop the startled prompt that rose unbidden. 'What ages are her children?'

'The little boy is six and the girl is three. Her name is Mary.'

He took an envelope from his pocket and held it out to her.

'Could you send that to her for me?'

Franny took the envelope, felt it with her thumb and forefinger and looked at him with one of her old impish smiles. 'I can guess what's in it! Do you mind my curiosity? The famous ring that got her into so much trouble with my mother! Am I right?'

'So you knew about that?'

'Of course! I was the family detective! But why don't you give it to her yourself?'

Guy had already thought of this, had envisaged calling on Ellen, had imagined her world, the home she had spent years creating, the contented husband, and knew that he could not do it, could not bear it. But now he thought of the little girl. Something in him suddenly bloomed, as though all the cynicism in his soul had deserted him. Three years old? It couldn't be possible, he told himself. Could it?

'Give it to her *myself* Franny? I wouldn't like to intrude on her life.'

'Guy, will you have sense! Fond as I am of you, do you think I invited you here just to re-hash memories? Ellen is staying with me at present. Yes, here in this house! She came ten days ago, just after her husband died. He had heart trouble and when they had their awful incident it fairly finished him.

'What awful incident?'

'Of course you couldn't know. The new police – down the country they call them the Black and Tans – searched their place and discovered that Brendan had a cache of weapons concealed in one of the outhouses. They arrested him, of course, and then they put Ellen and the children and the little maid out in their nightclothes and burned the house down. Brendan died in custody a few days later. Neighbours took in Ellen and the children. She sent me a wire and Liam went down to bring her here before he left for Paris. The poor girl is exhausted and completely traumatised. Today is the first day I managed to get her to take some air. And so, Guy dear, you can restore the ring to her yourself!'

'Where is she?' Guy rose nervously from his chair and looked towards the door.

'I didn't tell her you were coming, in case anything happened to detain you. But if you were to take a stroll down the avenue you might find a young woman with two small children returning from a walk.'

Guy left the room. Franny heard the front door open and watched through the window as he hurried across the forecourt.

'Well, Harry?' she whispered. 'What do you think?'

Outside, she saw Ellen approach with the two children. She was carrying Mary but suddenly stumbled, stared at Guy as though he were a spectre, set the child down carefully and put out her arms.

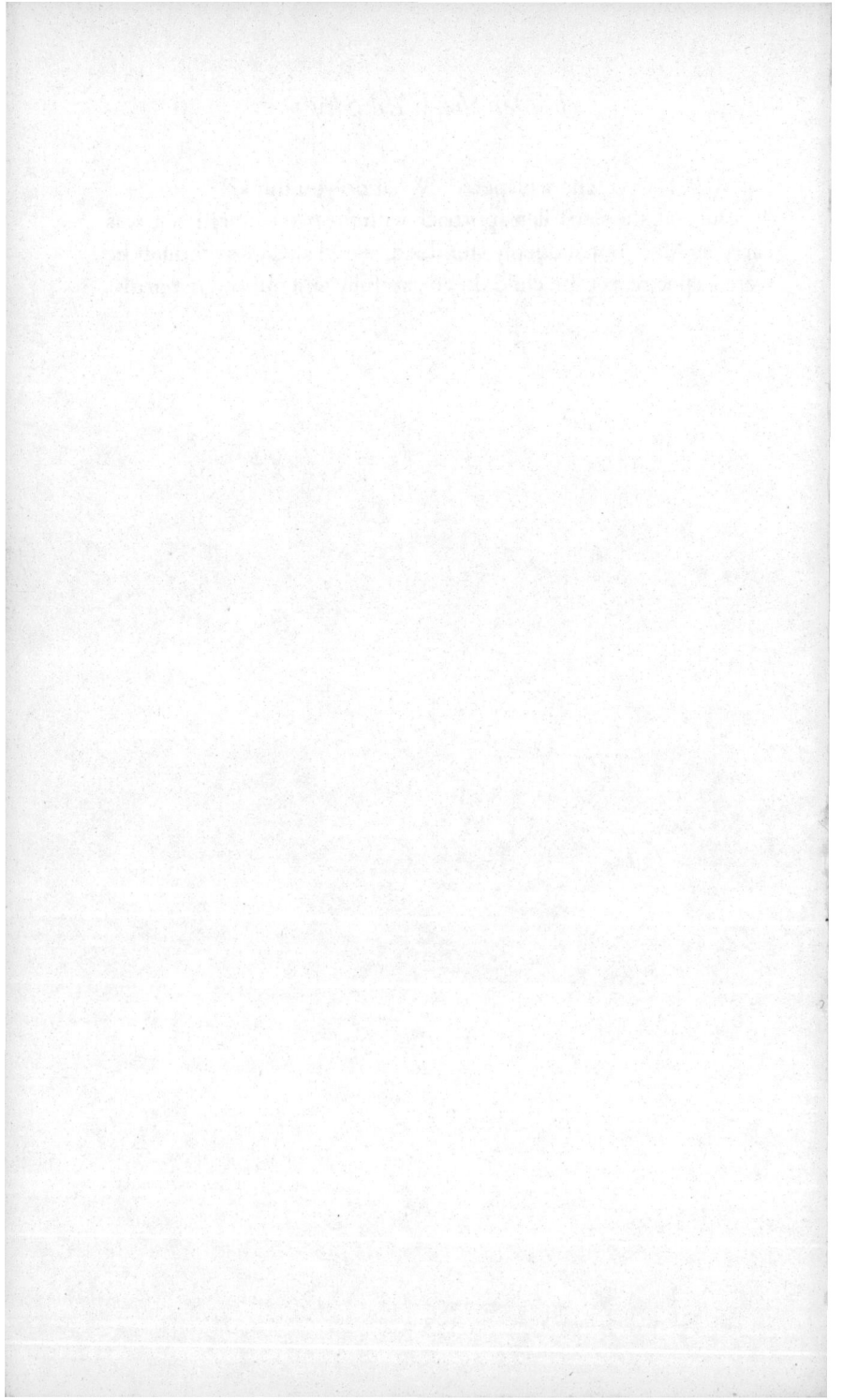